THE ART OF
HOLDING ON

BETH BURGOON

Editor: Blue Otter Editing

Cover design: Wicked By Design

❀ Created with Vellum

1

Sam Constable is back in town.

No surprise. I knew he was coming.

Not because he told me or anything. Sam hasn't initiated a conversation with me since he dropped out of my life almost a year ago. He hasn't called, texted or sent so much as an email. But that hasn't stopped me from hearing all about him and his fabulous new life in sunny California, my information coming from social media comments, snatches of overheard conversations and local gossip.

There are no secrets in a small town.

Sooner or later, the truth always comes out.

Still, I'd hoped word of his return was just the idle talk of those who missed him. Who were anxious to see him again.

Only to have my hopes cruelly dashed last week when Sam's mom went through my sister Zoe's checkout line at Top-Mart. During what had to be an awkward, stilted and overly polite chat, Dr. Constable-Riester confirmed her middle son's imminent return.

According to Zoe, the usually reserved doctor was almost giddy about having Sam home for a few weeks over the summer.

Made sense. She'd never wanted him to leave. No one had.

But he'd done it anyway.

Shortly after Zoe's conversation with Dr. Constable-Riester, Sam's friends started with the throwback pics of him. Every day for a week, my Instagram feed was filled with Sam, Sam and more Sam, the captions variations on the same theme: *So glad you're coming home! Can't wait to see you! All is right in the world again!*

Once he came back, it'd only be a matter of time until we ran into each other. Like I said, it's a small town.

Nowhere to hide.

That I'd considered it—quitting my job and staying tucked away in our trailer for the rest of the summer—left the unmistakable taste of resentment in my mouth.

Why should I hide? I wasn't the one who changed everything.

I wasn't the one who left.

And if I quit my job, my other sister, Devyn, would kill me dead.

So, no hiding. Not for me. Which meant I'd resigned myself to the fact that I would, at some point during Sam's visit home, see him. I'd be walking down Main Street and he'd be in his black SUV at a red light. Or he'd be leaving Drip 'n Sip, his usual large ice coffee with cream in his hand, when I was walking in. Or Zoe would send me to Top-Mart to get more diapers and baby wipes because even though Zoe works there six days a week, we're still forever running out of diapers and baby wipes, and Sam and his friends would be there buying plastic cups, pop, Hawaiian Punch and Red Bull, because in the summer there's always a party and there's always need for mix-ins for the vodka, tequila and rum.

There's no way I'd be able to avoid him completely. Before he went on his merry way again, I knew we would have at least one totally uncomfortable, completely unwanted encounter.

But it's supposed to happen days, maybe even a week or two from now. After I've had time to prepare. To mentally go over everything I'll say. Practice how I'll act. It's supposed to happen when I'm dressed to kill, my hair smooth and straight and shiny. My makeup perfect.

Not when I'm hot and exhausted from an eight-hour shift spreading mulch over the raised garden beds in Mrs. Benton's huge, perfectly landscaped lawn. Not when my clothes (khaki shorts that reach the knees, work boots and a green tee sporting the Glenwood Landscaping insignia) are covered in potting soil and grass clippings and I'm wearing a backpack approximately the size of a small car. Not when my hair—pulled through the back of my battered Pittsburgh Pirates baseball hat—is huge and frizzy from the humidity. Not when the only makeup I have on is lip balm and I smell like the worst combination of dirt and sweat and the 50 SPF sunscreen I slather on at least six times a day.

It's not supposed to happen today. Not like this.

But it is. Sam Constable is walking toward me.

Nothing ever goes the way I want it to.

It's so annoying.

Especially since I can't seem to move. I just stand in the middle of the parking lot like a statue while Sam closes the distance between us. It's so familiar, me waiting for him, watching him approach, that for a moment I forget everything that's happened between us. What we said. What we did.

For a moment, it's like it's always been.

But it's not real, this sense of connection. It's just memories of how we used to be.

He looks the same, which is another reason to be mighty ticked off. His dark, thick hair waves wildly around his handsome face and he's wearing the Warriors T-shirt he got after they won the championship. But the closer he gets, the more I notice the slight differences. His hair is longer than before, the curling ends brushing the collar of his T-shirt. His shoulders are broader, his stride more confident.

He stops a few feet away from me. "Hadley."

That's it. Just my name. But the sound of it in his soft, deep, familiar voice has my stomach tugging with longing.

Has me wanting to forget the past eleven months ever happened.

He knows it, too. He's always seen through me. Knew me better than anyone. Wasn't that the problem?

I let him get too close. Gave him too much.

And still he wanted more.

He must sense my vulnerability because he steps forward.

Reaches for me. I remember what it's like to have his arm slung around my shoulders as he squeezes me to his side. How he'd give me a quick, friendly hug whenever we said goodbye.

Except the last time he pulled me toward him, it wasn't so quick. Was way more than just friendly.

And when he said that final goodbye, he didn't touch me at all.

I cross my arms and Sam stops, clearly reading my *Hands off!* body language. Accepts it as his due. Part of his penance.

But not fully, because there's a flash of disappointment on his face, a brief glimpse of hurt in his eyes.

I refuse to feel guilty for either.

He shoves his hands into the pockets of his gray basketball shorts and gives me one of his stupid lopsided grins that he knows damn well is adorable. "Hey."

I don't smile back. "Hey."

"Uh...how's your summer going?"

Seriously? He thinks I'm going to play the nothing-happened-and-nothing's-changed-between-us game?

So much for that whole *he knows me better than anyone* thing.

"Fine."

"Good." He clears his throat. "That's...good."

I nod. Yep, everything with me is just hunky-dory. Living the dream and all that.

If living the dream means being basically friendless, spending forty hours a week working a job I hate and constantly scrimping and saving and still never having enough, then yeah, I'm there, standing on top of a brightly colored rainbow tossing handfuls of golden confetti to a bunch of dancing unicorns.

From the garage behind me, someone—sounds like Cody—calls Sam's name, diverting his attention.

"See ya," I say.

Keeping my pace slow and steady, I walk away. I won't let him think seeing him has me running scared. That being close enough to him to smell his cologne, to pick out the strands of hair highlighted by the California sun affects me in any way.

You know, like in a palm-sweating, heart-racing, stomach-twisting sort of way.

"Where are you going?" he asks, catching up to me.

Guess one more thing about him hasn't changed.

His persistence.

Comes with the territory of always getting your own way.

If at first you don't succeed, try, try again. Eventually, all opposition will fall away, leaving you an open path to whatever your little heart desires.

At least that's how it works for Sam. For regular schmucks like me who don't come from a life of privilege and entitlement? We learn early on how stupid and useless it is to want things beyond our grasp, so we don't even bother trying.

I slide my glance to Sam's strong profile.

Even when those things are close enough to touch, they're still out of our reach.

"Hadley?" His arm brushes mine.

I shift away. Hitch my backpack higher. "I'm going home."

"I can give you a ride. I just need to see Mr. G for a minute but you can wait in the car."

"I have my bike." I refuse to ask why he needs to see the owner of Glenwood Landscaping. Mr. G. is my boss. Not Sam's.

Sam quit working for him last summer.

Sam quit a lot of things last summer.

"We can put it in the back," he says, pulling his key from his pocket. He presses a button and his SUV's lights flash.

"I'd rather ride my bike home."

He skirts around me, walks backward so he can see my face. "It's five miles."

"I know. I ride it every day. Twice."

Now he's frowning. "No one picks you up in the morning? Takes you home after work?"

Like he used to.

"No."

After Sam left, a couple of our coworkers offered to drive me to and from work each day, but after my constant refusals, they finally stopped.

He tries that grin of his again because...yeah...adorable. "Come on, Hadley. Let me drive you home. We can stop at the Tastee Freeze for a milkshake. My treat."

The boy knows the way to my heart, that's for sure, and honestly, if he throws in an order of fries, I might just take him up on it.

What can I say? I'm weak.

But it's not really the food that's tempting me to say yes. After spending the entire day out in the sun, the humidity pressing down on me like a giant thumb, the idea of sitting in Sam's air-conditioned car—instead of pedaling my way home—sounds like heaven. But worse, and far more dangerous, I'm tempted by Sam. By his voice and smile. By his broad shoulders and dark eyes and pretty, pretty face.

This is how he got to me seven years ago. He wore me down—with his looks and dogged persistence, his seemingly endless kindness and charm.

And after he patiently chipped away at all my defenses, gained my trust and made himself indispensable to me, to my happiness, as if I couldn't possibly live one freaking day without him in it, he left.

He. Left.

Now, I may not have a 4.0 GPA like good old Sammy-boy here, but I can be taught.

Especially when the lesson is so clear.

And painful.

"No," I say and it comes out sharp. Too sharp. Gives away too much. I clear my throat. Modulate my tone before adding, "Thank you, but like I said, I'd rather ride my bike home."

There. That's better. All calm and casual and carefree and not the least bit bothered by his return to town, his presence or his very existence.

He stops me with a hand to my elbow.

I go completely still, my breath locked in my chest, and stare down at his hand. The sight of his fingers, so dark against my pale skin, his palm so wide on my arm, causes something inside of me to pinch painfully.

I tug away.

But even though I'm free, the skin he touched still tingles.

He shoves both hands through his hair, keeps them there, fingers linked behind his head, elbows wide as he looks down on me. The pose makes it impossible to ignore his rounded biceps, how they stretch the material of his sleeves.

I hate myself for noticing. I hate him, too. Just on principle.

"I was going to call you," he says.

"Why?"

"To tell you I was coming home." He lowers his arms and leans toward me, his voice dropping. "To tell you I wanted to see you."

His words, the exact words I'd spent so long wanting to hear—*I'm coming home. I want to see you*—skim along my nerve endings. Cause my scalp to prickle.

No. No, he does not get to do this. Not now. Not after all this time.

"But you didn't." My tone is flat. I just hope he doesn't notice it's also unsteady. "You didn't call me."

His gaze drops briefly then meets mine again. "I wasn't sure you'd want to talk to me."

I stare at him. He's nervous, I realize. Cool, confident Sam Constable is nervous.

Huh. Must be Karma.

Better late than never, I guess.

"Eleven months ago I would have answered your call," I tell him.

Back then I would have given anything to hear from him. God, I was such an idiot. Praying and wishing and hoping for things to be different. Waste of time. Life happens. It just is. It's like being on a roller coaster. There's nothing you can do to steer it in any given direction. Nothing you can change. You can't avoid the dips and turns, the nausea-inducing loops or the slow, painful climbs.

All you can do is hold on and go along for the ride.

"But you didn't call or text," I continue with a shrug. "And now we have nothing to talk about."

I finally reach my bike but it's no relief, not with Sam behind me, big and broad and silent as I crouch and unlock the chain, unwrap it from the post. Standing, I slip one strap off, then swing my backpack around so I can put the chain in a side pocket. Usually I change into sneakers before heading home but that's not happening today.

I just want to go.

I slide my arm back through the strap and shrug the backpack on, catching the end of my ponytail between it and my shoulders. I reach back...

And brush my fingertips over Sam's knuckles.

I don't move, barely breathe as Sam gently pulls my hair free and sweeps my ponytail over my left shoulder. Head bent, hand inches from my pounding heart, he wraps a few strands around his finger and I'm mesmerized by the sight, the strands seeming brighter, redder against his tanned skin.

"Give me five minutes," he murmurs. His breath washes across the side of my neck and I shiver. "Please."

But I can't. I can't give him anything. Not my time. Not my attention.

Not my forgiveness.

If I do, he'll take them all and ask for more.

And I'll be left with nothing.

Shaking my head, I step away from his touch and grab my bike's handlebars. Put up the kickstand. Then, wordlessly, I walk away from him.

Just like he walked away from me eleven months ago.

2

SAM IS NOT THE FIRST PERSON TO DISAPPEAR FROM MY LIFE WITHOUT A word, a care or a backward glance.

That dubious distinction goes to my dad, some guy named Billy Wheaton, who met my mom while she worked in the office of a local construction firm one summer.

Mom never had much to say about him so the only things I know for sure are his name (assuming Billy Wheaton is his *real* name and not an alias used to throw off the cops and/or a woman or two scorned, looking to collect child support), that he was originally from New Hampshire (which sounds even more suspicious than his name. I mean, New Hampshire? Do people even really live there?) and he had red hair and green eyes.

I also know that when Mom told him she was pregnant (over a blooming onion at Benedict's Steakhouse downtown), he excused himself to use the restroom and was never heard from again, sneaking out the back and sticking Mom with a fifty-dollar dinner bill and another kid to raise on her own.

By that time, at the age of twenty-one, she was three-for-three in that department.

Not that she was totally alone. She had Gigi, her own mother, who'd babysit us when Mom worked nights or went out—which she did in equal amounts. And when Mom got antsy or bored or overwhelmed with her lot in life (a frequent occurrence), she'd drop us on Gigi's doorstep, then take off to parts unknown, staying away for days. Weeks. And on a few occasions, months.

Until that last time when I was ten, when she never came back.

Skipping out on me, Zoe and Devyn the same way all three of our fathers had. Forcing Gigi to pick up the pieces, a resigned and resentful caretaker.

Life wasn't perfect—there still wasn't enough money and Gigi had never exactly been the warm, fuzzy, sweet grandmotherly type—but it was better than it'd been with Mom. I mean, yeah, we had to move into Gigi's tiny trailer and she constantly snapped at us and reminded us of how grateful we should be for her taking us in, but we were together—me, Zoe and Devyn. And together, we could handle anything.

Even being left again.

Which was what Gigi did the day after Devyn graduated from high school. She came into the bedroom Zoe and I shared, woke us up and told us that since Dev was officially an adult, we were her problems from now on. Her responsibility.

Then she picked up the suitcases she'd already had packed and waiting by the door and walked out. She moved in with her sister down in Florida but let us stay in the trailer.

The only time we hear from her is if we're late with a rent check.

Which is more often than we hear from our mom.

Having the people who are supposed to love you the most, who are supposed to take care of you, choose to go? It sucks.

And something I have a lot of experience with.

So, no, Sam wasn't the first person to disappear from my life.

But he was the first person I cried over.

He wasn't the first person to walk out on me.

But when he did, I swore to myself he'd be the last.

———

By the time I reach Hilltop Estates—which is indeed on top of a hill but decidedly less fancy than the name implies (Hilltop Trailer Park doesn't have the same ring)—my chest is tight and my quads aching. Biking five miles in heavy boots will do that, especially when that last mile is all uphill.

I live in northwestern Pennsylvania. Everywhere you turn it's hills, hills and more hills.

I could have stopped and switched into my sneakers. Could have gotten off my bike and pushed it up that last long incline. But I'd wanted to put as much distance between me and Sam as quickly as possible, so I'd pedaled as hard, as fast as I could.

It didn't even work. The whole distance thing, I mean. I can still feel his hand on my arm, his breath on my neck. Can still smell his cologne.

I turn onto Winter Street and stand and pedal when our trailer comes into view.

I just want to be home.

I pull into the gravel driveway behind Zoe's ancient blue Toyota, and brake hard. Too hard. My rear tire wobbles and skids, the bike lurching to the side. Swinging my right leg over the seat, I try to jump free but the bottom of my backpack catches on the seat and I tumble to the ground, landing with an *Oof!*, my bike falling on top of me, the pedal scraping my shin.

Catching my breath, trying to get my bearings, I stare up at the cloudless sky.

And see Sam's expression when I told him we had nothing to talk about. That it was too late.

Like he was devastated.

Like I'd broken his heart.

Again.

Frustration boils up inside of me, a toxic brew of fury and fear, and my hands curl, my nails digging into my palms. I hate that after all this time, after everything he did, everything he said, he still affects me this way. Like I'm some simpering idiot willing to toss aside all pride and self-respect just because he smiles at me.

Terrified I'll do that tossing all the same.

That's what the boy does to me: He makes me weak.

Worse than that, he makes me want things I'll never have.

I try and thump the back of my head against the pavement a few times but it doesn't reach. There'll be no knocking some sense into myself today.

And where does Sam get off being upset? To act all hurt and disappointed. He was the one who ended us. He was the one who left.

As always, he'd gotten what he wanted. Me, out of his life.

He doesn't get to change his mind now.

Tears sting my eyes. Clog my throat.

And as much as I'd like to blame them on the pain shooting up from my wrist, the sharp gravel digging into my lower back and the scratch just below my knee, I can't. So I take several long, careful breaths. Blink the tears back.

I will not cry over Sam Constable.

Not ever again.

Why did he even come back?

I roll my eyes. Okay, yeah, that's a stupid question.

He came back because this has been his home since he was ten years old. He has friends and his family here—his mom and stepdad and younger brother, Charlie. His older brother, Max.

Another Constable boy I'd be happy to never see again.

It's not fair. After Sam left, my days were all the same: Wake up, think of Sam. Go to school, imagine seeing Sam in hallway. Eat lunch alone, tucked into an empty corner of the cafeteria, remember sitting across from him every day. Get home, wait for him to return one of my many, many calls or texts. Go to bed, wonder what he's doing. If he thinks of me at all.

Wake up and repeat, repeat, repeat.

It all changed on Christmas, the last time we saw each other. I stopped waiting. And eventually, he was no longer the first thing I thought about every morning. No longer the last thing going through my mind before I fell asleep.

I got over it. Got over Sam.

And I refuse to backslide just because he's in town for a few weeks. We probably won't even see each other again. But if we do, I'll keep my distance.

It's what I should have done in the first place.

"Are you okay?"

I turn my head and my hat shifts forward, blocking my view. Lifting my chin so I can peer under the brim, I see Whitney McCormack at the end of my driveway.

Great. Just what I need. Stunning Whitney of the beautiful face, glossy black hair and perfect, petite body witnessing me on my back like a turtle flipped onto her shell.

Some days just suck.

I have more than my fair share of them.

Sitting up, I push the bike off my legs. "I'm fine," I say, getting to my feet. "Thanks."

We both reach for the bike, but I get there first.

"I've got it," I say, noticing that under the hem of her long, flowy skirt, her feet are bare.

Must be a Southern thing, going barefoot all the time. She and her mother moved into the double-wide mobile home across the street two weeks ago and I've yet to see her wear shoes. Whitney, that is. I'm assuming her mother wears them, though to be honest, I've never checked.

I walk my bike toward the trailer, stepping carefully on my sore ankle.

Whitney follows. "You're limping."

I lean the bike against the front post of the carport. "Just twisted my ankle a little."

"Do you need help getting inside?"

"I've got it," I repeat, an edge to my tone that I can't stop.

Look, I'm not trying to be mean, but I'm tired, my shirt is clinging to my sweaty back and my thighs feel like they're on fire. My shin is bleeding, my palm stings and both my wrist and my ankle hurt.

I'm not in the mood to be friendly.

Which, okay, is nothing new, but usually I can muster up a cool politeness.

But today, this is the best I can do.

"Oh," Whitney says. Her accent is soft, her voice husky. "Are you busy tonight? Maybe you could come over? We could watch a movie?"

Whitney moved here from one of those down-South states that ends in *a*—Georgia or Alabama or Louisiana—two weeks ago. One week after school let out, so she hasn't had a chance to meet anyone in town yet.

Other than me it seems.

And I am *not* welcome wagon material.

It's that whole not-friendly thing.

But Whitney is friendly. Always waving and smiling and asking how I am whenever she sees me. Now she's inviting me over so we can spend some good, old-fashioned quality teenaged-girl time together.

God, she must really be desperate.

Or lonely.

It's that last thought, that she might be lonely, that has me thinking I should ask if she wants to spend the evening watching Taylor with me. I made pizza dough last night and she could eat with us. Maybe we could make some cookies later, too.

But what would be the point? It's not like we're going to be friends.

Something she'll figure out soon enough.

"I can't," I say. "I'm watching my niece."

She keeps right on smiling because she is probably the kind of person that never gets down, disappointed or disheartened.

"Okay," she says. "Maybe another time?"

"Yeah. Maybe."

She waves and heads back across the street and I turn and walk past the carport and around the back of the trailer. I doubt there'll be another time. The only reason she even asked is because we live across the street from each other. I'm convenient.

She has all summer to meet people. She can join a club or get a job or just start hanging around the pool or the Tastee Freeze. I mean, I'm hardly well-versed in the art of friendship making but those seem like practical options.

And when school starts, she'll have our entire senior class of two hundred and thirteen students to choose from. She'll meet people who have more in common with her than living in the same trailer park.

Even if I was in the market for a new BFF, which I'm not, there's no point in Whitney applying for the job. A year from now, we'll graduate and then she'll go her way—probably to a college in some city like Philadelphia or DC or where she used to live before—and I'll go mine.

And by that, I mean I'll stay here.

That's how it is. Those who can get into and afford college or who are brave enough to join the military, they leave. And don't come back.

The rest of us, the ones with below-average grades, below-average incomes and generations of stupid decisions?

We stay.

We have to. We don't have anywhere else to go.

3

I climb onto the back deck, open the door and step into the kitchen. Sitting at the table, I take off my boots and socks, then set them on the mat next to the door before crossing to the sink and wetting a paper towel. I wipe the blood from my leg, then carefully wash and dry my hands. The scrape isn't as deep as I'd thought and my palms are only slightly abraded, so good news all around.

After tossing the dirty paper towels into the garbage, I go into the living room, which is separated from the kitchen by a short eating bar. Eggie (short for Egbert, our squat, muscular Rottie/boxer mix), is on his ratty blanket in the corner. He lifts his golden head, tail wagging, and I bend and give him some love before moving on to stand in front of the clanking AC unit in the window. Arms spread, eyes closed, I let the cool air wash over me.

Behind me, Zoe and Taylor are sound asleep on the grubby sofa, Zoe against the back of the couch, one arm wrapped around Taylor's tiny middle to keep her from rolling off. *Frozen* is playing on the TV, the part where a sobbing Elsa hugs the iced-over Anna.

There's nothing like the bond between sisters. Nothing.

God knows I'd be lost without mine.

Lost, in the foster care system and totally, completely alone.

I head down the short hall, the air getting thicker and hotter with each step. We had another AC window unit that we rotated each year between our bedrooms, but it broke two summers ago, and even with Dev picking up extra hours at the hotel, we can't afford a new one because her ten-year-old Focus needs new brakes if it's going to pass inspection in two months, and we're still saving up to have the roof redone. So during summer this entire half of the trailer is like a sauna, my room at the end of the hall especially.

I set my backpack on my bed, take my hat off and toss it onto the dresser. I'd planned on showering before making dinner, but if I don't get Taylor up now, she won't sleep tonight. And as I'll be the one watching her while Zoe tends bar at Changes Bar and Lounge (more bar than lounge), and Devyn works the front desk at the Red Dog Inn, I'd really like her to go to bed at a decent time so I can have a few hours to myself.

With my sisters both working two jobs and ever since Sam left town and our friend group—I mean...*his* friend group—decided they no longer want anything to do with me, I spend a lot of my time alone.

Not going to lie. It sucked at first, being a pathetic loser with no friends to sit with at lunch, no one to hang out with on the weekends, but I got used to it.

Now I like being alone.

I don't have to worry about how long someone is going to want to be in my life. Knowing there'll come a day when they decide they're better off without me but not knowing, exactly when that day is.

I was too content before. Too trusting. I let myself get too comfortable being Sam's friend, being a part of his group.

I was stupid, veering out of my lane. Believing things would be different with Sam. With the others. Forgetting all the lessons my life had taught me.

It's better the way it is now. Easier.

Safer.

Back in the living room, the movie's now at the part where Anna and Kristoff are in a serious lip-lock, because the *only* happy ending allowed is when boy and girl wind up together. Love conquers all.

Such a nice sentiment.

Such a nice, delusional sentiment.

I turn the TV off. They shouldn't fill little kids' heads with that crap. It just sets them up for disappointment when they're older and realize that in real life royalty doesn't fall for commoners.

Not even if that commoner is a cute Viking with wide shoulders, floppy blond hair and an adorable reindeer sidekick.

Kneeling next to the couch, I rub Taylor's arm. "Hey, baby girl."

She doesn't wake, but Zoe does. "What time is it?" Zoe asks, her voice husky with sleep.

"Almost five." I brush back Taylor's pale hair. Even though the only thing she's wearing is a diaper and the AC is on full blast, she's sticky and sweaty, the curls at her temple damp. "Come on." I lift her. "Time to wake up."

She whines and snuggles against me, her head on my shoulder, her hot breath against my neck. She's deadweight in my arms, all skinny arms and legs. I rub her back, can feel the tiny bumps of her spine. God, it seems like just yesterday she was a baby, round and squishy soft, the rolls of her legs and arms settling on each other, making her look like the Michelin Man.

Now she's less baby and more real person.

A mini, real person with thoughts and opinions and absolutely no interest in learning how to use the toilet.

I kiss the top of her head. "Want some juice?"

"Juice," she repeats. She wiggles, trying to get closer to me, her toes digging into my rib cage. "Juice!"

"I'll take that as a yes."

We walk into the kitchen and I get a sippy cup and matching lid out from a lower cabinet, then open the refrigerator. Taylor keeps her head on my shoulder, wraps my hair around and around and around her finger, the way she has since she was nine months old. It comforts her, holding on to my crazy, frizzy hair.

That's me. A walking, talking security blanket.

Glad I'm able to do something useful with my life.

It's a production, getting a toddler juice while holding that toddler, your hair in her death grip. I pour apple juice into the cup, cross to the sink to water it down, then heft Taylor higher. Holding the cup in my left hand—the one under her butt—I twist the cap on with my right.

Mission accomplished.

"Here you go," I say.

She takes it, her head still on my shoulder, hair still in her other hand. "Juice," she whispers, a solemn prayer to the nectar of the gods as she holds the cup up like a holy sacrifice.

I bow my head—seems like the appropriate thing to do. "Amen."

She guzzles it. I mean, the child chugs it down in mere moments then shoves the cup at my face. "Mowah."

She hasn't quite mastered *r*s.

"More *please*," I say.

She's now pressing the cup against my cheek, pushing my head in the opposite direction of the hand still holding my hair. "Mowah please."

I take the cup from her before she rips out a chunk of the hair she loves so and repeat the juice-getting process. While she's drinking this second cup, I put the bottle back in the fridge and take out the bowl of pizza dough and set it in a sunny spot on the counter to warm up.

Curled up on the couch, Zoe's reading something on her phone, smiling. She's still in her black pants and red Top-Mart polo, her light brown hair falling out of the French braid I'd given her this morning, pieces clinging to her neck, sticking out above her ears. The nubby material of the couch left its imprint on her cheek and her mascara is smudged.

Ah, the life of a Jones girl. So much glamour. Such excitement.

"What's got you so happy?" I ask.

"Just a text from Rob."

"Who's Rob?"

She's still focused on her phone. Still smiling. "A guy I matched up with last night."

"Matched up with? You're on a hookup app?"

"Please. I don't need an app for a hookup," she tells me, as if being hit on by guys at the bar all the time is a proud accomplishment. "It's a dating app."

I switch Taylor to my other hip. "You really think you're going to meet Prince Charming on a hookup app?"

"Dating app," she corrects in a singsong tone. "And maybe." She shrugs. "You don't know unless you try, right?"

Uh...wrong. Certain things are set in stone and all the effort in the world isn't going to change them.

Then again, Zoe's always been the optimistic Jones sister.

Even after being abandoned by her dad (Devyn, Zoe and I all have different fathers, the same backstory and Mom's last name), getting pregnant at sixteen, then dumped by the father of her baby, and never having a guy stick around longer than a few months hasn't put her off the opposite sex.

My sister's addicted to love. She's either chasing after it, falling into it or recovering from losing it.

But at least she's finally moving on from Ethan the Ass. Four weeks of her moping around heartbroken was more than enough for any of us. Devyn warned her that hooking up with her boss— although he isn't, like, the boss boss at the store, he is assistant manager and, therefore, Zoe's superior—was a mistake, but Zoe prefers to learn her lessons the hard way.

Hopefully this one will stick.

If only because Ethan broke things off with her so he could get back together with his on-again, off-again girlfriend and refuses to speak to Zoe unless it relates to—and this is a direct quote—Top-Mart business.

Hence his nickname.

"I'm going to shower," I say, but when I try to hand Taylor over to Zoe, Taylor screeches like I'm about to drop her into an active volcano and clings to me, arms around my neck, legs around my waist and juice dripping steadily down my back. "Or I could stay sweaty and stinky for a little bit longer. No problem."

Getting her way, Taylor loosens her grip on me and finishes her drink. When she's done, she throws the cup onto the floor, looks me in my eyes and says, "Stinky."

"She's right," Zoe says as I join her on the couch. "You're pretty ripe."

"Yeah? Then why don't you peel your kid off me?"

Zoe sets her phone on the side table. Holds out her arms to Taylor. "Come sit with Mama."

"No!" Taylor yells and turns her head away from Zoe. "No want you, Mama! Want Haddy!"

It's nice to be someone's favorite.

Even if that someone is sort of a terror.

Zoe shrugs and stretches, arms straight over her head, bare toes pointed, then stands. "Sorry I let her fall asleep. She refused to nap for Mrs. Richter and was so whiny I couldn't take it."

Mrs. Richter watches Taylor during the day, which is pretty much why Zoe tends bar five nights a week. To cover the cost of daycare.

"How long was she asleep for?" I ask.

"Maybe half an hour," Zoe says, going into the kitchen for a ginger ale. She opens the can, takes a sip. "She should still go down for you tonight."

I reach back and gently untangle my hair from Taylor's fingers. Turn her so she's sitting on my lap. "Is that right, baby girl? You going to go to bed on time tonight?"

She's shaking her head before I even finish my question. *No* is a big part of our lives. Saying it almost constantly to Taylor: No touching this or that. No coloring on the furniture. No yanking the dog's tail. Hearing it from her even more often: No, no, no!! complete with fall-on-the-floor, leg-kicking, body-thrashing tantrum.

Those are tons of fun.

"No bed, Haddy," she tells me. "No."

I give her a gentle squeeze because tiny, terrible-two terror or not,

I'm crazy about her. "Okay, no bed. But how about hanging out with Mommy so Haddy can take a shower?"

And that's what happens when you're around a toddler all the time.

You start speaking in the third person.

Taylor wiggles off me. "I showah, too," she says, shoving at her saggy diaper. "I showah with you, Haddy."

"Great," I say flatly. The past two years have taught me why, exactly, when my mom was still around, she used to spend so much time in the locked bathroom when Devyn, Zoe and I were little. That place is like a sanctuary, a tiny oasis—complete with waterfall if you turn on the shower—and a great place to hide when you live with anyone under the age of ten. "Just what I was hoping for."

Trying to step out of her diaper, Taylor nods. Sarcasm is lost on her. Too bad. It's one of the few things I'm really good at. But no matter how many times she does her march step—lifting and lowering her legs—the diaper stays on her ankles. Finally, she sits down and kicks it off. It arcs in the air, flying across the room. Eggie, with an excited bark, gives chase.

Me, too. Minus the excitement. And the bark.

I've seen what our dog can do when he gets a hold of a diaper. It's ugly.

And I'm in no mood to clean it.

"Egbert! No!" I yell at the same time Zoe lunges for Taylor and says, "Don't even think about peeing on the floor."

We're both too late as Eggie, snarling in pure bliss, shakes the diaper so hard pieces of it fly. And Taylor does, indeed, pee in the middle of the living room floor.

4

————————

I'M WASHING DISHES WHEN DEVYN SHUFFLES INTO THE KITCHEN IN A black tank top and blue boy-cut underwear.

"The coffeepot's all set up," I tell her.

Eyes half-closed, she grunts her appreciation, grabs a clean mug from the drying rack as she brushes past me and heads to the pot to turn it on. I'm scrubbing the pizza pan when the machine starts gurgling. A moment later, the scent of coffee fills the air.

I rinse the pan and set it in the rack, then let the dishwater out of the sink. When I turn to reach for the towel to dry my hands, Devyn's staring at the pot like she's been hypnotized by the slow *drip, drip, drip* of the magical brew.

Devyn hates mornings.

Except it's not morning. It's after ten p.m.

Guess it's just waking up that she has a problem with.

Probably because it means facing reality once again.

On nights she works at the Red Dog, Dev tries to catch a couple hours of sleep after she's done at the nursing home where she's a nurse's aide. She crashed the moment she got home, so Taylor and I ate without her. True to her vow of *no bed*, Taylor fought going to sleep despite my letting her lie down in my bed, reading her four bedtime stories and scratching her back for twenty minutes. When she finally drifted off half an hour ago, I didn't even bother moving her to her own miniature bed in Taylor's room. What's the point? She'll just find her way back to mine in the middle of the night, and this way, she won't wake me.

Except for the dozen or so times she kicks me in the face.

That child is a flopper.

The dripping coffee slows and then stops but Dev doesn't move. Doesn't even blink, just stands there, barefoot and sporting a serious case of bedhead, empty mug in her hands. Out of the three of us, she looks the most like Mom. Same dark hair and brown eyes. Same sharp cheekbones and heart-shaped face.

That's not to say Mom didn't leave her mark on all three of us. Dev looks like her, Zoe laughs like her and I have her sweet tooth.

And all three of us have crappy track records when it comes to guys.

Just keeping it all in the family!

When Dev continues to stand there, I take the cup from her hand —which does cause her to blink, once, so slowly I'm pretty sure she falls back asleep for the few seconds her lids are closed—then get the vanilla flavored creamer from the fridge. I pour some into her mug, top it with coffee, then press the cup back into her hands.

God. Sometimes I wonder if I was put on this earth just to make sure my sisters and niece are well-fed and hydrated.

Dev makes another sound, more groan than grunt, and lifts the cup to take a cautious sip. While she fuels up on caffeine and artificial colors, flavors and very real chemicals, I go about my business.

Except, everywhere I turn, there she is, in my way. Blocking the oven when I go to preheat it. Giving Eggie a pat in front of the cupboard that holds the cookie sheets. Holding the refrigerator door open with one hand, searching for something when I'm ready to get the cookie dough out.

I give her a gentle hip nudge to move her out of my way and she stumbles to the side like I just rammed into her with the car.

My sister. The drama queen.

"Creamer," she grumbles, voice husky with sleep, as I pull out the mixing bowl.

"Right there," I say, nodding at the creamer that's on the counter right where I left it not three minutes ago.

Seriously. What would these people do without me?

Setting the bowl on the counter, I use my foot to close the refrigerator door Devyn's left open, then take the plastic wrap off the dough. I turn to get a spoon from the drawer only to rear back in surprise to find Dev crowded even closer to me.

That's the thing about living with sisters. They're always borrowing your clothes, butting into your private business and invading your personal bubble.

"Give a girl some room, would you?" I say as I nudge her again—this time with the drawer to her butt—which moves her a few inches, just enough for me to get a spoon. "Don't you have to get ready for work?"

She shakes her head. "Not yet."

At least she's waking up enough to stop with the grunts, groans and grumbles. Before you know it, she'll be speaking in full sentences.

"If you're going to stay in here," I say, "could you at least sit down?"

I'm not used to people being in the kitchen with me when I'm baking. I like my space. It's why I bribed Taylor with two episodes of *Paw Patrol* earlier so I could mix up the cookie dough while the pizzas baked.

"What are you making?" Dev asks.

Not only has she *not* sat down, but she's moved even closer to me and is on her toes, pressing against my back as she tries to peer over my shoulder. Doesn't work. I'm taller than both of my sisters and Dev's the shortest of us all.

"Chocolate chip cookies."

Though I'm busy scooping rounded balls of dough onto the cookie sheet and don't actually see her face, I swear I can *feel* her expression brighten.

Dev loves my chocolate chip cookies.

She lowers down to her heels. "Will they be ready for me to take to work?"

"Possibly. If you give me some room to work."

She immediately crosses the few feet to the table and takes a seat.

Both my sisters appreciate my baking and are usually good at leaving me in peace to do it. Though tonight, for some unknown reason, Dev stays in the kitchen, sipping her coffee at the table, giving Eggie a belly rub with her bare foot while I fill the sheet tray, then sprinkle the dough with flaky sea salt. The oven beeps, letting me know it's reached the right temperature, and I put the first tray in and shut the door. Set the timer, then start scooping dough for the second sheet.

"Heard you ran into Sam today."

I go still at Dev's words, my hand tightening on the spoon handle.

Guess there's a reason for her sticking around after all.

"Zoe has a big mouth," I mutter.

"Was it a secret?"

Sighing, I lay the spoon down and face her. "No. And it's also not a big deal."

It's why I told Zoe in the first place. Just a calm, casual, *oh, hey, guess who I saw after work?* sort of thing.

Yeah, okay, so at the time I calmly, causally mentioned it, she just so happened to be walking out the door for work—and was already ten minutes late.

What can I say? Just because it's not a secret, or a big deal, doesn't mean I want to talk about it.

"Not a big deal, huh?" Devyn asks sounding less than convinced.

"Nope. I saw Sam. We talked for a few minutes. He went his way. I went mine." I force a shrug. "No. Big. Deal."

"You sure about that?" she asks softly.

My throat gets tight and I drop my gaze. Rub at the dot of dried pizza sauce on my tank top.

Both my sisters know what really happened between me and Sam last summer. How our friendship imploded. Why he left.

They witnessed firsthand what a mess I was. How heartbroken. How pathetic.

They got me through.

Jones sisters stick together. Always.

But they don't know everything.

And they never will.

I lift my head. Nod. "I'm sure."

She studies me, searching and intense, trying to see in my brain. Trying to dig out my truth.

But there are some things not even a sister can know. Some mistakes too huge. Too humiliating. Some feelings too private to share, even with her.

Like how I felt—how I still feel—after seeing Sam today. After hearing his voice. Angry that he came back, that he approached me after ghosting me for so long.

Confused that a part of me—a big, huge, loud part—was so relieved to see him again. So happy.

Scared that relief and happiness might shove aside everything I need so desperately to hold on to—all the bitterness I've felt for almost a year, the pain—leaving me weak. Giving him an opening he'll take advantage of.

One he'll use to hurt me again.

"Are you going to hang out with him again?" Dev asks.

Jeez. I hope my fake nonchalant tone is better than hers because hers sucks.

"I didn't hang out with him today. It was an accidental meeting."

"Uh-huh. So he didn't ask you to spend any amount of time with him?"

I roll my eyes. "I'm not going to hang out with him," I say, leaving out the part about Sam offering me a ride home. About him saying he wanted to talk to me. "I doubt I'll even see him again while he's in town."

"Make sure you don't," Dev says, standing. "The last thing you need is him messing with your head again."

I snort softly as she walks down the short hall off the kitchen toward her bedroom on the far side of the trailer.

Too late for that warning. I've spent less than ten minutes with the boy and already my mind's a tumbling, freaked-out mess.

But it doesn't matter because, like I told Dev, I probably won't even see him again. I'm sure he has plans to keep himself occupied for the week or two that he's in town. Spending time with his family. Catching up with the friends he didn't completely ditch last year.

And if I do just so happen to see him again, I'll ignore him.

Sam will not hurt me again.

I won't let him.

5

MY ARM LYING ON THE OPEN TRUCK WINDOW, I REST MY HEAD ON THE doorframe as we drive down School Street. The morning air is cool and damp on my face and forearm and I breathe in deeply, letting it fill my lungs. And pretend I'm somewhere else. Anywhere else—the wilds of Alaska or a Hawaiian beach. Somewhere far, far away from northwestern Pennsylvania.

Anywhere except the passenger side of one of Glenwood Landscaping's pickups.

Miles and continents and worlds away from Sam Constable.

I'm not. Far from Sam, that is. Nope, I'm super close. Well, closer than I'd like considering there's only about two feet of space between us. Empty space.

Where's Kyle when you need him?

Oh, that's right, Kyle Caldwell, the college kid I've been working with for the past two weeks, is now happily mowing, weeding, trimming and mulching with John Butler and Cody Finlay. Because, as has been noted, Sam is back in town.

And back working for Glenwood Landscaping.

If it wasn't for crappy luck, I wouldn't have any luck at all.

Yeah, I know, whine, whine, whine. But I'd talked myself into believing the only time I'd see Sam again was in passing. So much for that hopeful thought.

Although I'm still giving that whole ignoring him thing my best shot.

I sure wasn't expecting him to be there this morning when I walked into the garage where Mr. Glenwood was assigning today's jobs. Didn't think he'd be wearing his green GL T-shirt and a pair of khaki cargo shorts looking like some poster child for hot yard boy. He'd been talking with my coworkers, all chatty and grinning and more comfortable around them than I ever was.

Like he never even left.

Am I the only one who remembers that he did leave? That we all got along just fine without him?

I guess so because not only were Kyle, John and Cody tickled pink to have their buddy back, Mr. G. was ecstatic at the return of his favorite employee. And he obviously thought I'd be equally thrilled to be assigned to work with Sam. Like we used to. After all, Sam's stepdad helped us get these jobs when we were both fifteen, and the previous two summers we always worked together.

As far as Mr. G. is concerned, it always has been, and always will be, Sam and Hadley. Hadley and Sam.

It's like we have our own freaking theme song, for God's sake.

So, yeah, there was much celebration and excitement at my work place this morning.

Whoopee.

And now, as has been noted, I'm in a truck with Sam, who, for some reason, thought it'd be a great idea to get his old job back.

Can't I have one thing, one simple, little thing, that's just mine?

Even if it's a job I hate?

I shift, pretend to check my phone but really sneak a glance at Sam's profile, his straight nose, the sharp line of his jaw. Yeah, definitely hottie poster child material. The kind that gives a girl all sorts of tingly feelings.

Stupid tingles.

He's driving in his careful, cautious way, both hands on the wheel, speed just under the limit.

No rule breaking for Sam Constable.

That's why I thought I was safe being his friend. I figured he'd keep to the rules of that friendship. Stay within the boundaries.

I hadn't expected him to toss those rules aside. To knock down those boundaries.

Hadn't expected him to ask for more.

Did I mention he texted me last night just after midnight?

Hey.

That was it. One word. One word more than I'd heard from him in close to a year. Three stupid letters meant to remind me he's here, in town. That he's going to be here tomorrow and the day after that and all the days next week and for God only knows how long.

I didn't need the reminder, thanks all the same. It's not like I forgot seeing him a few hours before. Worse, memories had bombarded me all night, sneaking up on me when I least expected it. Memories of all the time we spent together.

I'd taken his friendship for granted. Had assumed he'd always be around, would always be a part of my life.

Lesson learned.

Long, painful lesson learned.

Now he wants...well...I'm not sure, but whatever it is, I can't give it to him.

I can't go back. I won't.

So I deleted his text without responding and despite the three dozen freshly baked chocolate chip cookies on the counter and the fact that I had to get up in six hours, I made a double-layer devil's food cake from scratch with chocolate Swiss buttercream.

Sometimes a girl just needs straight-up chocolate. Lots and lots of it.

Which I had in the form of two huge slices at three a.m.

And a third for my breakfast less than two hours ago.

Now that delicious breakfast cake is sitting like lead in my stomach.

Boys ruin everything.

We still have three miles before we get to Mr. Lucco's house outside of town, and even though it's less than ten minutes, I can't take one more second of silence. Sam hasn't said anything to me other than a quiet, "Morning, Hadley," when I arrived at work.

He barely looked at me while Mr. G. told us we'd be assigned together, "Just like old times."

What is with adults thinking old times were the best times? Does no one remember life before vaccinations, electricity, and the internet?

Reaching over, I turn on the radio. "Love Shack" is playing and I grind my back teeth together. The truck is ancient, older than I am, and only gets the local a.m. station, which plays what they like to call classics from the '70s and '80s.

Oh, well. As Devyn loves to tell me, beggars can't be choosers.

Dev's not big on the whole *build your younger sisters up with positive affirmations and inspirational quotes* thing.

She's more of a *tell them the harsh truth so reality doesn't kick them too hard in the ass* believer.

"Wow," Sam says, "you're more pissed at me than I thought."

I stiffen. Tell myself I'm not going to respond because...ignoring him...but then hear myself ask, "What?"

I give an inner eye roll. Why do I even bother?

He nods toward the radio. "You hate this song but you'd rather listen to it—and get it stuck in your head—than talk to me."

Folding my hands together in my lap. I stare primly out the windshield. "I'm not pissed."

If I was, that'd mean he had the power to make me angry. That he still had the power to hurt me.

Not giving him that power, remember?

Besides, I'm over him, so nothing he says or does means anything to me.

Totally, completely over him.

"Liar."

At Sam's softly spoken word, my mouth dries. I feel caught. Trapped. Worse, I feel exposed.

But then I realize he can't actually hear my thoughts, so he's not accusing me of lying about being over him. About my feelings for him.

Thank God.

"You can always tell me the truth, Hadley," he continues, glancing at me. "Always."

I look down at my hands. No, I can't tell him the truth. Not about this.

Not about a lot of things.

I reach over and turn up the radio until it's so loud the singer's *Bang! Bang! Bang!* reverberates in my head. Sam's right. I do hate this song. And it is definitely going to be stuck in my head all day long now.

And it's all his fault.

A lot of things are his fault.

But most of them are mine.

6

"IF I JOIN YOU," SAM ASKS ME ON OUR LUNCH BREAK, "ARE YOU GOING to run away from me again?"

"I haven't run away from you," I mutter, which is such a lie I look up at the sky in the hopes of evading the lightning bolt I'm sure is headed my way.

So I ran from him yesterday when he surprised me in the parking lot.

And, yes, I may have done my best to avoid him all morning, but it wasn't running away. I was working. Push-mowing the flat part of Mr. Lucco's yard while Sam tackled the hill. Running the Weedwacker along the edges of the driveway while Sam was in the backyard weeding the huge flowerbeds that surround the house.

Maybe I pretended to nap when we drove to the Sullivans' house on the top of Rutherford Run, but only because I was up late baking, didn't sleep well when I finally did go to bed and really was so tired I had to shut my eyes for a little while.

Is it my fault doing so conveniently meant I couldn't talk to him?

Sitting on the open tailgate, I shrug. "I'm not going anywhere," I say, "whether you're here or not."

Unlike him, I don't have anywhere else to go. When Sam wanted away from his life, he moved in with his dad, a plastic surgeon out in Los Angeles.

I don't even know where either of my parents are.

Have no desire to find out, to be honest.

Head down, the brim of my green, Nike ballcap shading my eyes, I watch Sam set his lunch pail on the truck bed next to the Weedwacker, then turn and, laying his hands flat on the tailgate, lift himself up to sit. The muscles in his arms flex and bunch and I jerk my gaze away, feeling overly warm and oddly breathless.

I shift ever so casually to the right, a tiny butt shimmy that puts a few more inches of space between us. He sighs, a soft, resigned sound.

He noticed my retreat.

I tense, waiting for him to call me on it. He doesn't. Just reaches back for his pail and pulls out the foot-long Italian sub he picked up during our nine-thirty break, when he drove to Joey's Deli.

He offered to buy me a sub, too—smoked turkey and provolone, my favorite. While I give three quarters of my paycheck to Devyn to use toward our expenses, Sam's money is just that. His.

And he can spend it however he wants. Can buy takeout coffees and lunch every day. Can pitch in for beer for every party. Can go shopping any day of the week and buy new clothes or sunglasses or sneakers. Doesn't matter whether it's money he's earned, cash that was given to him by his mom or the bank card his dad funds.

It's his to do with as he pleases.

But even when we were still friends, I was always careful about not letting him spend too much on me. I didn't want him to think I was using him or liked him because he bought me things.

I didn't want to owe him, either.

Not when our friendship always felt so lopsided. Like he gave me way more than I ever gave him.

So when he'd offered to buy my lunch, I'd politely declined. Now I'm sneaking glances at him again, unable to believe he's back. That he's here, next to me, once again.

Unable to look away.

His hands are big and tanned, his fingers long, and I can't tear my eyes from them as he pulls the sub out of the paper sleeve and unwraps it. He lifts the sandwich to his mouth and my gaze follows as he bites and chews, his eyes hidden behind dark sunglasses as he looks straight ahead.

"Not hungry?" he asks, as if only mildly curious.

As if he doesn't realize I'm staring at him.

Heat floods my face but I keep my movements slow and controlled as I open a bottle of water and take a sip. Mr. G. makes sure each truck is stocked with plenty of water, Gatorade and sunscreen.

Though I'm the only one who appreciates the sunscreen. The guys don't bother with more than a thin layer of the stuff on their noses and the backs of their necks, but I apply and reapply the SPF 50 on every inch of my skin not covered by clothes.

Just one of the joys of being a pale, freckled, redhead: higher risk of sunburns and skin cancer.

I set my water aside and get a piece of leftover pizza from my insulated lunch pail. Chewing my first bite, I follow Sam's lead and look out over the valley.

I should have said something when he turned onto the old lease road instead of heading to our next work site. Should have told him to stop.

We used to eat lunch here whenever possible. Ten minutes from town, it cuts our lunch hour down to forty minutes, but it's worth it. It's like we're on top of the world. Like this field overlooking town, surrounded by the lush rolling hills, is our private oasis.

Our spot.

I used to love it here.

Used to. Until that hot, humid day last July when, sitting in this same exact spot with this same exact boy, everything changed.

My throat threatens to close and I carefully swallow my bite of pizza. Take a sip of water to wash it down. There's another slice in my pail, along with a banana, some chips and four chocolate chip cookies. But I've lost my appetite.

Sam's fault.

All Sam's fault.

"Want half?" he asks, holding out a huge orange.

We used to share our lunches all the time, would spread the items out on a clean dishtowel like a picnic. Sam always brought the produce section of our meal (Dr. Constable-Riester keeps their house stocked with an assortment of eat-a-rainbow fruits and vegetables) and I provided the cookies and brownies and cupcakes. Not exactly health food, although some of them had fruit *in* them. Banana bread. Apple fritters. Lemon cupcakes. That has to count for something.

"No," I say, staring over the valley once again. "I don't want half."

He starts peeling the orange. I smell it, juicy and sweet.

I think of the chocolate chip cookies in my pail, and for a moment, I seriously consider eating one. Not because I want it but so I can purposely *not* offer any of them to Sam. That should make it super clear that our sharing days are over.

But even I'm not that spiteful. Or mean.

And I really don't want to hurt Sam.

Not again.

"Is this how it's going to be?" he asks quietly.

"How what's going to be?"

He doesn't look up, just picks at a small bit of peel still on the orange. Flicks it away. "You and me. Is this how it's going to be from now on? This" –he looks up and gestures between us— "distance?"

I twist the cap off my water bottle. Twist it back on. "I don't know what you mean."

"Bullshit. You won't talk to me. You barely even look at me. Do you..." He inhales deeply. "I can tell Mr. G. we don't want to work together anymore."

That is an absolutely fabulous idea. But I can't get the words out. Can't even nod or make any sort of noise in affirmation.

"If that's what you want," I finally manage.

Not quite the emphatic declaration I intended.

"You know what I want, Hadley."

His voice is low and gravelly and it rubs against my skin. Rushes through my blood. I tell myself I have no idea what he means. That after so long, after his silence and his easy dismissal of me, there's no way I can possibly know what's in his head. In his heart.

But I do.

Sometimes I think I've always known.

Unable to sit still, I jump off the tailgate, and he gets to his feet as well. I'm not sure what to do. Where to go, and I end up twisting this way, then that.

Looking for an escape.

Looking to run from him once again.

Leaning over the tailgate, I drag my lunch pail toward me. "We can't go back to how we were."

"I don't want to go back."

I whirl around to face him. "You don't?"

He shakes his head, the sunlight glinting on the dark strands. There are flecks of grass clinging to his shirt and the hair on his forearms. A tiny piece sticks to his cheek, just below his temple.

I curl my fingers into my palms so I don't reach out and brush it away.

"I don't want to go back," he repeats, bending so he can see my eyes under the brim of my hat. "I don't want to be your friend, Hadley."

"Best friend," I blurt, then press my lips together. "You were my best friend."

He drops his gaze to the ground for a beat then returns it to my eyes. "I don't want to be just your friend. Not even your best friend."

There's a rushing sound in my ears and I realize it's my pulse. That I'm breathing shallowly. I suck in a deep breath and hold it. Count to five.

No. He's not doing this to me. Not again.

He doesn't mean it. If he did, he would have texted me at some point during the past eleven months. Would have called me. He wouldn't have stayed away so long.

He wouldn't have been with another girl at Christmas.

I cross my arms. "When did you get back?"

"What?"

"When did you get back to town? Yesterday? The day before?"

His mouth flattens. "Sunday."

Sunday.

Five days ago. He's been in town for days and didn't text me. Didn't come see me. I hadn't even known he was home.

You know what I want, Hadley.

Obviously I don't.

"Did you come to the garage yesterday to see me?" I ask.

He hesitates and I wonder if this is it, if this is the moment Samuel Joseph Constable lies to me for the first time.

I almost wish he would. It would make us more equal. Would make it so much easier for me to hold on to my anger. If he lied, I might even be able to let go of him. For good.

"No," he says. "I didn't go there to see you."

I hate how much it stings, finding out he's been home for days. That I wasn't the first person he sought out.

That he didn't seek me out at all.

"Why here?" I uncross my arms and wipe my damp palms down the sides of my shorts. "Why did you bring me to this spot for lunch? Was it to hurt me? To rub my nose in what happened?"

His brows lower and he steps closer. "You know I wouldn't do that."

"Actually," I say, my voice quite calm and cool, if I do say so myself, "the past eleven months, along with this conversation, prove I don't know you as well as I thought I did."

I grab my lunch pail and water, then brush past him and climb into the truck. A minute later, he slides behind the wheel and turns on the ignition.

"I didn't bring you here to hurt you or to try and get back at you," he says, watching the movement of his thumb as he rubs it along the outer edge of the steering wheel. "I wouldn't do that." He shakes his head and puts the truck into Drive. "I really hope you believe that."

I don't respond. If I open my mouth, I'll say something I shouldn't, an admission I can't take back. A truth that will give him even more power over me.

He has way too much as it is.

I do believe him. How could I not? He's too honorable to have hidden motives. Too kind to set out to hurt someone. And he's way, way too honest.

I'm the only liar in this truck and we both know it.

7

SAM AND I WERE NEVER MEANT TO BE FRIENDS.

Us, together—Sam and Hadley, Hadley and Sam—went against the natural order of things. Was in direct opposition of how society has run since the beginning of time. A fact of life I understood clearly even at the tender age of ten.

Royalty did not cozy up to the servants.

And the second-born, golden son of wealthy parents did not befriend the granddaughter of the woman his family paid to scrub their toilets.

But that's exactly what Sam did.

Because he's like that. Friendly. Personable. Kind.

Incredibly stubborn.

For some reason I've never understood, he's wanted to be my friend since he moved here. The first day he joined Miss Melton's fourth grade class, he walked up to me, introduced himself and asked me to sit with him during lunch.

I ignored him.

And sat by myself like I always did.

For the rest of that school year, I kept right on ignoring him while he kept right on trying to befriend me.

It wasn't like he needed me to be his friend. Within a matter of days, he was buddy-buddy with most of our class. But that didn't stop him from trying to get me to play with him and his new pals during recess. Or talking to me whenever he got the chance. Picking me for his team in gym class though I never gave much effort at sports and still never spoke to him. Inviting me to play kickball at recess, and asking me to be his partner in the math Olympics or reading competition despite my grades being nowhere near as good as his.

Either he felt sorry for me because I didn't have any friends, or he couldn't stand the thought of someone *not* liking him.

More than likely, it was a combination of both.

Eventually he would have seen me for the lost cause I am and given up.

I wish he had. I wish I'd kept right on ignoring him until we graduated high school and he moved away to some fancy, expensive college never to be seen in town again.

I wish I'd protected myself better.

Even as kids we'd been too different. He was cheerful, confident and optimistic—as people living blessed lives often are. And I've always been serious, skeptical and pragmatic. You know, the usual side effects of having both your parents walk out on you, being one of the few kids in your class to qualify for free breakfasts and lunches and always being aware that no matter how hard you work, how many jobs you hold and how hard you wish things were different, there's never enough. Never enough money. Never enough time.

I'd known getting involved with Sam Constable in any way, shape or form was a bad idea.

I'd known I'd end up getting hurt.

What I hadn't considered, what hadn't even crossed my mind, was that he'd get hurt, too. And it would be all my fault.

———

The rest of the day, Sam and I keep conversation to the bare minimum.

I hate it.

Hate having him so close and not being able to talk to him. Hate how things have changed between us. But it's for the best. Talking sure didn't help either of us feel better, so might as well quit while we're ahead.

Now, finally, after the longest day in history, it's just past four and Sam pulls up to the huge two-story garage Mr. G. uses to store equipment. I open the passenger-side door before Sam even has the engine turned off.

I practically run inside, relieved Mr. G. isn't in his office so I can fill out my time card and leave it on his desk without having to talk to him. I'm even more relieved that Sam stays outside with Kyle and John, who both wave as I head toward my bike.

Sam doesn't even look at me.

Which is good. Great, in fact. And exactly what he'd done all afternoon. What he'd done ever since walking out of my life last summer.

Pretended I don't exist.

Perfect. Now I can go back to pretending he doesn't exist, either.

Is this how it's going to be from now on? This distance?

Uh, yeah, Sam. This is how it's going to be. How it has to be.

He had no right to ask that. No freaking right. He was the one who left. He doesn't get to come back and act surprised I'm not falling into his arms.

He doesn't get to act like he's still hurting.

We're both just going to have to deal with this new normal. Him being home and us not being friends.

Hey, I got used to him not being here. I survived him leaving me.

I can survive him being back.

"What do we have here?" a male voice calls out. "Hot Hadley. In the flesh."

I stumble. Great. For the second day in a row, in almost the exact same spot, I've come face-to-face with a Constable boy.

A Constable boy I was hoping never to see again.

Which, okay, was stupid, me thinking I'd never see Max

Constable again, that I'd only see glimpses of Sam all summer, but come on. At least these encounters could have been spread out a bit.

What is with this parking lot? Is it some sort of weird portal where I'm destined to encounter the people I want most to avoid?

I look over, squinting against the sun, and yep, there's Max, home from his first year at Pitt, sitting behind the wheel of Sam's SUV, grinning at me.

"Actually," I say to Max, my tone so dry I'm surprised dust doesn't poof out of my mouth, "I go by just Hadley. Only my grandmother called me by my full name, and only when I was in really, really big trouble."

His grin amps up. I amuse him. Always have.

Plus, he likes to toy with me.

I think it's because I'm a challenge.

I wonder if that's another part of the reason Sam worked so hard to earn my friendship for so long.

After all, he's like his older brother in at least a few ways.

Though neither one of them would ever admit it.

Max gets out of the Explorer, shuts the door behind him, then leans against it, arms crossed as he gives me the patented Max Constable Checkout: a slow up-down look that starts at the top of my head, then drifts down to the toes of my boots only to drag back up again, lingering on my hips...my breasts...my mouth. It's blatant and sexual but at least it's honest.

With Max, you know exactly what he wants from you.

"You look good walking toward me," Max says in a low rumble. "Real good. Then again, you look good walking away, too."

I roll my eyes, and though I know I should do as he said, I should walk away, I don't.

I'm afraid to wonder why not.

"And here I thought you'd learn something in college. Like a come-on that actually works."

Straightening, he laughs because, again, I am just soooo freaking funny and never fail to entertain the hell out of him. "My come-ons work just fine, Hot Hadley."

True. So very, very true.

"I guess when you have the prettiest face around," I say, "it doesn't matter what you say."

He sighs dramatically, his expression all aw-shucks and innocent. He's neither.

Seriously, the boy should be in movies—his act is always on.

"It's a curse," he says with a shrug. "But what's a guy to do?"

"Wear a paper bag over your head?"

"And deny the ladies all this?" He circles his face then winks at me. "That'd be cruel."

I can't help it. I smile.

That's the thing about Max. Yes, he's egotistical and a player, but he's also funny and can be charming.

And just when you think he's the biggest dick in the world, that he's all arrogance, selfishness and a complete horndog, he says or does something that has you reconsidering.

Has you thinking maybe he's not.

Has you thinking maybe he's not all bad.

It's what makes Max Constable so freaking dangerous.

That and his broad shoulders, wide chest and too-handsome face.

I nod at the SUV. "Stealing your brother's car?"

"Borrowing it while mine is being serviced. Contrary to popular belief," he says in his silky, smooth tone, "I don't want everything that belongs to my brother." He edges closer, his voice low and intimate. "Especially not after I've already had it."

My head snaps back. Yep. Max Constable is definitely the biggest dick in the world.

He looks up, free of care or guilt. Must be nice, not having a conscience. "Hey. You ready?"

And I know without turning that Sam is behind me.

I can't face him. It ticks me off that I'm such a coward I can't even look at Sam for fear he'll see the truth on my face. Or worse, that I'll see something in his eyes, in his expression that tells me he heard what his brother said.

That he knows what it means.

So, nope, not looking at Sam. Going to keep my gaze right where it is, on the ground. Huh. What do you know? There're grass clippings on my boots. Better brush them off right away.

I do, taking my time, even as I feel Sam watching me. Finally, he says, "Yeah. I'm ready."

But he doesn't move, and from my vantage point, I see him shift his weight from foot to foot. I hold my breath, wait for him to offer me a ride home like he did yesterday. And wouldn't that be a boatload of awkwardness? Me in a car with Sam *and* Max Constable. God, just the thought of it makes me sick to my stomach.

Or that could be all the blood rushing to my head.

"Were you waiting for me, Hadley?" Sam asks.

"Nope," I say, still brushing, brushing, brushing at my boots with my fingertips. "Not waiting for you."

I'm wondering if I can stay down here forever—or at least until they leave—but I've pretty much gotten the boots as clean as they're going to get without a scrub brush and a hose and yet the brothers are still here.

"Hot Hadley came over to say hi to me," Max says, like the smug douchebag he is.

I jerk upright fast, too fast, and sway.

Both brothers reach out to steady me, Sam taking my left elbow, Max wrapping his hand around my upper right arm. And I have the stupid, irrational thought that one good yank and I'll be torn in two.

I shake them both off and step back, but though I'm no longer between them, I still feel stuck. Trapped with a grinning Max on one side and a solemn, watchful Sam on the other. They're so similar with their dark hair and eyes, their straight noses and the shape of their mouths. But there are differences, too. Subtle ones in their appearances. Overt ones, bigger ones, in their personalities.

Important ones.

Max's hair is a shade darker, his eyes more hazel than brown. Sam is an inch taller and a bit leaner. Max has a shallow dimple to the left of his mouth and there's a slight bump in Sam's nose from when he broke it during a basketball game in eighth grade.

They're both popular and well-liked, athletic and smart, but Max is more outgoing and loves being the center of attention. Sam is less showy. Friendlier. But the biggest difference between them is that Max has an edge, a sharpness to him that draws girls to him like a magnet.

They all think they can change him.

What they really want is for him to love them enough to change for them.

Good luck with that.

Max's phone buzzes and he checks it. "See you later, Hot Hadley."

He climbs back behind the wheel and rolls the window up. A moment later the muted sound of Frank Ocean surrounds us. Sam is watching me, waiting for me to say...something. A confirmation of Max's claim? A denial?

Who knows? Boys are weird and mysterious creatures.

Since I'm not talking, Sam gives me a nod—an all-encompassing boy gesture for *yes, hello, what's up?* and *goodbye*—and gets in the passenger side.

A moment later Max pulls up next to me as I head toward my bike and rolls down his window. "I almost forgot to tell you; Beemer's having a party tonight. Sort of a welcome home for me and Sammy. You should come. No offense, Had, but you look like you could use a little fun."

Why do people say no offense when they're purposely trying to offend you?

Glancing at him, I keep walking. "Shows what you know. My life is one endless joyride."

He smiles and it's different than the other times. More open. Real. He's only a year older than Sam and me and I remember when we were younger. Chubby and goofy, Max spent most of his time entertaining the other kids, making sure everyone liked him. He was fun and funny and, as hard as it is to believe now, nice.

Then puberty set in and Max grew taller, started working out more, and suddenly, he went from class clown to class heartthrob. He became That Guy. You know, good-looking, confident and cocky, but also a bit lost.

The most enticing combination ever.

Ah, adolescence. The end of many of a perfectly decent boy.

"I bet you'll have a great time," Max says, trying to sell me on going. He turns to Sam. "Tell her she'll have a great time."

He doesn't even look at me. "She doesn't want to go."

"Sure she does," Max argues.

"No," I say, stopping because walking and talking wasn't working for me. Maybe the movement interfered with how clearly and concisely I enunciated. "She doesn't."

But the word no isn't one Max hears very often. "If it's because you don't have a ride, no problem. I'll pick you up."

Sam's expression darkens, his jaw works but he keeps silent. Doesn't look our way.

"At least think about it," Max continues when I don't jump at the chance at arriving to the party on his arm.

"It'll be hard to think of anything else. After all, it's not every day I get invited to a party by the great Maxwell Constable. What a treat for little ol' me. Wait until all my friends hear. They'll be so jealous."

"Ha! Now I know you're joking."

I wrinkle my nose. "The part about you being great gave it away, huh?"

He shakes his head. "Nope. It was the part about you having friends."

With that and a salute, he takes off, dust billowing behind the tires.

Leaving me standing in the middle of the parking lot, an odd ache in my chest.

Max knows just what to say to inflict the most damage.

The truth usually does.

8

"How about *Beauty and the Beast*?" I ask Taylor that night, holding up the DVD and giving it a little wiggle, you know, to make it more enticing and all. "It has a talking teapot," I continue, my tone indicating there's nothing better than—and not the least bit terrifying about—inanimate objects walking and chatting amongst us. "And there's singing. Lots and lots of singing."

"No, Haddy," Taylor says, her little face scrunched into a frown, and God help us all, even the scowl is cute on her. Especially with her being fresh from her bath, her hair curling into ringlets, her pajamas a cute pink-and-white-polka-dot short set. "The beast is bad."

I feel desperation take hold. I have to come out ahead in this battle of wills. Have. To.

After the day I had, I deserve a win.

"He's not really bad." Although he does hold a young woman captive for weeks on end, won't let her touch his precious rose and flies into uncontrollable rages at the drop of a petal. Nope. Nothing scary, mean, abusive or misogynistic about any of that. "He's nice. At the end he even stops being a beast."

Yes, yes, it all happens after a particularly violent scene where he gets stabbed, and okay, handsome Gaston *does* meet a gruesome end, but hey! Belle and whatever-the-beast's-real-name-is kiss! Love conquers all! Happy, happy, joy, joy!

"Please, Taylor." There's a whine to my voice. Clearly, I've lost my mind. It's humiliating to admit but I am, indeed, pleading with a two-year-old. "It'll be fun. You'll like it."

Devyn comes into the living room, carrying a sippy cup of chocolate milk for Taylor, and looks at me like I'm one step below Gaston on the creepy, evil scale.

"She can't watch that," my sister reminds me. "It gives her nightmares."

"I'm the one who's going to have nightmares if I have to watch *Cinderella* again." I flop onto the couch with a rather dramatic sigh. A prince and a peasant girl? Please. "If I have to listen to those talking mice squeak 'Cinderelly! Cinderelly!' one more time, I'm going to dig my eardrums out with a fork."

"Or," Dev says, handing Taylor the cup, "you could *not* watch it. You could stay in your room--"

"It's too hot in there," I say, the whine in my tone increasing with each passing moment.

"What about that new pie recipe you wanted to try?" Dev puts *Cinderella* in the DVD player. Pushes Play. No win for me. Not today. "You could bake it while we watch the movie."

I cross my arms, realize I'm still holding *Beauty and the Beast* and toss it onto the coffee table. "It's too hot to bake, too."

Dev straightens and raises her eyebrows at me. Dev not only looks the most like Mom, but they also share an intolerance for whiners and complainers.

"Go sit on the porch then," she suggests. "It's a nice night. Take a book out there and enjoy it."

"I don't feel like reading and I don't want to enjoy anything." I sink farther down into the cushions, tip my chin to my chest. "I'd rather stay right here and be miserable, thanks all the same."

"What's going on with you?" Dev asks, not unkindly but with more than a little exasperation. Then again, her life has pretty much been one major irritation after another, especially after Gigi took off.

She threw away her own future to become my and Zoe's legal guardian so we didn't go into the system.

She stepped up. Devyn always steps up and does what's right. What needs to be done.

So I can hardly complain that I'm a pathetic nobody who's spending yet another Friday night at home with my two-year-old niece and my sister when that sister should be going out herself on one of the few nights she has off.

She shouldn't even be here.

"Nothing's going on," I say, pretending great interest in the movie I just said I never wanted to see again. "It was just a long day."

Her expression softens and she nods in commiseration. Long, sucky work-days she understands.

And it's enough of a believable explanation for her not to ask any more questions.

No, I didn't tell her or Zoe about working with Sam today.

They have more than enough on their plates without worrying about me.

Especially Devyn. She's given up way too much for me to add to it, even a little bit.

I'll figure this thing with Sam out. On my own.

"They mean sistas," Taylor tells no one in particular—or possibly everyone in the universe—in her angry voice which, again, super cute. On the screen, Cinderella's nasty stepsisters are teasing her and that is an injustice Taylor cannot stand. She snuggles back against me and whispers, "I don't like them sistas. I like Cinda-ella."

I brush back Taylor's soft hair. Kiss the top of her head. "That's because you're a good girl."

Taylor nods, still watching the movie. "I good and nice and pwetty and smawt and stwong."

Well, she's got all the bases covered.

Not sure the order's correct but whatever. Dev, Zoe and I will work on that with her.

Strength has to come first.

A girl has to protect herself. Her physical self, yes, but just as important, she has to protect her heart.

While Devyn curls up on the armchair with a thriller she picked up at the library and Taylor continues to alternately narrate the film and give her own commentary on the characters, I tip my head back against the couch. Stare at the ceiling.

This—my feeling so down, so unsettled and, well, left out, I guess —is my punishment for hurting Sam last summer. For what I did at Christmas.

That's the thing about Karma. It doesn't play favorites. And no one escapes it.

It's life's way of keeping things balanced. Sam and I never should have been friends in the first place and this is Fate's way of showing us the error of our ways.

Mess with Fate and you get slapped upside the head.

In the movie, Cinderella's fairy godmother is making all her dreams come true when someone knocks on our front door. Eggie races over, barks, then runs back to us, quivering with excitement at this unexpected occurrence: a visitor on a Friday night!

Then again, a visitor at any time, on any day, is cause for surprise and wonderment.

One of us really needs to get a friend or two.

Devyn gets up and crosses to the door and opens it. Eggie darts out to greet whoever's on the other side.

"Hey, Dev," Sam says.

Sam! Sam is here, at my house. Now.

Crap.

"Sam," she says, and I hear her surprise. Her suspicion. "Hello. Haven't seen you for a while."

"No, uh..." He clears his throat and I imagine him shifting uncomfortably. "Is Hadley home?"

My eyes widen. Wow. He must really be nervous, or at least, anxious. Usually he'd give Devyn his whole charming spiel—asking her how she is, apologizing for showing up unannounced, offering to take out the garbage or mow the lawn.

But tonight he got straight to the point.

That can't be good for me.

I try to mentally link minds with Devyn. *Tell him I'm not home. Tell him I'm not home.*

"Of course she's home," she says, her tone implying *where else would she be?*

I hang my head. Well, the whole ESP thing was a long shot anyway but she didn't have to say it like that.

As if I haven't left the house since Sam left.

Which is basically true but she doesn't have to let him in on that little detail.

I shift Taylor onto the couch and stand, ready to bolt out the back door because you can bet your sweet bibbity, bobbity boo I wish I wasn't here. I wish I was out, somewhere, anywhere with anybody, preferably an entire group of people who enjoy my company, laugh at all my jokes and hang on my every word.

But I'm too late to escape. Sam's already stepping inside thanks to my sister opening the door wide and gesturing for him to come on in.

Even for Karma, this latest bit seems excessive.

"Hadley," Devyn says as she leads Sam into the living room, "look who's here."

Ugh. Yes. I can see who's here. You don't need to use that fake chipper, this-isn't-awkward-at-all tone. The boy is six feet tall and so shiny and pretty it's as if a holy light is shining down on him.

He's hard to miss.

And it is sooo awkward.

For Sam, too, it seems, who is usually comfortable and at ease in any and all situations. His hands are in the front pockets of his jeans, and under the material of his green V-neck T-shirt, his shoulders are tense. Eggie, thrilled to have some reprieve in his life filled with estrogen, bumps his head repeatedly against Sam's leg and Sam bends down to scratch behind Eggie's ears, sending my dog into ecstasy.

"Hey, Eggie," Sam murmurs. "Hey, boy." Still petting Eggie, Sam looks up at me, his gaze skimming over me, and I remember I'm in my Friday night outfit—soft gray gym shorts and a black tank top. No bra. He clears his throat. "Hi, Hadley."

My face burns and I cross my arms over my chest. I open my mouth but my throat is dry and nothing comes out.

"Sam," Devyn says a bit too loudly, as if her increased volume will somehow make up for my lack of verbal skills, "would you like something to drink? Chocolate milk? Or something to eat? Hadley made cookies last night."

I wince because, yes, my sister did just offer Sam milk and cookies.

I look up at the heavens. Seriously. Enough is enough already.

"No, thanks," Sam says as he straightens. Eggie leans against him, his new favorite person. I glare at my dog. Traitor.

Sam smiles softly at Taylor. "Hey, Taylor."

She squeaks in distress and clambers to her feet, her cup falling to the floor. "Up, Haddy!" Arms raised, she bounces on the couch cushion in frustration and fear. "Up, up, up!"

I lift her and she buries her face in the crook of my neck, her legs around my waist. She's like a python, squeezing the life out of me, but her little body is vibrating and she's making small noises in the back of her throat.

"Shh...shh..." Swaying side to side, I jiggle her. "It's okay. It's just Sam."

Her grip tightens.

Taylor's life is filled with women. Zoe and Devyn and me. Mrs. Richter. Rebekah and Christine, Devyn's friends from the nursing home where she works as a CNA, who sometimes come over for a glass of wine and a *we hate men* bitch-fest. And Carrie, Zoe's coworker at Top-Mart, a single mom of a four-year-old daughter, who Zoe and Taylor hang out with sometimes.

Taylor's aware the male species exists, but to her, they're *out there*. At the store or park or McDonald's. In cartoon form in her movies. They're not here, in our house, taking up too much space, speaking in their deep voices, so much bigger than all of us. So different than we are.

So confusing and heartbreaking and exciting and terrifying all at once.

"Sorry," Sam mumbles. "I shouldn't..." He shakes his head. "Sorry," he says again, then he turns and walks out.

"It's okay," I tell Taylor as the door shuts behind him softly. "He's gone."

I rub her back and she lifts her head. As soon as she sees for herself that the living room truly is male-free (not counting Eggie, of course), she wiggles to be put down.

"I wanna watch Cinda-ella, Haddy! Cinda-ella," she calls, as if Cinderella is going to step out of the TV and beat me with her ugly glass shoe until I obey the two-year-old tyrant. "Cinda-ella!"

Talk about ungrateful.

I set Taylor on the couch, where she settles back, queen of her castle once more. "Next time a boy shows up here," I tell her as I pick up the sippy cup, "you're on your own."

But the joke is on me because...ha ha!... this is probably the last time a boy shows up here. I sure don't plan on inviting one over any time soon.

I look at the door. No boys for me, at least not in the foreseeable future.

Just as soon as I get rid of the one who's here tonight.

9

"I'LL BE RIGHT BACK," I MUMBLE, AVOIDING DEVYN'S EYES AS I HEAD toward the front door.

"Hadley..."

But I pretend I don't hear her. I know she has questions—and, knowing Devyn, many, many thoughts, opinions and suggestions she wants to share—but I can only handle one thing at a time.

First on that list is seeing if Sam really is gone.

In the hall, I grab Zoe's black hoodie and put it on, tugging the zipper up as I step into the muggy night. Sam's standing at the top of the porch stairs, his back to me, his hands once again in his pockets.

I exhale soundlessly.

He's still here. He didn't leave.

He didn't leave, and instead of being disappointed, instead of being resigned that I have to deal with him, I'm relieved.

My fingers tighten on the zipper. This is all wrong. I'm not supposed to be relieved he stayed. I'm not supposed to be the slightest bit happy he came to see me. Not the least bit curious as to what he has to say.

But I am. I am all those things. I'm also nervous and frustrated and angry.

Boys. They sure know how to mess with a girl's head.

The only way to resolve this, to get him out of my head, is to send him on his way as quickly and painlessly as possible.

I pull the door shut with a soft click and he stiffens but doesn't face me and there's something in his posture, the tension in his neck, the way his shoulders are rounded, that gives me pause. He looks so dejected. So alone.

He's not, of course. He's Sam Constable, friend to everyone.

Everyone but me, that is.

His decision, I remind myself. Everything that happened between us was his doing. His choice.

But only after you'd made yours, a small voice inside reminds me.

I lick my lips. "Sam--"

"Taylor's scared of me," he says, his voice a low rumble.

There's something in his tone, a note of self-disgust or maybe self-pity, and I can't send him on his way yet.

"It's a phase," I tell him. "She's been nervous around guys...men... boys" –yep, that should cover the entire human, male species— "for a few months now."

Across the street, past Whitney's trailer, the sun sets behind the rolling hills, leaving streaks of pinks and purples in the sky. Sam seems to glow where orange light touches him—his head, his shoulders.

Great. Just what I need. Yet another reminder that Sam is all light and goodness and everything right in the world.

Everything I don't deserve.

Finally, he faces me but he looks over my head. His expression is unreadable. Or maybe I no longer have the ability to read him. To know what he's thinking, what he's feeling, by looking at him. That thought gives me an odd ache in my chest. Makes me feel hollowed out and empty.

And this, this right here, right now, is another reason why he shouldn't have come back. Should have left me alone. Every time we're together, every time it's not like it used to be, it's as if I'm losing him all over again.

"It's not you," I continue. "I mean, it is, but it's not personal." I push the sleeves of the sweatshirt up but I'm still sweating, itchy and uncomfortable from the heat and Sam's silence. "She's just not used to guys coming to the house, that's all."

Now his gaze meets mine, seeking and intense. "You haven't hung out with any other guys?"

That's not what he's asking. He's asking if I've gone out with anyone. If I've hooked up with any boys since he's been gone.

I think about that cold night last winter when I made such a huge mistake. How desperate I'd been. How broken.

I can't lie to Sam. Not again.

But I can't tell him the truth, either. Not ever.

Besides, what I've done, who I've been with—or haven't been with —is none of his business.

"That's not the point." Avoidance. My favorite coping mechanism. "The point is that *you* haven't been around for almost a year. That's a long time. I mean, it's, like, half of Taylor's life. She doesn't even remember you."

"Yeah, that's clear." He sighs. "She's grown so much."

"Life went on without you," I say, shooting for an easy tone, one with just a hint of smugness because, hey, all those months ago, I'd told myself he'd regret leaving. It's nice to be right once in a while. "Did you think it wouldn't?"

"No," he says, all quiet and gruff. "I knew it would."

All my righteous vindication shrivels up and dies at the pain in his eyes. As I'd predicted, he regrets his choice, but I can't enjoy it. I don't feel victorious. Just small and mean.

Damn him.

"Charlie's four inches taller," he continues. "How the hell did that even happen? I just saw him at Christmas..." He trails off, obviously not wanting to talk about that specific time in our lives. Guess I'm not the only one in love with avoidance. "He's pissed at me for leaving, too. So you don't have the market on that cornered."

I doubt that. Charlie, Sam and Max's twelve-year-old half-brother, worships them both. "I can't imagine him ever getting mad at you. And even if he is, he won't stay mad. Not for long."

"Yeah, well, like you said," Sam says, his mouth curving into a soft, sad smile, "life goes on. Things change."

It's the smile that gets me. It's so unlike Sam and I realize I haven't seen him smile for real, haven't seen him happy since he's been back. That I can't remember the last time I heard him laugh.

I move toward him without meaning to, without conscious thought or decision, hand raised to touch him, to offer him some comfort. Except, that's not my job anymore. Not my place. And I stop and curl my fingers into my palm and lower my arm.

I stare at the porch floor, the wood cool beneath my bare feet, my heart racing. "Why are you here, Sam?"

He's quiet so long I don't think he's going to tell me, but then he blurts it out, his words quick and pleading and not at all what I'd expected. "Come to the party with me."

"What?"

"At Beemer's," he clarifies though I know what party he's talking about. "Come with me."

He hasn't moved, isn't crowding me in any way, shape or form, but I need more space, so I take a step back. "I'm not exactly a part of that social group anymore."

Not since Sam left.

"Neither am I."

"Please. It's being thrown in your honor. Everyone is going so they can see you. Hail the conquering hero and all that."

"I was in LA. Not fighting terrorists."

"Ah, but you survived your junior year at a private school, surrounded by the sons and daughters of the rich and famous. All those super-white, super-shiny teeth! The spray tans and fake boobs." I give a fake shudder. "The horrors."

"Some of the teeth really were blindingly bright. It was a risk just to go to calc class without sunglasses."

"Wow," I deadpan. "So brave."

He tugs on his ear. "But the...uh...the boobs weren't so bad." He grins. Shrugs. "I mean, if you're into that sort of thing."

I fight my own smile because he *is not getting to me.* "Well, seeing as how at least half of your friends are guys and all but one heterosexual, then I'd say you'll have plenty of people who'll be thrilled to hear all about your exciting, boob-filled life in LA. Me? I'll pass."

"Come with me anyway," he says when I turn to go back into the house. "Mackenzie and Tori will be there. Mackenzie says she hasn't seen much of you lately."

I whirl around. "You talked to Kenzie about me?"

"I just asked her how you were doing. That's all."

"As you can see, I'm doing just fine. No need to discuss me with anyone else. Ever."

I turn back to the door.

"She said she didn't really know how you were," Sam says, stopping me once again. "That you two haven't been hanging out."

"That's right."

"Why not?"

Tucking my hands into the sweatshirt pockets, chin lifted, I face him. "Because after you left, it became crystal clear that *our* friends were really *your* friends."

"What does that mean?"

It means that Sam brought me into his world of friends and parties and group outings.

Then he took it all away.

"When a couple gets divorced," I say, "their friends have to decide which side they're on. And Mackenzie and Tori and T.J. and Jackson, all of them, they chose you."

He steps closer. "Hadley, I swear, I didn't say anything to any of them."

"Well, then, I guess they figured it out."

"Figured what out?"

My throat tightens. "That I'm the reason you left. They figured it out," I repeat, "and they blame me for it."

He blinks, but he doesn't deny I'm the reason he moved in with his dad. "I didn't know."

"It doesn't matter."

"It matters to me," he insists because he's too honorable to let any insult go unchallenged. Any hurt to go unhealed. Any except the ones he caused, that is. "I'll talk to them--"

"No." God, it's bad enough he feels sorry for me. Poor Hadley, friendless and alone since he left. I don't need the entire school to know it. I mean, I'm sure they suspect, but having him confirm it? Gah. "Don't say anything to anyone."

He watches me for a moment, then exhales harshly. "Fine."

But that mutter didn't exactly sound reassuring. "I mean it, Sam. Not a word. To anyone."

"I won't say anything." But he must see the worry on my face because his tone softens as he adds, "I promise."

Before, I never would have doubted him. Before, I trusted him with everything.

Things change.

Still, I don't have much choice. He'll either keep his mouth shut or he won't, and like everything else that Sam does or doesn't do, the choice isn't up to me. What I want doesn't matter.

"Okay," I say, the only answer I can give. I almost add *thank you* but stop myself in time. "Have fun at Beemer's."

"I don't want to go alone."

I frown. "What?"

"I don't want to go the party alone," he repeats, "but more than that, I don't want to go without you."

"You've been to plenty of parties without me. Or are you going to try and tell me you sat home every weekend while in LA?"

"That's different."

"Yeah, because unlike out there, you're going to know every single person at this party. Have known them half your life."

"It won't be the same. Nothing's the same," he says and his voice cracks like it hasn't done since he was thirteen. "I knew if I came back, things would be different, but *nothing* is how I thought it would be. Charlie barely speaks to me, Mom stares at me as if I'm going to disappear if she blinks and any time I try to hang out with Max, he brushes me off. I've only seen Jackson once since he's with Fiona now —and how did that even happen? And all Travis and Graham talk about is what a hardass the new basketball coach is and the girls they met at some party they went to a few weeks ago... Everything's different now."

He's right. Things are different. His choice. And he doesn't get to be all frustrated and irritated by it now just because he feels left out. Left behind.

Welcome to my world.

So why do I feel bad for him?

Oh, right. Because I'm an idiot where Sam is concerned.

"My going with you to Beemer's isn't going to magically change it all back," I tell him.

"No, but if you come, if we go together, things will be like they used to. At least for one night." He stops and I watch his throat move as he swallows. "We both know we can't go back, but we can move forward, right? And maybe for one night, a few hours, we can pretend..."

"Pretend what?"

"Pretend things haven't changed. That I never left." His voice drops to a low, rough note. "We could pretend you don't hate me."

"I don't hate you," I say, the words tumbling out of my mouth in a heated rush. I snap my lips together. I shouldn't give him even that bit of truth, not when he can turn it around, use it against me. "I don't hate you," I repeat because I can't lie. Not about this. "I wish I did. It'd be so much easier."

He holds my gaze. Nods. "I know."

It hits me that he *does* know. He understands exactly what I'm going through. What I'm feeling. He gets me. Always.

But it's more than that. He knows, he understands, because it'd be easier on him if he hated me, too.

My throat burns with unshed tears and I find myself weakening. Waffling. I can't go to that party with him. Shouldn't go anywhere with him. Spending time with Sam will only remind me of what I've lost. Of how much it hurt when he turned his back on me.

How hard it was to get over him.

Except all that *I'm over him* is a lie.

I'm not over him. And I doubt I ever will be.

Yeah, complete and total idiot.

Because instead of telling him no again and sending him on his way, I hear myself say, "Give me ten minutes."

10

THE FIRST TIME THINGS CHANGED BETWEEN ME AND SAM WAS WHEN WE became friends. But I didn't finally give him a chance because of his charm, friendliness or dorky sense of humor. Or because I felt guilty about ignoring him all through the school year. It wasn't even because I felt particularly nice that day.

It was because he had a pool.

Not exactly a deep and noble reason to finally talk to someone who'd been trying to befriend you for months, but in my defense, I was ten and going through a rough time. And it's a huge, in-ground, kidney-shaped pool with a waterfall at the shallow end and a two-story curved slide at the other.

It was the summer after fourth grade and Zoe was in Erie for two weeks visiting her grandmother. None of us had our dads in our lives: Devyn's father died while serving in the Marines in Afghanistan when she was a baby but he'd walked out on Mom and her years before that, Zoe's dad spent most of his time in prison and mine took off to parts unknown before I was even born. But Zoe had something Devyn and I didn't.

Another family.

Grandparents and aunts who kept in touch with her, called her every weekend, sent cards on her birthday, presents at Christmas, and always had her visit for a few weeks each summer.

Nice for her. Not so nice for me.

It didn't help that Mom had been gone for two months—the longest she'd ever stayed away before. Or that Devyn had gotten a job doing dishes at a local diner and wasn't around very often.

Without her to watch me, Gigi took me with her to work cleaning houses.

I hated it. Hated having to sit still and be quiet, reading in a corner while Gigi scrubbed someone else's toilet or mopped their floors.

Hated how jealous I was that Zoe got to escape our life for a few weeks. That her dad's family wanted to spend time with her. That they wanted her.

Hated that Devyn was gone all day and that when she got home, she was too tired and grumpy to play with me.

Hated that Mom had taken off again. That she didn't love us enough to stick around. Hated that, even then, I knew this time she wasn't coming back.

So, no, I hadn't been feeling particularly nice that day. Or friendly.

What I'd been feeling was hot and sweaty and itchy with boredom.

And more than a little sorry for myself.

I'd sat on the edge of that fancy pool, my bare feet in the cool, clear water, and shut my eyes, breathing in the sharp, strong scent of chlorine, the rush of the waterfall filling my head.

It wasn't fair.

Zoe didn't have to stay in our stupid little town all summer. She got to spend two weeks somewhere new. Somewhere else. Her other grandmother took her shopping and bought her new clothes even though she could just wear Devyn's hand-me-downs. And her aunts took her and her cousins to the zoo and a water park and the lake.

I didn't even have any cousins. Not that I knew of, anyway.

Gigi didn't yell at her, didn't tell her that when they got home she had to spend the rest of the day in her room and be in bed by eight o'clock.

And I hadn't even done anything! All I'd said was that I was bored. Okay, so maybe it wasn't the first time I'd said it, and yes, Gigi had warned me what would happen if I complained or asked what time she was going to be done again, but still...

Eight o'clock? I wasn't a baby. And my favorite show was on at eight thirty.

There was no sense hoping she'd forget about the punishment, either. Gigi never forgot. And she never went back on what she said.

She was so mean.

I hoped she was looking for me, wondering where I went. She probably wasn't. She probably thought I was still upstairs in the hallway with my book. Ha. I showed her. As soon as she took the sheets downstairs to the laundry room, I snuck outside. To the pool. To that waterfall and the promise of that slide.

Even though she'd told me not to.

I kicked the water, had it showering down on my legs. It felt good. I bet if I got in, the water would wash away all the mixed-up feelings inside of me. Would make my anger and jealousy melt away.

I peeked at the door leading into the big, bright kitchen. No sign of Gigi. I could do it. No one else was here except us, so no one would know. And it'd only be a minute or two, just long enough to cool off.

Biting my lower lip, I started a slow slide into the pool, ankles then calves then knees--

"You're not allowed to be here."

I jerked in surprise and lifted back onto the edge, my heart racing. Sam stood over me in gym shorts and a Nike T-shirt, his bare legs skinny and tan, both knees scabbed over. Squinting against the sun, I raised my gaze to his face. "What?"

His braces flashed when he spoke again. "You're not allowed to be here."

My entire body got hot, but not from the sun, from someplace inside of me. "Yes, I am. I'm with my grandma. She's inside cleaning."

He shook his head. "I mean you're not allowed at the pool."

"Why not? Because you're rich and I'm not?"

He took a step back as if I'd hit him. "No. Not because of that."

"I don't believe you."

Some of the kids in our school thought they were better than us just because Gigi's car was old and rusted and we lived in a trailer. Just because Mom had us when she was young and disappeared for days...weeks...at a time. Because Gigi cleaned houses for a living and we had to wear clothes from Top-Mart or Goodwill.

Just because we all had different fathers.

Zoe called them stuck-up pricks and told me to ignore them.

Devyn said the next time they said something mean to punch them in the stomach.

But I'd never thought Sam was like that.

I'd known he was one of those kids, the kind who paid for their lunches instead of getting them free, who started every school year with brand-new clothes whether they needed them or not, who went on vacations to places like Disneyland and Mexico.

But he'd always been so nice—to everyone, not just me. I'd thought he was different.

That was before I saw his house. It was like a castle. The outside was stone, the windows were tall and gleamed as if no dirt dared get on them, and it sat on top of a hill. All rich people lived on hills. It's, like, a rule, allowing them to look down on the rest of us poor schmucks. Besides the pool there was a fenced-in, full-sized basketball court, a trampoline Gigi said I was absolutely *not* allowed to go on no matter how bored I got and a real tree house that looked like a pirate ship.

Sam probably thought I wasn't good enough to touch his stupid pool.

"I don't lie," he said after a long moment. "You're not allowed out here because it's a rule. No one's allowed to be by the pool alone."

"Oh." The heat inside me subsided but was replaced with a weird, fuzzy feeling. A happy one that Sam wasn't a stuck-up prick. That I didn't have to punch him in the stomach. I dropped my gaze to my feet, swished them around to make small waves. "I'm not alone now. You're here."

"An *adult* someone."

I kept staring at my feet, their image distorted and fuzzy in the water. "My grandma said it was okay."

He toed off his sneakers and tugged off his socks. Set them aside and sat next to me, this dark-haired boy with his skinny arms and legs, kind eyes and friendly smile. He was the opposite of scary or mean. He was always polite. Always nice.

I was terrified of him and had no idea why.

"You don't have to lie, either," he said quietly. "I won't tell on you."

"I wasn't going to get in or anything," I said quickly then winced. *You don't have to lie.* "I just wanted to put my feet in. That's all."

"Do you know how to swim?"

"Yes."

When Gigi was younger than me, she'd almost drowned in some pond outside of town, so each summer, she paid for us to have swim lessons at the local pool until we're twelve.

But this year she couldn't afford them because the water heater broke, even though I would be the only one going.

Another reason to be mad.

Another reason life was so unfair.

Not that there was anything I could do about it. About life or swimming lessons. At least I learned how to tread water and do the breaststroke and the safety rules of being around a pool.

The first one being to never go swimming alone.

"I said I wasn't getting in," I told Sam, my stomach feeling all twisty with guilt. "I'm not stupid."

"I know."

"You know what?"

"That you're not stupid," he said, as if it was a guaranteed truth, as if he knew me so well. As if he saw me. He noticed me. "We could get in," he continued, his face turning red. "The pool, I mean. Uh... together. I can ask Laura if she'll watch us."

"Who's Laura?"

"Our babysitter. My little brother fell asleep in the car, so she's taking him up to his room."

"I don't know how much longer I'll be here," I said, disappointed because I wanted to go in that pool, down that slide more than anything. "My grandma has other houses to clean after this."

"Oh. Maybe...maybe you could stay here. Laura said I could have a friend over."

A friend.

Me.

After all those months of me being mean to him, he was giving me another chance.

I looked at him and he seemed so nice, so harmless that I couldn't remember why I'd never wanted to talk to him before.

Couldn't remember why I didn't want to like him.

Mistake number one.

Mistake number two was smiling at him and saying, "I'll ask Gigi."

Mistake number three was pretending that we were going to end any other way than badly.

11

_____

When I come out of my room, Devyn's waiting for me in the hall.

Arms crossed, she flicks her gaze over me, then tilts her head to the side. "Going somewhere?"

I consider lying, saying I've made some new friends and we're going to the movies or some such nonsense, but quickly discard the idea. Not because I'm above it or anything—I think it's been well established that me and lying are not only well acquainted, but good buddies. I don't lie because Devyn can see Sam's SUV in the driveway and knows darn well he's waiting for me.

And because she wouldn't believe the whole new-friends thing anyway.

I nod. Switch my phone from my left hand to my right. "To Beemer's."

"With Sam."

It's not a question.

More like a declaration of war.

I switch my phone back to my left hand. "He's giving me a ride."

She drops her arms with an extremely long, drawn-out sigh. "Do you think that's a good idea?"

Nope. It's a terrible idea.

But when has that ever stopped me?

"It's just a ride," I say, shooting for easy, breezy but coming across more nervous and wheezy. I clear my throat. "It doesn't mean anything."

I won't let it.

"We're not going to be friends again," I add firmly, hoping to convince us both as I step toward the door.

I don't want to go back. That's what Sam told me today at lunch. *I don't want to be your friend.*

He wants more. He wants too much.

For a while, after he left, I thought I could give it to him. Thought I could be what he wanted. Then everything changed between us again. And now it's too late.

I'm turning the doorknob when Dev takes a hold of my arm, stopping me. I frown at her, and for a moment, I think she's going to yank me back inside, lock the door and forbid me from leaving.

Which is crazy. And a complete turnaround from how our lives have been so far. She's never stopped me from doing anything. I've never had to ask permission to go out or had a curfew. As long as I'm here to watch Taylor when they need me, both she and Zoe have always let me come and go as I please.

But there's no yanking. No forbidding.

Just a warning.

"Be careful," she says. "Boys like Sam..." Mouth turned down, she shakes her head. "They don't stay. Not in this town. Not with girls like us."

Don't I already know that? Haven't I said, time and time again, that he's not here to stay, that in a few days or weeks, he'll be gone again?

I know all that and yet I find myself defending him. "He came back."

Yes, he left me just like everyone else.

But unlike everyone else, he's here now.

He's the only one who came back.

The look Dev gives me is so sympathetic, so condescending it sets my teeth on edge.

"Just because he came back doesn't mean he won't leave again." She draws her hand away, her voice dropping to a soft whisper. "And it doesn't mean he won't break your heart again, either."

She walks away.

I should do the same. The smart thing, the safe thing would be to follow her. To not just listen to her good advice but to take it, maybe have it tattooed on my forearm where I can see it each day.

But I've never been smart where Sam is concerned.

And I've always been willing to risk more than I can afford to lose.

Inhaling a deep, fortifying breath, I open the door. The sun is lower in the sky than when I was out here earlier. But it's still shining. The air is still thick and warm.

And Sam is sitting on the top step looking at his phone. He's still here.

I wasn't sure he would be. Not after the ten minutes I told him I needed to get ready turned into twenty, plus another couple spent with Devyn.

Twelve extra minutes that weren't just due to me being unable to settle on an outfit and changing clothes three times. I was testing him. To see how badly he wanted me to go to the party with him. To see if he really did want to make amends.

To see if he'd lose patience and interest and walk away from me again.

He stands when I step onto the porch and I see it all on his face, in his eyes. He was worried I'd lied to him, that I'd stay inside, hiding in my bedroom. He's surprised I came back.

Happy I'm going to the party with him.

I am, too. Surprised and happy.

Oh, we are both so messed up.

He slides his gaze over me, and it's different than how he used to look at me, quick and glancing, as if afraid I'd notice. Afraid he'd get caught.

It's slow. Deliberate. Forthright and challenging.

Changed.

I'm unable to move. With him looking at me like that, it's tough just to breathe. I wipe my palms against the sides of my shorts. After much deliberation and those three outfit changes—which necessitated changing my bra twice—I'd settled on my favorite jean shorts, an emerald-green halter top and strappy, slip-on sandals. Nothing fancy. Certainly nothing that could be misconstrued in any way, shape or form that I was trying too hard.

Or that I was trying to impress anyone. Least of all Sam.

But the longer Sam stares at me, the more uncomfortable I become. The more exposed I feel. Which is stupid. The jean shorts are no shorter than the cotton ones I'd had on when Sam first arrived. But they are tighter, the bottoms of the front pockets sticking out. And the halter top is looser than the tank I'd worn, but the hem barely reaches the waistband of my shorts.

Indecision grips me and I almost turn to run back inside, to change once again, but I force myself to remain still. No, this outfit is fine. The perfect blend between casual, comfortable and cute. Besides, I didn't choose it for him—even if dark green is his favorite color and, I realize with a blush, matches his own shirt. I chose it because I like it. Period.

I left my hair alone because it would have taken too long to straighten it, not because it air-dried after my shower all wavy and tousled.

And, yes, okay, I put on mascara. And lip gloss.

I'm not an animal. I may not have been to a party in almost a year but I still know how to dress for one.

Sam exhales, long and low, and I realize I'm not the only one holding their breath. "You are so pretty, Hadley."

His voice is soft, gravelly, and it rubs against my skin, has goosebumps rising.

Leave it to Sam to say something so direct. So stunning. No half measures for him. No *I like that top* or *You* look *pretty.*

You *are* pretty.

So pretty.

No wonder I can't freaking breathe.

"Thank you," I manage, but it's barely a whisper and I know he can hear how unsettled I am. How nervous.

But he doesn't call me on it. There's no gloating for Sam Constable. No pushing.

The last time he pushed, I ran.

Then he did.

"Ready?" he asks.

I consider telling him no, that I need to duck back inside, let Devyn know I'm leaving, kiss Taylor good night. But I've already done both of those things, and if I go in now, I won't come back out.

And I'm getting tired of being a coward. So I take a deep breath and hope I'm not making mistake number four where Sam is concerned.

"Ready."

12

WALKING DOWN THE STEPS, I FEEL SAM BEHIND ME, BIG AND SILENT AND dangerous to my peace of mind. My resolve. His fingers brush against my lower back, like he's guiding me. Like we're on a date.

Panic bubbles in my stomach. No. This isn't a date. This is...oh, jeez...I don't know but I do know it's *not* a date.

I'm not going to Beemer's so I can be with Sam as a friend or anything else. I haven't forgiven him. This isn't like when we were kids and he wore me down with his charm and persistence. He hasn't won me over again with his patience and kindness.

Unlike that hot summer day when we were ten, sitting along the edge of his pool, I don't want anything from him. I'm not using him.

I owe him.

And things can't be over between us, for good, until I pay him back.

He's having a hard time readjusting to being back. Feeling left out. And while I'd love nothing more than to be all vindicated and superior knowing he's suffering even just a little bit, I can't.

Because it's Sam.

Because it's my fault he left.

I'll go with him tonight. Help him ease into being a part of the group he walked away from.

And we'll be even.

He's not parked in our driveway but across the street, in front of Whitney's trailer, and when I go around the front of his SUV to the passenger-side door, a movement on her porch stops me and I look up. Whitney's there on a wooden swing, gently swaying back and forth. Smiling, she waves, but in her eyes I see it, the same thing I saw yesterday afternoon when she stood in my driveway.

Loneliness.

The guilt I felt for declining her invitation, for not inviting her to my house intensifies. Mixes with shame.

Before I can decide what I'm doing, I start up the porch steps.

"Where are you going?" Sam calls after me.

"I'll be right back," I tell him. I cross the wide porch and stand in front of Whitney. "Uh...hey."

"Hello, Hadley." Her gaze flicks past me and I know she's looking at Sam, that he's probably standing by his car waiting for me, ever the gentleman. She leans forward, stopping the swing, and lowers her voice. "Is everything all right?"

"Yeah," I say, wondering if she's worried that Sam is a stalker or a kidnapper or, at the very least, an unwanted presence in my life. God, if only that were true. The problem is, he's not unwanted. Not completely. "Everything's fine. Sam and I" –I jerk my head in the direction of the SUV— "are going to a party."

"Oh." She sits back, sets the swing moving again with her foot. "That's nice," she says as if I came up here just to inform her of my whereabouts, my comings and goings. But I stay silent too long because she adds, "Ya'll have a nice evening."

"Thanks." I shake my head. "I mean, no, that's not why I'm telling you. I thought... Do you want to come? With us, I mean. To the party," I add just in case she thinks I mean to the moon or something.

She seems to be having a hard time following me.

"You want me to come with you to a party?" she asks, stopping the swing once again.

Definitely having a hard time following me. "Am I talking too fast? I mean, I know you talk slowly, but does that mean you hear slowly, too? Or maybe you're not quite getting my northern accent."

"I understood you just fine," she says, speaking so slowly a normal-paced talker could have given a dissertation in the time it took for her to say those five words.

I think she did it on purpose.

I like her even more for it.

She may have understood me, but she still hasn't answered me.

"Well?" I ask, regretting this impulsive decision. But, hey, what's one more added to the list? "Do you want to go or not?"

Pursing her lips, she studies me, her head tipped to the side so that her long fall of hair brushes over her shoulder.

I fidget. Glance back at Sam, who is still waiting ever so patiently for me. For us. The silence grows and sweat forms at the base of my back. I've never done this before. How pathetic is that? I've never invited someone to do something with me. Sam made all the overtures. Asking me to his house, seeing if it was okay if he came over to mine.

Once I became a part of his group of friends, Kenzie and Tori were the same way, including me when they went shopping in Erie or picking me up so we could go to a football or basketball game together.

I've never had to put myself out there in any way. In this way.

Not sure I'm going to make it a habit after this.

The waiting, the possibility of being rejected, is terrifying.

But when she speaks, it's not to send me on my way. And it's not to gleefully, gratefully accept my invitation, which was sort of how I'd pictured this whole thing going.

"Is this a joke?"

I frown at her. "What?"

"A joke? Or a prank? You invite me to a party where you and your friends get the hottest guy in school to flirt with me. He'll talk me into going into a dark bedroom with him, tell me how much he likes me, and just when I'm tipping my head up, eyes closed, for our first kiss, the lights will turn on and we'll be surrounded by people who pour pig blood over my head."

Pig blood?

I glance at Sam but he's looking at his phone, giving no indication he can hear our conversation.

Our very weird conversation.

"Wow," I say. "That was oddly specific. What kind of lives do you people live down there in the South?"

She blushes. "I read a lot. And watch a lot of movies."

"I guess. But you've got it wrong. For one thing, the people at the party aren't my friends. For another, the hottest guy in school would never set you up that way." Sam holds that title and he's way too decent for anything like that. "And honestly, I can't imagine anyone there going through all that trouble to do something so mean. And pig blood? Forget it. Look, there's no joke or prank. I just thought maybe you'd like to go with me."

"If they're not your friends, why are you and your boyfriend going to the party?"

And wouldn't that take all night to explain?

"They're Sam's friends. And he's not my boyfriend."

Words I've said hundreds of times over the years. But this is the first time they give me a pang. But not the first time I've wished things could be different.

Whitney is looking at me like I'm ten pounds of crazy in a five-pound bag. "You're going to a party with people who aren't your friends with a boy who is not your boyfriend?"

Well, when she puts it like it, it does sound a bit...off.

"That's the plan."

"You," Whitney tells me, "are a very confusing person."

"I'm *trying* to be nice, here," I say, even as part of me thinks that if I was really being nice, I wouldn't have to point that out. Then again, nice is overrated. Dangerous.

And a good way to get hurt.

But I'm not mean, either. And I want desperately to prove it.

"Look, I saw you sitting here and I felt bad for you. If you don't want to go, just say so."

To my surprise, her shoulders straighten. Seems little Miss Southern Sunshine has some pride. And a backbone. I can't help but admire both.

"This is a pity invite?" she asks, her accent thicker in her affront.

"You are spending Friday night at home."

No sense telling her that until Sam showed up, I was in the same situation. Had been in that same situation every weekend for almost a year.

Except Whitney's dark trailer and empty driveway tell me she's alone. At least my night came with Devyn, Taylor and Cinderella's mice friends.

"And I'm going to a party," I continue, "with people who aren't my friends with a boy who is not my boyfriend."

"Ah." She links her hands together at her waist, a wise and sage Southern belle in a long, floral skirt and ruffled sleeveless top. "I'm a buffer."

"That's also part of it. But the main reason I came over here, is because I know what it's like."

"What what's like?"

"What it's like to be alone."

To be lonely.

Once again she studies me but this time it's thoughtful. Knowing. And I can't help but think that, in that moment, something shifts between us. We understand each other.

I may not be nice, but I can be kind.

She may be sweet, but she's also strong.

Don't judge a book by its cover and all that.

Another of those lessons learned.

"I'd love to go," she finally says. "Thank you so much for inviting me. I'll just run inside and leave my mom a note. Will I need a sweater?"

"Probably not, but you'd better grab some shoes. You don't want to be barefoot around these people," I warn her as I head back down the stairs. "God only knows what you could step in."

The sad part? I'm being serious.

Sam straightens as I approach. "Everything okay?"

Yet more proof he's not a normal guy.

He doesn't get angry that he's being kept from his friends and, if memory serves me correctly about Beemer's parties, copious amounts of alcohol and weed. Sam doesn't get upset about waiting for me—and now another girl, one he's never even met. He doesn't lose his cool or his patience.

My life would be so much easier if he did. If he wasn't so freaking *good* all the time.

"Fine." There's a breeze, a warm one, but it could cool off before long. Maybe I should have told Whitney yes on the sweater. Maybe I should have grabbed one for myself. "Whitney's coming with us."

He shifts his gaze to the trailer, then back to me. "Whitney?"

"Whitney McCormack. She moved here last month." I realize how much Sam and Whitney have in common. It doesn't sit well. "You'll like her."

He raises his eyebrows at my pissy tone. "Yeah?"

"Yeah." My voice is strangled and I'm blushing so hard I touch my cheek just to make sure my face hasn't caught fire from it. No such luck. Guess I'm stuck finishing this conversation. "She's..." Gorgeous, with her shiny hair and those big, brown eyes. But more than that, she's sweet. Polite. Friendly. Everything Sam is. Everything I'm not. "Southern."

He's silent a beat. "Southern?"

I nod. Tug on my right earlobe, which has started to itch. "Right. She's, you know, from one of the Southern states--"

"Hadley," Sam interrupts, his mouth twitching from fighting a grin, "I know what Southern means."

"Right." I force my hand back to my side. Set it on my hip. Take it off. "Right," I say again. "Well, anyway, like I said, she moved here— like you did. And she's very polite—like you are. And she has an accent. A Southern one..."

"A Southern one, huh? Imagine that."

I shut my eyes on a groan and wish a sinkhole would open and swallow me whole.

Of course Whitney's accent is Southern. Hadn't I just made it very clear she was from the Southern United States of America? What other kind of accent would she have?

"Are you okay?" Sam asks, a thread of humor in his voice.

I open my eyes. "Fine."

And that's what does it. My growly tone and do-*not*-mess-with me scowl. Sam finally gives me the full-out real smile I'd been missing only minutes ago. And it doesn't matter that he's laughing at me or that I sound like an idiot. An irritated, jealous idiot.

None of it matters because I really, really like his smile.

That, in a nutshell, is the problem with me and Sam, has always been the problem.

Liking him too much.

Wanting more than I can have.

And being unable to stop either one of them.

13

As I predicted, Sam has nothing to worry about.

The moment Whitney, Sam and I step into Beemer's backyard, a cheer rises above the music.

"Hey!" Travis shouts, holding up his plastic cup in a victory toast. "Sammy is back!"

Yes, the conquering hero has returned. Let's all get trashed and make bad choices in celebration!

Then again, at the time of my biggest mistake, I was stone-cold sober, so maybe they're all onto something. Blame it on the alcohol.

"Sam...me," Graham chants, like we're in the stands at a basketball game and Sam has just won the game for us. "Sam...me! Sam...me!"

As most people don't seem to be as drunk as him, only a handful of others join in but Graham keeps going, adding a hip gyration on the *Sam* and a pelvic thrust on the *me*.

"Eww," Tori says, her face scrunched up. "God, Graham. No one should see that. Ever."

"Amen," I murmur as I walk between Sam and Whitney toward the crowd.

Whitney nods in agreement.

When it counts, us girls stick together.

Without missing a beat—or a *Sam...me! Sam...me!*—Graham turns his gyrating and thrusting on Tori, arms in the air *Dirty Dancing* style.

He's never been one for picking up social cues, even when those cues are stated. Give him a few beers and all bets are off.

Luckily, Tori's never been one for subtlety.

She gives him a two-handed shove, and he stumbles back. Would have landed in the fire if not for Travis, his perpetual wingman, catching him by the arm.

"Again...eww." Tori jabs a finger in his direction. "Do not bring that crap around me."

My lips twitch and Sam nudges me. "Guess not everything has changed after all," he says softly and I can't help but smile at him because he's right.

Because, for a moment, being here with him, with these people we've known for so long...it's like old times.

He smiles back, surprised and pleased, and I know he's thinking the same thing I am. It's almost like it was between us. When we did everything together, shared everything.

Except he didn't share his secrets. Not all of them. He kept one from me, the most important one.

And now I'm keeping one from him. Two, but who's counting?

I look away. Guess plenty's changed.

Way too much for things to go back to how they used to be between us. I can't get sucked in by Sam's charm or memories of the good old days.

Can't waste time wishing for those days to return.

We're passing the huge wooden deck when the sliding glass door leading to the kitchen opens and Abby O'Brien steps out.

"Sam," she breathes, stunned by her good fortune and the beautiful boy at my side. "Sam!" she repeats, this time on a squeal because she's a squealer, the type of girl who hugs her friends (of which there are many) each time she sees them, then again when they say goodbye. Who jumps up and down and gives a high-pitched girly yell at the slightest bit of good news.

Abby is a very excitable person.

She runs toward us—*runs*—racing down the steps, boobs bouncing beneath her silky V-neck tank top, shoulder-length blond hair flowing behind her, and then throws herself into Sam's arms.

Arms, I note, that go around her and hold her close, his large hands just above the waistband of her tight dark jeans.

Whether the squeal was some sort of call to the herd or if she proved with her hug that Sam really was here and not a figment of everyone's alcohol-muddled imaginations, a stampede starts.

No, really, it's a rush of people, a wave of them surging toward us, drawn together in their zest for life and their zeal to welcome home the prodigal son.

Whitney and I both step back. Then back again when Danielle Webster totters by, almost dumping her beer on us.

We walk up the steps to the empty deck. Stand at the railing and watch the scene below. Guys slap Sam on the back while girls line up to hug him, shooting hopeful, please-look-at-me-in-that-special-way glances at him from under heavily mascaraed eyes.

Whitney tips her head as she takes it all in. "Your friends--"

"They're not my friends," I mutter as Jackson thrusts a beer into Sam's hand.

"Excuse me," she says, not the least bit sarcastic, which is a feat unto itself. "Your *not friends* seem very happy Sam's here."

"He was gone for a while," I explain, though honestly, even when Sam lived here, he always had quite the warm welcome wherever we went.

One of the many, many perks of being a golden boy.

"Gone on vacation?"

Below us, Abby presses against Sam's side and lays her hand on his chest, all the better to bat her eyelashes at him as she gazes adoringly at his handsome face.

I wish I'd stayed home.

Regrets. Yeah, I've got a few.

And they just keep on piling up.

"No," I say, turning away from the sight of Sam and Abby. "He lived with his dad in LA. Went to school out there last year."

He and Max had gone out there for their annual summer visit two weeks after Sam stopped talking to me. At the end of the month, only Max came back.

"I see," Whitney says softly, sympathy in her tone, understanding in her eyes. She gets it. What I'm feeling. What's going on in my head.

Sam left. He left me and his mom and stepdad, his brothers and his friends.

He. Left.

And I'm the only one who can't forgive him.

I really, really wish I'd just stayed home.

"What are *you* doing here?"

I turn as Mackenzie Porter steps out of the house, her scrunched-up face reminding me of Taylor's ticked-off expression, her anger toward Cinderella's mean sistas.

The scowl looks just as cute on Kenzie, with her short, spiky white-blond hair and delicate features, as it did on Taylor.

Life is so unfair sometimes.

Though it's not even nine o'clock, Kenzie's already on her way to being trashed—her words slurring, her steps extra-cautious as if the ground keeps shifting and rolling under her feet. At barely 105 pounds, she's a complete lightweight.

She's the first person to acknowledge my presence here, but there are no shouts of joy or beer toasts. No cheerful greeting, happy back slaps or warm embraces.

No one is happy to see me.

I firm my mouth when my lower lip wants to tremble in self-pity. Nope. Not going there. I knew this would happen if I came. I can handle it. I'd gotten used to Kenzie and Tori looking through me when we passed each other in the hall during school. Had become as good at ignoring them as they were at ignoring me in the two classes we shared. Told myself I didn't care when I rode my bike home and they drove past, music blaring as they sang along, laughing and smiling and having a grand old time.

Convinced myself that it didn't hurt, the way they left me out.

How they'd just pretended to like me because of my friendship with Sam.

I feel Whitney watching me and my face burns.

Should. Have. Stayed. Home.

"I'm here with Sam," I tell Kenzie.

Her eyebrows draw together in confusion. "Why?"

I roll my eyes. Does everything have to be studied and dissected and questioned to death?

God.

"Because he asked me to come with him."

"You and Sam are back together?"

No point mentioning we weren't ever *together*. Not in the way she means.

Kenzie had always insisted that Sam and I were Meant to Be.

She has a wild imagination and an extra-wide romantic streak.

I should set her straight. I should remind her that Sam and I were only ever just friends, but I can't. Well, I could. I mean, it's not like I have anything against lying. But I don't want to.

And I am not going to even consider why not.

"This is Whitney," I say, gesturing toward my new neighbor. It's a diversion tactic, which is like avoidance but sneakier.

It takes Kenzie a moment to process this turn of events—and turn in conversation.

Whitney smiles and sticks her hand out. "Nice to meet you."

Kenzie pulls up short, as if instead of a friendly handshake, Whitney's just jabbed a knife in her direction. She looks my way for reassurance or clarification or something. "Who?"

Forget on her way to being trashed, Kenzie is there. I look around for Tori—she needs to shut her best friend off—but she's on T.J. Hopkins' lap near the fire, having a serious make-out session.

No help from that corner.

"She's Whitney," I say as Whitney lowers her offered hand. "She moved in across the street from me," I continue but Kenzie's still frowning so I keep going. "She's going to go to our school this fall." Still nothing and I'm floundering, wondering if I should knock Kenzie's beer out of her hand or just let this whole awkward conversation die and walk away. "She's from Mississippi."

Kenzie's eyes light up and she whirls toward Whitney.

Beer sloshes over the side of Kenzie's cup.

That's right. Whitney is *not* from Georgia or Louisiana or Alabama of any other state that ends with an *a*. She's from Mississippi, is an only child, and she and her mother moved here because her parents recently got divorced and her mom, a teacher, has a friend in town who helped her get a job up here.

I'd insisted she sit up front with Sam for the drive to Beemer's, telling myself it was the polite thing to do.

Ha ha. So funny! Me, worrying about manners and whatnot.

More like I'd been worried about getting too close to Sam again. I'd needed space and had wanted to prove that this, us going to the party together, changed nothing. Meant nothing. And the best way to do that had seemed like hopping in the backseat and telling Whitney to go ahead and climb in up front.

But like so many of my decisions and most of my choices, it backfired in spectacular fashion.

We hadn't even gone a block before Sam and Whitney were laughing over some YouTube video they've both seen, the happy, oh-so-carefree sound of their combined chuckles filling the SUV. They became fast friends who, by the end of the night, will be sharing secrets, making playdates and swapping BFF necklaces.

Kenzie leans toward Whitney, all excitement and unsteadiness. Whitney, God bless her, holds her ground and her soft smile— though her eyes look a tad panicked at the drunk girl invading her personal space.

"You're Southern?" Kenzie asks, words painfully slow and, to be honest, not all that easily decipherable. "Do you have an accent?"

"Not at all," Whitney says, her accent thicker than I've ever heard, all long vowels and soft consonants that seem to take forever for her to form. "But all y'all sure do talk funny up here."

"*All* y'all?" I ask. "Is that grammatically correct? Because you seem like the type of person who cares about that sort of thing."

"Y'all means one or two people," Whitney tells me, serious as a heart attack. "All y'all means more than two, so yes, it is correct. And of course that's important. What are we? Neanderthals?"

I can't help it. She's so adamant and serious with her hippie clothes and Southern drawl and strict English-teacher tone. I smile.

She smiles back.

"I don't understand," Kenzie says to me. "Does she have an accent or not?"

Before I can answer, Whitney turns her smile to Kenzie, her expression softening. "I do have an accent. I was just teasing."

"Oh." Kenzie nods, her mouth pursed to the side. "Okay. Ohmigod," she says again, this time louder and with more feeling, "you have to meet Tori! She loves accents."

Kenzie takes Whitney's hand and tugs her down the steps. Whitney glances back at me but doesn't stop. Doesn't pull away.

Doesn't ask me to join them.

Whatever. That's why I invited Whitney. So she could meet people and get started forming those lifelong friendships high school is so flipping famous for.

Leaning my hip against the wooden railing, I watch the party below, shooting for carefree and nonchalant. It doesn't work. I'm grinding my teeth and my shoulders are rounded and tight with tension—a redhaired, hunch-backed troll in a tower watching the beautiful people below living it up.

I roll my eyes. Ugh, that's more self-pity than even I can justify.

Straightening, I stare up at the darkening sky, count stars as I exhale and wiggle my jaw. I get to fifty and lower my gaze again. It snags on Sam's. Though he's in the center of a group of people all vying for his attention, a brilliant sun for them all to orbit, he's watching me.

He doesn't look away like he used to when I'd catch him staring at me, a guilty flush staining his cheeks. No, he holds my gaze, lets me see everything he kept hidden from me for years. How he feels about me. What he wants from me.

It's too much, way more than I can handle, and I drop my gaze.

From my peripheral vision, I see him say something to his fans... er...I mean his friends...and extricate himself from Abby and head toward me.

I keep my eyes on the fire. Tori is standing next to the chair, T.J. beside her, his arm around her waist, while she talks to Whitney and Kenzie who is now without a cup, thanks, I'm sure, to Tori.

I keep watching them when Sam joins me. He rests his elbows on the top rail and gazes out over the yard with me and I wonder what he's feeling. What he's thinking. Is it different for him, too? Being here, no longer a part of this, not the way he used to be? Separated from these people by time and distance and his own choices? Or does it feel familiar, like coming home at the end of a long day? Like no time has passed at all?

Does he regret leaving?

Does he regret coming back?

I wonder. But I don't ask.

"You want to go down," he asks after a few minutes, "talk to Kenzie and Tori?"

His tone is quiet. Kind.

I shake my head.

He turns to me. "I'll go with you."

Why does he have to be so sweet? So thoughtful?

He tempts me, that's for sure. Tempts me to forget what he did. How much he hurt me.

"I already talked to Kenzie," I say, keeping my tone mild as if this whole conversation bores me. "Besides, they're talking to Whitney right now. I'd hate to interrupt the beginning of a BFF threesome— that'd be rude."

And I don't go where I'm not wanted. Not anymore. I never did fit in with Sam and those like him. Popular, smart, athletic. But it seems they've taken to Whitney fast enough.

She'll be one of them by the night's end.

That thought leaves me unsettled, the idea of her being so easily accepted when I was only tolerated. I'm reminded, once again, why Sam and I weren't meant to be friends.

It's those differences between us. Too many differences.

"That was nice of you," he says. "Inviting Whitney to join us."

"Yeah, well, you know how much I love bringing people together. Gives me a break from polishing my halo."

Elbows still on the railing, he links his hands together. "I thought you invited her so you wouldn't have to be alone with me."

I shrug. "That, too."

And then Sam does the darnedest thing. He grins. Like he's thrilled I admitted it.

Like he's happy I chose to tell him the truth when I could have easily lied.

"It was still nice," he insists, like it's important for me to believe it.

Or maybe that's not it. Maybe it's more important that he convinces himself.

Then he can say he was right about me. That there's more to me than snide comments, social awkwardness and a boatload of cynicism. He can claim to have seen something inside of me, deep, deep down, that everyone else missed. That proves I really was worth his time all those years we were friends. That I was deserving of his feelings.

I'm not. I'm too guarded, too stingy with how much I offer other people, too careful with my emotions.

I make too many mistakes.

But from the time we were little kids, Sam has seen good in me.

For a while he'd even managed to get me to start seeing it, too. And then he hurt me and left me and I did the worst thing ever.

So, no. Not nice. Not good.

Just me.

14

"You okay?" Sam asks.

I snort softly and cross my arms. "Don't."

"Don't what?"

Don't be nice to me. Don't look at me like there's something special about me.

Please, please don't ever leave me again.

That last thought, the one that popped up unbidden, unwanted, remains, stuck on a loop, spinning around and around in my mind.

Please don't leave me. Please don't leave me. Please don't leave me.

Oh, God, I've been such an idiot. So stupid to believe things were over between me and Sam. Naïve to think I stood any chance against his honesty and patience and kindness. Against my own conflicted, confusing, terrifying feelings for him.

"Hadley," he says, touching my arm, bending so he can see into my eyes. "What is it?"

"Sammy!"

At the sound of his name, Sam and I both turn. Abby is calling for him.

I could kiss her.

Which, honestly, would be a big hit with this crowd.

In that moment, Sam's attention is diverted from me, from what I'd been about to say. Thank God for Abby O'Brien and her deep and abiding obsession with Sam Constable and her never-ending quest to separate him from me.

She must've been in her own version of heaven these past eleven months, what with Sam being far, far away from me.

Abby's dream come true.

She grins widely and gestures for him to join her, her head tipped to the side, hip thrust out slightly, coy look on her face.

Ugh. Does she practice that pose in the mirror? And what's with those under-the-lashes glances she keeps tossing his way? Subtlety, thy name sure as heck isn't Abigail O'Brien.

He holds up a finger to Abby, indicating he'll be with her in a minute. She nods, smile amping up, all but shooting sunbeams from her fingertips and hearts and flowers from her eyes.

Until Sam turns to me. Then her smile fades, her fingers curl into fists and she glares at me, trying to kill me dead on the spot with one vicious look.

I'm the bane of her otherwise perfect existence.

And what she sees as the only true obstacle to happiness as Sam's girlfriend once again.

Yeah, they were together sophomore year, from mid-November to just after spring break. For four months it wasn't Sam and Hadley. Hadley and Sam.

It was Sam and Abby. Abby and Sam.

Four months, two weeks and four days.

Not that I counted or anything.

Or celebrated their breakup with a huge slice of chocolate fudge cake with mocha frosting that I might or might not have made to commemorate the event.

It'd been so awkward, sharing Sam with another girl. He'd gone out with girls before, but nothing serious. Not until Abby. It'd been the first time one of us had another person in their life who was more important.

A person he wanted to be with more than he wanted to be with me.

She blames me for the breakup. Blamed me for most things that went wrong when they were together, too. Any time I spent with Sam was dissected, analyzed and argued over. Any texts to or from me were read so she could try and decipher some hidden meaning. Any comment about me was questioned.

It was the second-worst time period in my life.

"Are you sure you're okay?" Sam asks me, clueless to the fact that, as we speak, his eyes on me, his body leaning over mine, his ex-girl-friend is a seething, writhing mass of jealousy, ready to rip my hair out because, for some reason, it's always the other girl's fault.

Boys. Not only clueless but also, apparently, blameless.

"I'm good," I say, sensing Abby staring at me, drilling a hole between my shoulder blades with the force of her hatred.

No love lost between us two, that's for sure.

I glance back at her and our eyes meet. I let my lips turn up slightly when her own mouth thins. After a long, tense moment, I face Sam again, satisfied and triumphant that he's still with me, by my side.

It's wrong. Wrong and mean and spiteful of me to feel that way, to be glad he chose me. But I can't stop it.

Even though it means my feelings for Sam haven't changed as much as I want to believe.

"You'd better go," I mutter. What is it about this boy that has me such a freaking mess? "We wouldn't want Abby getting upset."

That was our mantra when they were a couple. Don't do or say anything that will upset, anger or sadden Abby.

Forget a short leash, Abby had kept Sam under her thumb. She'd kept track of his whereabouts and, especially, every moment he spent with me. And if that time equaled even one more minute than the time and attention he'd given to her, there was hell to pay in the form of tantrums, tears and sulking.

And, okay, there may have been a bit of whining, complaining and hurt feelings on my end, too.

"I'm not here with Abby," he says, and it's as if the entire party disappears, the sounds of laughter and conversation muting, people fading into shadows. It's as if Sam and I are the only two people on the deck. The only two people in the entire world. "I'm with you." He takes another step closer, his voice going husky. "I'd rather be with you."

His words, the way he's looking at me make me jittery and confused and excited. Before he left, he never would have said something so flirtatious. So honest.

Would never have looked at me with such hope and longing, as if I'm the only thing he needs. The only thing he wants.

My resolve weakens even more and I sway toward him, unsure of everything, especially my intentions. Uncertain about what's right and wrong between us. What's smart.

"Hey, Hot Hadley! You made it."

Max's voice jars me and I stumble back, the world once more coming into focus. A reminder that we're not alone, Sam and me. A harsh warning of why I can't let my guard down around Sam. Why things between us can't ever be what he wants.

What I want.

Max saunters up to us, a trio of sophomore girls trailing behind him, and wraps me in a full-body hug, lifting me off the ground.

Max is very touchy-feely with me.

But only when Sam is around.

The Constable brothers are extremely competitive with everything. Basketball. Grades. Their mom's affection. Their dad's attention.

Me.

Not that Max is interested in me. What he's interested in is bugging Sam and nothing bothers Sam more than Max flirting with me.

Max is still hugging me when behind him, there's a wave of disappointed sighs. The sophomore girls had high hopes, and I have dashed them.

More like I saved them a lot of time, effort and heartbreak.

The Constable brothers can do a number on you, that's for sure.

"Couldn't stay away, huh?" Max asks as he sets me back on my feet.

He keeps his arms around my waist, like we're dancing, and I twist to see Sam. He's all scowly, his eyes on Max's hands, which are palming my back just above my butt. I face Max again. "Sam asked me to come with him."

It's the truth. And the only reason I'm here.

Because of Sam.

Sam takes me by the arm and tugs me free of his brother's hold. "You just get here?" he asks Max.

"A few minutes ago."

"I thought you were leaving the house right after I did." Which, considering Sam spent thirty minutes at my house, means Max should have been here much, much sooner.

Max smiles. "Had to make a pit stop."

More like a pot stop. The boy reeks of it, his eyes glazed, his grin sloppy.

Sam's eyes narrow. "Did you drive after you smoked?"

"Relax," Max says, patting Sam on the head like he's a puppy and not his brother who's his equal in breadth and taller in height. "I've got it under control. And you've got enough on your mind without worrying about me." He pulls me to his side, settles his hand on my hip and winks at Sam. "Like how you're going to get your girl back after you royally fucked things up."

Sam flushes, color climbing his neck up to his face. He takes a step toward us and I have a premonition of him taking my arm again, of being the rope in a tug-of-war between the Constable brothers. Winner gets Hadley!

I elbow Max in the side. Hard. With a grunt, he lets go of me and rubs his ribs, giving me an injured look. "What'd you do that for?"

I roll my eyes at him. High or not, he knows why I did it. "Because you're being a dick."

Now his hand goes to his heart and he stumbles back as if I've knocked him a good one. "Ouch. Hot Hadley, you sure do know how to hurt a guy." He slings his arm around Sam's shoulders, all broth-erly solidarity and understanding. "Isn't that right, Sammy boy?"

Sam shrugs him off, the move jerky and aggressive and very un-Sam-like, as he whirls on his brother. "Knock it off."

A hard gleam enters Max's eyes. So much for pot mellowing people out.

"Poor Sammy. All tied up in knots because Hot Hadley's put you firmly in the friendzone. You know what they say about that, don't you? Once you're in the zone, you never get out." He claps Sam hard on the back. "Take my advice, little brother, cut your losses." Max looks at me long and steady. "Some people aren't worth it."

My head snaps back. My breath lodges in my chest.

Ouch.

Something's going on with Max, something more than just sibling rivalry or him messing with Sam. He's always been quick with a joke or a teasing comment. But he's never been mean.

But now...he's different. Harder. Angry.

And I'm terrified of what this new Max is going to do. What he's going to say.

Someone calls Max's name. Touching two fingers to his forehead, he salutes me and Sam. "Have fun, kids. Don't do anything I wouldn't do."

"Sorry about that," Sam mutters as Max joins a group of kids he graduated with by the fire.

Ugh. That makes everything worse. This thing with Max, how he's acting, the things he said, it's not Sam's fault.

It's mine.

"Is Max all right?" I ask.

Now Sam looks at me. "Other than being stoned?"

"Yeah. Other than that." Which isn't anything new. He smoked pot occasionally when he was in high school. "He just seems..." Angry. Bitter. Lost. "Different."

Sam shrugs, then clears his throat. "You didn't correct him."

"What?"

"What he said about...about me getting you back," Sam says in a rush. "You didn't correct him. Didn't tell him you weren't my girl."

He's right. For years people have said similar things to us, have called us a couple, had assumed we were boyfriend/girlfriend or, at the very least, hooking up regularly.

I always set them straight, as quickly and emphatically as possible.

I'm not Sam's girl.

We're not together.

We're just friends.

But tonight, I hadn't. And Sam noticed.

I lick my lips and open my mouth but no matter how badly I want to stammer out some lame excuse about it not mattering or a lie about how I hadn't even realized Max had said that, nothing comes out.

"He was right about one thing," Sam says.

Take my advice, little brother, cut your losses. Some people aren't worth it.

I go still. And though it was what I thought I wanted, the idea of Sam cutting his losses, of him giving up on me, makes me sick to my stomach. "He was?"

He nods. "He was right about two things actually. I fucked up. And I'm going to do whatever it takes to get you back."

15

I RAN.

Okay, so I didn't technically *run*. But it was close. More like speed-walking, complete with pumping arms and wiggling hips, all the better to put as much physical distance between me and Sam as quickly as possible.

What was I supposed to do? Stand there, gaping at him all night, Sam's words playing over and over in my mind while he stared at me, intense and calm, as if what he'd said was no big deal?

I'm going to do whatever it takes to get you back.

It was a big deal. It was a huge, ginormous, gigantically big big deal.

Seriously. How's a girl supposed to resist those particular words said in that particular deep, husky voice coming from that particular dark-haired, dark-eyed boy?

How am *I* supposed to resist?

I couldn't. But I couldn't give in, either. Could hardly jump into his arms with a huge grin and an *all's forgiven now let's completely change the dynamics of our relationship and see how that works out for us!*

I already know how it would work out. It wouldn't. It would blow up in our faces and we'd be even worse off than we are now.

So, yeah, I took off. Right after I blurted out that I had to pee.

Not one of my finer moments.

I spent the next ten minutes locked in the bathroom. Would have stayed in there longer, staring at my reflection and trying to talk some sense into myself, if Katelyn Hainsey hadn't knocked on the door.

I consider going back there, to that sink and mirror, and possibly never coming out again, when I rejoin the party and see Abby glued to Sam's side.

He sees me, too, of course. There's always been a sixth sense between us. An awareness. That hasn't changed. The moment I step onto the deck, Sam looks over Abby's head and meets my eyes.

I'm going to do whatever it takes to get you back.

I shiver at the memory of those words. The way he watches me now. How he looks at me, confident and determined. So differently than how he used to.

Head down, gaze averted, I skirt around Sam and Abby.

"Hadley," he says softly, not letting me off the hook that easily. Not letting me keep running.

"I'm going to look for Whitney," I say, still walking. "Make sure she's okay."

It's as good an excuse as any and, better yet, one he can't argue with, me checking on the welfare of our new friend. I make my way oh so slowly and super casually toward the fire. That's me. Calm and controlled and not the least bit freaked out.

Maybe I'm blowing this whole thing out of proportion. Maybe Sam didn't even mean it the way it sounded. How it came across.

I'm going to do whatever it takes to get you back.

Okay, so there aren't that many other ways *to* take that, but it doesn't make sense. He can't get me back. I wasn't his. Not in the way that implies. We were friends. Just friends.

Only friends.

Except we're not friends. Not anymore. And that makes this whole situation even more confusing. More frightening. I need that label, that well-defined, easily understood definition of what we mean to each other. There are rules to friendship. Set lines that can't be crossed. Firm boundaries that can't be broken.

It's that friendzone Max was talking about. Not that I agree with his assessment of once you're in the zone, you never get out. Some do. But they shouldn't. Friendship isn't a punishment. It's a neat and tidy box keeping everything where it's meant to be. Safe. Secure.

Once you're out of the box, out of the zone, it's too much. Too much open space. Too much freedom. Too many chances for things to go wrong.

I want those boundaries. I need those rules.

Someone bumps into me and murmurs an apology. I shift to the right and glance at the faces around the fire. No sign of Whitney, but I spot Kenzie talking to Jeff Spittler near a wooden picnic table at the edge of the woods.

I walk up to them. "Where's Whitney?"

"Who?" Kenzie asks, as if she's never heard the name before. Never met the girl or dragged her away to share the wonders of her Southern accent amongst friends.

I sigh. Kenzie is wasted.

Thanks, I'm sure, to Jeff refreshing her drinks after Tori shut her off.

He's a get-a-girl-drunk kind of guy.

"Whitney," I say to Kenzie, hoping to jog her memory or maybe spark a few of her still-sober brain cells. "My new neighbor?"

She stares at me blankly.

Kenzie is beyond being any help to me.

But that doesn't mean I can't be of some help to her.

I take her cup.

"Hey," she says, making a clumsy attempt to grab it back from me. "That's mine."

Holding the cup out of her reach—being five eight has its advantages, especially when dealing with someone who's barely five two—I dump the beer, then set the cup onto the picnic table.

I take her hand. "Come on."

"Whoa, whoa, whoa," Jeff says, leaping to snag Kenzie's other hand. New tug-of-war game. "Where're you going, babe?"

I'm guessing he's not talking to me.

Kenzie sways, though we're all standing nice and still now. "I don't know." She looks at me. "Where are we going?"

"To find Tori. She wants to talk to you."

"Oh. Okay." She shakes her other hand but Jeff holds on. She leans toward me and whisper-shouts, "He won't let go."

"He'll let go." I keep my eyes on her face, but my words are for him. "If he doesn't, I'm going to scream so long and so loud, not only will every guy here come running, but the neighbors will surely think a murder is taking place and call the cops. And won't those cops find it interesting when they get here to discover a bunch of drunk teenagers and one, just one, mind you, guy over the age of twenty-one."

He lets go.

"Kenzie and I are talking," he says, getting in my face. "And you interrupted."

"Sure did. And now, since we're narrating this little scene, let me say, we're leaving."

"Bitch," he calls after me.

I don't turn back, don't stop walking, just raise my voice. "Dude. You're twenty-three. Stop coming to high school parties. It's sad and pathetic. Find people your own age to hang out with."

Kenzie leans heavily against my side. "Jeff's a creeper."

"Yes," I say, wrapping my arm around her waist—the better to help her stay upright and keep her moving at a decent clip. "And what do we do when a creeper gives us alcohol?"

She looks up at me, big-eyed and earnest. "We just say no."

"That's right. Next time, just say no."

"I will," she vows, giving me her drunk word. Hooray. It'll be carved in stone. She lays her head against my arm. "I didn't want to hurt his feelings. Boys are sentasive, you know."

"*Sensitive.*"

"That's what I said. Sentasive."

I can't help it. I laugh.

And it hits me, how much I've missed her. Her and Tori. And for a moment, I let myself wish things could be different. That they could go back to how they used to be, at least between the three of us.

But like I told Sam, there's no going back.

Not for any of us.

We walk around the crowd gathered at the fire. "Tori's over there," I say, pointing to where Tori and T.J. are plastered against one another near the above-ground pool. "Do they ever come up for air?"

Kenzie squints in the direction of my point. "No. They're like animals."

"Think you can make it to them by yourself?" I ask, not wanting to come face-to-face with Tori and her sharp tongue. Not tonight.

"Of course." She takes one careful step, wobbles, but catches her balance and turns to look at me. "You're not a bitch, Hadley. You're just..."

I wait, breathlessly anticipating the great wisdom of the badly intoxicated.

"Hard," she settles on as if that's the nicest thing she can come up with. Which, if it is...ouch.

"And sort of," she continues, wrinkling her nose, deep in thought for another long moment, "cold. Not, like, temperature wise," she clarifies, "but feeling wise, you know?"

I wince. Double ouch.

Drunk or not, she hit the nail on the head. My head. "Gee, thanks."

She nods solemnly. Like toddlers, sarcasm is lost on the wasted. "You're welcome."

I watch as she bobs and weaves her way to Tori and T.J., waiting until she arrives safely at her destination—like I do when I take Taylor to Mrs. Richter's, standing by the door to make sure Taylor is happy and safe before I leave.

Kenzie says something to Tori and gestures my way and they both look at me.

I turn and walk away.

Consider not stopping until I'm home.

First Abby hanging on Sam, then Max and his thinly veiled insults and now Kenzie telling me I'm hard-hearted and emotionally cold.

The fun. It never ends.

I wander the yard for another five minutes before going around the garage and onto the porch, then in through the front door. It's a quiet search. I get a few curious glances and a couple of Sam's buddies give me the guy nod, but no one slows me down with a friendly greeting or stops me for a quick chat.

Whatever. We hard, cold, unworthy people don't need that kind of validation to feel good about ourselves. We have inner acceptance.

I step into the kitchen and finally find Whitney.

With Max.

Her back is against the counter, a cup in her hand and a stunned, how-did-I-get-this-lucky look on her face. Max is towering over her, one hand on the counter next to her side, allowing him to show off the play of muscles in his arm every time he moves. He's in full guy-on-the-make mode, leaning close to speak in her ear, trailing the finger of his free hand down her arm, giving her long, soulful looks.

Blech.

She's eating it up, lips parted, eyes wide as she takes in the glory that is Maxwell Constable.

I really, really, really don't want to go over there, don't want to talk to Max, not after he goaded Sam that way earlier, as if trying to pick a fight. Not after he was such a prick to me.

Some people aren't worth it.

I'm in no hurry to put myself through that awkwardness again, thanks just the same.

Whitney seems smart enough. Capable of taking care of herself. I'm sure she can decide on her own whether to give a guy like Max the one—the only—thing he wants from a girl.

I'm not the moral police, for God's sake. Not even close. If Whitney wants to hook up with Max, well, that's her right. Her choice.

I already jumped into someone else's business tonight, making sure Kenzie was free of creeper Jeff. I should just buff the imaginary gold star on my chest and go on my merry way, content that my good deed for the day is done.

But I can't, in good conscience, leave Whitney at Max's mercy.

The least I can do is make sure she knows what she's getting herself into.

I walk toward them when Whitney tears her attention from Max and smiles at me.

"There you are," she says. "I was looking for you."

I glance behind me, but nope, she's not talking to someone else. "You were? Why?"

"Because I came with you. I can't just abandon you. That would be rude."

She and Sam must have read the same party-etiquette rulebook.

"So you decided to look for me in Max's eyes?" I ask.

"Actually, Maxwell suggested it would be better if I stayed in one place and let you find me." She beams at him, proud that so much pretty also came with half a brain. "He was right. And he's been kind enough to wait here with me."

"Yes," I say, tone flat, eyes narrowed on Max. "Well, that's *Maxwell* for you. A regular Boy Scout."

If the Boy Scouts are into getting high, drinking to excess and hooking up with as many girls as possible.

Max sips his drink, watching me over the rim, not quite as buzzed, it seems, as earlier.

Give him time and he'll get that high back. Give him time.

"It's like you don't really mean that, Hadley," he says, no *Hot* to be found before my name.

Yep. Definitely on the make.

"Listen," I say to Whitney, "I get that this" –I gesture from the top of Max's perfectly tousled, dark hair down to his sneakers then back up to circle my forefinger around his face— "is nice to look at. He really is all kinds of pretty--"

"Flatterer," Max murmurs.

"And," I continue, "I realize you and I don't know each other that well, but I feel it's my duty as a female and the person who is ultimately responsible for you being here and therefore responsible for you meeting him--"

"*This*," Max says, eyebrows raised, "*him*. I'm not just a sexual object, here for you to ogle and fantasize about. I have a name."

I roll my eyes and barrel on. "I feel it's my duty to warn you that *Max*" –I glance at him and he nods— "is not the guy for you."

There's a beat of silence while that all sinks in.

Silence broken when Max laughs, long and low.

Once again, I've amused the heck right out of him.

Still chuckling, still holding his cup, he raises his hands as if in surrender. "No need for warnings. I was just keeping Whitney company until you showed up. And now that you have, I'll just take this *all kinds of pretty* and get myself another drink." He tips his cup to Whitney in a toast. "Nice meeting you."

He gets only halfway across the kitchen before a pretty junior in a crop top is by his side.

The Constable brothers. Never lacking for female attention.

"I don't know whether to thank you," Whitney says, her expression unreadable, her tone mild, "or pick you bald-headed."

My hands go to my head, as if she'd reached up to start yanking out strands. "You should thank me. Unless you're totally into players who get trashed every weekend."

"No," she says slowly, thoughtfully, as she watches Max pull the same moves on Miss Crop Top that he'd tried with her—the leaning, light touching and deep looks, "I'm not into players." With a deep and what I'm thinking is a cleansing inhale, she turns to me. "Thank you."

It's a moment of sisterhood. Of female empowerment. And possibly, of budding friendship. For once, I don't run. For once, I don't mess it up.

I smile back. "You're welcome."

16

As soon as Sam pulls to a stop in front of Whitney's place, I unbuckle with one hand and grab the door handle with the other, ready to jump out and dart across the street to the safety of my own home. There's only one teeny tiny problem.

The door won't open.

Sam has engaged the childproof locks. It's almost as if he read my mind. Sensed my need to escape.

This boy knows me way too well.

It's so annoying.

I try the handle again. Then the lock. No good.

"Sam..." I say in warning, knowing he knows that I know what he's doing.

He ignores me. He's too busy typing his number into Whitney's phone to be bothered with the prisoner behind him.

My own fault for jumping into the backseat when we left Beemer's. Then again, it would have been worth sitting next to Sam for the ten-minute drive if that meant I'd have freedom now.

Sweet, sweet freedom.

Huffing out a breath, I cross my arms and sit back. I refuse to demean myself by begging to be let out. Really, this whole thing is childish and I will not be a part of it.

Even if I do stick my tongue out at the back of Sam's stupid, stubborn, thick head.

He hands Whitney's phone back to her, then opens his door because, you know, he can and all.

I straighten and lean between the front seats. "Swear to God, Sam, if you leave me locked in here--"

Not so much as looking at me, he shuts the door.

"This is illegal," I yell but he's walking around the front of the SUV, not paying me any attention.

Whitney clears her throat but even in the dark, I can see she's fighting a smile. So glad my being held against my will is funny to her.

"Goodnight, Hadley," she says when Sam opens her door, like some guy from the 1950s or something. "Thank you for the lovely evening."

"We saw two girls puke," I remind her. "Graham dropped his pants to his knees and peed in the middle of the yard, and we walked past a blowjob in progress in the driveway." Out of the three, Graham's pasty, flabby butt really was the most disturbing. "You call that a lovely evening?"

"It was nice meeting your not-friends," she insists. "And I enjoyed talking with you."

A warm feeling spreads in my chest. She likes me? I don't know what to do with that.

It doesn't happen very often. The liking me part.

Not that it'll last. Once she has some time and space to go over everything, she'll realize we don't have much in common and there's no point in talking to me again. Especially now that she's met Sam and Kenzie and Tori, people better suited for the whole friendship deal.

People more like her.

Zoe says I don't get close to people because I'm judgmental. That I have preconceived notions of others based on how I think they're going to behave, but that's not true. I'm not judgy.

I'm careful. Smart. And I'm able to read people. Which comes in handy. If you know what to expect from someone, they can't surprise you.

Can't hurt you.

I knew Whitney was sweet and polite and assumed that sweetness would be sickening. That politeness boring. I was wrong. She's fun and funny with a dry sense of humor I can't help but appreciate.

Great. Just what I need. A girl crush on my new neighbor.

Feeling like an idiot, I slump back only to rear up again when my door opens.

"It's about time," I say, but when I get out, Sam is there—right there—blocking my way, one hand on the top of the open door, the other on the side of the SUV. Whitney is waiting at the edge of her yard, her back to us.

I step forward but Sam doesn't move. I try the right, but he shifts to block me. Eyes narrowed, I go left but it's no use.

"Excuse me," I say pointedly.

I can be polite, too.

But I should have just pushed past him because he is not cooperating with me and my manners.

"I'm going to walk Whitney to her door," he tells me, the first thing he's said to me directly since my great bathroom escape from the deck over two hours ago.

It'd been nice while it lasted, but my reprieve is over.

"Yeah? Good for you. Very gentlemanly."

I shift to the right again, planning on just ducking under his arm only to freeze when he edges closer, taking away even more space and any ducking ability.

"Wait for me here, then I'll walk you to yours."

He'd always done that, escorted me to my door whenever he brought me home. It was the kind of thing a girl got used to.

Like having him around all the time.

Look how well that worked out for me.

"Not necessary," I say. "I've managed to get myself safely home for the past eleven months. I'll do it tonight, too."

"Wait for me here," he repeats because he is a stubborn, stubborn boy. "We need to talk."

Oh, no. Not going to happen. After what he said at the party, I'm too confused. As always when it comes to him, I'm too weak.

"Actually, I'm really tired." To prove it, I fake a yawn so wide my jaw cracks. "And I have to watch Taylor in the morning, so I'd better get to bed. We'll talk tomorrow. Or next week. Or, you know, never."

With only the faint glow from inside the car and the moon and stars overhead, it's hard to see him clearly, but I swear there's a glint in his eyes. Like instead of refusing him, I've issued some sort of challenge.

One he's more than glad to accept.

He straightens and even drops the hand to my right. A clear sign he's letting me go. Granting me this minor victory.

"Don't run," he murmurs, because as I've noted, he knows me way, way too well. "If you do," he continues in that same soft tone, "I'll come after you."

It's another promise, a vow, like the one he'd made earlier.

I'm going to do whatever it takes to get you back.

Or maybe it's his own version of a challenge.

Whatever it is, it leaves me uneasy, my face hot, my knees trembling, while he turns and walks away.

I want to believe he's bluffing. But just the slight possibility of it, of him knocking on my door and possibly waking Devyn and Taylor all so he and I can have a late-night chat, keeps me glued to my spot.

I shut the car door, then lean against it as I watch Sam and Whitney go up the steps to her porch, his hand lightly touching the small of her back. Laughing at something Sam says, Whitney unlocks the door. She turns, leans against it and smiles up at him.

A lump forms in my throat. I swallow but it remains, hard and constricting. They're all smiles and laughs and easy postures, neither in a hurry to leave the other's company. I try to read their lips but it's too dark and they're too far away and I have no idea how to do it anyway. Whitney's probably thanking Sam for the ride, which will prompt Sam to thank her in return for thanking him. Or else they're bidding each other a good night, a restful, happy-dreams-only sleep and for tomorrow a cheery wake-up call and good hair day.

Just say goodbye already so we can all move on with our lives.

Sam leans in closer, nods at something Whitney says, and I realize I have both palms flat against the door behind me.

Realize my vision has taken on a definite green tint.

Which is stupid. I'm not jealous. I wanted Sam and Whitney to hit it off. I just hadn't realized they'd do it like freaking gangbusters.

No surprise. They have so much in common. Though we haven't even started our senior year in high school, they're both already thinking of the future. On the way home, they talked nonstop about the lists they'd made of colleges they want to apply to. Lists they'd both broken into three tiers: Dream Schools, Doable Schools and Safe Schools.

It was like they were made for each other.

Even their plans for the future match up. Sam wants to follow in his parents' footsteps and become a doctor, possibly a surgeon. Whitney is going to study elementary education at whatever fabulous, hard-to-get-into, far-away-from-here, expensive college she attends.

Of course her dream is to educate the children of the world. Teaching is, after all, the noblest of professions.

I mean, not quite as noble as performing life-saving surgery, but pretty darn close.

And me? My greatest wish, my secret dream is to one day own a bakery, where I can sell my homemade cookies, cakes and donuts to the masses.

Just doing my part to add to America's growing obesity and diabetes rates!

One of these things is definitely not like the others.

I don't get why Sam wanted so badly to be my friend when we were kids. Why he's doing this now, acting like he wants me back in his life. He's the one who walked away.

Now he doesn't want to let me go?

It's messed up. And not fair.

Whitney finally goes inside, shutting the door behind her, and I push away from the car, debating whether or not to dart across the street.

I'll come after you.

Wonder if that's what I want. To see if he really would chase me.

But Sam is heading my way, as if he had no doubt I'd be here, right where he left me, waiting with bated breath until he returned.

But when he gets closer, I see his shoulders are tense, his expression wary. Nervous.

I'm not the only one out of sorts. Not the only one confused. I might not even be the only one who's scared.

And instead of finding comfort in that fact, it makes everything that much worse.

"You waited," he says when he reaches me.

I shrug. "You asked me to."

It's the wrong thing to say because it's not just me stating the obvious, it's not just the truth. It's the real reason I waited. The reason I went to the party.

Because I'm too curious about what he has to say.

Because I'm an idiot who can't tell him no.

He knows it, too. His mouth kicks up in a shy, adorable grin and my scalp tingles, my stomach tumbling in the very best way.

Stupid handsome boys and their stupid adorable grins. They make a girl forget why she's not supposed to get all tingly and tumbly. They make a girl forget why she's supposed to be smart and stay as far away from them as possible.

"Thank you for waiting," he whispers, then he steps closer and my breath locks in my chest. I don't move, not even when he's so close I can feel his body heat, can smell the lingering scent of campfire smoke clinging to his clothes. Not even when he lifts his hand, his fingers trembling, and lightly touches my cheek. "I missed you. Christ, Hadley, I missed you so much."

I freeze, my body wanting to lean into his touch. My heart leaping at his words.

Oh, this was such a mistake. Going to the party, waiting for him now. I need to go before he says something else I don't want to hear. Something that will make the resolve I've built up over the past eleven months weaken even further.

I have to go before he does or says something that will push me into admitting how much I missed him, too.

But I can't give him those words, that truth. He already has too much of what's mine. He knows too much about me, knows *me*, better than anyone. My likes and dislikes. My hopes and dreams. My doubts and fears.

He knows. And he walked away.

He doesn't get to have my secrets, too.

I turn and walk away, make it halfway across the empty street before he catches up to me. We've done this a hundred times, maybe even a thousand, walked side by side in the dark toward my trailer, the porch light guiding us. But it's different now. New. We're quiet when before we were always talking and joking and making plans for the next day. There's a space between us, a physical distance I do my best to maintain so there's no brushing of arms. Things between us have changed. I need to remember that. I need to accept it.

But it's hard to remember when the air is warm and thick with the scent of an oncoming rainstorm, reminding me of so many other summer nights with Sam. It's even harder to accept when there are so many other things that are the same. The way he walks, the steady sound of his breathing. How he follows me up the sidewalk and then the steps, big and protective behind me. How he leans his shoulder against the side of the trailer, hands in his pockets, watching over me while I dig out my key.

Sam. My friend.

Last summer I thought it would always be like this. That it would be Sam and Hadley. Hadley and Sam. Forever.

Now I can't imagine it ever being that way again.

My hands are unsteady. So unsteady I can't get my stupid key into the stupid lock.

A growl of frustration rises in my throat but I hold it back. Not that it matters. Sam, the super observant, notices I'm being a complete doofus who can't even unlock her own door. He takes the key from my hand and steps forward. I stare at his broad back, his wide shoulders, while he unlocks my door, the click of it loud in the silence.

He turns, gives me my key back, then stands there. Broad chest, wide shoulders and immovable body.

I curl my fingers around the key, the edges biting into my palm. "This new habit you picked up in LA of blocking my way is extremely irritating."

"If I don't block your way, you'll run. And I want to talk to you."

My chest burns and there's a roaring sound in my head, echoing in my ears, that makes it hard to think. Makes it impossible to keep my mouth shut.

"It's always what you want," I say, my words quiet but heated. "And that's not fair. I worked with you today, I went to the party with you, I waited for you but I can't...I can't do any more. Not tonight. It's my turn to get what *I* want."

To my everlasting horror, my voice cracks. My eyes sting. Because I'm tired. And frustrated. And angry. Because I spent the night surrounded by people who haven't spoken to me in almost a year. Because the past two days have drained me emotionally.

And because Sam Constable is back, once again pushing me for more.

"Shit," he breathes, shoving a hand through his hair. He exhales and lowers his hand, fisting it by his side. "You're right. It's your turn. What do *you* want, Hadley?"

So many thoughts whirl through my mind. What I wanted for so many months battles with what I want now, but none of that matters. There's only one answer I can give.

"I want you to let me go."

"I don't think I can."

His voice is low. Stark in its honesty. He's taking my words as something more than me going inside to bed. He thinks I want him to let me go forever. For good, this time.

I don't correct him. No matter how badly I want to.

"You can," I tell him. "You did it easily enough before."

He flinches. Nods. And finally, thankfully, steps aside.

I brush past him, open the door and step inside.

"Hadley."

Shutting my eyes, I stop, my hand still on the doorknob. I stop because hearing him whisper my name in the dark, like a secret, like a prayer, has tears forming again. I stop because even after all this time, I'm still too used to giving Sam everything I have. Everything I am.

His next works are even softer. And rip the breath from my lungs.

"Letting you go wasn't easy. It was the hardest thing I've ever done."

17

I HADN'T SEEN IT COMING.

I should have. All the signs were there. The long looks when he thought I wasn't watching. The way he touched me, a brush of his fingers across the back of my hand or a quick squeeze of my knee. How he held me when we hugged goodbye, his arms tight around my waist, his face against my neck.

Signs? They'd been freaking billboards. And I'd ignored them, choosing instead to believe Sam would never do or say anything to put our friendship at risk.

After Sam moved to LA, I went over and over everything that happened. What led up to it. If I'd been more careful, more proactive, maybe I could have stopped it before it got too far. Then I realized none of that would have changed anything. Delayed it perhaps, but in the end, we were always meant to wind up here.

It was inevitable.

———

It'd been hot the day everything changed between us for the second time, hence, my whining when Sam and I stopped for lunch about how forcing us to work under such conditions wasn't just dangerous but possibly criminal.

"All I'm saying is that I'm not sure it's legal." Sitting on the tailgate of the truck, I finished my bottle of water and reached for another one and set it next to me. I bit into the turkey and provolone sub Sam bought me hoping it'd help improve my mood—ha ha, no such luck, my friend—and spoke around my mouthful. "There are child labor laws against this sort of thing." I took another bite, waving the sub for emphasis. "This is exactly why workers have unions. So we're not exploited."

Sam didn't answer and I glanced behind me. He'd finished his lunch five minutes ago and now laid back on the truck bed, legs dangling over the tailgate next to mine, hands linked on his steadily falling and rising flat stomach, his face covered with his ball cap.

I poked his thigh, just above his knee. "Are you listening to me?"

"Illegal," he murmured. "Child labor." He lifted a fisted hand into the air. "Organize. Fight the power."

I took another bite, chewed while I glared at him, then swallowed. "Scoff if you must, but I'm trying to save our lives. It's inhumane, making us work outside in triple-digit-heat--"

"It's eighty-six degrees."

I finished the sub and crumpled up the paper it came in, then tossed it at his chest. It hit him and rolled off.

He didn't move.

I crossed my arms. God. Must be nice to be that relaxed, that at ease with life. Didn't matter what we were doing, where we were, or who we were with, Sam was laid-back, bright as sunshine and filled with good humor, kindness, and patience all. The. Freaking. Time.

And I, to put it simply, wasn't.

Sam was way, way too good for me.

Did he have to prove it so often?

Irritated with that thought, I stared at my bare toes—I'd taken my boots and socks off the moment we'd gotten into the truck—and swung my legs back and forth. Remembered the first time Sam and I had talked, really talked, that warm day at his house, us sitting side by side like this at the edge of his pool.

His legs were no longer skinny, but thick with muscles and covered with dark, springy hair. Mine were still slim and ghostly pale compared to his tanned skin. His feet had grown, too, in order, I guess, to match his body, and his size-twelve work boots looked big and rough and extremely masculine next to my narrow feet with their pink, sparkly toenails.

Turning slightly, I bent my left leg under my right one and opened my water while I let myself do something I normally avoided at all costs.

I drank in the beauty that was Sam Constable.

I had to. The boy was laid out before me like a free dessert buffet filled with my favorites, and the willpower I usually relied on melted away, taking along any resistance I might have felt with it.

Sipping my water, I scanned his legs. Bits of grass clung to the hair on his calves and both knees had scabs—just like that day at his pool when our friendship began—though these marks were courtesy of him being knocked to the pavement during a vicious pickup game of basketball at the park. His khaki cargo shorts ended just above his knees, hanging low and loose on his waist, and the hem of his polo was bunched up, exposing the gray band of his boxers and an inch of his toned, tanned stomach.

My fingers twitched. I'd never touched him there, that low on his belly, had never touched him anywhere on his bare stomach or chest or back, only casual, friendly touches to his arms or hands. What it would it feel like, to trace my fingertips along the elastic of his boxers? Would his muscles twitch? Would his skin be soft? Warm?

Would he like it, me touching him?

I wiped my damp palms down the front of my shorts. Those thoughts were dangerous. Dangerous and inappropriate and had been occurring way, way too frequently for my peace of mind. They left me jittery and uneasy, scared and confused.

Jerking my gaze upward, I watched the steady fall and rise of his chest, my eyes on his interlaced hands as I counted each breath he took. Matched my own breathing to his until the jitteriness soothed. The uneasiness calmed.

But the fear and confusion remained.

They'd always been there, lingering in the background, coloring every moment I had with Sam. But lately they'd been pushing to the forefront, demanding more and more of my time. My attention.

If I wasn't careful, they'd take over and everything between us would be ruined.

"Let's go swimming," I blurted and Sam twitched in surprise. Well, my words had been sort of sudden. And loud.

After pushing his hat back on top of his head, he rose onto his elbows. "Now?"

I couldn't meet his eyes, not when I'd just been imagining what it'd look like, my hand on his stomach, so I hopped off the truck, kept my back to him as I pretended to brush something from my leg. "Yeah. We can swing by your house, go for a quick dip, then go to the McClains'."

"No time. Our lunch break is over in twenty minutes."

I turned, the dry grass prickly under my bare feet, as he pulled an apple out of his lunch pail and offered it to me. But it wasn't the fruit that tempted me, it was him. Him and his stupid, sweaty ball cap, dark, watchful eyes and grass-stained clothes.

Adam and Eve we weren't. Though if I thought about it, the stereotypes fit.

Wasn't Eve the one who led Adam down a path of sin and rebellion?

Not quite the same as trying to get Sam to take a few extra minutes at lunch, but still...

I shook my head at the apple and he shrugged and bit into it himself.

"That's plenty of time. And no one's home at the McClains'," I pointed out. "They'll never know if we're a few minutes late."

The more I thought about it, the better my idea sounded. A swim would cool me off and clear my mind of any more thoughts about touching Sam.

"Come on," I said. "It may be eighty-six degrees now, but it's only noon. It could climb into the hundreds within a few hours."

It probably wouldn't, but it could. Anything's possible, right?

Even talking Sam Constable into stepping just one toe outside the lines of good behavior.

"We'll be quick," I continued as he munched away on the apple, not the least bit enticed to go with my plan. This was so not how the whole Adam and Eve thing went in Eden. "Ten. Fifteen minutes, tops."

"Mr. G.'s counting on us to be back to work at one."

Why did he have to be so stubborn? So endlessly, continuously perfect?

"Mr. G. doesn't have to know," I said, and yeah, I pouted a bit. Sue me. "No one does. And if we are caught—which isn't going to happen—we'll say we had trouble with the truck or that one of us wasn't feeling well."

Sam looked at me as if I'd suggested we knock Mr. G. over the head with a shovel and hide his body in the compost collector.

"What?" I asked, that single judgmental look making me defensive and, I might add, seriously ticked off.

Not quite the emotions I'd been hoping to get to, but I'd take them.

"We're not going to lie to Mr. G," he said, sounding like my dad or something—if my dad had bothered sticking around long enough to use that disappointed tone, that is. The only things missing were a *young lady* and *this is the end of the conversation.*

"It's not *lying*. It's a little fib about being a few minutes late."

If he'd stop arguing with me, we could be halfway to his house by now instead of wasting even more of that time he's so worried about.

"It's lying," he said, his tone quiet and final. And more than a little holier than thou. "And I don't lie."

That was the problem. And part of the reason I didn't want to let this go. Not because I wanted him to lie, necessarily. I just wanted him to be a little less perfect. Just once I wanted us to be more equal.

Maybe then I'd stop feeling like I was so far beneath him.

I snorted. Like that would ever happen. Sam was everything good —honest, trustworthy, responsible, kind.

He was so much better than me.

"Hey," he said, getting to his feet. He ducked his head to see my face beneath the brim of my hat. "We'll take water breaks every twenty minutes this afternoon. And I'll let you work the shadiest parts of the McClains' yard."

The goodness never ended.

Was it any wonder my feelings for him were so confused?

If he'd just be a dick every once in a while, I wouldn't have this problem.

My movements jerky, I turned and grabbed my backpack, rifled through it for my sunscreen. "So I can feel guilty when you're burnt to a crisp, dehydrated and dying of heat stroke? No, thanks."

Putting the apple in his mouth, he lifted his hat off with one hand, ran his other hand through his hair, then turned the hat and put it on backwards, a few tufts of dark hair sticking out from under the edge. All the while he watched me, like I was one wrong word away from ripping his head off and drop-kicking it off the side of the hill.

Which, yeah, wasn't that far from the truth.

After taking another bite, he took the apple out of his mouth. Chewed and swallowed. "Is something wrong? You're acting..."

I froze, sunscreen bottle in one hand, eyes narrowed to slits. "How am I acting?"

I already knew. I was acting like a crazy person. A hot, sweaty, cranky bitch who couldn't control her thoughts or feelings. I wouldn't even blame him if he asked if I was PMSing.

I'd go ahead with that head-ripping-off, drop-kicking thing, but I wouldn't blame him.

"Off," he finally settled on because even when I was at my worst, Sam was at his best.

And he deserved way better than me taking some weird mood out on him. It wasn't his fault I wanted something I couldn't have.

I sighed, contrite and embarrassed to have lashed out at him for no reason.

Well, no reason I could give to him, anyway.

"I'm fine," I said, my gaze on the sunscreen I squeezed into my palm. "Let's just forget it."

Bending over, I rubbed the sunscreen into my calves.

"We'll go swimming after work," Sam said, leaning one hip against the tailgate. "I'll even let you pick what we get for dinner."

Friday nights we got takeout and while Sam's choice was always pizza (and I mean *always*) I liked to vary mine.

"You won't *let* me pick," I said, straightening and squirting more sunscreen into my hand, then setting the bottle on the tailgate so I could apply it to my arms, "it's my turn. But it's going to have to wait until next week because I'm not coming over tonight."

"What? Why not? Because I won't take an extra-long lunch and lie about it?"

I rolled my eyes, rubbing my arms so hard I was surprised sparks didn't shoot off my skin. "Hardly. I have other plans."

"Plans?"

"Yep."

"Care to share what they are?"

I didn't much like his amused, disbelieving tone, as if I was making the whole thing up to get him to give in to me or beg me to spend the evening with him or something.

"Sure," I said, squirting a small amount of sunscreen onto my fingertips. "I'm hanging out with Colby."

"Colby Bricker?"

Dotting the sunscreen on my face—chin, cheeks, nose and forehead—I nodded.

"You're hanging out with Colby Bricker?" he repeated. "Tonight?"

"I'm not sure what part you're having a problem with," I said, rubbing the sunscreen in, "but the answer to both your questions is yes. I'm hanging out with Colby Bricker. And that hanging out is happening tonight."

"Since when do you hang out with Colby Bricker?"

"Since now."

Or, more accurately, since thirty seconds ago when I realized I couldn't spend the evening with Sam. Not when my feelings were so confused, my thoughts twisted and tangled.

What I needed was space. Time to find a little clarity.

And what better way to ignore my confusing, twisted, tangled emotions for the boy in front of me than spending time with another guy?

"You don't even know him," Sam said, as if *he* knew everyone I was, and wasn't, personally connected with.

Which, yeah, he did, but jeez. I can make new friends without him being part of the vetting process.

"Actually, we've been texting since we hung out at Ryan's party last weekend. So I do know him."

Sam turned and winged the apple core over the hill with enough force to have it landing in the middle of Main Street. "Blow him off."

"What?"

"Text him and tell him you can't hang out with him tonight."

I raised my eyebrows. "That would by lying. And as you so helpfully pointed out a few minutes ago, lying is a no-no."

His mouth thinned. He edged closer and there was a shift in the air, a change in the energy surrounding us, one that had goose bumps rising on my arms, apprehension climbing my spine.

One that had me wishing I'd never brought up Colby's name.

"It won't be a lie," he said. "Tell him you're with me."

"It's one Friday night. You'll be fine without me. And now you can have pizza two weeks in a row."

Watching me, he shook his head slowly. "No. Tell him you're *with* me."

There was something in his soft tone, in the gruffness of his voice that had me on edge. That left me breathless.

Tell him you're with me.

With him as in...as in...him and me. Me and him. Together.

Not just friends but something...more.

Panic swept over me like a wave and I scurried back, needing to get as far away from Sam—his words and the intent in his eyes—as possible.

I stepped on a sharp stone, the pain making me gasp and stumble. Sam caught me, his fingers wrapping around my arms just above my elbows, and I knew there was no escape. No way to stop this.

Because he didn't let go. Didn't give me a there-you-go-pal pat on the shoulder.

He held on, his fingers tightening. He pulled me closer, tugging me ever so slowly, ever so steadily toward him, until my bare toes touched the tips of his work boots.

"You ever wonder?" he asked, the soft rumble of his voice vibrating through my body, the heady thrum of it settling low in my belly.

I stared at our feet, unable to look at him. Afraid of what I'd see in his eyes. More afraid of what he'd see in mine. "Wonder what?"

Without meaning to, my own tone matched his. Low. Husky. Thick with longing.

He heard it, he must have, because his hands slid up my arms. "Do you ever wonder what it would be like to be with me?"

My head snapped up, my eyes wide.

But he wasn't done. Nope, rocking my world with that single question wasn't enough for Sam Constable. Not nearly enough.

"Do you ever wonder," he continued, watching his left hand as he skimmed it down my arm, those wonderful work-roughened fingers gliding across the sensitive skin of my inner forearm, past my wrist and scraping lightly against my palm, causing my fingers to twitch, "what it would be like to hold my hand?" He settled his hand on my waist, his thumb against my hip bone, fingers spread wide at my lower back. "Do you ever wonder what it would be like to touch me?"

I trembled, my body instinctively answering when I couldn't.

He inhaled sharply and widened his stance, drawing me between his legs. "Do you ever wonder," he repeated, his voice going even softer, dark and seductive as he slid his other hand up to cup my head, his palm cradling the back of my scalp, his fingers delving into the hair just under my hat, tipping my face up as he lowered his, "what it would be like to kiss me?"

The air shuddering out of me, my gaze flicked to his mouth for one long second before I wrenched it back up to his eyes. "No."

I didn't give him the answer he wanted, but he already knew the truth. We'd both known it, had hidden from it, for six years.

Yes. Yes, I'd wondered what it would be like to be with him. Just as I knew he wondered, that he wanted to be with me in the same way. We were never meant to be just friends.

But it was all we could be. All I could give him.

And now that he'd brought it all out into the open, he wanted more. Sam would always want more.

"Don't be scared," he murmured, his breath brushing against my cheek. "I won't hurt you."

I shut my eyes against the sudden sting of tears. Of course he would hurt me. It was unavoidable now that he'd said too much, had changed things between us by touching me this way.

If I didn't stop this, I was going to lose him.

Worse than that, *I* would hurt *him*.

"Sam..."

My words died in my throat, my hands going to his chest as he lowered his head, ducking under the brim of my hat before hesitating, his mouth inches from mine. Eyes open, breath held, I waited, the sound of my pulse beating in my ears, my body tight with tension until, finally, he brushed his mouth over mine.

He raised his head, just far enough to meet my eyes, his forehead bumping my hat. "Kiss me back, Hadley."

I shouldn't. It went against everything I needed to do to stop this madness from going any further. Would only make it that much harder for us to get past what had already happened, what had already been said.

But his voice was so quiet, his tone almost a plea. And when he lifted his hand to tug off my hat and toss it aside, his fingers were unsteady. Under my palms, his heart beat wildly, as did the pulse at the side of his neck.

He was nervous. Scared. Maybe as scared as I was, but he wasn't going to let fear stop him from going after what he wanted. He was so much braver than me.

For once, he was reckless.

"Kiss me back," he repeated in a whisper right before he settled his mouth against mine.

His lips were soft and warm and firm and he tasted like apple—crisp and tart. But his kiss was sweet and edged with a need I couldn't refuse.

Rising onto my toes, I linked my hands behind his neck, pressed against him and kissed him back. He made a noise deep in his throat and held me tighter, one hand tangled in the hair at the nape of my neck, loosening my ponytail, the other dipping under the hem of my shirt, his fingers skimming over my skin.

Heat wound its way through my system and I stroked his shoulders and down his arms. He was broad and solid, the light scrape of the sparse stubble on his cheeks and chin a wicked contrast to the softness of his mouth. He deepened the kiss, his tongue stroking mine, and my mind blanked to everything but Sam. The feel of his mouth. The strength of him under my hands. His touch on my back, slow and sure and hypnotic as he trailed his fingers up my spine to my bra strap and then back down to the waistband of my shorts.

But it wasn't enough. Now that this moment was finally happening, I was greedy for more, my body working purely on sensation and instinct. I wiggled against him, trying to get closer. Wanted to tug him to the ground and pull him on top of me.

Slipping my hands under his shirt, I pressed my palms against his stomach, against that band of skin I'd been so tempted by only minutes ago, finding it as soft and warm as I'd imagined. His muscles quivered and I curled my fingers slightly, scraping my nails against him. Drew them lower...

Lower...

His belly hollowed as he captured my wrists and tugged my seeking hands away. Lifted his head. We stared at each other, both breathing hard. In his grip, my hands shook and I cursed that telltale sign of weakness. The proof of how far gone I was over him.

How far gone I'd always been.

Sam smiled at me, that wonderful, crooked smile of his. "Guess that answers my question."

Do you ever wonder?

All. The. Time.

Except, now I didn't have to wonder anymore. I knew.

And knowing, having a taste of what I'd been missing, of what I could never have again, was so much worse.

I stepped back. "Take me home."

Instantly, his smile was replaced with concern. "What's the matter?"

Sidestepping him, I headed around the truck. "I don't feel well. I want to go home."

He sighed the drawn-out and patient sigh of the long-suffering. "Hadley--"

"I want to go home," I repeated, shrill and desperate and on the brink of tears. I sniffed and yanked open the passenger-side door, then reached in for my phone in the console. "If you don't want to take me, I'll call Devyn. Or Zoe."

He held up his hands, pacifying the crazy, overly emotional girl, his tone meant to soothe. "Okay. I'll take you home."

I nodded and got into the truck. Fought those stupid tears as I waited for him to shut the tailgate and climb in beside me. We drove in silence, him shooting me glances, me staring out the passenger-side window.

He pulled into my driveway and I unbuckled and grabbed my phone. Opened the door and got out but his voice stopped me.

"Hadley."

I shut my eyes. It wasn't fair that out of all the boys in the entire world, Sam could reduce me to a puddle just by saying my name.

I waited, expecting him to get out and walk me to my door, insisting we talk about what just happened. But he was full of surprises today, this boy who, fifteen minutes ago, I would have sworn I knew better than anyone. Whose every move I thought I could predict.

Guess not.

"I'll tell Mr. G. you went home sick," he said. "Feel better."

It was a momentary reprieve, one I couldn't refuse.

So I shut the door and turned.

And for the first time, I ran from Sam Constable.

18

LETTING YOU GO WASN'T EASY. IT WAS THE HARDEST THING I'VE EVER DONE.

Freeing myself from the sheet, I carefully roll onto my stomach so I don't wake Taylor and pull my pillow over my head. But it doesn't muffle the sound of Sam's voice echoing in my thoughts. Nope, it's as clear this morning as it was last night when he spoke those words. As clear as it was for hours after that, the memory of it spinning around in my mind while I tossed and turned in bed.

Figures the only time I have perfect recall is when it comes to Sam Constable and the things he's said and done.

I stretch out my right arm and leg to the side, let my hand and foot dangle off the edge of my bed. Eyes squeezed shut, I try to even my breathing, calm my mind and think of the most boring, mind-numbing things I can—algebra class and the Weather Channel and baseball.

It's no use. Sleep isn't returning anytime soon.

Sam is ruining my life. Not only did thoughts of him keep me up half the night, but now I'm wide awake before seven a.m. on a Saturday because I'd been dreaming of him.

Stupid, vivid dreams of him kissing me again the way he did that day last summer. Of me kissing him back.

I can't even escape the boy when I'm asleep. He's always there, hiding in my subconscious, ready to jump out and show me all the things I can't have.

The things I could have had if I hadn't been so scared last summer.

If I hadn't done what I did at Christmas.

With an inner groan, I pull the pillow down, curving the ends over my ears, and push my face to the mattress until my lungs burn.

I lift my head with a soft gasp, then take a deep inhale of the stale, hot air. It's like a sauna in my room, the morning sun heating it up despite my fan whirring like mad. And I have my own little human furnace next to me, warmth pouring off her.

At least Taylor's still conked out, her breathing deep and even, her hair sweaty at the temples, her pudgy hands curled together under her round cheek.

I set the pillow aside and slowly roll onto my back. Push the hair out of my eyes. I might as well get up. I want to shower by myself, which will only be accomplished if I do so before Taylor wakes up since Devyn left an hour ago for her early shift at the nursing home and Zoe didn't get in until after three.

So, yeah. As much as I'd like to put off facing the current situation that is my life for just a little while longer, I can't.

I stare up at my ceiling, eyes narrowed as if I can see through it to the sky and whoever's running things up there. "Let's see what fresh hell you have in store for me," I say under my breath, then I get out of bed.

A new day awaits.

Hooray.

I grab some clothes then step out into the hall, leaving my door open an inch behind me. I tiptoe past Zoe's room toward the bathroom, each creak and groan of the floor beneath my feet making me wince. Nobody wants Zoe awake before she's had at least seven hours of sleep.

She doesn't have my bright and sunny disposition.

Fifteen minutes later, I'm showered, wearing shorts and a bra, wet hair combed away from my face and dripping down my back. Steam coats the mirror above the sink and I'm wiping it off with my damp towel when the bathroom door opens.

I don't even glance over.

You know how you're not supposed to make eye contact with an unfriendly dog or they'll take it as a sign of aggression on your part?

The same theory holds true with a sleep-deprived Zoe.

"I barely made a sound," I say, because when it comes to dealing with this particular sister of mine, the best defense is a good offense, and the last thing I need is her yelling at me about waking her up. "So don't start."

"I'm not starting anything."

Leaning over the sink, I freeze. My fingers tighten on the towel. Guess I should have glanced over after all, because that wasn't Zoe's voice.

I turn my head to find a skinny, shirtless, heavily tattooed guy standing just inside the door, his low-slung jeans unbuttoned.

"Unless," he continues, giving me a slow-once over that is the creepiest thing I've ever experienced, "you want me to."

And he grins.

Okay. The once-over was the second creepiest thing I've ever experienced. That smile of his is number one.

Keeping my eyes on his, I ease back, holding the towel in front of me like a shield. I dart my gaze to the door but he's blocking the way. He's wiry, the muscles of his arms, chest and stomach well-toned, his expression telling me he'd enjoy me trying to get past him. Especially if it means he gets to try and stop me.

I consider screaming, but that would only scare Taylor and I'd rather she not know there's a strange man at our house.

Plus, she might say something to Devyn about it and then all hell would break loose.

Right on Zoe's head.

Then again, I'm standing in our cramped bathroom in shorts and a bra while some creeper is edging closer and closer to me by the second.

Hell breaking loose seems pretty fitting.

"Zoe," I whisper-shout, hoping that while *she* can hear me, the sound doesn't travel over to my room. "Come and get your sleepover pal."

His smile amps up a few degrees and I see it, why Zoe brought him home. The sexy grin, the long, light brown hair and sharply planed face, the faded jeans and hard body covered in ink. He's got the whole bad-boy vibe down pat.

And Zoe loves nothing more than falling for a guy who'll never fall back.

Guys like she used to hook up with in high school, who strung her along until they got bored or found some new girl to mess with. Guys like Taylor's father, who spent months lying to her and cheating on her, always begging her to take him back, promising he'd change, that he loved her and wanted to be with her forever.

Until she told him she was pregnant.

Forever. Not as long as you think.

I skim my gaze over shirtless guy. Gah. Her taste hasn't improved.

"No need to be scared," he says, still coming at me. The hard edge of the counter digs into my lower back. "I'm just being friendly."

I open my mouth to yell for Zoe again when she steps into the room. My hero has arrived and she's wearing a faded Minnie Mouse T-shirt that barely covers her white underwear, her hair is flat against one side of her head, sticking out on the other, and last night's makeup is smudged and smeared around her eyes, making her look like a raccoon after a bender.

Wonder Woman she's not.

Zoe's gaze narrows. "What's going on?"

I incline my head toward the guy. "He's being *friendly*."

Mouth thinning, she crosses her arms, her lips barely moving when she speaks. "Get out."

My jaw drops. "Hey, I was in here first."

She rolls her eyes but then holds her head with both hands as if afraid it'll fall off her shoulders with any other movement.

Hangovers: Nature's Karma.

"Not you." She jabs a finger at the guy. "You."

I frown as that processes. Nod. "Okay. Yeah, that makes more sense."

Sisters over misters and all that.

Shirtless guy holds up his hands as if in surrender, but he's still sending me *I'd love to eat you up* looks, like he's the Big Bad Wolf and I'm Little Red Riding Hood. Next thing I know, he'll lick his lips and start howling.

I tug the towel around myself tighter. Wish I could drop it long enough to put on my tank top but I'm not giving this guy any more glimpses of my skin than he already has.

"Come on, babe," he says to Zoe in a low, and what I'm assuming is supposed to be seductive, tone. "Don't be jealous. The three of us could have some fun."

Oh. Blech.

"I'd rather lick the toilet brush," I tell him. "Which should give you a huge clue about what I think of that idea."

The gleam in his eyes makes my skin crawl but it's nothing compared to the fear when he winks at me, like I'm flirting with him or something. "I bet you'd like it just fine."

"Get out," Zoe repeats in an icy tone that means she's nanoseconds from ripping your heart from your chest and shoving it down your throat.

If shirtless guy wasn't a freaking sexual predator trying to talk me into a threesome with him and *my sister*, I'd almost feel bad for him.

Obviously he and Zoe hadn't spent the past few hours discussing their personality quirks, their likes and dislikes, because he smiles at her, like she's the cutest thing he's ever seen with her bare legs and crazy hair and scary scowl.

"I bet you're that fiery, too," he murmurs to me, his gaze flicking to my slicked back hair. "Aren't you, Red?"

"Don't look at her," Zoe says, yanking his arm and whirling him around to face her. "Don't talk to her." She shoves his chest hard and he stumbles back, landing against the doorframe with a dull thud.

Before he can fully catch his balance, she's pushing him out into the hall. "Just leave."

As soon as he clears the room, I drop the towel and yank on my shirt, then hurry after them in case he starts pushing her back.

Leaving him by the bathroom door, Zoe goes into her bedroom. A moment later, a motorcycle boot is tossed out, landing next to his toes with a thump that has him hopping out of the way and me wincing and glancing at my bedroom door. I peek through the crack. Taylor doesn't even stir.

The second boot flies out of Zoe's room, landing next to the first one and I quickly pull my door shut. A wallet follows, then his phone. Last comes a balled-up T-shirt that he snags out of the air.

A T-shirt I bet has the logo of some metal rock band from the nineties on the front and is missing its sleeves—the better to show off all that ink on his arms.

Shaking it at her, he steps forward and I move over to stand by Zoe's side.

As always, it's the Jones' girls against the world.

Or, in this case, against one wannabe biker badly in need of a haircut.

"What the fuck is your problem?" he growls.

He's glaring, a greasy, riled-up dude whose morning is not going the way he'd hoped and that's ticking him off but good.

Though she's six inches shorter and fifty pounds lighter, Zoe is not intimidated.

My sister is fearless.

The reckless usually are.

"My problem is you're still here." She points dramatically toward the door, arm straight at shoulder height, chin lifted—a hungover queen in underwear and a Disney shirt. "Leave. Now."

He swipes up his things. "Whatever."

But as he passes her, he knocks into her shoulder, pushing her back a step. She makes a low sound and leaps at him, fingers curled, nails ready to do some serious damage to his face. I grab her around the waist and haul her back before she can reach him. Hold on while she kicks and swipes at him.

He sneers at her, like she's so far beneath him, and I want to scratch his eyes out myself.

"Crazy bitch."

He stomps down the hall in full temper tantrum, reminding me of Taylor when she feels the world has treated her unjustly. Eggie comes racing over, barking like mad, tail wagging in excitement about this new, interesting person in the house, wanting to get to know him better. Is he a head patter or a belly scratcher kind of human?

Neither, it seems. Shirtless guy ignores our dog and keeps going. A moment later, the front door slams shut.

His potential new buddy gone, Eggie runs over to me. Males. So fickle.

Zoe sags against me, the fight in her gone. I let go of her and she slides down to sit, back against the wall.

I frown at Eggie. "Some watchdog you are. You need to be more discerning about the people you want to be friends with." His tail wags harder and I crouch so I can pet him. "It's not your fault. You get it from Zoe."

"Shut it," she says, head back, eyes shut.

"You're right. I shouldn't be so darn quick to judge. I'm sure once I get to know your new pal, I'll see how nice he is. It's already clear he's a class act. I mean, he did want me to join you two in bed. That was super polite of him, making sure I wasn't left out of the fun. Hey, where'd you two crazy kids meet? A church social?"

"Not in the mood." Opening her eyes, she swallows carefully. "Why didn't you lock the bathroom door?"

I raise my eyebrows. "Silly me, thinking I was safe in my own home and could take a shower without having to barricade myself in the bathroom in case some greasy-haired pervert waltzes on in and tries to molest me."

Like we used to have to do when Mom was still around and brought one of her male friends home for the night.

"Axel wouldn't have hurt you," Zoe says.

"Axel? What happened to the guy from the hookup app?"

"Dating. App. And he lost interest once he found out about Taylor."

Of course he did.

Jerk.

But that doesn't excuse her for bringing home some random guy. "When did you meet Axel?"

Getting to her hands and knees, she pushes to her feet, then lurches toward the bathroom.

"Too hard of a question?" I ask as I follow her. I lean against the counter while she fills a paper cup with water from the sink. "Let's try something easier. What's his last name?"

She takes a tiny sip. Inhales slowly and deeply through her nose.

And doesn't answer.

Un-freaking-believable.

"Please," I say through gritted teeth. "Please, please, please tell me you know his last name."

"It didn't come up." Her lips roll inward and she swallows again. "Don't look at me like that."

Turning to face the mirror, I pick up my hairbrush and pull it through my already combed hair. "I'm not looking at you at all."

"You are." She takes another sip of water. "You're judging me."

I whirl on her. "You brought a man home! A man I'm guessing you met just last night, whose last name you don't even know. You had sex with him two doors down from where your daughter is sleeping. What if she would have woken up and needed you? What if his tastes don't just run to teenage girls but to toddler ones?"

Zoe blanches and makes a choking noise and I wonder if I've gone too far but I push the worry aside. She's the one who went too far. But at least what I said seems to have gotten through to her. She stares at me wide-eyed, a hand over her mouth, her face sickly pale.

Good. She should feel sick over what she did. But then I look closer and she doesn't look just sick. She looks ready to pass out.

Which is the last thing I need.

"Are you okay?"

She turns, drops to her knees in front of the toilet and throws up. Definitely not okay.

I set the brush down and gather her hair in both hands, holding it out of the way while she heaves. Rub her back with my other hand.

"Done?" I ask when she stops gagging. She nods and leans back against the tub, tears leaking from her closed eyes, face drawn.

I straighten and flush the toilet, then refill her cup at the sink. When I turn back, Zoe's head is on her bent knees, her T-shirt tugged over her legs.

I hand her the water. "Here."

While she rinses her mouth and spits into the toilet, I wet a washcloth with cool water then take the cup and set it aside. Sitting next to her, I brush her hair back, curling my finger under a few sweaty strands sticking to her temple, then dab her forehead and cheek with the cloth.

She tips her head onto my shoulder, her voice raw when she speaks. "Thanks, sissy."

"Better?"

"Yeah."

I start to rise. "I'll get you a ginger ale."

She grabs my hand. Holds on, her palm clammy. "Can you just... can you sit with me? For a few minutes?"

I settle back and we sit there, side by side, shoulders touching, hips pressed together. I give her hand a squeeze to let her know I'm not mad at her anymore. To let her know everything will be okay.

That I'm here, beside her, no matter what.

19

AFTER SITTING ON THE BATHROOM FLOOR FOR A GOOD TEN MINUTES, I helped Zoe back into bed, leaving the washcloth on her nightstand and the garbage can from the bathroom on the floor near her head. Then I let Eggie out back to do his business and grabbed a can of ginger ale for Zoe. I was making my second trip down the hall when Taylor padded out of my room, crying that she was thirsty. I picked her up only to discover she was soaking wet.

As was my bed and, thanks to me picking her up before checking for any dampness, my shirt.

Devyn's fault. She insists on putting Taylor in pullups at night even though they're not as absorbent as diapers. But she thinks Taylor will get tired of sitting in her own pee and start being more agreeable to potty training.

Because two-year-olds are known far and wide for their logic.

Taylor's logic tells her that the tiny plastic toilet next to the bathtub is a torture seat that will suck her soul from her body if she sits on it.

I gave Taylor a quick bath, changed my shirt and stripped my bed, throwing the sheets, Taylor's pajamas and my tank into the washing machine before getting Taylor her juice and finally letting Eggie back inside.

Now Taylor and I are on the top step of the porch, Eggie lying next to me. It's not so awful, sitting out here on a warm Saturday morning, Taylor's tiny body curled against me.

Morning Taylor is my favorite. She's cuddly and sweet and it reminds me of when she was a baby.

Morning Taylor is only around for a limited time, though. Like a Shamrock Shake. You have to be quick or you'll miss it completely. After thirty minutes, forty tops, she wakes up enough to start talking.

Right now, though, she's content to stay quiet, the back of her head resting against my chest, the fingers of her left hand idly stroking my arm as she sucks down her second cup of juice.

Eggie lifts his head and looks down the road, his tail thumping against the wooden floor boards. A moment later, a car approaches and I think it's our neighbor, Mr. Keane, but as the vehicle gets closer I see I'm wrong. It's an SUV.

A black Explorer that slows then stops in front of my house.

I'm not even all that surprised. Not after everything he said last night.

I'll come after you.

I missed you.

I'll do whatever it takes to get you back.

Nope, not surprised Sam's at my house, bright and early on a Saturday morning to have his say.

Problem is, I'm not exactly unhappy about it, either.

The bigger problem? I'm way too interested in hearing him out.

I tip my head back and glare at the sky. "Seriously?" I mutter while the stupid Fates laugh their butts off at my lot in life. "You haven't messed with me enough so far today?"

Guess not, because when I lower my head, Sam is strolling up the sidewalk. Eggie races down to give him a proper, enthusiastic greeting, which includes running in circles around him three times, then shoving his nose into Sam's crotch.

Taylor whips around, whacking me so hard in the chin with her sippy cup, my teeth clack together.

"Ow." I rub the spot then take the stupid cup from her. "Be careful."

Paying no attention to my stern tone—like her mother, she only hears what she wants to hear—her knees dig into my stomach as she turns and stands, her bare feet on my thighs. Capturing my face between her two sticky hands, she leans forward until our noses touch. "Who dat?" she whispers.

"That," I whisper back, sensing him getting closer and closer and closer, "is Sam. He was here last night. Remember?"

She jiggles my face side to side as she shakes her own head fiercely, her face scrunched up in a tiny scowl. "No, Sam, Haddy. Don't want Sam here."

Taking both her wrists in one hand, I gently tug her hands from my face. "You and me both, kid. You and me both."

This is as good a time as any for Taylor to learn the most valuable of all life lessons: You don't always get what you want.

I sure don't.

Especially when it comes to Sam Constable.

Except, when he stops at the bottom of the steps, his hand on my adoring dog's head, I'm not sure what that is anymore. What I want from him.

All I know is that he's here, looking way too good with his hair still damp from his shower, his face clean-shaven, his eyes clear and bright and studying me in that searching way of his. Like he's trying to read my mind. Wanting to know my every thought. My feelings.

Everything I can't let him see.

"Good morning, Hadley," he says and the sound of his deep voice causes Taylor to squeak and put me in a chokehold as she presses her face against my neck.

Since speech is beyond me—what with my trachea being crushed and all—I nod in greeting.

He shifts his weight from one side to the other. Looks so nervous, so unsure, I can't help but soften toward him. And isn't that what makes him so dangerous to me? How easily he can get to me. How I feel about him even after everything that's happened between us.

"Do you want to go to out?" he asks. "Get some breakfast?"

I reach back and loosen Taylor's grip. "I can't. I'm babysitting."

"She can come. We can go to the bakery."

The Davis Bakery is my favorite place to go and breakfast is my favorite meal to go out for.

Which Sam darn well knows.

I'm more tempted than I should be. All part of his dastardly plan.

Just because he's pretty doesn't mean he's a dummy.

"I don't think that's a good idea," I say, my self-protection instincts kicking in.

Better late than never, right?

He nods as if he expected no less than my refusal. As if he came all this way just to give it a shot and now that he has, well, he tried. No harm done. "Okay."

He turns and walks away.

And I bite my tongue so I don't call him back.

Maybe he's not so stubborn after all.

Or maybe he's gotten smart and is finally giving up on me. For good.

Which was what I'd wanted. What I'd always known would happen.

But knowing it and experiencing it are two totally different things.

Taylor lifts her head. "Him leaving?"

"Yeah," I say, as Sam waits for a car to pass before stepping onto the street, leaving Eggie at the curb. "Him's leaving."

Though it's already in the seventies, I'm suddenly chilled. I want nothing more than to go inside, curl up on the couch under the blanket and hide there for...oh...the rest of the summer should do the trick. But that would be admitting how disappointed I am that Sam is getting into his SUV. And if I admitted that little nugget of honesty, then I'd also have to admit how, deep down, I'd secretly hoped he meant everything he'd said last night.

I'll do whatever it takes to get you back.

Stupid, silly, delusional me. I know better than to believe the pretty words some guy spouts. Boys will say whatever it takes to get what they want.

They'll say whatever a girl wants to hear.

Actions speak louder than words. Which is why I don't go inside and hide under a blanket. I force myself to sit there so I can watch Sam drive away.

Actions over words.

Except, he doesn't. Drive away, that is. Oh, he opens the driver's-side door and even climbs in, but he doesn't turn on the ignition. Instead he leans down as if reaching for something then straightens, slides out of the vehicle and shuts the door.

And once more, heads my way.

This time carrying a bakery box.

I stand, settling Taylor on my hip. "What's that?"

"I stopped at the bakery on the way over here. In case I needed something to convince you to talk to me."

He doesn't. Isn't that obvious? He doesn't need to bribe me—or any girl—to talk to him. To listen to that deep voice of his. To spend time with him.

That's only one of the many, many reasons why he's so flipping dangerous.

He opens the box's lid. There are half a dozen donuts, three scones, two muffins, two pieces of apple strudel, two croissants, and a huge, frosted cinnamon roll.

I try to play it cool but it's not easy when my stomach is rumbling and my mouth watering. Even Taylor has lifted her head to goggle at the wonders before us. "Wow," I say, "when you bribe a girl, you go all out."

He shuts the lid. "I didn't want to take the chance of you saying no."

As if that would even happen. This boy knows the way to my heart—through my stomach.

I shouldn't give in. No matter how badly I want one of those scones.

"I don't know," I say, as if thinking it through. "I didn't see any bear claws in there. That might be a deal breaker."

"It's not."

"No? Because you're hiding one in your pocket?"

He shakes his head. "Because you don't like bear claws."

True. And trust him to remember that.

He's sneaky. Knowing me better than anyone, bringing treats here to lure me into conversation.

Sneaky *and* smart.

But the donuts, scones, muffins and cinnamon roll aren't what get to me. It's him.

He's always gotten to me.

"Let's go inside," I grumble, a less-than-gracious hostess to my uninvited company, way less than grateful for the box of sweets I'm dying to dive into like a pool. "If we're going to talk, I'm going to need some coffee."

20

MAKING COFFEE WITH A TWO-YEAR-OLD CLINGING TO YOUR NECK LIKE A spider monkey isn't easy but, like so many Jones' girls before me, I do what I have to.

Sam offered to make it but I'm not in the best headspace to have him moving around our tiny kitchen like he belongs here, familiar with where we keep the coffee and filters and cups. It would just remind me of...well...everything. How much time he used to spend here. How he used to pitch in to help me do the dishes or fetch and grab ingredients while I made cookies or cupcakes.

How it was between us.

Bad enough he's at the table, sitting the way boys do, taking up too much space with his legs wide, his feet planted on the scuffed floor, watching me. I wonder what he's thinking. If he's planning what he wants to say or if, now that he's gotten his way, he's changed his mind and doesn't want to go through with an early-morning chat.

"Juice," Taylor says. Seeing Sam, a real live actual boy, looking at us, she tries to bury her head in the crook of my shoulder. Her words are muffled against my hair. "Mowah juice, Haddy."

I shift her higher. "No more juice. You already had two cups. I'll get you some water."

This is an injustice that will not stand. She lifts her head to glare at me. "Don't want watah."

Sam snorts out a laugh.

"Don't encourage her," I say. "She already thinks she's a princess and you laughing will only give her the idea she's a funny one."

"Sorry," he says, trying to hide his grin behind his hand. "But she sounds like Mark Wahlberg in *Ted*."

Huh. He's right. "You been hanging out in Boston lately?" I ask Taylor. "Is that where you left all your *r*s?"

She's not amused. Then again, she hasn't seen that movie. "Juice, Haddy! Juice!"

"The first step in getting over an addiction is to admit you have a problem. You need a twelve-step-program for juice-aholics."

"No pwogwam," she says, not the slightest bit fazed. This is not the first time we've had this conversation. "Juice!"

I shouldn't give in. If I let her have her way now, it will only make it harder to tell her no the next time.

But I'm tired. And honestly, I've already dealt with enough today. I glance at Sam. Still have more to deal with.

Sometimes a girl needs to take the easy way out.

"What do you say," I ask Taylor, "when you want something?"

"I say please," she tells me, switching from demon child to angel baby. "Juice, please, Haddy."

I pour her more juice. "Want a donut?"

Already sucking down her drink, she nods.

"You have to sit in your chair at the table to eat it."

She glances at her booster seat. Then at Sam. Shakes her head. "No, donut, Haddy. No, thank you."

Well, at least she's being polite.

Good to know a few of the things we're teaching her are getting through.

"You don't have to be afraid of Sam," I tell her. "He's nice. Look, Eggie likes him."

Understatement of the year. Eggie lies on his back at Sam's feet, belly exposed. You know, in case Sam should feel so inclined to give it a good rub.

My dog has no pride.

Taylor studies the boy and then the dog as if gauging Eggie's trustworthiness on this issue, then turns back to me. "You like him."

I blink. Blink again. Try to figure out if that was a question or statement. Sam's watching me, hands fisted on the table, waiting for my response. "Uh..."

Taylor sighs because I haven't answered her and am straining her patience. Ha. Welcome to my world, kid. "Haddy, you like him?"

Definitely a question. One that makes my palms sweat. One that's a lot harder to answer than it should be.

"Sam's nice," I repeat lamely and he drops his gaze. He caught what I did there—how there had been no admission of my liking or disliking him. Yep, that's me. Super clever. "He brought you a donut."

He gets the hint and opens the bakery box, taking out the frosted donut covered in rainbow sprinkles and putting it on one of the paper plates I set on the table earlier. "I got this one just for you," he tells Taylor.

"See?" I say, hooking my hands underneath her bottom. But when he holds out the plate to her, she whimpers and turns her head to my shoulder.

Sam slowly lowers the plate.

He's not used to people—the female population, especially—not liking him.

Poor baby.

"How about we turn on Disney Jr.?" I ask Taylor—a rhetorical question as there's only one way she'd ever respond to that.

"Yes, Haddy! Yes. Disney Junaw." She kicks her legs in excitement, starts bouncing in my arms. "Mickey! Goofy! Pluto! Dai--"

"No need for roll call," I say, before she can list every character she knows. "We get it. The gang will all be there."

I take the plate without looking at Sam and carry Taylor into the living room. Set her up in front of the TV, her juice and donut on the coffee table. I shouldn't use the TV as a babysitter, blah, blah, blah, but...

Drastic times and all that.

It takes approximately thirty seconds for her to be transfixed by the crazy—yet educational—shenanigans of Mickey and his gang and I go back into the kitchen.

I pour my coffee, add vanilla creamer to it then fill a tall glass with milk and carry them both to the table. And realize as I set the milk in front of Sam that I didn't ask him what he wanted to drink.

"Sorry," I say, my face heating. "You don't have to drink that if you don't want it. You can have coffee or apple juice or--"

"This is good." He pulls the glass toward him. "I'm just...I'm surprised you remember what I like." He lifts his gaze to mine and I can't look away. "I'm glad you do."

"It's no big deal," I say, shooting for cool and casual when it's so hard being either around him now. "I mean, we were friends for a while."

His mouth thins and I feel bad, like I've dashed some high hopes he'd had. But I don't take anything back. Don't assure him that I remember more than just his preference for milk when he eats something sweet.

I remember everything.

I pull out a chair, move it as far from him as possible—which is about six inches but hey, give me a break, I'm working with a tiny square table in a small kitchen here—and sit down. Wonder if he sat where he did, across from Taylor's booster seat, on purpose, taking away my ability to put the table, and even more physical space, between us.

Feeling him watching me, I choose a cinnamon scone and break it in half. I take a bite and, as much as I'd love to just enjoy its melt-in-my mouth, buttery, sweet deliciousness, I can't. I'm too anxious about what Sam has to say.

It hits me that once I've heard him out, that'll be it. Things between us, our friendship, and that tiny possibility of more I could never even admit to myself I wished for will be over.

We'll be over.

The scone turns to dust in my mouth. My heart starts racing and I'm having a hard time catching my breath. Which is stupid. And makes no sense. Us being over is what I want.

I'm not Zoe. I don't fall for guys I can't have.

I've always known I can't have Sam. Not forever.

So I have to let him go. Now. While I still have the strength to do it.

I set the remainder of my scone on my plate and link my fingers together in my lap. "You...you wanted to tell me something?"

He nods. Wipes his palms down the front of his shorts. "I owe you an apology."

There's a lump in my throat, something small and hard, like a pebble. Something suspiciously like disappointment.

I take a sip of coffee to wash it away.

I'm an idiot. That's the only explanation for feeling this way. For thinking Sam was here to convince me to take him back. For being terrified I wouldn't be able to resist him if he did.

I'll come after you.

I missed you.

I'll do whatever it takes to get you back.

Words. Nothing but meaningless words said in the heat of the moment. He's not here to renew our friendship. He's not here to win me back. He's here to clear his conscience.

Of course Sam wants the one thing I said I'd never give him.

Forgiveness.

But maybe I should. Maybe, instead of it making me weak, it'll give me the power to move on.

Maybe it'll free me from our past, from our mistakes, as much as it does him.

I open and shut my mouth—twice—before I finally get the words out. "It's okay."

He frowns, which, can I just say, is not the reaction I expected. A little gratitude wouldn't be uncalled for. I'm being magnanimous here. God.

"What's okay?" he asks.

Now I'm frowning, too, and completely confused. He wants me to spell it out when he didn't even get to the *I'm sorry* part of his whole spiel? Seriously?

Wait...that's right. He didn't say what, specifically, he wanted to apologize for. And here I am, tossing forgiveness at him all willy-nilly. "Whatever you did. It's okay."

That should cover him ruining our friendship, leaving, not calling or texting me, and for being so mean to me when I went to his house Christmas night.

All-encompassing absolution.

"Hadley," he says, his gaze intense, "last night...I lied to you."

My fingers tingle and I realize I'm squeezing them together too hard. I let go, straighten them. "What..." I lick my lips, and when I speak, my voice is hoarse. "What about?"

I'll come after you.

I missed you.

I'll do whatever it takes to get you back.

"I told you I wanted you to go with me to Beemer's because I was nervous about being around everyone, but that wasn't true."

"You weren't nervous?"

"No. I..." He scoots forward, sitting on the edge of his seat. Rests his arms on his thighs, his hands clasped loosely between his knees. "I told you that so you'd go with me because...because I didn't want you to go with Max."

His confession comes out quick and fierce and my head snaps back. "What?"

"He said he'd pick you up--"

"He wasn't serious."

"Yes, he was. He told me later, when we were home, he was going to stop by your house on the way to Beemer's, see if he could talk you into going with him."

"He was messing with you. And even if he wasn't, even if he had come here, I wouldn't have gone anywhere with him."

"I couldn't take that chance," Sam says quietly. He lifts his head, his eyes locking on mine. "Not with you."

My breath escapes me in a soft whoosh. It's as if his words are knives, slicing my skin, drawing blood. His confession slowly killing me, his guilt shredding me into tiny pieces.

I should feel vindicated right now. Should be thrilled to discover he's not always honest. Not always virtuous.

Not always better than me.

"It's not that big a deal. It's barely even a lie. The only thing you should feel bad about is letting Max get to you—which I'm sure is what he wanted and the only reason he even said he'd stop here. But," I hurry on when he opens his mouth, because there's no way I can take it if he apologizes again or, God forbid, offers up any more admissions of guilt, "if it'll make you feel better, I officially forgive you of the one and only time you told a fib." I give his knee a quick pat meant to convey forgiveness and acceptance of what this conversation means. The end of us. "Now, go on your way and sin no more."

The pat was a mistake. Because Sam—of the cat-like reflexes—grabs my hand before I can pull away. Stares down at it, where his dark fingers are joined with my pale ones. "That's not the only time I lied," he murmurs.

The nape of my neck prickles. My fingers twitch in his. When I try to tug free, he holds on and my apprehension grows, turns into the premonition that I don't want to hear what he says next.

That it'll change everything between us. Again. And my brilliant plan about letting him go will no longer be possible.

"Sam..."

"I lied all the time," he says, still looking at our hands, his thumb rubbing back and forth across my skin. "Before. I lied when I said I just wanted to be your friend."

Oh, God. I wrench my hand free and stand up so quickly, my chair wobbles, almost tips over, but Sam reaches around me to steady it.

Always steadying things.

Except I don't feel steady. I'm trembling, my skin prickling with heat. And Sam is too close, holding the chair, trapping me between his arm and the table.

"I lied," he continues, relentless and driven, it seems, to break down every one of the barriers I've built up over the past eleven months, "every time I pretended I didn't care when you went out with another guy. Every time I ignored the jealousy eating at me at the thought of you being with someone else when what I really wanted was for you to be with me."

I feel them, those barriers that I built, brick by brick, crumbling under the weight of his words, the look in his eyes.

But I need those walls. Need their protection.

I can't let him hurt me again.

"Why are you doing this?" I ask hoarsely.

He frowns as if he has no clue what I'm talking about but that, too, is a lie.

Sam Constable doesn't make a move without thinking it through, weighing the pros and cons.

"Doing what?"

"This." I wave my hand in a huge arc, one large enough to encompass everything—us, every word he's spoken, every action and choice he's made since he came home—and he steps back to save himself getting slapped on the chin. "Confessing all this now. What's the point? In a few weeks, you'll be back in LA and I'll be here."

"I'm not going back."

Everything inside of me goes still—all except my stupid heart which races with panic. And hope. "At the end of the summer--"

"I'll be here. I'm not home for just the summer. I'm back for good." He once again closes the distance between us. "I'm back for you, Hadley."

21

I'M BACK FOR YOU, HADLEY.

Great. One more emphatic statement I can add to my growing list of Things Sam's Said To Rock My World and Keep Me Up At Night.

I tip my head back and glare up at the Fates, who, it seems, have nothing better to do this morning than ruin my life.

Sam follows my gaze.

Probably wondering when I lost my mind.

Which would either be the moment I saw him walking toward me two days ago or the day at his pool when I threw caution to the wind and became his friend.

Sam being the common denominator in both situations.

He's why the whole point of this conversation has gotten away from me. I'm supposed to let him go, not have my feelings twisted and tangled like ropes, tying me even tighter to him.

And I'm definitely not supposed to have any hope that somehow, someway Sam and I can finally work things out.

That we can be together.

I push past him and pace the length of the room. Once. Twice. Stopping, I whirl around to point at him. "Don't say things like that to me."

"Why not?"

Because it only confuses me when I've spent so much time trying to get over him.

Because it makes me want things I can never have.

"Because it's too late." From the living room, the soundtrack to our little drama is Taylor singing along to the Toodles song. "You said so yourself. On Christmas. Remember?"

He blanches, as if thinking about what he said to me, how he treated me Christmas night makes him want to throw up.

That makes two of us.

"I shouldn't have said that." He moves toward me and I take a quick step back. No way can I let him get close to me again. He stops. "And I shouldn't have stayed at my dad's. I should have come back. I should have fought for you."

I shake my head, denying his words. Denying the way they make me feel because there's that dumb hope again, floating around inside of me, trying to burst free. "But you did. You said it. And you left. You can't take it back."

Just like I can't take back the choices I made.

No matter how much I want to.

"You're right," he agrees so readily, I'm immediately suspicious because, as nice a guy as Sam is, he's still a guy.

And he hates being wrong.

I eye him warily. "I am?"

He nods.

I sense a trap and yet I keep right on going, barreling ahead without thought or care about the snare that's ahead.

"Okay," I say slowly. "If I'm right, then what's all this about?"

All this crazy talk about coming back for me. About fighting for me.

"I can't take it back," he says, holding his hands out to his sides as if to show he's harmless. He's not. He proves that by once more closing the distance between us in his slow, confident way. "But I can move forward."

He's doing that, all right. Literally. And with each step he takes, I take one back.

Until the edge of the counter digs into my spine.

"I want to move forward," he continues, stopping a foot away. He sets his hands on the counter on either side of my waist, leans down so that we're eye to eye. "With you."

Once more this morning I'm trapped by a guy, my stomach twisting with nerves, my heart racing. But unlike what happened with greasy, inked Axel, these nerves aren't from fear, but anticipation. The fluttering in my chest from excitement.

"We're not going to be friends again," I tell him and, unbelievably, my voice is steady. Firm. Like that of a woman who says what she means and means what she says.

And how does Sam respond to my unequivocal statement?

He grins. Like I'm the funniest thing ever.

"No," he says, an undercurrent of laughter in his soft tone, "we're not going to be friends again."

His words from yesterday come back to me, how he said he didn't want to be my friend. Or, more specifically, that he didn't want to be *just friends*.

I open my mouth but he rushes on. "Don't tell me it's too late. And don't tell me you don't feel the same way about me that I feel about you, because I know you do."

I cross my arms—not an easy feat when he's so close, but it allows me to stick my elbows out, making sure he doesn't get any closer. "Wow. Someone's ego grew nice and big out there in the California sun."

"Don't say no," he continues as if I haven't spoken. "Give us a chance."

I mean to tell him, clearly, concisely and calmly, that there is no us. The days of Sam and Hadley, Hadley and Sam are long gone. And that chance he wants has passed by. Instead, when I speak, my voice is thin.

Unsure.

"I can't."

Sam, of course, notices my hesitation. "You can."

I don't have his confidence. His courage. Or his belief that things will work out. Don't have the strength to lose him again.

"I'm sorry," I whisper, unable to look at him.

His arms next to me stiffen and he slowly lets go of the counter and straightens. I stare at his knees, peeking out from underneath the hem of his shorts, waiting for him to storm out.

He steps back. This is it. The moment I've been waiting for since Sam and I first became friends. The moment when he realizes I'm not worth it—not worth his time, energy or feelings.

The moment he gives up on me for good.

My lower lip trembles and I bite down on it. Hard.

I'd been prepared to let him go. That'd been the plan, right? To let him have his say as some sort of closure between us. I'd even thought it would somehow be easy, what with everything that's happened between us. That it would be painless.

It's not. Not easy. Far from painless.

And, it seems, the whole process is going to be dragged out way longer than necessary because Sam hasn't moved. I can feel him watching me, his gaze on the top of my head. Why doesn't he get on with the walking-out part, already? The least he can do is make this quick. God.

But nobody can make Sam Constable do something he doesn't want to do. And that includes leaving after his welcome has run out.

"There's one more thing," he murmurs, his breath ruffling the hair at the top of my head. "One more thing I need to tell you."

"Remember our discussion last night? The one about how it's not fair for you to always get what you want?"

"I'm tired of being fair and always doing the right thing. I'm still in love with you, Hadley, and I'm tired of pretending I'm not."

My head whips up so fast, my neck cracks. Eyes wide, I stare at him, fingers touching my throat, silently begging him not to say any more.

Secretly hoping he does.

Sam loves me. He still loves me.

In all my wildest fantasies, I never, not once, dreamed this could happen. That not only would Sam return to town for good, but that he could still have those feelings for me. But he does.

How am I supposed to resist him?

Am I an idiot for even trying?

"I...I don't know what to say," I admit.

"You don't have to say anything," he assures me quickly. "I'm not asking you to tell me you love me, too, or to make me any promises about...well...anything."

Okay, good. That's good. Because I can't do either. Not now, when I can barely think straight, my emotions going haywire. Possibly not ever.

And that scares me, shames me, because Sam deserves the words. Deserves a promise or two. One more very good reason for me to end this here and now. To not say or do something that will take this any further.

But I can't. Not when what I want is there, right there, in front of me, handsome and honest and earnest. It's heady stuff, knowing a boy like Sam feels that way about me. That he wants to be with me so much.

I lick my lips. Take a deep breath. "What are you asking?"

Small as it is, it's an opening. One that tells him I'm listening. I'm considering what he's saying.

I'm not saying no.

He realizes it, his eyes widening slightly as he straightens to his full height, encouraged and hopeful. "That you don't push me away. That you let me back into your life so we can see where, if anywhere, this can go between us."

I hesitate, unable to find the words to tell him what's inside of me. Too cowardly and selfish and self-protective to share what's in my heart.

"Don't be scared," he says, quiet and intense, and I'm right back to last summer when he kissed me.

Don't be scared, Hadley. I won't hurt you.

He had. Just like I'd known he would. And, like I'd also predicted, I'd hurt him, too.

But maybe...maybe this time we won't make those same mistakes. *I* won't make them. I can be more open. I can give more of myself, my thoughts and feelings. I can be the girl he deserves.

Maybe, for once, I can have what I want most.

No, I don't have his confidence or his courage. But I can try and have at least some of his faith. Can choose to believe that things will work out.

And if we don't, if I lose him again, I'll deal with it then.

In the meantime, I'll hold on to him for as long as I can.

"Okay."

He frowns. "Okay you won't be scared?"

I wince. *Okay* is an extremely lame response to everything he's said. And it tells him exactly nothing as to what I want.

Giving him more of my thoughts and feelings is harder than it sounds.

"I..." Much, much harder. "I'm still scared."

His expression softens. "Me, too."

His admission is quiet. Gruff. And makes me realize I'm not alone in this. In my fears.

It helps. It helps a lot.

"Maybe we could go out sometime," I say, but I can barely hear myself over the pounding of my heart. "Uh...get something to eat or...something..."

More lameness. Well, at least I'm good at it.

"Tonight?" he asks.

Tonight? As in twelve hours from now? Like a date?

Yes, yes, I realize that what Sam wants, what I'm agreeing to, isn't for us to be just friends and that going out together, as more than friends, will likely be a part of that. I just hadn't realized it would happen so quickly.

The panic I've been trying to pretend doesn't exist rears its head as if reminding me it's there, burrowed nice and deep inside of me, but is more than happy to pop out any time.

Great. Good to know.

"Uh...maybe not tonight," I say.

"Why not?"

"Because we need to take our time with this. Not rush things."

He grins slowly and I'm glad the counter is behind me because I feel a real-live swoon coming on. "Had, we've known each other since the fourth grade. Have been friends for seven years. If we went any slower, we'd be going in reverse."

He has a point.

"I can't tonight," I say. "I...uh...already have plans."

His grin fades, his expression darkens. "With a guy?"

I roll my eyes. Trust that to be his first thought.

Teenage boys. Such fragile creatures.

"No. With Whitney." Before he can ask what we're doing or if I can ditch her, before he can break me down with his persistence and charm, I hurry on, "What about tomorrow afternoon? We can go to the Tastee Freeze."

It's a bit sooner than I'd prefer, but I did say I was going to try.

This is me trying.

But the gleam in his eyes tells me he knows exactly what I'm doing. Getting ice cream on a Sunday afternoon is a very non-date-ish, non-sexy thing to do. And a good way to ease into this.

"I'll pick you up at three," he tells me. He checks the time on the microwave. "I've gotta go. Coach scheduled a conditioning session at ten."

"You're trying out for the team?"

Though basketball tryouts aren't until late fall, the team does conditioning all summer and most of the boys play on a travel team. All of the coaches at our school like their players to prove their dedication by forgoing other silly pursuits like jobs, family vacations and sleeping in on Saturday mornings.

Eggie, sensing that his good buddy is about to leave, pads over to us and butts his head against Sam's leg. "Yeah," Sam says, giving Eggie a few pats. "Not sure how it's going to go. I haven't played for a year. Well, nothing other than a few pickup games in my dad's driveway."

It's so unusual for Sam to be worried about...well...anything, to have anything less than total confidence in himself, I give his arm a quick squeeze. "You'll do great."

He flushes. "Thanks," he says, straightening. "I'll...uh...see you tomorrow then."

He makes it sound like a question, like he's worried I'm going to back out.

"At three," I say, wanting to reassure him—and myself—that I won't. "I'll be ready."

He smiles, gives me a nod goodbye and walks out of the kitchen and past Taylor who is hypnotized by the antics of Mickey and his gang. I count to twenty, then go into the living room and look out the front window. Watch him pull away from the curb. Count to twenty again.

Then pick up Taylor and hurry out the door.

22

Mrs. McCormack is an older, curvier version of her daughter in a pair of black capri pants and a white T-shirt. Her dark hair is cut into a chin-length bob, her makeup perfect even at the ungodly hour of not-quite-nine a.m.

She's also, it seems, horrified at the sight greeting her on her porch this fine Saturday morning.

Well, I didn't bother changing, so my cupcake-themed cotton shorts, faded pink sweatshirt with the coffee stain and ratty flip-flops might give someone so well put together pause. And Taylor *is* screaming as if I'm trying to murder her, so there's that. Plus, she has frosting from her donut smeared across her shirt, her cheek and chin, and even in her hair. Though the sprinkles sticking here and there give her a festive look.

"Are you okay?" she asks, leaning out to look behind us. "Did someone hurt you? Is someone chasing you? Come in, come in. We'll call the police."

I see where Whitney gets her wild imagination.

"We're fine," I say, but I have to yell to be heard over the banshee in my arms and it comes across sort of aggressive, like I'm mad she's asked about our well-being. My face heats. Parents—the normal kind, the ones who stick around and actually raise their own kids—make me nervous.

I try jiggling Taylor to get her to calm down but that only makes her madder. She stiffens her entire body and lets out a howl guaranteed to have every dog on the block barking in commiseration. "She's upset because she wants to watch a TV show."

Mrs. McCormack frowns. Glances at Taylor, who, for the first time, seems to notice we're no longer in our own yard but on the porch of the house across the street and, yes, another strange person —though this time of the female species—is close by. She buries her face in my neck, her screams turning into sobs.

Really loud, completely pitiful sobs.

It's not an improvement.

"Looks like someone's not used to being told *no*," Mrs. McCormack says and now that Taylor is somewhat quieter, I can hear that her Southern accent is way more pronounced than Whitney's.

But not nearly as nice.

I grind my back teeth together. Adults love sharing their thoughts on parenting, their rules and wisdom and, most especially, their judgment when they think you're doing it all wrong. It's so annoying. For one thing, Taylor's not my kid. Even though I may not always agree with the choices Zoe makes regarding her, I keep my mouth shut. Which more people—especially the woman in front of me —should do.

For another, I'm doing the best I can. God.

And I'm seriously not in the mood for a lecture.

"*No* is the single most used word at our house," I assure her, trying not to sound bitchy, but come on. Taylor's only two. "Is Whitney home?"

"She's eating breakfast," Whitney's mom says and steps back, opening the door wider. "Would you care to come in?"

She's as polite as her daughter.

Or, you know, vice versa seeing as how Mrs. McCormack was here first and all.

Taylor must have caught her breath—or remembered she's

mighty ticked off—because she chooses that moment to start screaming again, starting with a cry that reaches a high pitch unbeknownst to man before this moment.

Mrs. McCormack and I both cringe.

"We'll just wait here," I say, unable to even imagine what it would be like to have Taylor's shrieks contained by four walls.

The word torturous comes to mind.

Mrs. McCormack gives me a quick, grateful nod. "I'll send Whitney right on out."

She leaves the door open and I watch her walk through a tidy living room. Then I cross to the top step and sit down. Eggie—who'd been checking out all the new and interesting smells of the McCormacks' yard—comes trotting up, circles three time to find just the right spot and lies down next to me. The rising sun is warm on my face and I close my eyes and tip my head back to soak the warmth in and try and get back to those few peaceful moments I had on my own porch before Sam showed up.

Just a girl, her dog and her sweet, cuddly niece enjoying a nice Saturday morning.

"I want Mickey!" Taylor wails, wiggling to be free of my hold. "No want you, Haddy! Want! Mickey!"

I sigh. Okay. Not so sweet. Not so cuddly.

"I'll remember you said that," I tell her, "the next time you're crying for me. Now knock off the bawling or I'm going to put you in timeout."

I should do so anyway, but trying to get a two-year-old to sit still and think about why their behavior is wrong isn't easy. And when I put Taylor in timeout, it usually descends into a wrestling match with me trying to hold her still while she screams and does her best to get away.

And she's already doing that so what would be the point?

"No timeout! No!" she says, pushing against my chest. See? With a huff, she glares up me. "I no like you, Haddy."

"Well, we're even because I'm not all that crazy about you right now, either."

She frowns, tear stains now mixing with the frosting on her cheeks, as she processes my words. "No. You cwazy 'bout me. I a good girl."

Ah, to have her confidence.

And delusions.

"You're not being good right now." Zoe read that you're not supposed to tell kids they're *bad* because that damages their psyche or something.

"I good!" Taylor screams. "I a good girl!"

I guess I walked right into that one.

Although it does prove Taylor's psyche is just fine.

Eggie gets to his feet a moment before Whitney walks out onto the porch.

I jump up—okay, more like I lurch up. Hey, it's tough to jump and do so gracefully while you're holding a squirming thirty-pound toddler who's yelling at you that she's good and nice and pwetty and stwong and smawt and that you're bad (Taylor obviously didn't get the memo about fragile psyches) and mean and not pwetty or stwong or smawt.

Why did we think it was such a great idea to teach this kid to talk?

But I must look like a maniac, even without the jumping, because Whitney stops and takes a small step back when I move toward her. "I told Sam we were hanging out tonight," I blurt. "You and me, I mean."

"Umm, okay," she says, slow and careful, like she's talking a jumper down from the ledge. "Why would you do that?"

I shrug, feeling antsy and hot, my arms tiring from holding Taylor. "He asked me out."

Her lips thin and I'd bet money she's holding back a smile. "I see. Here," she continues, handing me a wet washcloth, "Mama said you needed this."

Of course she calls her mother *Mama*. They're probably really close and do things together because they actually want to. She probably warns her that boys only want one thing and tells her she can do anything she wants with her life and asks her about her friends, her job, her dreams of the future, and never forgets her birthday.

Or that she's alive and living in the very same trailer where she walked out on her.

Not that I'm envious or anything.

When I try to clean Taylor's face, she shrieks and wipes tears, frosting and snot across the front of my sweatshirt.

And that's it. That's the moment I give up.

"You win," I mutter to the Fates, my throat tight with tears. "You broke me. Happy now?"

"I win what?" Whitney asks, courageously edging closer even as she follows my gaze upward.

"Nothing. I wasn't talking to you."

"Are you all right? You don't seem like the type of person who usually talks to herself."

I open my mouth to tell her I'm fine, that I have wonderfully deep conversations with myself all the time about the meaning of life and politics and the Kardashians. I'll tell her all that then ask her to pretend I was never here at which point I'll run back to my house, where I'll be safe. Where I'll be alone.

Yes, I open my mouth to say all of that, but nothing comes out except a small squeak.

Because I don't want to be alone.

I don't want to lie.

Hey, there's a first time for everything.

And I can't run from this. I've tried and all I did was end up right back where I started.

"No," I say, and unbelievably, after holding it all together in front of Sam, my voice breaks. "I'm not all right. I'm freaking out."

She nods as if she completely gets what I'm saying, even though I haven't, technically, said anything, then lightly touches Taylor on the back to get her attention. "Hi, Taylor. Remember me?"

Taylor lays her head on my shoulder. Sniffs loudly. "Moana."

From the moment Taylor first saw Whitney on the day they moved in, she's insisted our new neighbor is Moana—the character from the Disney movie of the same name—in the flesh. It's the long, dark hair, I guess.

Or maybe it's the bare feet. Moana never wears shoes, either.

Plus, you know, they're both gorgeous, so there's that.

Whitney smiles and holds up her phone. "If you stop crying and let Hadley wash your face, you can watch your television show on here."

Guess Mrs. McCormack filled her in on all the pertinent details of our quick conversation.

Taylor, never one to turn away a good bribe, tips her head back for me to wash her face. When I'm done, she faces Whitney again. "I not cwying. I watch Mickey now."

"Good girl," Whitney says and Taylor shoots me an *I told you I was a good girl* look. "What show?"

I tell her and in less than two minutes we're all sitting on the front step, Taylor on my lap watching Mickey and his pals, Eggie's head on Whitney's thigh. Peace reigns over the land again.

The only problem with peace? It comes with silence. Lots and lots of heavy-duty, expectation-filled silence broken only by the occasional yuk yuk of Goofy and Taylor counting along with Mickey—at least until he gets to three.

But I'm okay with that. I don't need conversation filling in the gaps. Don't want Whitney asking me a bunch of personal, nosey questions.

Silence is good. It's great. It's just what I need to get a hold of myself, to gather my thoughts and dissect them, bit by bit. To figure out the crazy, messed-up feelings inside of me. I could sit here all day, just like this, and be perfectly content.

All day or, you know, two minutes, which is approximately how long I last before asking, "Aren't you going to ask me why I'm freaking out?"

Whitney scratches behind Eggie's ear. "No."

"The real Moana would've asked," I grumble.

Whitney smiles, but when she speaks, her tone is gentle. Understanding. "I'm not going to ask because I don't need to. You're freaking out because there's something between you and Sam. Something complicated."

"It is," I agree, because that's the perfect definition of me and Sam. "It's very complicated."

"Do you want to talk about it?"

I've never been big on the whole *let me tell you every thought in my head, every feeling inside of me* thing so many girls my age live for. Not even with Tori and Kenzie. Sharing secrets with someone else is dangerous. Better to keep them hidden where no one can use them against you.

Better, safer, to handle everything on your own.

But I did tell myself not thirty minutes ago that I would try and be more open. That I would give more of myself. And while I meant I'd do all of that with Sam, for him, maybe it wouldn't hurt to...I don't know...practice a little.

"I don't know where to start," I say, which is slightly less embarrassing than admitting I have no idea *how* to do this. That I'm afraid I'm going to be bad at it—because if I was good at it, wouldn't Tori and Kenzie still be my friends?

Or maybe I'm just afraid, period.

"Why don't you start at the beginning."

That's a good idea. And makes perfect sense.

I take a long, deep inhale and start the story of me and Sam.

"We were never meant to be friends..."

23

I TOLD WHITNEY EVERYTHING.

At first, the story came out in bits and pieces, starts and stops, but the more I talked, the more fluent I became. Don't get me wrong, it was still terrifying, opening myself up that way. Letting someone other than my sisters in. Someone I barely even know.

It was also a relief.

And way more freeing than I thought it would be.

I think the fact that Whitney is practically a stranger helped. Or maybe it's because she's new in town. She hasn't known me her entire life like everyone else. Doesn't have preconceived ideas about me based on what I was like in kindergarten. Hasn't had a chance to observe me and Sam together other than a few hours last night. Never gave me a knowing, smirky *oh, please* look when I insisted Sam and I were just friends.

That neutrality made it easier to tell her what really happened between us. How, when someone asked me why Sam left, I told them he wasn't getting along with Patrick, his stepfather, and decided to live with his dad.

When they asked what happened between us, I told them we drifted apart.

When they asked how I was, I told them I was fine.

That I didn't miss him.

But sitting on Whitney's porch, the sun warming my skin, Eggie snoring softly, Taylor singing along to Mickey, I told the truth.

How our friendship started.

How we used to do everything together.

How much I counted on him. How much I trusted him.

I told her I was the real reason he left his family, his friends and his home.

That he kissed me and changed everything between us.

That losing him was the hardest thing that's ever happened to me.

I told her everything.

Well, *almost* everything.

Some secrets are too private, to shameful to share. Ever.

Like what happened at Christmas.

Some secrets aren't mine to tell.

Like Sam telling me he was still in love with me.

And some secrets are too precious, too intimate to put into words.

Like how I felt when he said those words to me this morning. How my skin prickled with heat, my heart raced with excitement, my stomach tumbling with fear.

Just like the first time he told me.

———

The night after Sam and I kissed, I stood on the sidewalk in front of my house and watched the taillights of Colby's car disappear down the dark road. My entire evening had been a freaking disaster.

And it was all Sam's fault.

Do you ever wonder what it would be like to be with me?

Ever since he'd said those words to me at lunch, I hadn't been able to think of anything else—not even when I'd been with another boy. All night, instead of paying attention to Colby, I was distracted and out of sorts, thinking nonstop about Sam and the way he'd looked at me. The way he'd kissed me.

He'd kissed me. And I'd kissed him back.

I wished I could do it again.

But there could be no more kissing. No more remembering the things Sam said. No more wishing for things to be different.

Not if I wanted to keep Sam in my life.

Hugging my arms around myself, I headed up the sidewalk, my steps dragging, my legs heavy. The air was still, the night dark with thick clouds hiding the stars. Mosquitoes and moths danced and buzzed around the porch light as I walked up the stairs and pulled my key from my pocket.

"Hadley."

I whirled around with so much force the key flew out of my hand. I pressed back against the wall, my heart racing, fear coating my mouth.

"Don't be scared."

The scream I'd been holding back died in my throat. Hadn't I heard those exact same words spoken in that exact same soft tone just a few hours ago?

Don't be scared. I won't hurt you.

I straightened and, eyes narrowed, peered into the darkness. Didn't work. I couldn't see a thing. But I heard him take one step. Then another, the sound seemingly loud in the night.

Ominous.

And though I knew it was Sam, when he appeared, stepping out of the shadows like a ghost, his dark hair and clothes blending in with the night, a chill gripped me.

"Sam!" Remembering how late it was and really, really not wanting either of my sisters to come out and see what was going on, I lowered my voice to a harsh whisper. "You scared the crap out of me. What are you doing here?"

He shrugged. The boy shrugged—like it was no big deal he'd been skulking around my trailer at midnight—and leaned against the wall. "I'm waiting for you. Like always."

I raised my eyebrows at how bitter that last part came out. "What's that supposed to mean?"

Another shrug, though only one shoulder lifted in a quick, ticked-off jerk. "It means exactly what you think it means."

His breath smelled like beer.

"Have you been drinking?"

He straightened, and while it wasn't exactly graceful, he remained upright, if a bit unsteady. "I had a couple beers."

His tone was belligerent and challenging, his voice slurred enough that I knew he'd had a few more than a couple.

This was bad. This was really, really bad. And I had a feeling—and a horrible fear—it was only going to get worse.

I grabbed his arm. "Did you drive here?"

The Sam I knew would never drive after he'd been drinking, but this wasn't that Sam. This was some continuation of the new version I'd encountered at lunch. A version who asked questions I couldn't answer. Who said things he had no right saying. Who kissed me and left me reeling and breathless.

He shook his head. "Jack dropped me off."

That at least was good, but the rest? Not so much. Sam Constable was at my house drunk, skulking, shrugging and muttering.

It was like the end of the world as I knew it.

Because it was so unlike Sam to be this way—moody and grumpy and just a little bit scary. Because I had a feeling him acting this way was somehow all my fault.

Realizing I was still touching him—and remembering what happened between us at lunch today—I dropped my hand and took a step back. Then another.

Getting too close to this version of Sam Constable was not a good idea.

But Sam seemed to think it was A-okay. For every step I took in retreat, he took one in pursuit until my butt hit the railing near the door. He kept right on coming, the porch light casting shadows on his face.

"Where were you?"

It was a simple question. One that didn't need any explanation or even clarification. It was why he'd drunk too much tonight. Why he'd come here at this hour.

Because I wasn't with him.

"Sam, I--"

"I called you." This close I could see his jaw was tight. His mouth a thin line. "I've been calling and texting you all night."

I go cold all over, suddenly, viciously nervous. "I...I don't have my phone with me."

I'd left it in my room because I knew he'd call. Knew he'd text.

And I knew I wouldn't be strong enough to ignore him once he did.

"You shouldn't be here," I continued, desperate to end this conversation before it went too far. Sam had changed the rules of our friendship when he kissed me. But it was what we said, here and now, that had the power to change everything else. For good. I edged toward the door. "I'll get Zoe's keys and drive you home."

Except when I faced the door, tried the handle, I remembered it was still locked. That my key was somewhere on the floor.

"Were you with him?" Sam asked. "While I was calling and texting you, were you with Colby?"

It was another simple question.

One Sam already knew the answer to.

Unable to face him, I leaned my forehead against the door. "Yes."

"Did you kiss him?" he asked hoarsely. "Did you kiss him like you kissed me?"

I hadn't. Hadn't even wanted to, not after thinking of Sam the entire night. Wishing I was with him instead of Colby. But I couldn't admit any of that. Not if I wanted things to go back to normal between us.

Biting my lower lip, I turned slowly and kept quiet, knowing my silence would be answer enough.

Knowing he'd think it was as good as a *yes*.

He flinched and dropped his gaze.

I stared at the top of his head, my fingers twitching with the need to slide through his hair. To offer him some measure of comfort and care. To give him just that small bit of truth.

I curled my fingers into my palms and kept my hands at my sides.

"What do we do now?" he asked, still staring at the ground.

"I take you home," I said, firm and resolute and certain it was the right course, "and we pretend this never happened."

He lifted his head. "*This*?"

"You coming here tonight and...and what happened earlier."

"Earlier?" he repeated, eyes narrowed. "You mean when I kissed you? When you kissed me back?"

Yes, Sam, that's exactly what I mean—as you well know.

God.

Linking my hands together at my waist, I nodded. "We pretend it never happened and we go back to how we used to be."

"I'm tired of pretending. And I don't want to go back."

He stopped as if surprised by his own words. Unsure. But then he shook his head, his spine stiffening, his chin lifted. As I watched, cold with fear and shock, he made the decision that would alter our friendship forever. That would end it.

"I won't go back. Not even for you."

It was an ultimatum. One given in a flat, set tone. One delivered without doubt or regret.

Anger flowed through me, washing away the fear, bursting through the shock with painful intensity. I welcomed it. Was grateful for it, the burn that heated my blood, the flash that had prickles stinging my skin. After everything Sam had done—after he'd asked me if I ever thought of being with him, after he kissed me, after he changed everything, every-freaking-thing between us, he had the balls to stand there and offer me an ultimatum?

No. Just...no.

I lowered my arms to my sides, reaching behind me to grip the slats of the railing, the wood rough against my palms. Held on so tightly my hands ached. "You won't go back to being my friend?"

"I won't go back to being *just* your friend."

"That's a problem," I snapped, "because I can't go forward as anything *but* your friend."

"You mean you won't."

I shrugged. Hoped it irritated him as much as his stupid shrugs earlier bugged me.

Hey, a girl had to take her revenge where she could get it.

"Can't. Won't. What difference does it make?" I asked. "The end result is the same."

He stepped forward, crowding me again, his expression pinched. "You want us to be friends?"

"You know I do."

"Do you kiss all your friends the way you kissed me? Do you touch them the way you touched me?"

I reared back but there was nowhere to go short of hopping over the rail and landing in an evergreen bush. "That was a mistake."

He set his hands on the rail on either side of me, his arms rigid. My heart pounded, my breath got short and choppy. Ducking his head, he held my gaze, his anger and frustration clear in the dark depths of his eyes.

"Do you have any idea how long I've wanted to kiss you?" he asked roughly. "Do you have any idea how much I want to do it again? And you're standing here telling me it was a goddamn mistake, and you want to be *just friends* again like nothing happened?" He shoved away from the rail. "Fuck!"

Whirling around, he stared out at my dark yard, hands fisted at his sides.

I fought back tears. Of frustration, I told myself. And anger. I'd skipped work that afternoon to get away from Sam. Had turned my phone off so I wouldn't get his calls and texts. Had gone out with Colby to get my mind off what happened between us. All to give myself some time and distance to deal with that kiss and the possible fallout from it. To figure out how to move past it.

I needed that time. Wanted that distance.

And Sam had taken them both away.

"I'm done," he muttered, his lips barely moving.

Great. More grumbling.

"Done acting like a dick?" I asked. "Because that would be awesome."

And to think, just a few hours ago I'd actually wanted him to stop being so freaking perfect all the time.

He faced me, all scowly and un-Sam-like, his gaze hooded. "I'm done with *you*, Hadley."

The quiet words blew through me, had me going cold and still. "What?"

He looked at the ground for one long moment before meeting my eyes, determination clear in the set of his shoulders, the line of his jaw. "I can't be around you. I can't be your friend. Not anymore."

My knees threatened to buckle. I locked them. "Are you really that spoiled? That conceited? You don't get your way, so you're done with me" –I snapped my fingers—a "just like that?"

"This isn't about me getting my way."

I snorted. "Please. That's exactly what this is about."

"Damn it," he thundered, whipping his hand through the air as if to erase my words, my opinions. "Do you think this is easy for me? Do you think this is really what I want?"

"Then don't do it." I hated how my voice shook. How he'd reduced me to pleading. But I couldn't help it. Couldn't let him go. "Please, Sam..."

"I have to."

"Why?"

"Because I'm in love with you!"

I stumbled back. "You don't...You can't..." I had no words, no breath left in my lungs. I stopped. Inhaled carefully. Held it for the count of three before letting it go. "You don't love me. You've been drinking--"

"It doesn't matter if I'm drunk or sober, the way I feel about you is always the same. Always there."

He didn't sound happy about it.

That made two of us.

"You're confused," I said, barely above a whisper, "because of the kiss--"

"The kiss didn't do anything other than prove what I already knew. I love you."

"God!" I stabbed both hands through my hair and tugged hard. "Stop saying that."

"I love you," he repeated, I'm sure, just to torture me. "I want us to be together, but I can't wait for you any longer. I can't keep loving you if you're never going to love me back."

I knew what he was really saying. What he wanted. For me to dispute his words. To tell him that I loved him, too.

But I couldn't. I couldn't be what he wanted. What he needed.

"I'm sorry," I said raggedly, my throat aching with unshed tears. "I'm so sorry, Sammy."

His gaze shuttered, he nodded once. "Yeah. Me too."

When he walked away, I didn't bother trying to stop him.

I watched him go.

I watched him and told myself that I wasn't a coward. Wasn't a liar. I'd done the right thing. Made the right decision, the smart one.

Sam deserved better than me. He deserved a girl who'd give him everything she had inside of her. Her thoughts and feelings. Her truth. A girl who wouldn't hide from him, who wouldn't constantly protect herself from him.

I wasn't that girl.

No matter how much I wanted to be.

24

AT 2:55 SUNDAY AFTERNOON, I STEP ONTO THE PORCH, SQUINTING against the bright sunshine.

"Going somewhere?"

I whirl around, hand covering my racing heart. "God! Give me a heart attack, why don't you?"

Devyn's curled up on the ratty wicker love seat, her book open and face down on her lap, her hair pinned back on both sides by bobby pins. And she's not alone. Eggie, of course, is at her feet, and both Taylor and Zoe are in the yard; Taylor, in a one-piece Moana swimsuit, is picking dandelions and singing to herself while Zoe's stretched out on her stomach on a beach towel next to her in a black bikini.

My black bikini.

But I don't call her on borrowing it without asking. Not when I have places to go and Sam to see.

Instead of being contrite—as she should be—for scaring the crap out of me, Devyn tips her head to the side looking thoughtful. And suspicious. "Why so jumpy?"

Uh, maybe because she's not supposed to be out here? None of them are. They're supposed to still be out back watching Taylor in her wading pool and Zoe and Devyn on the tiny back deck, Zoe painting her toenails and Devyn engrossed in her book.

Or maybe it's because I was so hoping I'd be able to leave with a *I'm going out!* shouted as I head down the driveway toward Sam's SUV.

"I'm not jumpy," I say with an eye roll, as if the mere idea of it, me, being antsy and anxious and nervous as all get out, is just laughable.

Ha ha ha ha.

But the sound of a car door shutting has me whirling once again. It's Mr. Keane, unloading his groceries. He catches me staring, gives me a nod of his gray head, and I smile weakly and wave.

"You didn't answer my question," Devyn says.

I sigh. Crap.

"What question?" I ask, facing her.

"Either one, but we'll stick with a variation of the first one. Where are you going?"

I shrug.

"You don't know where you're going?" Zoe asks, chin resting on her folded arms. "Or you couldn't possibly say?"

I shoot her a mind-your-own-self look. "I'm going to the Tastee Freeze."

My sisters both eye me from head to toe then look at each other.

But I don't have the time or energy to decipher that loaded, silent passage of disbelief because I really *am* going to the Tastee Freeze.

Though I should have spelled it out instead of saying it.

Because Taylor has scrambled to her feet. "I go, too, Haddy!" she squeals, racing over to me. "I go with you!"

I wince. Double crap. "Sorry, baby girl. You can't come with me today. I'll take you to the Tastee Freeze tomorrow after work."

She stomps her foot. "No, Haddy! No! I go today!"

And she throws one of her cars at me then bursts into tears.

Zoe groans and buries her face in her arms.

"Any reason you can't take her today?" Devyn asks as if she doesn't already know the answer to that question.

Which, naturally, is when Sam pulls up.

He's always on time.

He gets out and rounds the front of his SUV and I'm not sure whether it's the quick shake of my head, Taylor's screeching or Devyn's death glare, but he stops, one foot on the sidewalk, the other in the road. Eggie races over to him.

Dev turns to me slowly, mouth thin. "Not going to be friends with him again, huh?"

Yep, that's what I told her not even two full days ago. My face is hot. "We're...trying something new."

"Right," she says with a snort as she gets to her feet. "Funny how it looks like the same old song and dance to me. It's going to end the same way, too."

I glance back at Sam. He's watching us, watching me—despite the fact that Zoe has gotten to her feet and looks way better in my swimsuit than I do and Taylor is breathless and sobbing and yet still screaming that she wants *ice queam*.

"It doesn't have to," I tell Devyn. "End the same way."

Maybe it won't have to end at all.

Dev shakes her head sadly as if I'm just a huge disappointment to her and womankind. "You're kidding yourself if you really believe that."

"Oh, lay off," Zoe tells Devyn. "So she's giving him a second chance. What's the big deal?"

"The big deal," Dev says from between gritted teeth as Taylor adds kicking to her tantrum routine, "is that not everyone deserves a second chance."

Zoe shrugs. "Even if that's true, it's not up to you to decide. Not in this case. Don't put what happened to you on Hadley. Sam's not Bryan. This isn't your story."

My eyes widen, and from the way Dev inhales sharply, she can't believe Zoe brought up Bryan, either.

Forget Voldemort. At our house, Bryan Rodgers is He Who Shall Not Be Named.

"My story *is* her story," Dev says, expression and tone ice cold.

"Hers and yours. The sooner you both realize that, the better off you'll be."

She turns on her heel and stalks over to the door, yanking it open so forcefully I'm surprised it doesn't fly off the hinges. When she's inside, she slams it shut, the sound startling Taylor out of her tantrum.

"What's that?" she asks, sitting up, her face streaked with tears. She pulls herself to her feet using Zoe's legs for balance, then tugs on Zoe's hand. "Mama, what's that?"

"That was Auntie Dev throwing her own tantrum." She picks up the towel and her sunglasses. "Come on," she says, holding her arms out for Taylor. "Let's go inside and get dressed."

Taylor once more flops onto the ground. "No, Mama! No thanks! I get ice queam with Haddy!"

Zoe shuts her eyes for a moment, looking so tired, so worn down, I step forward. "She can come with us." I glance at Sam, once more waiting patiently for me. "I'm sure Sam won't mind."

But Zoe's already shaking her head. "She can't always get her way. And she sure doesn't deserve to be rewarded for having a fit like this."

"I was thinking more of it giving you a break."

Bending to lift a squirming Taylor into her arms, she shoots me a small, sad smile. "I'm fine." She straightens, holding Taylor diagonally across her body while Taylor flails and kicks. "Go on. And for God's sake, don't worry about us. Have some fun. While you still can," she mutters before carrying her screaming, sobbing, thrashing two-year-old into the trailer.

Pursing my lips, I turn and slowly make my way down the sidewalk toward Sam.

Devyn's mad at me—worse, she's disappointed.

Zoe looks ready to fall over at any moment.

And Taylor is still screeching and, by the sound of it, trying desperately to kick down the front door.

Me? I'm headed out for ice cream with the boy who changed the rules of our friendship, deserted me and crushed my heart.

What's there to worry about?

25

Sam and I are both quiet as he drives through town. The only words we've exchanged so far were when I reached his SUV and he asked if everything was okay and I said it was.

Lying. It's what I do best.

Not sure why he's not talking, but I'm too busy replaying Devyn's words over and over again in my head to strike up any sort of conversation.

My story is *her story.*

It's the story of all Jones girls, from Gigi's grandmother on down. Always searching and struggling for more than they'll have. Left behind. Left alone.

Just...left.

It's what happened between Dev and Bryan. They were together from the time they were fourteen until Bryan left for boot camp two weeks after they graduated high school. He promised he wouldn't forget her. That he'd always love her.

He promised he'd be back for her.

The last we heard, he married some waitress he met while stationed overseas.

She hasn't dated anyone since.

I glance at the handsome, confusing, frustrating, wonderful boy beside me.

She might be onto something.

Sam doesn't even have music on, so the silence seems more oppressive. And way more obvious.

Five minutes in and I'm already confused, irritated and scared.

Most Awkward Date Ever.

Not that this is a date, I assure myself, shifting in my seat. We're going out for ice cream. We used to do it weekly, starting the first weekend the Tastee Freeze opened in the spring until it closed again on Labor Day.

Wasn't that the whole reason I suggested this specific activity? It's familiar. A way for us to ease into the whole *let's see where things go between us* thing Sam asked for. We can't jump into being more than friends, not after spending the past eleven months not speaking to each other. This is better. Safer.

And definitely not a date.

I mean, yeah, Sam did open my car door for me but that's just because he's polite. And, yes, we're both dressed a bit nicer than our usual Sunday afternoon Tastee Freeze trips—Sam in slim dark blue shorts and a white, short-sleeved button-down, his damp hair combed back and drying into perfect waves. Me in a snug, short, floral print skirt, strappy sandals and a lime-green tank top with a web of crisscrossing straps in the back, my hair straight.

I tell myself Sam wore that outfit to church with his family and didn't have time to change—conveniently ignoring the fact that he's obviously freshly showered. Just like I tell myself the only reason I'm wearing a skirt is because all my shorts are in the dirty laundry.

Okay, most of my shorts.

I give myself an epic inner eye roll. Technically only two pair of my shorts are dirty, but they were the only ones I wanted to wear, and since I couldn't, I chose this skirt. And this is the only shirt that looks right with it. It's not like I wore it because it's Sam's favorite color. Or because it shows off my back and shoulders. Or because this shade of green brings out my eyes and looks really good against my pale skin.

Those things are just coincidences. I did not dress up for Sam. This is not a date.

Just an extremely awkward, nerve-wracking, so-far-tensely-silent jaunt to the local Tastee Freeze with an insanely attractive, incredibly appealing boy who makes me forget everything, including, but not limited to, how badly he hurt me, how I responded to that pain, and all the many reasons why we shouldn't give this whole more-than-friends things a try.

I'm soooo glad I agreed to this! It isn't uncomfortable or terrifying in the least!

Tugging on the hem of my skirt, I slide a very casual glance at the speedometer. Thirty-two mph. That's not too fast. Not fast enough to do any major damage should someone...oh, I don't know...jump out while we're rounding a curve or something.

Hypothetically speaking.

But even as I reach for the door handle and remind myself to tuck and roll, a teeny tiny voice inside of me suggests that perhaps bolting out of a moving vehicle isn't the best option.

Or the best way to prove I really do have faith like I told myself I'd have when Sam tossed out his *I'm still in love with you* yesterday morning in my kitchen.

I curl my fingers and rest my hand on my lap. Having faith is a lot easier said than done.

No wonder I haven't tried it before.

Sam slows and turns into the Tastee Freeze parking lot. It's packed, all the lined spaces taken, and we inch along, passing the dozen or so people in line to place their orders, then a few cars and two motorcycles parked at the edge of the grass. We drive behind the building and I see the picnic tables are crowded with people. Kids and dogs run around the grassy area.

Stopping by for a cone or sundae on a lazy, sunny, summer Sunday afternoon was such a freaking fabulous idea.

Sam's waiting for a pickup to back out of a space, his fingers drumming on the steering wheel, when someone pounds on the back of the car, scaring the crap out of me and making Sam swear under his breath. A moment later, a grinning Graham appears at Sam's side of the SUV, arms raised in victory. "Sammy!"

Graham has spotted Sam out in the wild. Back pats and high fives all around!

Sam nods at his friend then looks straight ahead, as if watching some guy take three times longer to exit a parking space than it should is the most riveting thing he's ever seen.

Graham, though, will not be ignored.

He's clueless like that.

"Sam-me, Sam-me, Sam-me!" Today's chant is accompanied by raps on Sam's window to the beat of a cha-cha.

Better than a hip thrust any day of the week.

Sam keeps looking out the windshield as if Graham hasn't lifted his shirt (he has) and isn't rubbing against the glass like a pasty human squeegee (he is).

"It's like he's made of play dough," I say, horrified and enthralled as Graham does a full body roll, his stomach rippling against the glass. "I want to look away, but I can't."

Sam laughs, a short burst of sound that startles me. Makes me realize I haven't heard him laugh in a long time.

Makes me want to hear it again.

He faces me, turning so his shoulders block most of the circus act outside his door. "Better?"

Graham now has his wide-open mouth on the window, like a fish stuck to the glass, and is puffing up his cheeks, his wiggling tongue in full, disturbing view. I wrinkle my nose. "Not really, no."

Sam glances behind him then sighs and finally rolls down his window. "Dude, how many times have I told you not to lick my car? You're washing off that spit mark."

With a *whatever* flip of his floppy brown hair, Graham leans against the open window, arms crossed against the ledge. "Come on, we've got a table near the creek."

"I'm with Hadley."

Graham flicks a surprised glance my way, as if just noticing me sitting there.

Because I'm so hard to miss, what with my bright red hair and even brighter green shirt.

"We can make room for her," he says with a shrug.

After an eleven-month banishment, I've once again been invited —with as little enthusiasm as possible, I might add—to the cool kids' table.

Hooray.

The pickup finally vacates the parking spot and Sam pulls forward Graham, still leaning against the window, walks with us as we move. "I'll save you a spot in line," he tells Sam then straightens and gives the SUV one more slap before loping off.

Sam parks but leaves the engine running. The *we* Graham referred to at the table near the creek is Jackson, Travis, and Kenzie, Kenzie's younger brother Ethan and Rachel Gerring, Melanie Reece and Wyatt Smith.

Hail, hail, the gang's all here.

Whitney's a new addition to that gang, sitting between Rachel and Kenzie, and she waves, all cheerful and smiling and, after our conversation yesterday morning, in full possession of many of my secrets.

That thought doesn't terrify me like it should. Whitney is too honest, too honorable and just too nice to tell anyone what I told her in confidence.

Or maybe I'm delusional and she's already told the entire table.

Guess we'll find out.

At the moment, I'm going with me being a great judge of character. We'd hung out last night—me and Whitney. She'd insisted on coming over so my telling Sam I had plans with her wasn't a lie. We hadn't done much. Just watched TV and played with Taylor, but it was fun.

No, Whitney won't tell my secrets. They're safe.

Sam clears his throat. "We don't have to sit with them if you don't want to. We can eat in here."

Eat in the Car of Silence? No thanks. I'd rather join the others. At least with them, I know what to expect: Everyone but Whitney will ignore me and I can eat my three scoops of mint chocolate chip in relative peace.

There's no peace here. Not with Sam so close, smelling so good. Not when he's acting so weird.

"I don't mind sitting with them," I say and his mouth thins. "Unless you don't want to."

He shrugs.

But he doesn't get out. Doesn't move except for his thumb, which is rubbing back and forth across the steering wheel.

"We don't have to do this. Be" –I gesture between us— "here. Together. Like this…"

"You're not changing your mind," he says when I trail off. "You told me you'd give me a chance." Leaning toward me, he takes my left hand. "Don't back out on me now."

My heart races. He's still afraid I'll run from him, and while I may have briefly considered doing just that, I wouldn't have gone through with it.

And not just because it would have meant jumping out of the car.

I've spent the past seven years running from Sam, from how he makes me feel. It hasn't worked.

Maybe it's time to try something new.

Time to have that faith for real.

"I'm not. I haven't." I stare at our hands. His is so big and tan. So warm and steady. But his touch still has the power to unnerve me. To thrill me. "I thought you changed yours."

"Are you ever going to trust me again?"

I lift my head. "What?"

"I told you I came back for you," he reminds me, his quiet tone laced with an edge I don't understand. He pulls his hand free and I have the strongest urge to grab it. To hold on to him. "Christ, Hadley, I told you I'm still in love with you! Did you think I was lying? That this is some game to me?"

"No! It's just...you didn't say a word the whole ride out here and you're acting like you don't even want to be here. You won't even get out of the car!"

"I'm nervous! I don't want to say or do something that will give you an excuse to be pissed at me again. You told me you want to take things slow so I'm trying not to push too far, too fast, but this?" He waves his hand to indicate the building, the people. "This isn't what I want. I don't want to be with Graham and Travis or any of those guys. I don't want to be reminded of how you and I used to be. I don't want to go back, Hadley. I want to move forward. And I need to know if that's what you want, too. Because if it's not, then there's really no point in us doing this at all."

His words are quiet.

And so final they shake me to my core.

For months I thought I was over him. Told myself that I was okay with him being out of my life. But now that he's back, now that I know how he feels about me?

I can't let him go.

He's right. This whole afternoon was a way to remind us of how we used to be. A way for me to keep us in the friend zone. I knew exactly what would happen if we came here. It'd be Sam and Hadley. Hadley and Sam. Two best friends together again.

Just like it used to be.

But we're not those people anymore. We aren't friends. Haven't been friends for almost a year.

We can't go back.

It's time to move forward.

It's time for something new.

In the console, Sam's phone buzzes. He checks it. "Graham wants to know what we want him to order for us." When I don't answer, he glances at me. "Mint chocolate chip?"

This is it. My leap of faith. Who knew it'd involve ice cream?

"No," I say.

Typing his reply, Sam stops. "You always get mint chocolate chip."

I lick my lips. "I know. I just...I think it's time for something different."

Something new.

"Do you want to get out of here?" I continue in a rush. "We could go somewhere else. Somewhere we haven't been before."

It takes him a moment to process what I'm saying, what I mean, but when he does, he grins, slow and swoon-worthy.

"Yeah," he says. "I'd like that."

He sets his phone in the console then backs out of the spot without looking. Someone honks and Sam brakes and lifts his hand in an apologetic wave, waits while they pass, then finishes backing up.

"Hey!" Graham's shout reaches us as Sam rounds the far end of the building. He keeps driving, though Graham is jogging our way, waving both arms to get Sam's attention. "Sam! Where're you going?"

I turn in my seat, look at the picnic table to see everyone watching us, Travis on his feet, Kenzie shading her eyes with her hand. Whitney grinning.

"Changed our mind," Sam tells Graham as he taps on the brakes at the edge of the parking lot. "I'll catch you later."

And then careful, law-abiding Sam Constable floors it, darting out onto the street with squealing tires. Barely slowing, he takes a sharp right onto Hillside Road. We fishtail, but Sam corrects it then speeds up once again, going so fast the houses outside my window pass in a blur.

It's so unlike the Sam I know, being rude to anyone, blowing them off. Going fast, acting even the slightest bit reckless. And I realize with a sharp pang, that's because I don't know him. Not anymore. He's changed.

The Sam I used to know no longer exists. He's gone, replaced by this new Sam. The one who spent eleven months on the other side of the country in a different time zone. He's had experiences I wasn't a part of. Hung out with people I've never met.

He isn't afraid to look me in the eye and tell me how he feels. What he wants.

Time for something new.

I roll down my window. The wind catches my hair, whips it around my face as we drive farther and farther away from the Tastee Freeze and his friends. Our hometown. Away from our past.

Time for something new.

Time to stop looking back.

26

BETWEEN THE TWO OF US, WE'VE BEEN TO EVERY DECENT DINER, restaurant, takeout place and ice cream shop in town, so when Sam suggests we keep driving until we come across somewhere neither of us has been before, I'm all for it.

Time for something new.

While we drive, Sam has me get his phone and I play DJ, picking songs from his playlist. His taste has always run to the classics—rock and roll mostly—but now his phone is filled with new songs, from alternative to rap. When I mention my surprise, he says he got into a lot of different music while in LA. The music scene out there is obviously bigger and better than Nowhere Pennsylvania.

Old Sam listened to Rush and Ozzy Osborne and Nirvana.

New Sam listens to Bryson Tiller, Kendrick Lamar and Chance the Rapper.

And the changes just keep coming!

Half an hour later, we end up at Mary's Trading Post, a burger and ice cream place overlooking the dam. It's as busy as the Tastee Freeze was except no one in line, at the tables, or working behind the order window knows who we are, is aware of our history as friends and then not friends, or wants our attention.

Being with Sam again, at an unfamiliar place, is different, and I wonder if this is how it's going to be between us. Him quiet and nervous and afraid to say the wrong thing. Me anxious and unsure and scared of letting him hurt me again.

Great. We're both completely messed up. Sounds like the basis for a strong, steady, healthy relationship.

In keeping with the Try Something New theme we've got going, I decide to get a peanut butter and marshmallow fluff sundae instead of three scoops of mint chocolate chip. Sam follows suit and instead of his usual hot fudge sundae, he tries the mint Oreo cyclone, Mary's Trading Post's version of Dairy Queen's blizzard.

Look at us, branching out in our ice cream choices. So brave! So bold!

Okay, not all that brave. Not completely bold, because Sam orders onion rings and French fries for us to share—like always.

I'm willing to give new and different a shot, but some things should never change. And that's eating hot, greasy, salty onion rings and French fries after we've finished our ice cream.

It's sort of our thing. A Sam and Hadley tradition.

And him doing it, placing the order like he always did, knowing it's what I want, too, makes me less anxious about being around New Sam. Surer we can move forward, leaving the past behind.

Takes some of the edge off my fear that this is a huge mistake.

We sit at a picnic table near the edge of the wooden deck overlooking the murky, fishy water. There are no waves, no crashing surf, and the pebbly area to our left is the closest thing we have to a beach unless you want to drive ninety minutes to Presque Isle at Lake Erie.

But it's still a popular spot. People are wading and splashing around in the roped-off area of water. A bunch of college-aged guys are playing volleyball near the concession stand and kids and moms are at the small playground next to the parking lot.

Old Sam always sat on the opposite side of the table. New Sam is next to me, straddling the bench and facing me, one leg bent and resting between us.

Boys. They love taking up as much space as possible.

I inch back, all casual like. Being close to New Sam, yes, even to just his knee, isn't good for my equilibrium or state of mind. And I'd like to enjoy my ice cream in a state of relative peace, thanks all the same.

We eat in silence. My sundae is soft serve vanilla covered in a thick, creamy peanut butter sauce and sticky, sweet marshmallow fluff.

But it's not mint chocolate chip.

Ice cream regret is the worst.

"Don't you like your sundae?" Sam asks.

One more thing that hasn't changed. Sam reading my mind.

Or else he noticed me staring at his minty, chocolate concoction with what I'm pretty sure is lust in my eyes. Either way, the boy still gets me better than anyone else ever has.

"No, I do." To prove it—and, yes, maybe to prove he doesn't know me as well as he thinks he does, to show I've changed over the past eleven months like he has, and there are new, hidden depths to me he's yet to discover—I take another bite. Speak around my mouthful. "It's good."

He smirks. He knows what I'm doing. Not lying, exactly.

Just not telling the truth.

Story of our lives right there.

"But it's not what you really want?"

And that is a dangerous question, especially when asked in Sam's deep voice, his gaze on mine. When I know he's asking about more than ice cream choices.

He's asking about us, about our previous friendship. How I was content to settle for it when I wanted so much more.

He's not the only one with a strong ESP game.

"No." Time for more of that faith. "It's not what I really want."

It was never what I wanted. It was what I thought I deserved.

I'm still not so sure I deserve more, but I'm going for it anyway.

He puts his leg down. Scoots closer. "Want to switch?"

I eye the cup of ice cream he's holding out. "Did you order that because you knew I'd like it?"

"Maybe." He skims his gaze over my shoulders, down my chest before oh-so-slowly dragging it back up again to my eyes. Despite it being a million degrees and the sun burning down on us, my insides get shivery. "Did you wear that shirt because you knew I'd like it?"

I open my mouth to deny it—like I'd denied it to myself when I put the stupid shirt on—but that would be pointless.

And cowardly.

Brave and bold. My new life motto.

I take his cup and, as I slide my ice cream toward him on the table, move closer to him. My thigh pressing against his knee, my stomach jittery, I meet his eyes. "Maybe."

The one word comes out husky and breathless but he doesn't seem to mind. He wipes his hand over his mouth and leans his upper body back, keeping his knee right where it is.

It's cute, that he's flustered. That I can make him nervous in a good way.

Cute and hot and very, very rewarding to know I affect him the same way he affects me.

"I don't suppose you have your swimsuit on?" he asks.

I raise my eyebrows then turn my back to him, gathering my hair over my shoulder so he can see that beneath the crisscrossed straps, it's all bare skin. Then I look at him over my shoulder. He's gone still, his jaw tight.

This isn't so hard. Flirting with Sam Constable.

In fact, it's incredibly easy.

"No suit," I say. "Why?"

"I..." He stops. Runs his palms down the tops of his thighs then up. Down. Up. He clears his throat. "I thought we could go swimming."

Brushing my hair back, I face him again and nod at his shorts. "Do you have your trunks on under there?"

He shakes his head. "In the car."

Digging out a chunk of mint Oreo with the long-handled plastic spoon, I wrinkle my nose. "The last time you left wet trunks in the car, it smelled so bad I had to ride with my head out the window like a dog for two weeks."

He laughs. Ah, time. The great equalizer when it comes to lessening the pain of heartache, grief, and how fast a pair of wet swim trunks can turn moldy in a hot car. Or how bad they can smell.

Especially when it takes an entire week to find them under the backseat.

"Man, that was rank." He digs into my sundae. "I learned my lesson. You can keep your head inside the vehicle and the windows up. These trunks were completely dry when I put them in there. We always kept suits and a few towels in our cars in LA in case we decided to go to the beach after school."

The Oreo gets stuck in my throat and I take a bite of ice cream to push it down. That's right. Sam spent the past eleven months in California.

So much for that whole *I will never forget how he left* vow I made three days ago.

The power of a pretty face. Turns a girl's memory to mush.

"Did you go to the beach a lot?" I ask.

The thing is, I know he went there a lot. At least, for the first few months. I stopped following him on Instagram after Christmas. Didn't see any sense torturing myself with the pictures he posted of himself on the beach, shirtless, tanned, windblown and smiling, arms around the shoulders of his new equally tan, equally buff buddies or curvy, bikini-clad girls.

Not something I needed to see on my Insta feed each day. Not if I wanted to get over him.

Of course, the boy is next to me, his knee warm and solid against my leg, so I guess that whole getting-over-him thing was a big, fat fail.

"Every weekend," Sam says in response to my question. "And a few times during the week."

I can see it now. Sam laughing and goofing off with his entitled LA friends as they jump into their shiny BMWs, Lexuses and Audis after school on their way to a sun-filled, fun-filled few hours of splashing in the waves and playing beach volleyball. While I was here. Alone.

Bitter? Me?

You bet.

Something I need to work on. To get over.

"Must've been nice," I say, trying to keep the resentment from my tone. Not sure I succeed, but I'd like a few points for the effort. "Being that close to the ocean. Going to the beach all the time."

He finishes my sundae and puts the crumpled napkin in the container along with the spoon. "It was cool at first, but it got old after a while."

I roll my eyes so hard, I'm surprised I don't see my brain. "Yes, I can see how all that sun, surf and sand would eventually get to be *super* boring."

"Not boring. Just...the same. After a while, no matter what you do, if you do it all the time, it becomes ordinary."

"I'd still take an ordinary day at the beach over any day here. Especially between the months of November and March."

The wind blows my hair and he reaches out, as if to brush it aside, but then curls his fingers into his palm and lowers it without touching me.

It's what I wanted. To take this slow. For him not to push me.

So there's no reason for me to be disappointed.

I tuck my hair behind my ears.

"I missed the snow. The snow and the rain and the leaves changing in the fall. I missed the hills and how green it is here." He slides me a glance. "I missed a lot of things."

"What about the friends you made in LA? Won't you miss them now that you're back?"

"A couple of them, yeah, but not like I missed everyone here."

"What about your dad?" I ask.

Before Sam can answer, the girl working the order window appears with our onion rings and fries.

"Here you go," she says, all chirpy and cheery, setting them in front of Sam. She's cute, with short, dark hair and light brown eyes.

But if she keeps batting her lashes that hard, the force is going to lift her straight off the ground. "Anything else I can get you?" she asks him, completely ignoring me.

"We're good," he says with a smile. "Thanks."

Old Sam would have prolonged the conversation. Would have puffed up with pride, his ego inflated to have a cute girl flirting with him. Old Sam would have flirted back.

Sometimes I think he did it to bug me. To see if he could make me jealous.

It did. He could.

But New Sam turns back to me before she's even walked away.

Major points for New Sam!

He moves the cardboard box so it's between us and lifts out the containers of ketchup and ranch dressing—ketchup for the fries, ranch for the onion rings.

"Dad was pretty pissed when I told him I wanted to come back here," he says, as if we weren't interrupted, "but it's not like he can force me to live with him. I never should have moved in with him in the first place. He works all the time, and when he was home, all he'd do was get on my ass about school."

This, too, is new. Old Sam never said anything bad about his dad. Always choosing to make him out to be some prince among men.

"I'm sorry," I say, because I know how important it was for him to believe the best of his dad.

"It was my own fault. I knew what he was like." He dips an onion ring into the ranch. "I knew a week into the school year going there was a mistake. I just..." He pops the entire onion ring into his mouth. Chews and swallows. "I didn't know how to fix it."

"You mean you didn't want to admit you were wrong."

It's Sam's greatest flaw.

Goes hand-in-hand with his stubbornness.

Everyone likes being right. For Sam, it's more like an obsession.

Picking up another onion ring, he shrugs. "It wouldn't have made a difference. Mom and Dad both said that if I made the move, I'd have to stay the entire school year."

He could have tried to talk them out of it. Could have whined and begged and complained and harassed them until they gave in.

If he had, he could have come home sooner.

I guess whining, begging, complaining and harassment are beneath New Sam.

And I realize what I'm doing. Looking for differences in Sam. Trying to figure out if all of this is a waste of time. If we should even attempt this now with all the months and distance that's kept us apart for so long. All the choices we've both made.

But as we share fries and onion rings, Sam making me laugh with the story of the first time he tried surfing, none of that matters. Because no matter how much has changed, so much has stayed the same.

Sam is still the same sweet, stubborn boy who invited me swimming all those years ago. Who broke through my walls and became my first real friend. Who shared his friends with me. Made me a part of their group. Who accepted me.

The same boy who's had my heart from the very start.

And that's something I don't think will ever change.

27

He hugged me.

When we got home from Mary's Trading Post, Sam walked me to my door and gave me a brief, platonic hug.

Like he used to. When we were *just friends*.

And then he straightened, smiled as if he was super pleased with life in general and himself in particular, and told me he'd call me later and went on his merry way.

Leaving me staring after him wondering what had just happened.

Not that I wanted him to do more. I mean, it was my idea to take things slow, so it was a relief he didn't kiss me.

It's already been well established I don't do my best thinking when he kisses me.

But there'd been a moment, right before the hug, when I'd been certain he was going to. That he wanted to.

And maybe a small part of me wanted him to as well, because I'd raised my head, my eyes drifting closed as anticipation, nerves and excitement warred inside me.

All of which shriveled up and died in embarrassment and disappointment when he wrapped his arms around me instead.

After his quick squeeze, I'd half expected him to pat me on the shoulder and call me dude.

Now, I glance at Sam as we turn onto the street where he lives. It's been five days since then and we've gotten into a rhythm. All part of our Try Something New plan. True to his word, Sam talked to Mr. G. and I'm back to working with Kyle, but Sam drives me to and from work, like he used to. But instead of texting me every night, he calls and we talk for at least an hour.

And until today, when he asked if I wanted to go to his house after work, we haven't hung out again.

Which is good. The whole take-our-time thing. My idea and all.

I just hadn't thought it'd be quite so...confusing.

Or that I'd want to pick up the pace a little.

We pull up the driveway to Sam's house, and though it's a hot, sunny summer afternoon—the opposite of cold, dark and snowing— I'm reminded of the last time I was here.

I push the memories aside.

Not thinking about that night. Not, not, not.

Sam parks in front of the left stall of the four-car garage and we get out to the sound of a basketball being dribbled. When we round the corner near the fenced-off court, Charlie tucks the ball under his arm and waves.

Sam had mentioned that Charlie had grown, but I'm unprepared for how different he looks. He's taller and thinner, his face losing its little-boy softness. His dark hair is longer, too, and flopping in his eyes.

"You need to call the police or the army or something," I whisper as Charlie jogs toward us. "Some strange, alien invader has taken over your brother's body and is turning him into" –I pause and give a dramatic shudder for effect— "a middle-schooler."

Switching the cooler he uses as a lunchbox from his left hand to his right, Sam shakes his head. "Can't stop adolescence."

"We could try. For Charlie's sake. God knows puberty has ruined more than one nice, sweet boy, turning him into..." I wrinkle my nose. "Well. You know."

"A teenager?"

"A teenage *boy*. It's a sad, sad time."

Sam leans down. "Oh, I don't know," he murmurs into my ear. "We're not all that bad."

I turn my head to look at him, my throat dry. With him this close, grinning down at me in a knowing way, all broad shoulders, wide chest, flat stomach and tanned, toned arms, I can't help but agree.

Or at least, my hormones agree. They're all for teenage boys—especially this one.

Puberty doesn't just do a number on the males of our species.

"Hey," Charlie says to Sam when he reaches us. "Want to play one-on-one?"

Guess he's over being pissed at Sam. And Charlie sounds the same, thank God. His voice isn't any deeper and there's no cracking yet. But he's still so different. So changed. Is this how Sam felt when he saw Taylor after so long?

Like he'd missed so much?

"You sure that's a good idea?" Sam asks Charlie. "The last time we played one-on-one, you didn't like the outcome."

Charlie flushes, splotches of color on his cheeks, and shoots me a glance before scowling at Sam. "You only spotted me five points," he mutters, sounding like a little kid—whiny and bratty because he didn't win. Hooray! Puberty hasn't fully gotten its clutches in him yet. "You could give me ten this time."

Sam, all six feet plus of natural athleticism, competitive edge and basketball talent, nods. He could spot Charlie twenty points and still beat the kid to twenty-one. "I could do that, but Hadley's here. Which I'm sure you noticed even though you haven't said hello to her yet."

Charlie's blush intensifies at his brother's not-so-subtle admonishment and I feel bad for him, being embarrassed by Sam twice in under a minute.

"I didn't say hello to him, either," I point out before turning to Charlie and holding out my hand. "Hello, Charles. Good to see you again."

One side of his mouth lifts, his brown eyes lit with humor, and he looks so much like Sam I wish I could take a marker and write DANGER on his forehead, just to give all the girls his age a heads-up about what's to come.

"Hello, Hadley," he says, mimicking my solemn tone as he shakes my hand, pumping it up and down three times before letting go. "Okay, we said hello," Charlie tells Sam. He bounces the ball once. "Let's go."

"Hadley doesn't want to sit around and watch us play basketball."

Charlie looks so disappointed, I step over to stand next to him. "How about a game of two against one?" At Charlie's confused look, I explain, "You and me against Sam."

He stares at me like I've offered to slice Sam's chest open and share his organs for dinner. "Uh, do you even know how to shoot a basketball?"

"I'm sure I could figure it out," I say with a shrug. "You just throw it." I pretend to hold a ball in both hands and jump awkwardly while pushing my arms straight out from my body. "Like that. Right?"

Poor Charlie. He goes from beet red to snow white.

"Can she be on your team?" he asks Sam hopefully.

"Any time," Sam tells him, but his eyes are on mine, and really, that husky tone, full of innuendo, is not appropriate around children.

I roll my eyes at him and his lame attempt at turning an innocent comment into something sexual.

His grin widens and he wiggles his eyebrows.

Doofus.

"If she's on my team," Charlie says, oblivious to anything other than trying to beat his brother, "then we get fifteen points."

Sam sets down the cooler. "Ha. No."

"Fourteen," Charlie says then, when Sam doesn't respond, "Thirteen."

"You're not doing much for my confidence," I tell Charlie as I untie my boots. I blink up at him, trying to look wounded. "Don't you want to be teammates?"

Instead of answering, he shrugs, which, let's be honest, is answer enough. He turns back to Sam. "Ten points.

"Shoes off," Sam tells him, tucking his socks into his boots then taking the ball from Charlie.

Charlie toes off his sneakers then hops on one foot to tug off his sock, switches sides and repeats the motion.

"Playing to twenty-one," Sam says, dribbling as we make our way to the court. "Half-court. And since it's two against one, I'm not spotting you any points."

"Aw, man," Charlie whines.

Seriously. His lack of faith is starting to get annoying.

We walk to midcourt, the pavement hot under my bare feet.

"You can stand over there," Charlie tells me, pointing to the far corner where, I'm assuming, he's hoping I'll stay out of his way and far, far away from the ball.

"Hadley's our guest," Sam says. "It's only polite that she gets the ball first."

And he turns his back to the basket we'll be using and tosses me the ball. I catch it, then tuck it between my legs so I can straighten my hat. Pull my ponytail tighter.

Then I send a bounce pass at Sam, who bounces it right back.

He crouches, knees bent, arms out, weight on the balls of his feet. I copy his stance except I keep the ball between my palms, elbows out. I watch his hands, his feet, so that when he tries to swipe the ball from me, I'm ready and swing it out of his reach.

I fake left then go right. Dribble for four steps then stop and shoot before Sam can block me, arm extended, wrist snapping. As the ball arcs up, I head toward the basket for the rebound, but Sam's already there, back to me, crouched low, butt out, arms extended to take away my space.

Doesn't matter as the ball hits the rim then tips in.

"Huh," I say, frowning up at the basket in fake wonderment. "It went in." I turn to Charlie, who's staring at me, mouth literally open. "Is that good?"

Charlie blinks. And closes his mouth. "Uh, yeah. That's pretty good."

"Please. Stop with all the flattery. You'll inflate my ego."

"Pretty good is being generous," Sam says as he scoops up the ball. "Your form sucked."

"Everyone's a critic. Or a coach." Which is accurate as Sam is the one who taught me how to play basketball. "It's not like I've had reason to shoot baskets the past year."

But my tone is mild and teasing instead of bitter, and he grins. Dribbles the ball twice. "Hopefully it'll come back to you soon enough."

It does. But not enough for an epic upset.

Charlie and I lose thirteen to twenty-one, which I take as a victory —even if Charlie doesn't. Sam is super competitive and doesn't take it easy on his opponents. He plays hard. All the time.

Like being right, Sam loves to win.

After the game, Sam and I go into the kitchen and he gets us both glasses of water. The kitchen is my favorite room in Sam's house. It's huge, with sunlight streaming in from the bank of windows in the breakfast nook overlooking the pool and, as every time I've been here, spotless.

Over the rim of my cup, I watch Sam gulp down his water, his head tipped back, his throat working. His hair is damp at the temples, the sweat darkening it to almost black. His shirt has wet spots under his arms and the collar, down the middle of his stomach.

There's a weird sensation in my chest and I rub my hand over it but it remains, a tugging inside of me.

Like my heart's falling at his feet.

Catching me staring, he lowers his glass. Gives me a quizzical look. "You're smiling."

"Am I?" I ask, lifting my hand to my mouth, and his gaze zeroes in on my fingers as they trail over my lips.

He clears his throat. "Yeah. It's nice. You look happy."

My smile falters at the surprise in his tone. "Don't I usually?"

As soon as the question comes out, I regret it.

Never ask a question you don't want to hear the answer to.

"No," Sam murmurs. "Not nearly often enough."

He holds my gaze and my breath catches and I want to tell him that I *am* happy. That being here, with him, in this new way, makes me very happy.

But I can't. It's too scary, sharing what I'm feeling. Makes me too vulnerable.

And gives him even more power over me.

So I stay quiet and unmoving as he sets his glass down and steps closer. Reaching out slowly, he curls his fingertip around a strand of hair stuck to my damp neck, his fingertips warming my skin as he pulls it free.

My lips part on a soft exhale and his gaze drops to my mouth. He wraps my hair around his finger once...twice...three times, taking a step toward me each time. Closer. Closer.

But not close enough.

It's frustrating.

Especially when he lets go of my hair and takes a sudden quick step back. He grabs his glass, refills it at the sink and drains it in three long gulps.

When he looks at me again, his expression is clear.

"I'm gonna jump in the shower," he says as if nothing happened. As if he hadn't looked like he wanted to kiss me. As if I hadn't wanted him to. "You can wait in my room."

I follow him out of the kitchen. I wanted to go slow and he's respecting that decision.

And now that be-careful-what-you-wish-for hindsight is kicking me in the pants.

28

Sam didn't make his bed.

He used to. All the other times I've been in his room it was made, all neat and tidy, the lightweight gray comforter pulled up and wrinkle-free.

Today the comforter is piled on the bottom corner, like he kicked it there at some point in his sleep. The white-and-gray striped sheets are rumpled. One pillow is lined up against the headboard, smooth and plump. The other is at an angle and still has a slight indentation.

It unsettles me, that unmade bed. Those rumpled sheets and slept-on pillow. I tear my gaze away, watch Sam get clean clothes out of his dresser.

He tosses a T-shirt over his shoulder, holds shorts in his hands. "I'll be right back."

He leaves and my gaze once again flicks to his bed.

Definitely unsettled.

I grab the corner of the comforter and pull it over the sheets.

That makes it worse. It smells of him. His bed, his sheets. Like the laundry detergent his mom buys, the body wash Sam uses and, faintly, the scent of his cologne. I'm literally leaning over, trying to get a good sniff of his pillow before I realize what I'm doing and jerk upright.

Everything about the boy messes with my head. Makes me weak.

But I'm here. At his house. In his room. Because no matter how much that weakness scares me, no matter how badly I want to protect myself, I want this more. Us, together.

I want him more.

I sit on the end of the bed, my bare toes grazing the carpet.

Something niggles at the back of my brain. Something's off with the room. Something's different, and not just the messy bed.

I slowly get to my feet. No, not different.

Missing.

Which doesn't make sense. Everything's where it's always been. Wide, three-drawer dresser next to the closet. Desk and chair across from the window. Bookcase against the far wall, arm chair in the corner. Nightstand with lamp at the head of the bed. Framed, signed Stephen Curry jersey and Warriors posters--

My mouth dries and I walk toward the wall across from the bed. Reaching out slowly, my fingers trail over the empty space.

I cross to the dresser. Ignore my reflection as I check out the items tucked into the edges of the mirror. Pictures and notes and ticket stubs from sporting events and concerts. Heart pounding, I move on to the desk next. There are framed photos on the surface, more tacked to the huge bulletin board on the wall. Pictures of Sam and his family, of Sam and Jackson and Graham in their basketball uniforms, of Sam and the friends he made in LA. One of Sam as Deb from *Napoleon Dynamite* (complete with side ponytail) next to Kenzie, who'd dressed up as Pedro, and Tori, who'd been Napoleon.

I slide onto the desk chair, try to catch my breath.

It's me. I'm what's missing.

I sit there, emotions rioting, until the sound of my name has me turning toward the doorway.

Sam, freshly showered and dressed, his wet hair combed back, steps into the room. "You want to get some dinner? We can try that new Mexican place."

Dinner. Right. Because we're moving on. Letting the past go. Exactly what I want to do. What I have to do in order to be with Sam.

I glance at the pictures on the bulletin board.

One of us is better at letting go than the other.

"You erased me," I say and, God, I hate that I sound so pitiful. So resentful.

Hate that I feel so small.

That it hurts so much.

"What are you talking about?"

"You erased me," I repeat. I get to my feet. "You erased me and you lied to me."

He sends a quick glance into the hall, then shuts the door. "I didn't lie to you."

"*I missed you, Hadley,*" I say, imitating his deep voice. "*I thought of you every day.* Lies."

His jaw tightens. "Truth."

"You took down Steph!" I cry, pointing straight-armed at the blank wall where the life-sized Steph Curry decal I got him for his sixteenth birthday used to be. "And you threw out all the pictures of us."

The pictures that used to take up the most space along his mirror. The ones that outnumbered everything else on his bulletin board two to one.

"I put Steph in the game room."

"Out of sight, out of mind, huh?" I know he moved the decal so he wouldn't have to see it. So he wouldn't have to think about me. "What about the pictures?"

"I didn't throw them away," he says quickly.

"But you took them down."

He nods, his gaze steady on mine. "I thought it would help me forget you. It didn't work." With a snort, I turn away, only to have him take a hold of my arm and turn me back to face him. When I refuse to look up, he ducks his head to meet my eyes. "It didn't work."

Doesn't matter that I believe him. Or even that I understand why he did it—that I'd done something similar by un-following him on Instagram, distancing myself from his friends.

He wraps his other hand around my free arm. Pulls me closer. "I thought of you every day," he tells me, his eyes searching mine. "Every. Single. Day."

I shrug free. "You wanted to pretend I didn't exist. That I'd never existed. Why even bother? It's not like you were here. But I was. I was stuck here, reminded of you everywhere I went. With everything I did."

He stills as my words hang in the air between us. My confession. "You...you thought of me?"

I want to deny it, but I can't very well be self-righteous and ticked off about him lying if I don't give him my own truth now.

"I thought of you," I admit. "I thought of you every day."

He reaches for me. "Had--"

I step back. "You got rid of me. It's like I was never a part of your life."

"I wanted to move on." His voice drops to a deep, frustrated tone, as if I'm the one being unreasonable here. The one who is wrong. "I couldn't go back."

"Was any of it real?"

"Was what real?"

"Us. You know, the years we were friends. The years I *thought* we were friends."

His face scrunches up into that stupid expression guys get when they think a girl's saying things just to piss them off. "We *were* friends. You were my best friend."

"I don't think I was. Because a best friend doesn't just stop talking to their friend because they had a fight. They don't walk away because they didn't get what they wanted."

"I never wanted to lose your friendship, but things changed for me and I couldn't hide how I felt."

"Exactly. Things changed *for you*, and when I didn't fall in line with your plans, you decided to erase me from your life."

He stabs a hand through his hair, leaving finger marks in the wet strands. "I didn't have plans."

"You did," I insist, my words, my suspicions and fears coming faster than my thoughts. Outpacing reason and control. "You planned all of it, right from the beginning. You never wanted to be my friend. Not really. You wanted this."

"Are you serious?"

I give a quick, jerky nod. "All those times when you tried to get me to sit with you at lunch, when you tried to talk to me, when you asked me to join you and your friends on the playground...all those months you were so nice to me, it was because you had feelings for me. And instead of just telling me that, you pretended you wanted to be just friends."

"You mean all those times when we were in *grade school*? So you're saying that when I was ten I came up with some grand plan to...what? Trick you into being my girl?"

Put that way, it sounds sort of idiotic. But I can't let it go. It's had a hold of me ever since he kissed me last summer. The sense that he'd been dishonest.

The feeling that while I'd spent all that time content with our relationship, secure in the knowledge that our friendship was rock solid, trusting that my heart was safe, he was biding his time until he could spring his feelings on me.

"I don't know," I mutter, blushing so hard I take off my hat and wave it in front of my face—pretending I don't care that I have the worst case of hat hair ever recorded. "It was your plan."

He grabs my wrist, lowering my hand and stopping all my hat fluttering and waving. "I told you, there was no fucking plan. I didn't have feelings for you when we were kids, or even when we first started being friends."

"Then why did you want to be my friend?"

Why didn't you give up on me?

"Because you needed one." He rubs his thumb across my inner wrist. My pulse flutters. "You were always so alone. Seemed so lonely. Jesus, Had, you needed a friend more than anyone I've ever known."

And that's it. The great truth I'd been seeking. The answer to my question. To so many of the questions I'd had since we were ten years old.

Sam Constable befriended me because he felt sorry for me.

So freaking glad I asked.

I tug my hand free and slap my hat back on my head. "This is a mistake."

"It's not," he says simply, as if he has utter faith we're right where we're meant to be, standing at the foot of his bed arguing about ancient history. "You're just scared. You're always scared." His words are quiet, his gaze intense. As if he's trying to see inside my head. Trying to get to the truth I keep hidden from him. "Always so terrified of opening up. Of letting someone see the real you. Or get close to you."

Yes, this boy knows me too well.

"Sam, I--"

"But you can trust me," he says and my own words get stuck in my throat. He lifts a hand as if to touch me and once again I'm unsettled, but not by his bed. By how much I want his touch. How disappointed I am when he slowly lowers his hand. "You can let me in. I swear I won't hurt you."

My heartbeat is echoing in my head, each pulse of it a painful thump in my ears. No. No, he doesn't get to say that. Doesn't get to sway me with his sweet words and pretty promises.

"You left me. You stopped talking to me." I sweep my hand around the room to encompass the missing Steph, all the pieces of me that are gone. "You erased me. God, Sam, don't you get it? You already hurt me!"

I'm breathing hard, my scalp tight and sweaty under my hat while Sam stares at me, lips parted in surprise, body stunned into stillness and silence.

"I know I hurt you, too," I continue hoarsely. "Everything that happened last summer...it all got messed up. The past and the present get so mixed up inside of me. And I want to be brave. I want to have faith. But I don't know if I can."

"You can."

There's that confidence again. That assurance that he's completely, totally, one hundred percent right.

"You're right. I can. But I don't know if I want to." I lift my head, meet his eyes as I give him one more weapon against me. A truth that will give him entirely too much power over me. "You broke my heart, Sam. And I'm terrified you're going to do it again."

29

S<small>AM TAKES A QUICK STEP TOWARD ME, BECAUSE NOTHING</small>—<small>NOT MY LIES</small>, my fears or my confession that he broke my heart—can stop him from going after what he wants. "I won't. I promise, I won't."

He's so earnest. Sincere. I want to believe him. I want to so badly. Isn't that the problem?

Wanting something impossible?

"You can't promise that," I say. "And neither can I."

"But that's what you want, isn't it? Promises. A guarantee. Jesus, Hadley."

He whirls around. Paces to the dresser, keeps his back to me, his hands on his hips, his head tipped up. I watch as he takes a couple of deep breaths. Then he faces me.

"Valentine's Day."

I look around, trying to figure out what corner he picked those two words out of and why he'd think an overly commercialized, barely-even-a-real-holiday is relevant to this conversation. "What?"

"Valentine's Day. Sophomore year. Do you remember it?"

"Sam, what--"

"Abby and I were together. I bought her a necklace and took her out to dinner. Do you remember?"

"I remember."

He'd showed me the necklace, a delicate gold chain with an open-heart pendant. He'd asked me if I thought Abby would like it.

She'd loved it—like I'd told him she would. Abby's the kind of girl who wants typical V-Day gifts—hearts and flowers and a box of chocolates.

"But I came to see you first," he reminds me. "Before I picked her up. I stopped at your place."

I nod, unsure where he's going with this. "You brought me croissants."

A dozen freshly baked, perfectly flaky, melt-in-your-mouth croissants from the Davis Bakery. He'd been so handsome in dark slacks and a deep blue button-down. His hair had been shorter then, the curl almost cut off, the ends waving wildly.

I was so jealous. Of that stupid, unimaginative necklace and the dozen roses in his SUV and the dinner. Jealous that Abby got to be the one to sit across from him, gazing at him in the candlelight.

I told myself it was because Sam was in a relationship and I wasn't. A pity party for the single girl, stuck at home with her sisters and a newborn on Valentine's Day. That it was because of the time he spent with her—time that took him away from me. From our friendship.

Oh, yeah. I'm a liar from way back.

"I gave you that box of croissants," Sam says, coming closer, "and it was like I'd given you a box of diamonds. You were so happy. So... bright." He stops inches from me and I tip my head back to maintain eye contact, looking at him from under the brim of my hat. "You hugged me."

"Did I?" I ask, shooting for nonchalance, as if I don't remember. As if a hug from me didn't matter.

Sam's having none of it, none of my games. None of my lies. Not now. "You hugged me. For the first time ever."

"We'd hugged before."

"No. I'd hugged you before. That night, *you* hugged *me*. You reached out to me, you touched me and...God, Hadley...I didn't want to let you go."

"But you did." I remember the moment exactly. I'd launched myself at him, knowing he'd catch me. "You let me go and you took Abby to dinner."

"I was freaking out. I had a girlfriend. And you were my best friend. I wasn't supposed to feel that way about you. I told myself that I didn't, that it'd been a fluke. But the whole night, the whole time I was with Abby, I wished I was with you and after I dropped her off..."

"You came back." But my words are barely a whisper of sound. I clear my throat. Raise my voice. "You came back to me."

"I had to know if it was real. I didn't want it to be."

I nod. "I know."

One more thing we share, the fear of losing what we had.

"When I got there, when you answered the door and saw it was me, you smiled. It's such a rare thing, your smile. It hit me" –he taps two fingers against the center of his chest— "here and I couldn't breathe. It was like my heart just stopped."

I know the feeling. I'm struggling to take in enough air right now, each inhale and exhale shallow and shaky. My heart pounding so hard I'm sure he can hear it.

That he knows it belongs to him and always has.

He lifts a shoulder. "That was when I realized it."

He doesn't have to finish. I know what his realization was. But I'm selfish enough to want to hear him say it. To want him to give me the words.

Even if I can't give them back.

"Realized what?" I ask.

"That I was in love with you," he says softly. "I didn't know when it happened—that moment when you smiled at me or weeks or months or years before. All I knew was that it was true. And you're right, there are no guarantees that we won't hurt each other again, but that doesn't mean we shouldn't try." He lifts my chin with his thumb and forefinger. "Give me a chance, Hadley. The one thing I can promise you is that I'm worth it."

I already know he's worth it. He's worth everything.

"I want to," I admit and my voice is hoarse. "I'm just... I'm no good at this."

"You're doing fine."

"I'm messing everything up. I get too caught up in the past, in our mistakes--"

"Fuck the past," he says, his rough tone at odds with how gently his thumb is moving over my jaw, the caress soft and warm. "Forget we were friends."

If only it were that easy. "Sam--"

"No more past. Whatever happened between us before this moment no longer exists. You and me? We start right now. We start something new."

No past means the choices we made during the last eleven months don't matter.

It means our mistakes are erased.

There's a warm, fluttery sensation in my chest. It fills me, lightens me, until I feel like I'm made of air, lifting off the ground.

Hope really does float.

"No past," I agree, covering his hand with mine.

There's freedom in that, in letting go of what's been. But I can't focus on what's to come, either. We have no control over the future. Fate runs that show.

What we have, all we have, is here and now.

And I want to make the most of it.

"You can kiss me."

I surprise us both. Sam draws in a quick breath, his fingers on my face tense and still.

I wait for one heartbeat. Then two. But he doesn't move.

Humiliation and disappointment wash over me. "In case you were wondering," I continue weakly, the Queen of Lame explaining herself. "If you could or not."

Angling his body over mine, Sam slides his hand down and around to cup the back of my neck, the pad of his thumb brushing under my jaw where my pulse races. "You wanted to take it slow."

I did. I definitely did.

And it's super fantastic that he's reminding me of that now.

"That was before we were starting new."

"So now that we're starting new, we don't have to go slow?"

I lick my lower lip and his gaze drops. Lingers on my mouth. "Just not as...as slow as we've been going."

"Hadley, do you want me to kiss you?" he asks and I shift closer, as if his gruff tone is a line, reeling me in.

"If *you* want to," I whisper.

It's a non-answer. One that takes control out of my hands. That will force him to make the choice for both of us.

"Tell me."

He's not going to make the choice.

He wants me to make it. To prove myself. My feelings.

But I can't. I can't tell him how I feel. What I want.

I'll have to show him.

Grabbing him by the front of his shirt, I yank him to me as I surge onto my toes. The brim of my hat jabs him hard on the nose and I cut off his "Oof" of surprise and pain by slamming my mouth against his.

My knees wobble, my calf muscles burn and I twist the T-shirt's material some more, fisting it in my hands to maintain leverage and balance. We stay that way, eyes open, mouths smashed together so hard I can feel his teeth behind his closed lips.

Worst. Kiss. Ever.

I fall back to my heels, stare at my hands still clutched around his shirt. "I told you I'm no good at this."

"We could try again," he says and I lift my head. He's touching the bridge of his nose, rubbing two fingertips over the spot I'd hit. One side of his mouth lifts. "If you want to."

He's teasing me, tossing my own words back at me, and I give him a small smile in response. Then I give him what I couldn't only a moment before.

The truth.

"I want to." Realizing I'm still holding his shirt, I force my fingers open. Smooth the wrinkles with my palms. "This would be easier if you weren't so tall."

He pulls the desk chair out and then sits, bare feet planted wide. "Better?"

With a nod, I sit on his lap for the first time ever. His left arm goes around my waist, his hand on my outer hip, his other hand on my knee. I start to lean forward when I remember my stupid hat.

I'm such an idiot, bringing up kissing when I'm still in my work clothes, a day's worth of sweat and sunscreen clinging to me. But I've come this far and I refuse to back down.

Must be some of Sam's stubbornness is rubbing off on me.

I straighten and Sam's arm around me tightens, keeping me close. I take off my hat, pull the band off my ponytail then put my hat back on backwards.

Not my best look, I'm sure, but the way Sam's looking at me, dark and intense, the way he's holding me, his fingers pressing into my hip, tell me he doesn't mind. I trace my fingertips over the red mark on his nose and he shuts his eyes on a soft exhale.

Then I finally kiss Sam Constable the way I've always dreamed. The way I was too afraid to kiss him last time. Long, slow, lingering kisses that have Sam pulling me closer, his right hand sliding higher on my leg, his left hand moving up to press against the middle of my back, turning me toward him.

I tilt my head and deepen the kiss, my tongue sweeping over his bottom lip then into his mouth when he opens for me, my hands delving into his hair, my nails lightly scraping against his scalp. Sam makes a sound in the back of his throat, the muscles of his legs tense under me, but he doesn't rush me. It's as if he's perfectly content to take whatever I'll give him. However much I'll give him.

Unlike our first kiss, there's no urgency. No worry about making the most of each moment because it would never, could never happen again. This time it's a slow, steady buzz that snakes its way through my system, warming my blood, drugging my senses until all I can feel are the spots where we touch. All I can think about is the next kiss. And the next.

Until the door opens and someone makes a gagging sound.

I jerk back, leaping to get off Sam, but it's too fast, too hard, and I almost fall flat on my butt. Sam's there to catch me, steadying me while I stand.

"You are so dead," Sam tells Charlie.

Charlie shrugs, not the least bit intimidated. "You told me to tell you when Mom's home." He chomps off a bite of orange popsicle. "She's home," he says around his mouthful.

"Shit," Sam mutters, glancing out into the hall as if expecting his mom to be there, ready to kill the both of us dead with one of her I'm-so-disappointed-in-you looks, and a long-winded, I-expected-so-much-more-of-you lecture.

Then she'd tell Sam's dad and his stepfather about it.

And Sam would be dead for real.

Or at least grounded for a month.

"You told me," Sam says, jerking his head toward the door. "Now beat it."

Charlie wipes the back of his hand across his mouth. "You owe me ten dollars."

Sam's eyes narrow. "I told you five."

"Five for telling you when Mom gets here," Charlie says with a grin so smug, so superior it's like looking at a shorter, rounder version of Max. Not good. Humanity can only handle one Max Constable among its ranks at a time. "And another five for *not* telling her that you had a girl in your room. Or what you were just doing."

Sam seems to consider this little blackmail routine. "Yeah. Okay," he says with a nod as he gets to his feet. "I'm definitely going to kill you."

Smugness gone, Charlie's eyes widen. He turns, but Sam's quicker and he takes a hold of Charlie by the ear and walks him out the door.

"Owowowowow," Charlie mutters, shoulders hunched. "That'll be fifteen dollars," he says, because while he may be cocky like Max, he's stubborn like Sam. "Five more for my pain and suffering."

Sam storms back into the room, grabs his wallet from the dresser and takes out a couple bills. Goes over and hands them to Charlie.

"Here's ten. If you get Mom out of the house for at least five minutes, I'll give you another ten. And if you get any ideas about telling her Hadley was in here, I'll have to tell her about that stash of magazines under your mattress."

Charlie goes red—neck, face, ears. Guess he's not hiding copies of *People* or *Entertainment Weekly*.

"Deal," Charlie says, taking the money and going to great lengths not to look my way. Thank God. No eye contact needed between us after hearing about his preferred reading material, thanks all the same.

Charlie walks away and Sam steps out into the hall. Holds out his hand to me.

I take it, without thought. Without hesitation.

And then I close the distance between us and I kiss him again, a soft, sweet kiss. Because I want to.

Because I can.

30

"You should come with me. It'll be fun."

Sitting on the floor of Whitney's bedroom, my back against her bed, I double-click a post on Instagram, then glance up from my phone. Whitney's at her vanity applying mascara in the classic eyes-wide, mouth-open, face-forward stance.

"No," I say. "I shouldn't."

But she's right about one thing, Tori's family's annual Fourth of July Extravaganza *is* fun. It's held at the lake house Tori's and Jackson's dads—they're brothers and run a construction company together—built for their families to share. Each year they throw a combined party for the Fourth and there's always live music, tons of food, games and activities, and a firework show at dusk.

Whitney sighs and caps the mascara. Meets my gaze in the mirror. "I just don't understand why you're being so stubborn about this."

I'm guessing she meant to come off strident and scolding, but that's tough to pull off when you look like a Disney princess and sound like a Southern belle.

Not intimidating. Not in the least.

As she would say: Bless her heart for trying.

"I'm not being stubborn. I wasn't invited."

I didn't make the guest list this year.

I knew I wouldn't.

But it still hurts, anyway.

Whitney waves my extremely valid excuse away then leans closer to the mirror, checking for any slight imperfections—of which there are none. I've yet to see her get so much as a pimple. It's unnatural. "Tori is not going to mind if you come along."

I stare at my phone, telling myself it's stupid to get my hopes up. To even wonder. The last time Tori invited me to do something with her was a month into the school year last fall when she asked if I wanted to go to that weekend's football game with her and Kenzie.

I told her I had to watch Taylor.

We haven't spoken since.

But still I ask, "Did she say that?"

"Hmm?" Whitney asks, turning this way, then that, checking the waterfall braids I'd given her.

They're perfect, too, if I do say so myself.

"Did...did Tori say she wouldn't mind?"

Whitney pauses and blinks. "Not in so many words..."

I was right. It was stupid to be hopeful. To wonder.

Stupider to be disappointed.

"You mean not in any words."

As I'd predicted, taking Whitney to Beemer's party that night resulted in Whitney making plenty of friends, foremost among them Tori, Kenzie, and...

Me.

Although that last one probably has more to do with me showing up on her doorstep that Saturday morning and spilling my guts about me and Sam. I figured us hanging out together that night was a one-time thing. Instead, we've become bona fide girlfriends complete with sleepovers and braiding each other's hair.

Crazy, I know. And unexpected. But that's life. Always with the unexpected. You just have to go with it.

And like so many girls before her, Whitney wants all her friends to be the best of friends, too.

Except I've been there. Done that.

Not interested in repeating that mistake.

Neither, it seems, are Tori and Kenzie.

Which is good.

Or so I keep telling myself.

"I could text Tori," Whitney says, hesitant and hopeful. "Ask her if you can come."

"No," I say again, this time firmly. The last thing I need is Tori thinking I asked Whitney to ask her if I can go to her family's party.

Talk about pathetic.

I'm feeling sorry enough for myself, thanks all the same. I don't need anyone else knowing how much I wanted Tori to invite me. How I feel like I'm missing out by not going.

How much I miss being friends with Tori and Kenzie.

But life is not only full of the unexpected, it's also stingy with the good things, doling them out piece by piece. Making sure to balance any high with an appropriate low so we don't fly too far, too fast.

I got Sam back, but Devyn's still mad at me for giving him a second chance.

Whitney and I are friends, but Tori and Kenzie still pretend I don't exist.

Piece by piece.

Highs and lows.

I stand when Whitney gets her bag from her neatly made bed. Tori's picking her up at ten and it's almost that time now and I'd really love to be tucked away inside my own trailer before she and Kenzie show up.

"Even if I had been invited," I say as we step into the hall, "I couldn't go. We're doing the family thing today."

It doesn't happen often, mainly because one, two or all three of us are usually working, but today's special.

Like a Fourth of July miracle.

"I thought Devyn had to work tonight," Whitney says.

We stop by her front door and I slip on my flip-flops. "Not until later." Which, in this case, means seven p.m. "We're having a cookout this afternoon."

Hot dogs, potato salad, chips, soda and the blueberry pie I made. Not exactly the variety of food the Vecellios will have at their party, but it'll still be festive.

And after we eat, Dev will go to work at the hotel, and Zoe and Taylor will meet Carrie and her daughter so they can watch the fireworks the country club puts on every year.

Zoe invited me to join them, but I'd feel like a third wheel, so I told her I'd rather stay home.

On the porch, Whitney makes sure the front door is locked before we head down the stairs. Her mom left an hour ago to work a 5K race at the YMCA, but she's meeting Whitney at the lake this afternoon.

"I don't have to go to Tori's," Whitney says, and while I know she's being nice, it only makes me feel even more pitiful.

"Uh, yes, you do. She'll literally be here any minute."

"Well, Mom and I could come home early, before the fireworks. I'm sure Tori and her family will understand."

"I'm fine." It's the same thing I told Sam when he offered to skip his family's trip to his grandmother's in Rochester. Not that his mom and Patrick would have let him miss it, but he has a tendency to hope for the best despite the odds against him. "Besides, that outfit would be wasted at my house."

She'd gone the patriotic route in a light blue strapless maxi dress, thin red belt and white sandals. Plus, it's already hot, the sun beating down from a cloudless sky. A perfect day to spend at the lake.

"But it's Independence Day," she says. "You shouldn't be alone."

I open my mouth to tell her I *like* being home alone, that it doesn't happen very often and I won't be the least bit lonely. But ever since that truth session in Sam's bedroom last week, I'm trying not to lie as much.

It's harder than it looks.

"It'll give me a chance to try my hand at croissants," I say.

Which isn't a lie at all. I've been wanting to make croissants for months.

I already have the dough chilling in the fridge, along with the butter I'd flattened out into a thin rectangle that I'll use to laminate it, which should, hopefully, result in a nice rise and tons of flaky layers.

"I'm sure it'll be nice for you," she says, accepting defeat the way she goes through life—gracefully, "not having to entertain Taylor while you're baking. Or staying up until two a.m. to do so."

"Nice? I dream of times like this. I might even make a cake."

I've had the idea for it ever since Sam and I got ice cream—our first official date.

Funny how easy it is for me to call it that now, two weeks after it happened.

Funnier still how easy it was, going from *just friends* to *more than friends*. Makes it hard to remember why I'd resisted the idea for so long.

"A chocolate cake," I continue, "three layers, with peanut butter filling and a marshmallow frosting. Oh! Or maybe marshmallow filling and peanut butter frosting. Or one of each."

I'm picturing them both now—the marshmallow frosting all sticky and peaked, the peanut butter frosting thick and creamy—and doing a mental review of my baking supplies when I realize Whitney is smiling at me.

"What?" I ask.

"Nothing." But she's looking at me like an indulgent mother. "It's just you're the only person I know who gets so passionate about cake."

I roll my eyes. "Please. Everyone loves cake. Except psychos."

"Actually, a dislike of cake isn't listed on the Psychopathy Checklist."

Spoken like the daughter of a psychologist.

Yes, her mother is an English teacher and her father—who she does *not* like to discuss...at all—is a professor of psychology.

It's a wonder she's turned out so normal.

"Not liking dessert, cake in particular, should absolutely be on that checklist," I say as I walk backward across the empty street. "Hey, you could do an experiment at the extravaganza. See which people avoid the dessert table and note their personality traits. I bet they all have similar antisocial views, hate kittens and pop little kids' balloons when they're not looking."

Even from across the street, I can see the epic eye roll she gives me. "You have antisocial views. And you love dessert."

Both true. Though now that I have Sam back in my life and have hung out with Whitney several times, I've been extremely social.

At least with the two of them.

I spot Tori's car at the stop sign a block away and start walking backward again, this time up my driveway. "I'm the thing that's not like the other things. The special snowflake."

"All snowflakes are special," she points out as Tori pulls to a stop in front of her. "You're the outlier."

Then she gives me a cheery wave, opens the rear driver's-side door and climbs into the backseat.

And even though I should walk away, even though it's dumb and useless, I stand there for a moment, the sun warming the top of my head, watching them, three pretty, shiny girls talking and laughing. I stand there, waiting for some sort of acknowledgement from Tori or Kenzie. A smile or wave.

Hoping I'll get that invitation after all.

I stand there, in my sleep shorts and ratty T-shirt, my hair in a messy bun, my throat tight as Tori takes off down the road like a shot.

Neither she nor Kenzie even glanced my way.

I stand there for one minute. Then two. Watching long after they're gone, waiting for something that's never going to happen, Whitney's words replaying in my head.

You're the outlier.

Yes, that's me.

On the outside looking in.

31

SAM AND I MAKE OUR OFFICIAL DEBUT AS A LEGITIMATE, HONEST-TO-God, yes-we-are-together-as-in-*together*-together couple a week after the Fourth at Danielle Webster's party.

We've once again arrived at a party together, and this time, we're holding hands. The looks start first, fleeting, could-not-care-less glances from most of them, outright stares of disbelief from a few and a pointed *oh, no he didn't* glare from Macy Fitzsimmons, Abby's best friend.

The truth is out.

Sam and Hadley, Hadley and Sam has taken on a whole new meaning.

"Want something to drink?" Sam asks me.

I nod and we head toward the refrigerator in the corner of the two-stall garage. It's twenty feet away but it takes us a good five minutes to get there, what with Sam being stopped and greeted— girls with hugs, guys with back slaps and playful punches to the arm. A curvy blond freshman presses up against his free side to give him a giggling hello. He gently disentangles himself from her and we continue on, Sam the belle of the ball.

And me. A trailer-park Cinderella.

Minus the fancy dress, impractical shoes, and fairy godmother.

I now get why Cinderella keeps those mice around. Gives her someone to talk to while her prince is being flirted with, hailed and chatted to and otherwise charming an entire room.

When we reach the fridge, Sam lets go of my hand and opens the door. Grabs a can of Coke, pops the top and gives it to me. He then gets a bottle of water, twists off the cap and takes a sip.

Then reaches for my hand once more.

As if he hated letting go for even a few moments. As if he wants to make it crystal clear to everyone here that we're together.

I link my fingers with his and step closer to his side.

Guess I want to make it clear, too.

But as we stand there, Sam talking with Bobby Piccoli, who just graduated and is attending Temple University in the fall, I start to wonder if that's such a great idea.

For three weeks it's been our little secret.

And now we're letting the world in on it. Giving others the chance to comment on us being together. Question whether it's a good idea.

I would've been happy putting this moment off for a bit longer, but this afternoon when Sam suggested we do something that involves leaving my trailer and hanging out with people other than my two-year-old niece, well, I couldn't tell him no.

Ever since that day at Sam's when we played basketball with Charlie then kissed in Sam's room, we've kept a low profile.

As in so low some would call it underground.

Whitney's the only person who knows. After spilling my guts to her that morning on her porch, it seemed pointless to keep Sam and me being together a secret.

Plus, she lives across the street. I'm sure she's seen him at my house.

He comes over during the week after work, stays until eleven or so. Saturdays he's there most of the day and he stops by on Sundays for a few hours between church and dinner with his family. We play with Taylor until she goes to bed, then we watch TV.

And on the nights when both Devyn and Zoe are working, we skip the TV and spend the rest of our time in my room, touching and kissing until we reach the point where we have to stop or go all the way.

We always stop.

Well, to be technical, I always stop him.

Just because we're no longer taking things at a snail's pace doesn't mean we should rush into that next step. I've always rushed before and it's never worked how I wanted it to.

I have it all figured out. We'll continue how we are, and in a few months, if we're still together and if things are still going well between us, then we'll have sex. There's no hurry. It's not like the attraction between is us going to disappear anytime soon.

As if reading my thoughts—or getting a whiff of some rebellious pheromones I'm releasing—Sam rubs the pad of his thumb against the back of my hand. Then, still talking to Bobby, he tugs me even closer, plastering me against his side.

I've got it so bad for this boy.

I slip my hand from his so I can wrap my arm around his waist. Slide my hand between his shirt and jeans so I can feel the warmth of his skin. Yeah. Stopping is getting harder and harder to do.

If I can hold out against Sam—against his kisses and touches and the things he says to me in the dark, the way he makes me feel—for another few weeks, it'll be a freaking miracle.

I'm not much on the whole willpower thing.

I'm more of a do-it-then-deal-with-the-consequences-later kind of girl.

Ha. Look how well that's worked out for me.

After finishing his conversation with Bobby, Sam once again takes my hand and we make our way through the party. I'd forgotten what being with Sam was like. He makes the rounds, goes from group to group, smiling and chatting with one and all.

About an hour in, I leave Sam's side for the first time and head into the house to use the bathroom. It's pretty much all the same people who were at Beemer's a few weeks ago. Still, it's not like I'm a part of them just because Sam and I are together.

I wish Whitney was here. At least then I'd have someone else to talk to. But she went out with her mom and her mom's friend to celebrate Mrs. McCormack's birthday.

I hope she likes the carrot cake I helped Whitney bake for her.

And I really, really hope Whitney saves me a piece. Or two.

I've been to a few parties here so I don't have to ask where the bathroom is. In the living room, I skirt around a couple making out and head down the hall then stop a few feet from the bathroom door. There's a line.

And it consists of Kenzie and Tori, both leaning against opposite sides of the wall, looking at their phones.

I start to turn, but they raise their heads in unison, look at me then exchange a glance that speaks volumes. At least to each other.

Best friends and their secret language. Very cute.

But they've seen me and they know I've seen them so...yeah.

More awkwardness in my immediate future.

Resigned to my fate, I head down the hall and take my place in line next to Kenzie.

It's silent. And as awkward as I predicted.

What I hadn't predicted was how I'd feel. You'd have thought I'd be used to them ignoring me as if we hadn't been friends for years. As if we hadn't texted each other every day, talked to each other in between classes at school and hung out together on weekends, attending parties like this together and, yes, taking group trips to the bathroom.

The three of us.

But, nope, not used to it.

"You and Sam, huh?"

I lean forward to look around Kenzie at Tori and ask, "Are you talking to me?"

"Who else would I be talking to?"

Considering she hasn't said more than two words to me in almost a year, I wasn't sure.

My initial reaction to her question is to deny it, but that's just habit, learned from many, many years of deflecting questions, of brushing aside comments. Of lying over and over again.

Sam and I are just friends.

Instead I take a deep breath. "Yes. Me and Sam."

It feels good, to say it out loud. To not pretend.

It feels so very, very good.

Kenzie holds out her hand. "I win," she tells Tori.

"I realize that," Tori grumbles, digging into her purse. She pulls out a twenty and slaps it onto Kenzie's palm.

Kenzie's small smile is smug, which only makes her look more adorable. It's like a curse, her cuteness. "Meant to be," she says in a singsong tone. "Didn't I say it?"

Tori rolls her eyes, but she's fighting a smile. She's tough as nails, that girl, but she adores her BFF. "You did."

Holding the money against her chest, Kenzie leans against the wall. "I love being right."

"You bet on whether or not Sam and I would get together?" I ask.

Kenzie shakes her head. "Of course not."

"Then what's with the *I win* and the money?"

"We bet on *when* you and Sam would get together. Not if. I said it would be before the end of July. Tori thought it'd take at least until Thanksgiving for him to convince you to take him back."

They didn't know. Had no idea Sam and I have been together for almost a month.

Whitney never told them.

"I didn't take him back. I mean, we weren't together before."

"You broke up," Tori says, not believing this not-friends version of Sam and Hadley is a recent development. "Sam left town and you ditched anyone and everyone connected to him." She shrugs. "Sounds like a breakup to me."

My breath clogs in my chest and I have to force myself to inhale. Exhale. "I...I didn't ditch anyone."

Tori snorts. "Please. You stopped responding to our texts. You didn't answer our calls. And if we did happen to be in the same vicinity, you refused to make eye contact. You made it perfectly clear that the only reason you hung out with us in the first place was because of Sam, and since he was out of your life, so were we."

"You were Sam's friends first." It's a weak excuse, but it's all I have. "You only hung out with me because of him."

The bathroom door opens and a girl who graduated last year steps out, gives the three of us a curious glance then goes on her way.

When we're alone again, Kenzie pushes away from the wall. "You're right. We were Sam's friends first. But we were your friends, too. At least, we thought we were." She lifts her chin, and though her tone is steady, it's also soft. Sad. "Guess you thought differently."

Brushing past Tori, she goes into the bathroom. Tori follows her but turns back to me, one hand on the doorjamb, her hip cocked to the side. "Now that you and Sam are a couple, we'll probably be seeing a lot more of each other, but don't feel like you have to pretend to like us again. We all know where we stand."

Before I can tell her I never pretended, she shuts the door in my face.

32

My heart is pounding and there's a sick taste in my mouth.

A taste very much like guilt, mixed with a big dollop of regret.

I want to knock on the door, apologize for how I treated them, but it probably won't make a difference. And I'm really not in the mood for one of Tori's putdowns. Don't think I can handle Kenzie's rejection.

No. The best thing to do is just let it go. Let them go.

Like I did last summer.

There's too much water under the bridge. Too much time has passed. An apology won't change anything.

I head toward the kitchen, head down, so I don't make accidental eye contact with anyone. I'm so over this party, so done with these people. I just want to go home.

But first, I want to find a bathroom.

I go upstairs and glance into the first room I come to. Do a double take then freeze. It's a bedroom done up in purple and white—purple and white polka dots on the curtains, wide, purple and white stripes on one wall and a purple and white quilt complete with ruffles covering the single bed.

Oh, there's one more thing on the bed, one extremely out-of-place thing.

Sam.

And a sobbing Abby.

Oops. Guess that's two things.

But hey, with the way they're sitting—Sam's arm wrapped around Abby's shoulders, Abby's head pressed against the side of his chest—you could say they're a single unit.

I can't help but think the entire conversation with Kenzie and Tori, and now this sucky discovery, never would have happened if only I'd stayed next to Sam.

Tonight's lesson? Stay glued to the boy's side. At least when any ex-friends and especially any ex-girlfriends are present.

I step into the room but Sam and Abby are so wrapped up in whatever they're whispering about, and extremely wrapped up in each other, they don't notice.

"Sam."

They both startle and look up. Abby leaps to her feet and takes a step as if to rush out on a wave of tears and heartbreak but Sam—you know, my boyfriend—grabs her hand, stopping her. Then he glances at me, holds up a finger in the universal just-a-minute sign.

And leans down and says something in Abby's ear I can't hear.

My eyes narrow. Seriously? Did the boy really just tell me to wait so he can whisper in his ex-girlfriend's ear?

What the hell?

I cross my arms and watch the mini drama play out. Whatever Sam said to Abby makes her shake her head. Still holding her hand, he speaks again, his expression one of concern and sympathy. She hiccups softly then sniffs. Finally, she nods and he lets go of her. She sits back on the bed, her face turned away from me.

Sam heads my way.

And ushers me out into the hallway, where he shuts the door behind him then blocks it. Keeping Abby safe from my presence.

I repeat: What. The. Hell?

"What's up?" Sam asks me, sort of impatient. As if I interrupted something important. Something he'd like to get back to as quickly as possible.

"I just caught you hugging your ex-girlfriend," I snap. "Maybe you should be the one telling me *what's up*?"

He frowns. "You didn't *catch me* doing anything. The door was wide open and all the lights are on. It's not like we were in a dark, locked room. And I wasn't hugging her. Not like you're making it sound."

"Oh, no. You don't get to act insulted here. I'm the one who left your side for five minutes only to find you snuggled up with another girl."

"I already told you, it wasn't like that."

"No? Then what was it like?"

He stabs a hand through his hair. Yes. Poor baby, it's so hard to deal with your unreasonable, overly dramatic girlfriend and her silly accusations. "She's drunk. And upset."

"Upset about what?"

Taking me by the elbow, he tugs me to the other side of the hall, keeps his voice low. "About you and me."

"You two broke up a long time ago."

"I know. I guess she thought..."

He trails off, looking uncomfortable. Embarrassed.

Caught.

My eyes narrow. "You guess she thought what?"

He flashes me an apologetic look. "That she and I would get back together."

"Have you been talking to her? Recently, I mean."

"No! I mean, yeah, she texts me sometimes--"

"Sometimes? Like once a month? Once a week?"

"A few times a week."

"Your ex-girlfriend texts you a few times a week," I repeat, trying to understand this truth. To accept it. "Do you respond?"

He flushes. Guilty as charged. "It doesn't mean anything."

"Maybe not to you. But to Abby? I bet it means a lot. Like that you still like her. Like there's a chance you want to get back together."

"I don't," he says, reaching for me. I step back but this is Sam and he keeps coming, not stopping until he's set his hands on my shoulders, his head ducked so he can meet my eyes. "I love you, Hadley. You know that."

I do know that. I do. But it's so much easier to believe when it's just the two of us. The past three weeks, we've been insulated from everyone and everything, happy and content in our own little world. A world where there are no ex-girlfriends. No fights. No past. Just us and the hope that being together isn't a mistake. That this whole thing isn't going to blow up in our faces.

That's the world I prefer. Sure, it's all fantasy, but I can live with that.

"I want to go home."

He hangs his head, a poor, defenseless boy beaten down by his mean old girlfriend's jealousy and harsh demands. "Yeah, okay. Give me five minutes to talk to Ab--"

"I want to go now. Right now."

"I can't leave her alone," he says, giving me a disappointed look, as if I'd suggested he toss a whimpering puppy out a third-story window. "Hadley, she's *crying*."

"A few tears never hurt anyone."

I know that better than anyone. I'd cried, too, when Sam left me. I'd survived.

"If you're that worried about her," I continue, "go find Macy."

"I will," he assures me quickly. "But I really think I should talk to Abby first. Explain things."

"Things?"

"Yeah. How I didn't mean to give her the wrong impression and that I'm with you now." He lowers his voice. "How I want to be with you."

"She'll get all of that by you taking me home."

"I can't leave her like that," he says, gesturing to the room. "Just give me five minutes. Please. Then we'll go."

And Sam Constable always does what he says he'll do.

Because that's the kind of guy he is. The kind who tells the truth.

Who's always there with a shoulder to cry on. Who's kind to everyone. Who always does the right thing.

I shouldn't be surprised he wants to make things right with Abby. That he wants to help her get through her heartbreak—pain he caused, whether knowingly or not.

I shouldn't be surprised, but I am.

I'd gotten too complacent. Had been lulled into a false sense of security. Things between me and Sam had been going really well ever since our kiss in his bedroom. Too well.

I should have known it was only a matter of time before reality came knocking.

Nothing that good lasts forever.

"Whatever," I grumble. "I'll wait in the car. But if you're not out there in five minutes, I'm finding another ride home."

As threats go, it's not a very strong one considering these are Sam's friends and none of them would ever give me a ride, especially if they knew we were fighting.

Also there's the little fact that I'd never ask any of them to.

Still, I make what I feel is a very dramatic exit...you know...chin lifted and righteous indignation in the set of my shoulders. It's not until I'm downstairs, have gone through the living room and am standing on the front porch that I realize it was all for nothing.

I didn't ask Sam for his keys and Sam always locks his car doors.

Waiting for him in the SUV is out. And I'm sure not going to wait inside surrounded by all those people. I could stand in the driveway until he comes out or, better yet, start walking home. Except it's raining. And dark.

Chewing my lower lip, I look at the house. Maybe going back inside isn't such a bad option. After all, it's brightly lit, warm and dry.

And filled with people.

People like my boyfriend, who is currently cuddled up with his ex in the purplest of all purple bedrooms.

I turn back again, walk to the stairs leading to the driveway. The wind picks up, blows rain onto my arms and face.

"What's it going to be, Hot Hadley?"

At the soft, deep voice, I whirl around, my heart in my throat. Great. I'm not alone. Stepping toward the far corner of the porch, I see a dark figure sitting on the porch swing.

My stomach does a loop, like I'm on a roller coaster. "What?"

"What it's going to be?" Max repeats. "You staying? Or going?"

Going. Definitely. I can't stay. Not with him.

It's like Fate is telling me to go back inside. To wait for Sam in some quiet corner like a good little girlfriend. One who's just so darn grateful to be with him that she lets him do whatever he wants and doesn't complain.

Even when he sits on a bed with his arm around his drunk ex-girlfriend, who he's been texting on the sly for only God knows how long.

I stalk toward Max. "Staying," I tell him, like I'm accepting a dare he's issued.

Which, let's be honest, he sort of has.

He's sitting in the middle of the bench seat, feet planted wide, legs spread, one hand holding a plastic cup, the other arm stretched out along the back of the seat.

The Constable brothers. Always taking up more than their fair share of space.

"You going to move over?"

"Plenty of room right here," he says, patting his thigh.

I kick the side of his foot.

Hard.

"Ow." He slides to his left. "No need to get violent."

I sit down and Max once again settles his arm along the back.

Then starts playing with my hair.

I slap his hand away. "I'm not in the mood for you, Max."

"And yet, here you are, sitting with me in the dark." He leans toward me, his voice dropping to a husky, seductive tone. "Bet I could put you in the mood."

I jump to my feet, setting the swing into motion, but before I can walk away, Max catches my wrist.

"Aw, come on. I'm just messing with you." He tugs gently. "Sit down. I'll behave. Promise."

Unlike Sam, Max's promises don't mean much.

I sit anyway. It's reluctant, and as soon as I do, I scoot as far away from Max as I can get and cross my arms. But still, I sit.

Because I am a glutton for punishment.

Or maybe just a complete idiot.

Max takes a drink then slouches, reclining against the hard seat. "What has you hiding out on the porch, Hot Hadley? Party not up to your usual high standards?"

"Just needed some air," I say. "What about you? No freshman girls inside to practice your pickup lines on? No buddies from high school to reminisce about the good old days?"

"Oh, there are plenty of girls for me to practice all sorts of things on." He meets my eyes. "As you well know."

My face goes hot. Yep. Staying was definitely a mistake.

Walking home doesn't seem like such a bad idea after all.

I've had more than enough of the Constable brothers tonight.

"You don't always have to be such a dick, you know."

"But I do. We all have our parts to play. I'm just better at playing mine than most. Sam's the golden one and I'm the fuck-up." He shrugs and gives me a grin. "And more often than not, that means being a dick."

He drains his drink. There's something off about that smile, something not right in his tone. Something that puts me on edge. Makes me nervous.

Makes me realize what a very bad idea this is, being with him.

I shift, suddenly uncomfortable. Wary of this boy I've known for years. Certain I should have waited for Sam inside.

"No one expects you to play the part of an asshole," I say.

He makes a tsking sound. "But I'm so good at it. You wouldn't want to take that away from me, would you?"

What I want to take away from him is his drink. But that's not my job. I'm not his girlfriend. I'm not even his friend. The only thing we have in common is Sam—who, of course, chooses that moment to join us.

So glad he could tear himself away from Abby's tears and heartache just in time to find me sitting in the dark with his brother.

Sam's gaze shoots from me to Max and back to me. Huh. That must have been my expression when I saw him on the bed with Abby: Surprised. Suspicious. Angry.

I liked it a lot better when I was giving that look, not receiving it.

"Sammy!" Max calls as if they don't live in the same house, have bedrooms next to each other and share a bathroom. "Come on." He slides over next to me—as in super close to me, our hips pressed together—and pats the now-empty space on his other side. "Join us."

Sam steps toward us, all stiff and robotic. Gives his brother the flint eye—either because Max is draining his drink or because he's put his arm around my shoulders. Nods at Max's cup. "You sure that's a good idea?"

"What? This?" Max holds the empty cup upside down. A drop lands on my thigh just below the hem of my shorts and I brush it away. Hard to believe he missed even that much. "Yeah, it's no problem. I came prepared."

He reaches across me, pressing against me as much as he can, and picks up another cup from a small side table, this one full and, I'm guessing from the smell, Coke and whiskey and not the beer everyone else inside is drinking. Then he takes his good old time easing back.

He lifts the cup in a mock toast. "See? It's all good."

Sam's mouth thins, and when he speaks, his lips barely move. "I meant do you think getting drunk is a good idea."

"Always, little brother. Always."

Sam's expression gets even more fierce. "Your flight leaves in nine hours."

"I'd better not waste any more time, then." He drains the cup in several long gulps.

"Where are you going?" I ask Max.

"You didn't tell her?" Max shakes his head at Sam. "Shame on you, Sammy boy. Always tell your girlfriend everything. No secrets and all that when it comes to true love, right?"

I tense, that sick taste back in my mouth, threatening to spill out.

"He's going to our dad's," Sam tells me.

"Mandatory annual summer visit," Max says and his attitude, and the heavy-even-for-him drinking, become crystal clear.

Max and his dad do not get along.

"Sammy gets to skip it," Max continues, "because he lived with the bastard last year. So it'll just be me and Pops for an entire month. Plenty of time for father-son bonding. Though I doubt we'll ever have that special relationship he and Sam have." Max nudges me, leans toward me to say in a loud whisper, "Sam's the old man's pride and joy."

Sam's the golden one and I'm the fuck-up.

For the first time in my life, I feel bad for Max.

It must be hard always being compared to the perfection that is Sam Constable. Especially when that perfect boy also happens to be your younger brother.

"Give me your keys," Sam tells Max.

Max smirks. "I won't drive."

Sam just holds out his hand. "Give them to me."

They stare at each other, a real, honest-to-god, Constable Brother stare down that seems to go on forever.

One of the few things they have in common is stubbornness.

Finally, Max gives another shrug and, holding his cup in his mouth, reaches his free hand into his front pocket, pulls out his keys and throws them at Sam, who catches them before they hit him on the nose.

Sam turns to me. "Had?" he asks in a low, rough tone. "You ready to go?"

Max takes his arm from around my shoulders to grab my hand. "You don't have to go with him," he says, an unreadable intention in his eyes. That's the thing with Max. You never know what's real. "You can stay here, continue our conversation. Sam's such a good brother, I'm sure he won't mind sharing you with me."

Oh, God.

I have no idea what game he's playing, but I have no intention of joining his team.

And there's no doubt in my mind that Max is playing at something. He doesn't do anything without a reason. One that benefits him.

Sam's shoulders are rigid, his hands fisted at his sides. And Max is loving every moment of messing with his brother.

Torturing me is just a by-product.

Brothers are so freaking weird, always giving each other a hard time, competing over everything.

But in this, there is no competition. Just as there's no question of who I'd rather be with.

I yank free of Max's hold and step closer to Sam. Take his hand.

I pick Sam.

Always.

I just hope that no matter what happens, Sam believes that.

33

NEITHER SAM NOR I SPEAK THE ENTIRE DRIVE TO MY HOUSE.

It's a tension-filled, nerve-wracking ten minutes.

I wish it could last forever.

"What the hell was that all about?" Sam asks the moment he pulls to a stop in my driveway.

And here we go.

"What was what about?" I shoot for nonchalant and innocent, as if I have no idea what he's referring to. Maybe if I play dumb, we can avoid this entire conversation altogether.

A girl can dream.

"Back there." He jerks a thumb in the direction we came from. "That...thing...with you and Max."

A girl can dream, but for girls like me, those dreams never come true.

"There is no *thing* with me and Max."

Sam glances at me but keeps his hands on the steering wheel. "You were sitting with him. In the dark."

"I was waiting for *you*. He just happened to be there."

"You could have waited inside."

"I didn't want to wait inside. I wanted to go home. But you couldn't tear yourself away from Abby--"

"I told you," he grinds out, his hands moving back and forth as if strangling the steering wheel, "she was drunk. And upset."

"Yeah? Well, so was your brother."

Now he stills. "Did he tell you that?"

"Yes. Max and I had a deep, honest, heart-to-heart conversation. He really opened up to me, told me all of his secrets and hopes and dreams and wasn't a jerk once."

Sam sighs, frustrated and impatient with me or Max or maybe his life in general at the moment. "He's just being an ass because he doesn't want to go to Dad's. He probably wanted you to feel sorry for him."

"He's spending a month in LA. Hardly a reason for me to pity him."

Except, I sort of do. Their dad is a complete tool.

And Sam really is his favorite.

Sam's the golden one and I'm the fuck-up.

No, it can't be easy being Sam Constable's brother.

"He had his arm around you." Sam stops trying to murder the steering wheel and unbuckles, then turns to face me fully. "Why did you let him put his arm around you?"

"First of all, I didn't *let* him do anything..."

"You sure as hell didn't stop him."

True. I didn't push him away like I had earlier, before Sam arrived.

Just like Sam hadn't pushed Abby away. Knowing Sam, he was probably the one who initiated their hug.

The only thing he loves more than being the good guy is playing the hero, swooping in to make things right.

"Max put his arm around me. Probably because he knew it would bug you. It's not like you walked in on us...oh, I don't know... embracing on a bed or something."

"Jesus, do we have to go through this again? She. Was. Up. Set. What was I supposed to do?"

"You were supposed to find someone else to babysit her," I cry, unbuckling my own seatbelt with jerky motions. "You were supposed to take me home when I wanted to go. And you sure weren't supposed to be texting her all this time."

"I don't text her. She texts me."

"Oh, well, that makes it all okay. So, if a guy texts me, I can text him back and you won't get mad. Good to know."

"That's not what I said," he mutters darkly.

"No? You mean, you don't want other guys texting me?"

"You know I don't."

"And I don't want other girls texting you!"

Sam tips his head down as if praying for guidance or patience or maybe just a miracle that'll make his silly, harpy girlfriend see reason. "I was just being nice. She's going through a hard time--"

"What sort of hard time?" I ask, because I am a suspicious person like that.

I know how people work, how they'll twist things to their advantage, say whatever they have to in order to get what they want.

Tell lie after lie to protect themselves, to hold on to the good things in their life.

"I can't tell you that," he says.

"You're sharing secrets with her?"

"Not sharing secrets." But he's hedging. Forthright, honest, Boy Scout Sam Constable is hedging over telling me what he and another girl chat about. "Just...keeping one of hers."

My throat is so tight I have to clear it twice before I can speak again. "How long?"

"What?"

"How long have you been keeping Abby's secrets? How long has she been texting you?"

"It doesn't mat--"

"A few weeks?" I ask and he presses his lips together. "Since you've been back?" He still doesn't answer and my mouth dries. "Did you talk to her while you were gone? When you were at your dad's?" He remains silent. "Sam?"

"Yeah," he says after a long moment. "We talked a few times when I was gone."

"A few times," I repeat on a hoarse whisper. "You...you talked to Abby a few times while you were gone." I straighten, shoulders rigid. "You talked to her, you texted her. God, you...you saw her over Christmas break, had her at your house, and when I came over..."

When I came over, he was cold. Unforgiving.

And crueler than I'd ever thought he had the capacity to be.

But I can't think about that now, not when my emotions are so messed up. Can't take the chance of a truth about that night coming out.

"You talked to her," I say again, "but you wouldn't talk to me."

It's too much. Too painful, remembering how he'd ignored me. Remembering how his walking out of my life had so completely destroyed me.

"No more past," Sam says. "Remember? We agreed the past doesn't matter. That we'd focus on the here and now."

"You mean the here and now where you chose staying with your ex-girlfriend over taking me home? Where you're texting her? Keeping her secrets and giving her your big, strong shoulder to cry on whenever she needs it? That here and now?"

His brows lower. His mouth turns downs at the sides. "It's not like you're making it sound. She just needs someone to talk to, that's all."

"If that was all, she wouldn't have thought there was a chance of you two getting back together."

"I told her I was with you."

"Did you tell her to stop texting you?"

He doesn't answer.

Which is answer enough.

I blink but it does nothing to erase the red haze covering my vision. "Are you kidding me?"

He takes my hand. "I couldn't tell her tonight," he says as if I'm an idiot for even suggesting such a thing. "But I will. I promise."

Another promise. One he'll keep because he's true-blue and honest.

As most heroes are.

But it doesn't matter if he's a freaking saint, Superman and Ghandi all rolled into one, because for the first time ever, I don't believe him.

For the first time ever, I don't believe *in* him.

I tug free and bend over to grab my purse from the floor. "You know what? Talk to her as often as you want. Keep all her secrets and cozy up to her as much as your heart desires. I don't even care."

With that whopper of a lie hanging in the air between us, I open the door and hop out. Hear his soft, vicious curse right before I slam the door shut.

I stomp up the sidewalk through the misting rain, so intent on my goal—which is more get away from Sam than actually get into the house—that I reach the top of the porch steps before he catches up. He once again takes a hold of my hand and I stop, all stiff and unyielding and not willing to give him an inch.

He doesn't deserve one.

"I'll talk to her," he tells me again, but I'm too angry to even look at him. "I swear I'll tell her tonight. As soon as I get back in the car to leave."

He sounds so sincere, is standing so close, I can't help but bend. A little. Just enough to meet his eyes. "You told her we were together?"

I hate how I sound, unsure and needy and jealous. Hate feeling those things even more.

"I told her I was with you." He leans down, speaks close to my ear, his breath brushing my neck. "I told her you're the only girl I want to be with."

I shiver as a thrill shoots through me, the warmth of his words defusing my temper. Being the only girl Sam wants is intoxicating and exciting and scary all at once. It's a huge responsibility, living up to his view of me. Being worthy of him.

I'm not. But I want to be.

"I'm sorry I didn't get up when Max put his arm around me," I say. "I should have."

"I shouldn't have gone into that room with Abby. I should have taken you home when you wanted to go." He searches my face in the dim glow of the porch light. "Hadley?" he asks, quiet and gruff and nervous. "Are we..." He stops. Inhales. "Are we okay?"

Once again it's up to me to define what Sam and I are to each other. Friends or not friends. Together or not together.

It's up to me whether to continue this new version of Sam and Hadley or end it before it's too late.

I give an inner eye roll. That's hilarious. Me thinking I actually have a choice.

When it comes to Sam and my feelings for him, there is no choice. There never has been.

Too bad. A girl should have more control over her life. Over her feelings. Should be more careful with her heart.

But if I had more control, I wouldn't have Sam.

And now that I do, I'm not willing to let him go.

"We're okay," I say, and even though it comes out grudgingly, even though there's still some anger and more than a little doubt in my tone, Sam smiles, relieved.

Guess I'm not the only one willing to take whatever I can get.

Like I said, there's never been a choice. For either of us.

34

TIME HEALS ALL WOUNDS.

That's what they say, anyway.

But four months after Sam left, I still thought of him every day. There was a hole in my life without him. Without Sam, nothing was right.

I missed him.

I missed him so much it was a constant ache, like a never-ending hunger—gnawing and relentless. I'd made a mistake in letting him go. In not telling him about my feelings for him.

And on Christmas night, I decided to change that. To fix things between us.

For the first time, I was going to go after what I wanted.

I'd been so proud of myself. So certain I was doing the right thing.

I thought Sam would be thrilled I wanted to be with him. That I was willing to take a chance on us.

I thought going there would fix everything between us.

Instead, it made everything worse.

I was halfway up Sam's driveway when it started snowing. Big, fat flakes floated from the sky, drifting in the breeze to cover the pavement. Sparkling like diamonds in the soft glow of the security lights on the upper corners of the garage and the matching sconces on either side of the front door.

It was pretty. Like a Christmas card. The beautiful house on the hill, with its yard covered in white, overlooking the quaint town below, the buildings and houses lit up with twinkling holiday lights. I stopped and stood there in the middle of the driveway, eyes shut, breath coming out in puffy clouds, and took it all in. Just absorbed it, tried to let it soak into my skin, seep into my bones. Hoped the stillness and quiet would soothe my nerves.

It might have worked, too.

If I hadn't been freezing my butt off.

Stillness and quiet would have to wait.

Shoving my gloved hands into the pockets of my coat, I ducked my head against that pretty snow, hunched my shoulders against the breeze and continued toward Sam's house. White lights outlined the roof and porch and electric candles flickered softly in every window.

I walked up to the porch and rang the doorbell. Stared at the huge evergreen wreath, complete with shiny, red bow, hanging on the front door while I waited.

And waited.

I pushed the doorbell again, held my finger against it, when the door finally opened and there he was. Sam, so darkly handsome and big and broad and good. Forget the stillness and quiet, it was Sam I wanted to soak in. Seeing him again had everything settling inside of me. Had my doubts and fears disappearing. It may have taken me some time, but I finally got it right.

Sam and I belonged together.

"Hadley," Sam said, his tone flat, his gaze cold. "What are you doing here?"

He was still angry. Still hurt by what happened over the summer. I'd expected him to be, but coming face-to-face with that anger and hurt had my carefully rehearsed speech flying from my head. Left me struggling to find the right words to tell him what I wanted. How I felt.

"I...You..." I cleared my throat and tried again. "Merry Christmas." I swept my gaze over him again because I could. Because he was there, right there in front of me. "Did I...Were you sleeping?"

His hair was mussed, like he'd been lying down, his T-shirt wrinkled, his feet bare.

He stepped toward me, right to the edge of the foyer, pulling the door almost shut behind him. "You shouldn't be here."

Of course I should be here. It was Christmas. A time for cheer and joy, peace and goodwill.

A time for miracles.

"I wanted to see you," I said, barely above a whisper.

His expression darkened. "You should have called."

Yes, that was becoming extremely clear. I should have called. Shouldn't have surprised him this way. But he hadn't spoken to me since that night on my porch when he told me he loved me.

When he walked away from me.

"Would you have answered?"

His mouth flattened. "What do you want?"

The tip of my nose stung from the cold. From unshed tears. What did I want? I wanted him to stop treating me this way, like some stranger whose evening I'd interrupted. Like someone who'd never said he wanted to be with me. That he loved me. I wanted him to stop being all hard and angry.

I wanted him to go back to being the boy I knew.

I inhaled deeply, breathing in the frigid air, drawing in courage. "I miss you," I said on my exhale, the words coming out soft like the falling snow, the truth of them drifting over us.

He shook his head. "It doesn't matter."

That wasn't right. None of this was right. He was supposed to smile when he heard that. Was supposed to tell me he missed me, too.

"It matters," I said, fighting tears. "If I could just--"

"Don't," he ground out. "Whatever you came here for, you wasted your time. It's too late."

I shivered from the cold, my teeth chattering. I'd walked from my house, having decided this was such a great idea, surprising Sam this way, needing to tell him what was in my heart. Not wanting to wait another moment to do so.

I should have waited.

At least until I'd had a ride.

But Devyn was working at the motel—she always worked holidays for the extra pay. And Zoe had taken Taylor with her to her latest boyfriend's house.

So I'd donned my long, puffy coat, pulled on my gloves and boots and headed out the door, determined and excited and nervous.

It wasn't until I'd walked a mile I realized I'd forgotten a hat.

"C-can I come in?" I asked, covering my ears with my hands.

"This isn't a good time."

"Are you...are you and your family doing something?" It *was* still Christmas. And Sam's family was a whole lot more traditional than mine. Maybe they were...I don't know...drinking hot chocolate and eating Christmas cookies while playing board games or singing carols around the fireplace.

Something wholesome and sweet. Something I was interrupting.

Something Sam would rather be doing than talking to me.

"Mom's at the hospital."

"Oh." I lowered my hands. "So you're hanging out with your brothers?"

Okay, that seemed a stretch. Not the hanging-out-with-Charlie part, but I couldn't imagine Sam and Max spending quality family time together without their mom insisting—and acting as a buffer. Season of miracles or not.

"Max is out. Charlie went with Patrick to his parents' house."

"Oh," I said again.

He wasn't busy. His family wasn't even home.

He just didn't want to talk to me. Didn't even want to hear me out.

I hugged my arms around myself but there was no warmth to be found. I wanted to apologize for showing up here unannounced. For not maintaining the distance he put between us. For breaking the silence.

I wanted to beg his forgiveness for not being the girl he wanted me to be four months ago. For not being able to give him everything he wanted.

But I was ready to be that person now. I was ready to give him everything.

"Sam," I said, reaching for him, "I--"

"Sam?" a girl's voice said from behind him. "Everything okay?"

I twitched, like I'd received an electric shock. My fingertips tingled. My scalp prickled painfully. Holding Sam's gaze, I shook my head slowly.

Please, please, don't let that be who I think it is.

His jaw tightened and he opened the door as Abby pressed up beside him. She was dressed for a date in dark skinny jeans and crop top the color of plums, shiny hair smooth, as if it'd just been brushed, her dangly silver earrings catching the light.

While I was dressed for braving the elements in a coat that made me look like a giant marshmallow and a pair of clompy boots. My hair was windblown and now damp from the still-falling snow, my nose and cheeks, I'm sure, bright red with cold.

"Hadley," Abby said, the triumph in her gaze making it clear she'd known I was what had been keeping Sam from her. That she wanted *me* to know she was what he'd been so eager to get back to. "What are you doing here?"

I couldn't answer. Couldn't speak even if I'd wanted to.

It hurt, God, did it hurt, seeing them together. Seeing the real reason why Sam's hair was messy, why his shirt was wrinkled. Knowing what they'd been doing, alone in Sam's house.

What they'd go back to doing once I was gone.

"Hadley was just leaving," Sam said, an unfamiliar edge to his tone, a hardness in his eyes when he looked at me that had never, not once, been there before. "Isn't that right?"

No. No! None of this was right. My Sam would never be so mean. Would never treat me this way. Would never hurt me like this.

Except, he wasn't my Sam. Not anymore.

Not when he put his arm around Abby's waist and pulled her against him.

I was still reaching for him, my arm outstretched, my hand seeking, trying to touch him. To hold on to him.

Lowering my arm, I stepped back.

And I let Sam go.

35

I'M CAREFULLY PULLING A TOOTHPICK THROUGH THE FROSTING OF MY Bakewell tart Wednesday evening when there's a knock on our back door. I turn to see Whitney through the door's window. Sam made a local travel basketball team and has a game in Jamestown, so Whitney and I are going to watch a couple episodes of *Friday Night Lights* after Taylor goes to bed.

I lift my free hand to motion for her to come in when Taylor and Eggie run into the kitchen, Eggie taking the lead and reaching the door first.

"No, Eggie! No!" Taylor cries. "I get it!"

"He can't actually open the door," I tell her. "He's a dog."

Ignoring me, she shoves Eggie aside.

"Hey," I say, using my sternest voice, "don't push Eggie. That's not nice."

She scowls. "I nice," she mutters under her breath, then she glares at Eggie, who is looking at her in pure adoration. "You not nice, Eggie."

He barks twice and licks her face.

Sap.

Taylor uses both hands to twist the knob and opens the door. "Whitty!" She throws her hands in the air, suddenly full of glee and good cheer. "Hi, Whitty!"

I wince. Good Lord, that child is loud.

"Don't yell," I tell Taylor, keeping my own voice low so she'll get the gist. "Use your inside voice."

"I no yell, Haddy!" she yells at me, all frowning and fierce and not getting the gist at all. "*You* yell!"

That's her new thing. Turning everything we tell her around so that it's never her fault. Come to think of it, her mother's the same way.

Zoe often thinks she's a victim of circumstance.

"You're a very excitable child," I say. "You know that?"

She lifts her little nose in the air and grabs Whitney's hand, pulling her inside. "I no talk to you, Haddy. I talk to Whitty." She gives Whitney the same love-struck look Eggie had given her. Whitney is officially at the top of Taylor's Favorite Person List. "Whitty, we made a tart!"

Except in the land of no *r*s, it comes out towat.

Whitney smiles and picks Taylor up. "You did? What kind of tart?"

"The most yummy kind," Taylor says, though she hasn't tasted it yet. Ah, the confidence of youth.

"It's a Bakewell tart," I say, carrying it over to the table. It really does look the most yummy. I did a feathering effect on the top, blending the white icing and thinly piped raspberry jam together. "It's raspberry jam topped with almond filling and then iced."

Whitney looks suitably impressed. "Wow. Fancy."

I cut a small slice of tart for Taylor then two bigger ones for me and Whitney, who sits at the table with Taylor on her lap.

"Mmm," Whitney says, taking her first bite. She gives Taylor a gentle bounce. "You're right, Taylor. This is the most yummy."

"Yes," Taylor says, forgoing her fork to drag her fingertip through the icing. She licks it off. "I always wite."

I take a bite of tart. It's definitely most yummy. The pastry is flaky and buttery, the layer of raspberry jam a good balance between sweet and tart and the almond filling is killer.

And worth every penny of that twelve bucks I spent on the puny bag of almond flour.

"This is so good," Whitney says, eating her piece slowly. She does that, talks and moves slowly, savors moments and bites of sweets. "You should really start selling these. Oh!" She sets her fork down with the wonder of her great idea. "You could get a booth at the farmer's market."

Taylor shoves her plate away and climbs down to go back to the living room, Eggie padding behind her. She only ate the icing, so I draw her plate over to me.

Like I said, that almond flour was twelve dollars. Not one crumb of this tart is going to waste.

"You probably have to rent those booths," I say. "And what happens if I don't make enough to cover it plus the cost of ingredients?"

She picks up her fork, taps the tines gently against her mouth. "Hmm. Okay. Well, maybe you could sell desserts to a local café?" She sits up straighter. "Or Good Grinds?"

I finish my piece of tart and move on to Taylor's. "Good Grinds' customer base is mostly hipster-wannabes. They probably only eat sugar-free granola and raw vegan cookies."

"You can still ask them if they'd be open to the idea," Whitney insists.

"What's the point? They're just going to say no."

Whitney looks like she'd really, really like to argue. Instead she sighs and focuses again on her tart.

I like to think it's because she's realized I'm right, but it's probably more because she hates any type of confrontation, no matter how small.

Or else she just knows her good intentions are no match for my pessimism.

We eat in silence a few moments. Well, relative silence as the clanking of the air conditioner has gotten louder as the summer progressed and Taylor is sing-shouting "Girls Just Want to Have Fun" in the living room.

Baby girl loves '80s pop music.

I'm chewing the last bite of Taylor's piece of tart and am considering a third slice when Whitney says, "My mom said you can come to Pittsburgh with us."

I frown. "Why would I do that?"

Whitney and her mom are doing the college tour thing, going down to Pittsburgh tomorrow and spending the night, then visiting both Pitt and Carnegie Mellon.

"So you can look at culinary schools down there," Whitney says as if this makes perfect sense.

"I don't even know if there are culinary schools in Pittsburgh."

She uses the side of her fork to cut her last bit of tart in two. "I'm sure there's at least one. We'll research it tonight. Mom says you probably won't be able to take a tour since it's late notice, but we can maybe look around, get information about their programs."

Appetite gone, I stack my plate on top of Taylor's. "I don't want to tour any schools or get information."

Lifting her last bite of tart to her mouth, Whitney stops and tips her head to the side to study me. "Why not?"

Because no one in my family has gone to college or even trade school. Mom and Zoe didn't even graduate high school.

Because college costs money. A lot of money. More than I have, that's for sure. More than I'd ever be able to afford.

Because there's no point in wanting something you're never going to get.

I stand, the stacked plates in my hands. "I just don't want to."

"It's not a commitment," Whitney tells me as I carry the plates to the sink. "It's just seeing what it's all about, what they offer in terms of courses and financial aid."

I rinse the plates, scrubbing harder than necessary at a spot of jam. "I'm not college material."

"Define *college material*," she says.

"Uh...you. Sam. Tori and Kenzie. People who get good grades, who are in school clubs and sports and actually want to spend another four years of their lives sitting in a classroom, surrounded by their age-appropriate peers."

I shudder. Ugh. That is so not me.

It's also people who can afford to pay six figures for an education. So, *so* not me.

"There are all types of schools," Whitney says. "Community college. Trade schools. It's not like high school. And if it's not for you, that's okay. But it doesn't hurt to look."

Drying my hands, I face her. Give a shrug, but my shoulders are so tense they barely move. "Even if I did want to go, I can't. I have to work. Unless we're sick, Mr. G. makes us give at least a week's notice if we take a day off."

Not that I ever do. If I don't work, I don't get paid.

Something Whitney obviously doesn't understand.

"Oh, right," she says with a blush and shake of her head. "Sorry. I wasn't thinking."

Why should she? She doesn't have to work, has only just started looking for a part-time job so she can have some spending money. It's times like these, times when Whitney seems so clueless as to what my life's really like, that I start to wonder if this, us being friends, isn't a huge mistake.

There's a loud crash from what sounds like my bedroom immediately followed by Taylor yelling, "Not me!"

Which means it was definitely her.

"Want me to check on her?" Whitney asks, already getting to her feet.

I nod. "Thanks."

Alone in the kitchen, I rinse Whitney's plate and fork and put the tart away, our conversation replaying in my head.

It doesn't hurt to look.

Where does she get this stuff? It does so hurt to look. Seeing what you want and knowing you can never have it?

Torture.

Better not to see all that's out there.

Safer not to get any crazy, useless, hopeful ideas about getting more than you could ever possibly have.

36

"I just don't get why she still hates me."

"She's two," I remind Sam as I pull my bedroom door shut behind me. I had to lie down with Taylor in her bed in Zoe's room to get her to fall asleep. Luckily it only took twenty minutes.

A new record. Usually it takes at least half an hour and I end up dozing off before her.

"The only things she hates," I continue, "are getting her hair brushed, broccoli and being told no."

"And me," he insists, sounding pitiful. Looking anything but, the way he's stretched out on my bed, back against the headboard, long legs straight and crossed at the ankles. His hands are behind his head, elbows out and his T-shirt pulls taut against his broad chest. I'm not sure if he's posed that way on purpose, but it's working for him.

It's working for me, too.

"At least she no longer cries when she sees you." Although she does tell him to *Go 'way!* whenever he shows up. I'm pretty sure Devyn taught her that. "You're making progress."

He gives an irritable shrug, hands still behind his head. "I guess."

I grin. He's adorable when he pouts.

And while I don't think Taylor actually hates him, it is true that she's *not* a fan, even after having Sam hang out here almost every night for the past month and him always bringing her little treats— toys and cookies and her new favorite, gum.

"You need to let her come to you in her own time," I tell him, crossing to stand at the end of the bed. The better for me to look at all that pretty laid out before me. "Don't worry so much."

He also shouldn't try so hard, but there's no sense telling him that.

Trying hard is the essence of who Sam Constable is.

That and wanting everyone to like him.

Even a two-year-old.

"Cheer up," I tell him, reaching up to take out the messy bun I'd put my hair up into when I'd given Taylor her bath. Sam's gaze tracks the movement. Darkens. "There's at least one Jones girl who likes you."

More than one, truth be told. Zoe and Devyn have always thought Sam was great. Devyn would just rather I'd kept him tucked safely away in the friend zone.

But even though he's out and running free, she's still nice to him whenever she sees him. And, thankfully, she's stopped acting so irritated with me and my life decisions.

"Yeah?" Sam asks, his voice a low rumble. He lifts his chin and uncrosses his ankles. "Show me."

I crawl onto the bed and onto his legs, straddling his thighs. He's smiling, looking confident and relaxed and very, very content. As if he has everything he's ever wanted, right here, right now.

Because he has me.

And it hits me, as it does at random times—when we're walking, our fingers intertwined, or sitting on the couch watching a movie, me pressed up against his side, or lying together on my bed, my head pressed to his chest, his heart beating beneath my ear, his fingers in my hair—that this, being with Sam, having Sam's heart, is real.

It's real and it's right and it's so good, so much better than I ever dreamed it could be between us.

And it scares me. God, it terrifies me, how much I feel for him. How much he means to me, to my happiness.

Sam's eyebrows rise as I study him. "Well?"

"Don't rush me," I say with a tsk. "I'm admiring you."

His grin turns cocky and he wiggles a bit, settling into the mattress. "Well, take your time, then."

"Oh, I plan to."

His arms are still behind his head and I rise to my knees, lean forward and lay my hands on his biceps, just above his sleeves.

The muscles under my fingers tense and get bigger.

"Are you flexing right now?" I ask.

The look he gives me is pure innocence. "This is just what they're like all the time."

With a laugh, I shake my head.

Boys and their egos.

His skin is warm and silky soft. I'm forever amazed at that, at how smooth parts of him are—the insides of his arms, the slope of his shoulder, the nape of his neck. How sensitive to my fingers. My lips. Just as I'm always surprised how often I want to touch him. How badly I want to.

I glide my hands up to his elbows and he twitches. "Tickles," he murmurs.

I drag my nails lightly up his forearms. "Better?" I ask on a whisper.

He nods on a sharp exhale.

He's only gotten a trim once since he's been home and his hair is the longest it's been in a few years, all thick and waving wildly. I smooth it back from his forehead then comb my fingers through it from his temples to where his hands are connected at the crown of his head. He inhales sharply.

I skim my gaze over his face. His eyes are hooded, his lips parted. I trace the outline of his mouth with my index finger then trail my fingertips over the sparse, patchy stubble on his cheeks. Leave them there, cupping his handsome face as I lean forward, the scent of his aftershave filling my nostrils. I press a soft, lingering kiss against the right side of his mouth, then skim my lips over his to repeat the process on the left.

I pull back and our gazes lock, and while his breathing has quickened, mine has stopped, caught in my lungs at the glittering, intense look in his dark eyes. The hunger. The yearning.

"Hadley," he says, my name a rough sound that could be a curse, could be a prayer. I'm not sure. Can't make myself care as he surges up, one arm going around my waist, the other hand going behind my head, his fingers spearing my hair as he holds me still for his kiss.

Like his voice, it, too, is a bit rough, but again, hard to care. Not when there's a pleasant humming in my head, an electric buzzing coursing through my veins. My skin tingling. My pulse racing.

Gone are the slow, indulging explorations of each other. The hesitancy. The doubts.

It's...freeing.

And I give myself over to it. To that freedom. To the heat. The urgency. Let it rush over me, through me, sweeping me along so I don't have to think about whether this is too soon. Don't have to worry about what this next step will mean for us. What it'll change.

If it's a mistake.

Kissing Sam harder, I slide my hands under the hem of his T-shirt. His hand in my hair trembles. I shove the material up and he pulls back, breaking the kiss so I can yank the shirt over his head.

He's so beautiful, all golden, tanned skin and lean muscles, and I smooth my hands over his chest. Down to his abs. It's a stark contrast, my pale hand against his darker skin, my slender fingers against the visible ridges of muscle.

"Hadley..."

This time my name is a question.

But I don't want Sam to ask if I'm sure. Or if I want to slow down.

So I kiss him again, pressing against him.

No, I'm not sure. Not at all. Part of me does want to slow down. Part of me thinks we should stop.

But another part of me wants to keep going. Because it's Sam. Because it feels so good to be with him this way.

And if we have sex here, now, I can blame it on being carried away in the heat of the moment.

If it happens here, now, like this, I don't have to take responsibility if it turns out to be a mistake.

If I lose my heart to him over it.

I kiss him again and again, my hands smoothing across his chest, his hand sliding from my hair to my jaw then down to my throat. Then lower, his fingers hot against my collarbone. Lower, rubbing along the neckline of my tank top.

Lower.

My heart is pounding and I wonder if he can feel it there, against his palm. He makes a sound in the back of his throat and his kiss gets deeper. His touch surer.

I tug on him, wanting, needing him closer, and he scoots forward, lifting me off the mattress. Still kissing, I wrap my legs around his waist as he gets to his knees then lays me on my back.

Except my bed is small, tiny even, and pushed up against the wall so Taylor doesn't roll out at night, and I hit my head against it.

Hard.

As Sam is still kissing me, my grunt of pain is muffled by his mouth, but the loud thud of my skull bouncing off the drywall gets his attention.

"Shit," he breathes, his hand going to the tender spot on my head. "Are you okay?"

Wincing, I nod but...ow. That hurt.

He lowers his forehead to mine and we stay that way for a moment, breathing hard, bodies warm and, in Sam's case, sweaty.

He exhales heavily and lifts himself onto his elbows. "Should I go?"

His hopeful tone and physical state make it clear he wants me to say no.

But now that I've literally had some sense knocked into me, I no longer have the excuse of that whole heat-of-the-moment thing.

If I decide to have sex with Sam, it's going to be because I made a careful, conscious decision to do so.

Oh, who am I kidding? There's no *if* about it. And when it happens, it's definitely going to change everything between us again.

Which makes the careful, conscious deciding part of it even more important.

"You can stay," I say and his eyes gleam until I add, "We can watch a movie."

And the way his expression falls would be hilarious if I wasn't just the tiniest bit disappointed, too.

But I'm also relieved.

He gives me a sheepish, good-natured grin. "A movie sounds good."

He kisses me, a quick, warm press of his lips, then pushes himself up and off me to sit at the edge of the bed.

I sit up and straighten my tank top as he looks around, combing his fingers through his hair.

"It's over there," I tell him, inclining my head to the other side of the room. Yes, we've become that couple that reads each other's minds and I know he's looking for his shirt, which I'd chucked aside like it'd personally offended me, covering up all that golden skin I'd wanted to get to. "On the dresser."

He grins at me over his shoulder and stands to take the two steps needed to reach his shirt, hanging from the corner of my dresser. When he picks it up, the brochure beneath it slides to the floor.

Tossing his shirt over his shoulder, he picks up the brochure and sits back down on the bed. "What's this?"

"Just some stuff Whitney left here."

"I thought Whitney wanted to be a teacher."

"She does."

He turns, setting his bent leg on the mattress. "Then why is she looking into Pittsburgh Technical College?"

I shrug. "She's not. I guess she thought I'd be interested in seeing the information."

I'm not. Whitney brought it over after her trip to Pittsburgh. Said she'd picked up the information just in case I changed my mind.

I won't. I mean, yeah, I may have looked it over once or twice or a dozen times but that's only when I get bored.

Or let my guard down.

Guard goes down, hope goes up, reality crashes in.

It's a vicious cycle.

Sam flips through the information. "They have a baking and pastry program. Had, this would be perfect for you."

He takes out his phone.

I frown. "What are you doing?"

And why hasn't he put his shirt on? His naked chest and those abs are super distracting, not to mention making me think watching a movie might not be the best use of our time together.

"Seeing how far it is from Pitt."

"Is that...is that where you're going?"

I'd always suspected as much, seeing as how it's his mom's alma mater and Max's current school, but I've never asked. If I ask, it'll make it real—Sam leaving. Moving on with his life after we graduate next year.

Moving forward without me.

"I hope so," he says, distracted by his phone. "If I can get accepted there."

Please. As if Sam Constable, with his doctor parents, high GPA, AP course load and upper-tier SAT score, couldn't go to any school he wanted.

There's a lump in my throat that tastes distinctively like bitterness.

I clear it away.

"Seventeen miles," he murmurs. "Not perfect, but doable."

"Doable for what?"

"For seeing each other." He puts his phone in his pocket and finally tugs his shirt on. "At least every weekend. And maybe a few times during the week, depending on our class loads."

I'm shaking my head before he finishes. "I'm not going to school. Not in Pittsburgh. Not anywhere."

He frowns, baffled by this development. "Why not?"

Why not? It's the same thing Whitney asked me when I told her I didn't want to tour any schools or get information on them.

Information she pushed on me anyway, I might add.

God. What is with these people? You'd think my best friend and my boyfriend would understand the reality of my life.

I swing my legs to hang over the side of the bed then stand, intending to tell him what I'd told Whitney: I don't want to. Instead, the truth comes out. "I just...It's not something I've ever even thought about before."

"So? Just because you never thought of it before doesn't mean you can't think about it now, right?" I give an irritable shrug and Sam reaches over and gently snags my wrist. Tugs me around the corner of the bed and into his lap, his big hand pressing against my lower back. "The future's not set in stone. We can shape it into whatever we want."

"Maybe *you* can."

He tips my chin up so he can meet my eyes. "Anyone can."

Of course Sam believes that. He's never *not* gotten something he's wanted. But there's no use explaining, no sense trying to get him to understand.

It'll only prove to him how different we are. How different our futures are going to be.

But what if...what if they're not so different? What if Sam's right?

What if I can have more than I ever dreamed possible?

There's a twinge in my stomach that I want to be irritation or frustration or disappointment, but I'm terrified it's not.

It's worse than any of them. And so much more dangerous.

It's hope.

Not much. Just a tiny flicker, like a match flaring to life.

I should snuff it. Should douse it before it grows stronger, brighter, but I don't want to. Not yet. I want to pretend, just for a few moments, that I can have more than I ever dreamed possible.

"I don't know how to do it," I admit.

"Do what?"

"Any of it. How to find schools or apply."

How to want something more.

How to believe in something good.

He settles both hands on my waist and draws me closer. "We'll figure it out."

Oh, to have his confidence.

But maybe I don't need it. Maybe him having it is enough.

"I guess..." I stop and take a long, careful breath. "I guess I can at least think about it some more before I make a decision."

Grinning, he tugs me onto his lap. "That's all I'm asking."

"What if I don't go?" I glance at him then drop my gaze to my hands in my lap, my fingers linked together. "What if you're in Pittsburgh and I'm up here..."

"We'll still be together," he says, quick and intent. "We'll always be together. You're my girl, Hadley. No matter what."

"Promise?"

The one word is soft. Pleading.

And something I have no right to ask for.

"I promise," he says gruffly.

I believe him. I believe him because this is Sam. He doesn't say things he doesn't mean. He doesn't lie.

And he doesn't make promises he can't keep.

But mostly, I believe him because I want to.

37

"PLEASE," I SAY TO DEVYN THE NEXT MORNING, HATING THAT I'VE BEEN reduced to begging for something so insignificant, but there you have it. My pride is always the first thing to go. "It's one afternoon," I continue, fighting to keep any whininess from my tone, but I have to admit, a teeny tiny bit of whiny sneaks through. "I haven't had a day off all summer."

Dev rinses her cereal bowl at the sink and sets it aside. "No? Seems to me you have every weekend off. Which is more than I can say for Zoe or me."

"What's more than you can say for us?" Zoe asks as she enters the kitchen in a pair of faded blue sweatpants and a loose pink sleeveless top, hair in a messy bun. Taylor, in her favorite Disney princesses nightgown, sits on her hip.

"Up, Haddy!" Taylor says, throwing herself out of her mother's arms in her enthusiasm to get to me. "Up! Up! Up!"

I take her from Zoe before she can do a faceplant on the floor.

"I was reminding your sister," Dev says, as if I've somehow ceased being *her* sister, too, by virtue of my wild, crazy, selfish request, "that she doesn't have to work weekends while we do."

"She watches Tay on the weekends," Zoe points out and I throw her a grateful look.

"Because we both *work*." Dev shakes her head as if I'm asking for the sun, the moon and a few stars, just for kicks and giggles. "She wants to take next Friday afternoon off."

Getting the apple juice from the fridge, Zoe glances at Dev. "So?"

"If she doesn't work, she doesn't get paid."

What goes unsaid is that we need every dollar, every cent from all our paychecks combined, just to make ends meet.

I know this. I know it, but I still want to take the time off.

I never should've brought it up with Devyn. Most of the time I come and go as I please—as long as I let either Dev or Zoe know where I'll be and when I'll be back—but I know how Dev stresses about money and I didn't want her to be mad at me.

Not when she's finally stopped being upset about me and Sam.

"It's a few hours." Zoe hands Taylor a sippy cup filled with watered-down apple juice. "What's the big deal?"

Dev gets this pinched expression that clearly says it's a big deal indeed and that Zoe's siding with me isn't swaying her in the least.

But I appreciate Zoe trying to help all the same.

"Please," I say again, shifting Taylor to my other hip. "It's the only time off I'll take all summer. I promise. And I won't buy baking stuff this week." I do some quick mental math. "Or next week. And I can ask Mr. G if I can pick up extra hours--"

"You can't pick up extra hours after five during the week or any on weekends," Dev says. "We need you here to watch Taylor."

My eyes sting with unshed tears. Ugh. It's official. I. Can't. Win.

I sniff. Blink back the wetness. "It's not like I take time off every week or even once a month. I don't do anything but work and babysit."

Unlike every other kid I know.

They go on vacations with their family and drive the cars their parents bought them to Ocean City or the Jersey Shore where they spend a fun-filled, sun-filled week with their friends. They go to Lake Erie or an amusement park a few times a month. And when they're not traipsing around? They get to sleep in until noon, work a few hours here and there, then spend their paychecks totally on themselves, on clothes and fast food and beer and pot.

They don't have to pay for their own school clothes and supplies, don't have to pitch in for groceries, or to help cover the electric bill because their family's one air conditioner uses twice as much energy as the newer, more efficient models.

The new, more efficient models we can't afford to buy.

And I'm okay with that. Most of the time. Just not right now.

All I'm asking for is one afternoon. A few hours where I don't have to work or watch Taylor or take Eggie for a walk or cook dinner or make sure Zoe's scrubs are washed or that there's plenty of that crappy bagged salad Dev likes to make her lunches out of in the fridge.

A few hours that are just for me.

But playing the *poor me* card with Devyn is the wrong way to go.

Even if I am feeling more than a little sorry for myself.

Dev gets a travel mug from the dish drainer and slams it on the counter. "You're seventeen," she says as she fills it with coffee, her movements irritated, her body stiff. "Not seven. You don't need entertained every day of the summer. We all work." She gestures to the three of us. "We all pitch in."

Taylor, sensing the tension, lays her head on my shoulder while she drinks her juice, her fingers twirling my hair around and around and around.

"Why do you want Friday afternoon off?" Zoe asks, opening a can of ginger ale.

Breakfast of champions, right there.

I shrug, feeling hot and itchy, uncomfortable and irritated. To soothe myself, I start swaying with Taylor. "I don't know."

Zoe, in the act of taking a sip of soda, stops. "You don't know?"

"Sam wants to take me somewhere," I mutter, defensive. "It's a surprise."

All he'd told me was that he wanted to do something special with me next Friday and to let Mr. G know I could only work until noon that day.

Devyn and Zoe exchange a knowing look and Zoe smirks. "Ah, the old I-have-a-surprise-for-you line. Yeah, I fell for that once." She nods at Taylor. "Got a seven-pound, five-ounce surprise that time."

"God, don't even joke about that," Dev says, then gives me a searing look. "And you, don't fall for that. Ever."

"It's not a line." I flop onto a kitchen chair and turn Taylor so that she's sitting on my lap. "And if it is one that other guys actually use," I tell Zoe, "you should be ashamed of yourself and embarrassed, because it's terrible."

"What can I say?" Zoe asks with another sip of her soda. "I love me a good surprise. Especially one that lasts a lifetime." She turns to Dev. "Let her take it off. She deserves it. If it bugs you, I'll give you the money for her wages for the day."

"That's not the point," Dev says but I can tell she's weakening—a rare sight indeed.

"No, the point is that she's seventeen. Let her have a little bit of fun."

Yes, yes, there's definitely weakening going on, I can see it on Dev's face. In how her shoulders lower. I bite the inside of my cheek, hold my breath, trying not to look too anxious. Too hopeful.

Finally, she sighs. "Fine. One afternoon. One," she repeats, holding up a corresponding finger.

I can't help but grin. Give Taylor a celebratory bounce that gets her giggling. "Got it."

"Woo hoo. A whole afternoon of freedom." Zoe stretches her legs out, points her toes. "A reprieve from this prison you've been sentenced to."

"A prison. Yes," Devyn says dryly. "That's exactly what it's like. Although, last time I checked, no one was forcing you to stay locked up here."

"And give up special times like this with my family? I couldn't possibly leave."

"That's what I'm afraid of." Dev gathers her things, then gives Taylor a kiss on the top of the head. "See you later."

I wait until I hear the front door close before saying to Zoe, "Thanks for getting her to ease up on the work assignment."

"What are big sisters for?"

"Up until this moment I thought they were for making younger sisters' lives miserable, reminding us how struggling will make us stronger, tougher and better able to cope with the world, and generally kill our spirit."

"All true. But we're also bad influences—walking, talking, living examples of what not to do to completely screw up your life." She nods at Taylor. "You're welcome."

Taylor starts singing softly to herself, some made-up song about Eggie and Cinderella and Olaf from *Frozen*—an interesting threesome for sure. She wasn't planned. Wasn't expected. Wasn't wanted. Not at first.

But then she arrived, all tiny and pink and wrinkly. Helpless and blameless for the challenges her existence created.

Another Jones girl ready to take on the world.

It's up to us to make sure she doesn't get totally crushed by that world first.

I hug Taylor closer and she snuggles in, curving her warm body against my chest, her uncombed hair all fuzzy in the back, like cotton candy. "Your life isn't completely screwed up."

Zoe snorts and turns the can of soda in her hands around and around and around. "Yeah, well, I'm not even twenty. Plenty of time left to mess up some more. Plenty of time," she continues softly, looking at Taylor, "to mess up both our lives."

There's an itchy sensation at the back of my neck, like a spider crawling over my skin, and I rub at it, but the feeling of unease remains.

It isn't like Zoe to be so serious. So somber.

"What's wrong?" I ask.

"Nothing."

"You're acting weird. Did you get fired or something?"

"Mowah juice, Mama," Taylor says, thrusting her cup at Zoe. "Please."

"I still have a job," Zoe assures me as she takes the cup and stands. "I still have two of them."

I wait until she hands Tay her refilled cup. "What is it then? Something's wrong, I can tell. You look..." Like a vampire—pale face, dark circles under her red-rimmed eyes. "Tired."

"I work until three a.m. and between my two jobs, I put in twelve hours a day, not to mention I have a two-year-old who tosses and turns all night and refuses to be potty-trained." She gives Taylor a significant look but Tay's too busy chugging apple juice to notice or care. "I look tired because I am tired. I'm always tired."

Guilt pinches me hard. "Maybe I shouldn't go with Sam--"

"Oh, you should go," she assures me. "The world isn't going to fall apart if you have fun for a few hours."

But now I'm not so sure. Not nearly so desperate to have those precious few hours to myself. Not when neither Dev nor Zoe get them. "What about Taylor? Who's going to watch her while you're at Changes?"

"I'll ask Carrie."

"What if she can't? Or won't?"

"Then I'll figure something else out." But I must not look convinced of her capability to do that because she rolls her eyes. "I've got this. Believe it or not, there are a few things I can manage to do all on my lonesome."

"I know," I say, but I'm biting my lower lip.

Because while I'm sure she could manage to work two jobs and raise a toddler on her own, she doesn't have to. Devyn and I are always there to help with childcare and extra expenses. There with shoulders to lean on when her heart gets broken yet again. It's not that she's lazy or stupid or incapable.

It's that she's too soft. Too open.

Way too vulnerable.

"But if something happens," I continue, "or if you can't find a sitter, then I'll cancel."

"Nothing's going to happen and I'm going to find a sitter. You worry too much."

"Maybe you don't worry enough."

She waves that away. "Why bother? It's a waste of time. What's going to happen is going to happen."

"Wow," I say, deadpan. "That's deep. And so inspiring."

"You want inspiring? Watch a TED talk. You want the truth? This is it," she says, leaning forward—the better to pin me to my seat with the intensity of her gaze. "All we have is what's in front of us. Here. Now. So when something good comes along—like the chance to take an afternoon off and spend it with a boy who's crazy about you—you need to go. You need to enjoy yourself. But mostly, you need to remember that the good things in life don't last. Not for us, anyway. Which is why you have to grab hold and hold on to them for as long as you possibly can."

38

When Sam pulls into the driveway over a week later, I run to the Explorer, getting there before he can get out. He reaches across the passenger seat to open my door for me from the inside. I flashback to another day, another car, and another Constable boy doing the exact same thing.

Not exactly who or what I want to be thinking about right now or, you know, ever, so I shove the memory aside.

Smiling, I climb in, then lean over and kiss his cheek. "Hi."

He slides his gaze over me, his voice a husky murmur. "You're beautiful."

Warmth fills me, a combination of embarrassment and pleasure. I want to insist I'm not. I'll never be beautiful, not like Whitney or Abby. My skin is too pale, my freckles too numerous. I want to point out the weird shape of the tip of my nose, that my face isn't symmetrical, my chin too pointy.

But Sam already knows all that. He's looking at me, isn't he?

He sees me. He knows me better than anyone else.

And he thinks I'm beautiful.

It's a gift. One I won't refuse.

"Thank you," I say. "You, too."

He laughs, but I'm not joking. There is no boy more beautiful than Sam Constable. His hair is combed back, all dark and wavy, and he's wearing khakis and a deep green polo. He'd told me to wear something "cute but not too dressy" and I settled on Zoe's sleeveless blue and floral print sundress.

"Okay," I say, after I've shut my door and buckled up, "enough with the secrecy. What's the surprise?"

It's been over a week, and no matter how many times I pester Sam about what this big surprise is, he hasn't let anything slip.

Who knew he had it in him to be so secretive?

Checking for traffic, he glances at me, then pulls out onto the street. "If I tell you, it won't be a surprise anymore."

"That's fine with me." I've never been big on surprises. I'd rather know exactly what's going to happen. "At least give me a hint."

"One hint," he says, taking a right onto West Washington Street. "We're going out of town."

"Not fair. I already knew that." There's nothing to do in town on a Friday afternoon wearing what Sam called "cute but not too dressy" clothes. "I get another hint."

"Nope. You'll just have to wait and see."

With an eye roll, I slump back against the seat. Wait and see?

Talk about torture.

We get on the highway and head south. Sam must sense my irritation, my unease, because he glances my way. Lays his hand on my thigh just above my knee. Gives me a light squeeze. "Trust me?"

I look at that hand, so warm and solid and steady, then move my gaze up to his face. Eyes on the road, strong, handsome profile to me, he brushes his thumb against my skin.

Trust him?

I settle my hand on top of his and answer the only way I can. "Absolutely."

———

It's raining when we arrive in Pittsburgh three and a half hours later, and continues, steady and hard, while we're stuck for another thirty minutes in Friday lunch-hour traffic. We're on the other side of one of the rivers, the city to our left looking gray and gloomy.

Inching forward, the wipers moving back and forth consistently, Sam checks the directions on his phone.

"Shit," he mutters, glancing up at the barely moving vehicles in front of us. "We're going to be late."

"Late for what?"

He just shakes his head. Sam's surprise is being ruined by the rain, the traffic, and his inquisitive girlfriend.

"At least let me help with the directions," I say and he shoots me a frown. "If you keep checking your phone, you're going to get into an accident. And then the surprise will really be ruined."

"Yeah, okay," he says because I am wise and right and convincing. He holds the phone out to me only to withdraw it when I reach for it. "Promise you won't look at the end destination. Just the directions on the way."

"I promise." He doubts, though, because he doesn't hand over the phone and I give him my most solemn, sincere look and make an *X* over my heart. "Cross my heart."

Once the phone is in my hand, it's a tough promise to keep but I manage.

It was so sweet of Sam, setting up this surprise, driving all the way to Pittsburgh for it. I don't even care what it is anymore and I doubt it'll be better than the drive down, talking to him, just being with him. It's already been one of the best Friday afternoons of my life. Whatever happens next is a bonus and I make another promise, this time to myself, to act properly thrilled, excited and grateful no matter what's at the end of these directions.

Even if it's a Pirates game and I have to spend the next six hours sitting in the rain watching baseball.

Please, please, don't let it be a Pirates game.

Ten minutes later, we cross one of the many bridges and head toward the city, then take a right onto Penn Avenue. A few blocks later, Sam pulls into a parking garage, gets his ticket, finds a spot and turns off the ignition.

"Come on," he tells me. "We're late."

I don't bother asking late for what—wouldn't matter if I did as Sam is out of the car and hurrying around the back to open my door.

"Come on," he repeats, holding out his hand. Even in his impatience, he's more patient than any real, live human boy should be.

Trust me?

That's what he asked when we started this little adventure.

That's what he's asking now.

It's always something with boys, isn't it?

I unbuckle, slide my hand into his and get out. He shuts my door and starts jogging through the parking garage and out the door.

Which wouldn't be a problem if I wasn't wearing a short dress, wedge sandals and, oh, yeah, it wasn't still raining.

Thrilled and excited and grateful, I remind myself as we hurry across the street. *Thrilled and excited and grateful.*

Head down, I let Sam tug me along and we weave around the few other people dashing through the rain, dodge umbrellas and puddles until he stops suddenly and I run into him with so much force, I bounce back a step.

"Whoa," he says, like I'm a horse and not his girlfriend he'd been dragging down the street. In the rain.

Thrilled and excited and grateful.

"We're here," he continues and pulls me into a narrow brick building.

I smell it first, the scents of yeast and baking bread and chocolate, but it's not until we're inside and it's safe for me to raise my head without the risk of drowning that I see we are, indeed, in a bakery.

It's housed in an old building, the vibe distinctly rustic with scarred, slanted wood floors brick walls and visible ductwork under the high ceiling. There's a glass case at the front of the building, another to the right, both topped with large glass jars filled with at least a dozen varieties of biscotti.

I look over the choices in the front case. What will it be? Biscotti, for sure, as that seems to be their specialty. What else? Apricot-filled croissant? Chocolate-covered macaroon? Cannoli? Decisions, decisions.

"This is great," I tell Sam, squeezing his hand, as I try to narrow my choices. "Thank you for bringing me here."

"What? Oh. No, this isn't your surprise."

"It isn't?"

Before he can respond, two women come in, one older with graying hair, the other younger and resembling the first one so much I guess they're mother and daughter. They smile at us as they walk past to an older bald man wearing a white apron.

"No," Sam says. "I mean, yeah, it is, but it's not."

"Sorry. Still not getting it. Maybe if you use small, simple words and speak slowly?"

He grins. Rolls his eyes at me playfully. "The bakery isn't the surprise, it's where the surprise is taking place." He pauses for dramatic effect and sweeps his arms out in a *ta da!* gesture. "We're taking a bread making class!"

Adrenaline rushes through me, hard and fast, a burst of joy I can't contain. I grab his arm. Shake it. "What?"

His smile widens. "Surprise."

I let go and press my palms against my cheeks. "Sam, I..."

But I can't speak. Can't get the questions out.

How did he find out about this?

Why did he go to so much trouble for me?

"Do you like it?" he asks, unnerved by my silence. Worried by my lack of response. He tugs on his ear. "I missed your birthday and I wanted to--"

Launching myself at him, I cut him off, my momentum knocking him back two steps. I'm kissing him before he can regain his balance and we stumble, but he braces us, holds us both steady and wraps his arms around me and kisses me back.

Thrilled and excited and grateful.

I am all that and much, much more.

39

I'M DOWNRIGHT GIDDY WHEN SAM PARKS IN FRONT OF MY HOUSE. IT'S just past three a.m. but I'm not the least bit tired. I'm all fluttery and there's a pleasant warmth in my chest, a tumbling sensation in my stomach and an overall sense of joy threatening to burst from my fingertips.

I don't want this day to end.

I don't want to let Sam go.

"Do you want to come in for a little bit?" I ask, my voice unintentionally husky.

He glances at my trailer. Hesitates. The porch light is on, but the windows are dark. "I don't want to wake up your sisters."

"Devyn's working. And Taylor's been sleeping through the night more often, and once Zoe's out, she's dead to the world. We'll just have to be quiet."

"You sure?"

I nod and bite my lower lip while Sam takes in what I'm saying, trying to decipher the meaning of my invitation.

Trying to decide for the both of us.

Go. Or stay.

"Yeah." He shrugs, as if he's all calm and casual about spending a bit of time with his girlfriend in her bedroom late at night. But when he unbuckles his seatbelt, he fumbles and has to try again. "Sure. I can come in."

Inside, Sam takes off his sneakers, leaves them on the mat in the hall as I lock the door. Eggie pads over to greet us and we give him a quick pet, then I take Sam's hand and silently lead him down the hall, past Zoe's open bedroom door to my room. Leaving him by the door, I turn on the lamp next to my bed.

I put my purse and phone on the nightstand then gesture to the dresser near the window. "You can put that there," I whisper of the bags he carried in.

One holds a dozen biscotti, the other the loaf of rustic Italian bread I'd made in class. We'd dug into Sam's loaf while it was still warm, eating half of it as we walked around the Strip, but I wanted to save mine.

Wanted to savor it.

While he sets the bags on the dresser, I open the window, let in the damp breeze. It doesn't do much to cool off the sticky interior of the room, but it does bring in the scent of rain, which is nice. I turn on the fan in the corner then go to the door, shut it...

And lock it.

Sam, his back to me, goes still and turns, ever so slowly to look at that locked door, then at my face. Raises his eyebrows, a silent question. This isn't the first time we've been alone in my room with the door locked. But he senses my intentions, realizes this time is going to be different.

Our gazes lock. Hold. He's waiting for me to make the first move. To decide what tonight is going to be. Nerves dance in my stomach, constrict my chest. Nerves, but not doubt. I'm sure this is right.

Possibly the rightest thing I've ever done in my life.

I step forward, holding out my hand. It trembles.

I don't do it enough, reach out for him. Touch him first. Not nearly enough. But he doesn't hold it against me. Just closes the distance and links his fingers with mine.

Palm to palm, we walk to the bed and I turn us so the backs of his knees are against the mattress. Letting go of his hand, I nudge his chest and he sits, feet planted wide, legs apart.

Always taking up so much room.

He watches me, patient and sweet, letting me take the lead. Giving me the choice, as he always does, of what we'll do, how far we'll go.

"Thank you," I tell him softly, "for today."

A muscle in his jaw twitches and he shifts, letting his hands dangle between his knees. "Hadley..." He clears his throat. "You don't...you don't owe me..."

It takes a moment for his meaning to sink in.

I smile. "I'm not sure what you think is about to happen, but I can assure you it's not in trade for a few loaves of bread and dinner."

He colors slightly and rubs a hand over his mouth. Drops it and gives me a sheepish grin. "Sorry. Guess I was having delusions of grandeur."

I step between his legs. Lay my hands on his shoulders. "You're not deluded. But you are confused about the reasoning behind it. Let me see if I can clear things up." I kiss his left cheek. "That's for taking me all the way to Pittsburgh for a bread-making class." I kiss his right cheek. "That's for buying me biscotti."

"Twelve different kind of biscotti," he murmurs. "I'm not saying that deserves a real kiss, on the mouth, but..."

I straighten. "I can go with a solid handshake instead."

"No, no." He settles his hands on my waist, tugging me even closer, as if afraid I'm going to step back. "This is good. Please continue."

"Who said I was going to continue?"

"Well, I did take you on the Incline..."

"Hmm. True. But it was raining."

"It was still pretty cool."

The Incline is a railway-type car that goes up Mount Washington and the view of Pittsburgh at night, all lit up, was very, very cool.

I kiss his forehead. "That's for taking me on the Incline." Then I kiss the bridge of his nose. "That's for dinner at Primanti's." When I lean back, his eyes are half-closed and I brush my lips across his smiling mouth.

"What was that one for?" he asks.

"That was for me." I trail my fingers from his temple to the sharp line of his jaw. "And so is this."

I kiss him again, a long, lingering kiss that goes on and on. His fingers twitch, tighten on my waist then relax, his thumbs rubbing circles across my hip bones. He gives me control, let's me set the pace, so I take my time.

I want to remember every moment of it. The scent of the rain, the heat in the room. The soft whir of the fan and the way its breeze tickles the backs of my legs. Flutters the hem of my dress. The feel of Sam, so broad and solid and warm. The contradictions of him: silky hair and roughly stubbled jaw. Smooth skin over hard muscles. Strong arms and gentle hands.

And in this moment, all mine.

Our kiss heats but stays unrushed, our lips clinging, our tongues touching. He slides his hands up my back, then down...up and down, up and down...dragging the silky material of my dress across my skin. I touch him everywhere I can—his arms and shoulders, his neck and face, his hair. But it's not enough. Not nearly enough.

Breaking the kiss, I take his hands and pull him to his feet. Grab the bottom of his shirt and shove it up. Under my palms, the muscles of his stomach clench. Tremble.

My touch makes beautiful, golden boy Sam Constable tremble.

It's amazing. Wonderful.

And so empowering I forget my intention of taking his shirt off and trail my fingers across the ridges above his belly button. Luckily, Sam's still with the program and tugs his shirt off himself. He tosses it aside, mussing his hair.

It's that slight imperfection, that and the way he's breathing, so heavily, as if he's having a hard time catching his breath, that makes the moment even better.

Gives me the courage to stand there, in that fan-made breeze, in the glow of the lamp and, lifting the hair out of the way, turn and offer Sam my back.

And the zipper that runs down the length of my dress.

He draws a sharp intake of air then steps closer. His exhale is a rush of breath against the nape of my neck. He tugs the zipper down and the sound echoes in the room, rings inside my head.

Warns me that after this, there's no going back.

It's not a mistake. It can't be. Each and every step Sam and I have taken over the years, our friendship and him leaving, the mistakes and choices we both made, have led us to this exact moment.

It's not a mistake because Sam already has my heart. He took it. Without thought. Without even having to work for it.

But now, this...this is me giving it to him.

And I'll never get it back.

My breath catches and the sense of rightness that'd filled me moments before dissolves into nerves and fear. Sam finishes unzipping my dress and steps back. I hold the front against my chest and slowly kick off my sandals, head down, hair shielding my face.

"Hadley," Sam says, my name a dark, husky caress, "we don't have to do this."

I shut my eyes.

Sam Constable, reading my thoughts again. Knowing me better than I know myself.

Isn't that part of what scares me so much?

Yes, taking such a huge step should make me nervous. But I'm not afraid of what's going to happen between us tonight.

I'm afraid of how much it's going to hurt if all my wishing and hoping for a future with him doesn't come true.

If he walks away from me for good.

But he hasn't left. He's here. He's with me.

Right here, right now, he's mine.

Which is why I face him and tell him the truth. "I want to."

"Are you sure?" he asks gently as I clutch my dress, holding it against me like a shield. "We don't have to do anything you don't want to do. I can wait. I'll wait as long as it takes."

I'm waiting for you. Like always.

It's what he said to me that night last summer on my porch. "Why?"

"Why what?"

My fingers tighten on the material of my dress. *You can have any girl you want. Why do you wait for me? Why do you want me?*

"Why me?"

He smiles, that lopsided grin that's been making me melt since I was ten, its effect no less melty now in the heat of my room with him shirtless and mussed.

"That's easy," he says. "I love you."

For Sam, it really is that easy.

I love you.

So easy for him to give me those words. A casual *love you* when we end a phone call. A smiling, confident declaration when I've made him laugh or reach for his hand. A whispered confession when we're alone.

I love you.

Three simple words.

I love you.

For me, there's nothing easy about saying them.

Nothing simple in giving them.

No matter how much I want to.

I loosen the hold on my dress, peeling one finger at a time away from the fabric. There's something about the stillness of the night, the quiet of my house, the thick, hot air and soft hum of the fan that seems to cocoon us here, in this moment. It's a spell I'm careful not to break even as I let go.

I let go of the dress and it slides down my body. Sam's throat works as he swallows but he keeps his eyes on mine. His breathing becomes ragged.

And I let go of my fear. Of my doubts.

I let go of them, but I hold on to what's in front of me.

"I don't want to wait," I whisper as I step over the material pooled at my feet. I lay my hand on his chest, feel the steady beat of his heart under my fingers. "I want to be with you, Sam."

It's all I can give him. A little bit of the truth that's in my heart, that's always been there between us. In me.

I love you.

I can't say the words.

So I take his hand, lead him to my bed.

And I show him.

40

"CANNONBALL!" CHARLIE SCREAMS RIGHT BEFORE HE LANDS IN THE pool with a splash so huge it reaches the lounge chairs.

The lounge chairs where Whitney, Sam and I are happily minding our own business, me flipping through *Bon Appetit* magazine's latest issue, Whitney scrolling through Instagram and Sam sleeping.

Sam doesn't move, but Whitney and I jump and shriek like we've just been pelted with hot lava. It's all for show. Charlie's been in rare form this afternoon, showing off for his buddy Evan—a short, skinny kid with a fauxhawk—and basically being as obnoxious as possible.

Preteen boys. So excitable.

But it's fine. Both Whitney and I caught on pretty quickly that our plans for a leisurely Saturday afternoon at Sam's pool were going to be anything but when we arrived to find Charlie and Evan already in the water.

No biggie. We've just been entertaining ourselves by egging them on, pretending they're getting to us.

At the end of the diving board, Evan doubles over in laughter as Charlie comes up for air grinning. He shakes his wet hair out of his eyes and gives Evan a completely unsubtle head jerk in our direction.

Grinning maniacally, Evan straightens then bends his knees, bounces on the board and launches himself into the air, then curls his knees and holds them against his chest.

"Woo hoo!" he cries.

Another splash—though not nearly as big as Charlie's—another round of us screeching and them yukking it up like it's the funniest thing in the world.

Pretty much been our life for the past hour.

"Knock it off," Sam warns his brother. He's lying on his stomach on my other side, arms folded beneath his head, facing me, eyes closed, tone more dreamy than threatening.

"Our hero," I whisper to Whitney with an eye roll and we both crack up.

"What's that?" he murmurs.

"Nothing." I pat his shoulder. "Go back to sleep."

Keeping his eyes closed, he slides one hand free, reaches over and settles it on my hip, his long, warm fingers pressing against my bare belly. "Not...sleepy..."

And he's out again.

Well, we did have a late night and he woke up at six thirty so he could get home to eat and change before going to basketball practice.

Also so he could leave before Devyn got back from work.

Not that she would've said anything about Sam staying the night.

But I didn't want to take that chance.

So, yeah, he went home and I went back to sleep. For all of half an hour before Taylor came into my room.

I yawn. Wish I could curl up next to him, but it would be rude to do so with Whitney here, not to mention someone needs to stay awake and make sure Charlie and Evan are safe.

Plus, I'm worried Sam's mom will come out and find us together, snuggled up on a lounge chair in our swimsuits.

I've always been intimidated by her, but when Sam and I became an official couple, the healthy respect I had for her morphed into out-and-out fear.

She can be one scary lady.

Charlie and Evan get out of the pool and run around to the gate —despite being told numerous times today not to run near the pool. They jostle and shove each other as they race to the basketball court.

Ah. A reprieve.

I flip the page in my magazine.

"Do you know him?" Whitney asks, holding her phone so I can see the Instagram account she's showing me.

"Michael Snyder? Yeah. I know him."

I don't bother telling her—again—that if it's someone within five years of our age, I probably know them.

Small towns.

"Why?" I ask.

She shrugs. "He sent me a DM."

I sit up. "What'd he say?"

"Hey."

"Huh. I thought he'd be more articulate. He's a musician. Writes his own music and everything."

She smiles, intrigued.

Musicians have that effect.

"But you don't want to go there," I tell her.

Her smile fades. "I don't? He's pretty cute."

I glance at Sam. Still sleeping. I lean over and whisper, "Michael's very cute." He's got that whole wannabe-rock-star vibe, is blond, tattooed and has a killer smile. "And he's a great musician. There are rumors he's had interest from recording companies."

"And I don't want to go there...why?"

"Because he's Tori's ex. They were together almost all junior year."

"Really?" She looks at Michael's account again. "She never told me that. And there aren't any pictures of them on here together. Or on hers."

I shrug and twist the cap off my water bottle. Take a sip. "Michael doesn't post that much. And Tori used to have pics of him but she deleted them after they broke up. It was messy."

At least, that's what I heard. That Tori and TJ hooked up behind

Michael's back before Tori finally broke things off with Michael to be with TJ.

Whitney sighs, long and disappointed. I don't blame her. Michael Snyder is hot.

And completely still in love with Tori.

Again, what I've heard.

"Sisters before misters," Whitney says, deleting Michael's message with a flourish.

I toast her with my water bottle. "Sisters before misters."

Sam's fingers twitch on my stomach and I look over at him. He'd gotten in the pool about half an hour ago to cool down and his hair is still damp at the nape and temples, the strands on top of his head all messy and wavy. He looks younger in sleep. Softer. I watched him sleep last night, too. His face close to mine, his breathing deep and even, and there'd been this swell of emotion inside of me. Like my heart was filling up, expanding with warmth and joy, growing bigger and bigger like a balloon.

Until it got so full I thought it would burst.

Kind of like how it feels now.

"Well, look at this. It must be my lucky day."

I jerk my head up to see a grinning Max sauntering onto the pool deck in board shorts and a Pitt T-shirt, his dark hair combed back, a pair of designer aviators hiding his eyes.

"What are you doing here?" I ask.

When he stops in front of me, his eyebrows rise above his sunglasses as he holds his hands out at his sides, all aw-shucks and innocent.

Neither of which he is.

"Just came out for a quick dip." Even though I can't see his eyes, I can tell by the way he licks his bottom lip that he's giving Whitney one of his smoldering looks. Thank God, she ignores it. And him. "If I'd known two gorgeous ladies were out here, I'd have come out sooner."

Whitney flushes.

I roll my eyes.

Okay, so she's not ignoring him as much as she should be.

"No," I say. "What are you doing home? I thought you were at your dad's for another week."

"Didn't I tell you?" Sam mumbles, eyes still closed. "Dad kicked him out. He got tired of his bullshit."

"No," I say again, teeth gritted. "You didn't tell me."

If he had, if I'd known there was even a chance of Max being home, I wouldn't have agreed to spend the day here.

And I sure wouldn't have brought Whitney.

The farther she stays away from Max and his smolder, the better.

"The old man and I had a disagreement," Max says with a lift of one shoulder. "So I cut my visit short."

Sam snorts, his thumb moving back and forth over my hip bone. "Dad kicked him out," he repeats. "Because he came home wasted every night."

"Every night?" Whitney asks, frowning at Max in concern.

I want to tell her not to bother, that the last thing Max Constable needs is her worrying over him, but to be honest, I'm starting to get worried, too. Max has always loved to party but he'd kept it contained to weekends. And he'd always hid it from his parents.

Despite the dull wash of color filling his cheeks, he grins at Whitney and crosses to the lounge chair on her other side. "Just living up to the old man's expectations of me. And if I hadn't, I'd still be there, under his thumb." He leans toward Whitney. "There's not much room under there," he says in a conspiratorial whisper. A whisper loud enough for his brother to hear. "Not with Sam taking up permanent residence."

Sam just lifts his hand and flips him off.

Whitney and I exchange a look. This time it's not just me who's caught between the Constable brothers.

Should be a lighthearted, fun-filled, tension-free afternoon.

Sam sets his hand back on my hip as Max lowers his sunglasses and peers over the top of them at Whitney—the better to take in the sight of her hot pink one-piece swimsuit.

Yep. Definitely smoldering.

"Your shoulders are getting red," he says to her, reaching out to trace his fingertip over the shoulder nearest him. "Want me to rub sunscreen on them for you? Would hate for you to get a sunburn."

"Please," I mutter. "I just threw up in my mouth."

Whitney has gone still. After a moment, she looks at his hand, lingering on her person, then to his face. Tips her head to the side. "Did I give you permission to touch me?"

She's as sweet and polite as ever but there's a hint of steel in her voice that has a smile tugging at my lips.

And Max slowly removing his hand.

He stares at her for one long beat, his expression shocked, as if he's never had a girl turn him down before. For anything. Which is probably true.

But it's the intrigue in his eyes, the spark of interest that has my ears ringing from some inner alarm.

The Constable brothers love nothing more than a challenge.

"Just trying to help," he assures her. "Would hate for you to get a painful sunburn."

"You're so considerate," I say flatly.

Taking off his sunglasses, he grins at me as he stands. Sets them on the table next to Whitney's water bottle. "You know me. Always thinking of others."

And then, because he's thinking of us—or at least, how to get Whitney's attention—he proceeds to make a big production of taking his shirt off—crossing his arms and grabbing the hem and then slowly, oh, so very slowly lifting the material as he tugs it up past his hard abs and sculpted chest before pulling it over his head. He arches his back and stretches, all his muscles flexing this way and that.

Whitney shields her eyes from the sun as she peers up at him. Smiles indulgently. "I see Charlie's not the only showoff in the family."

I laugh. Max is stunned for a moment, almost embarrassed. But then his mouth twitches into a crooked grin, and he looks younger. Healthier.

Less angry.

He tosses his shirt onto the chair. "Where do you think he learned it?"

And he winks then takes the few feet necessary to do a perfect, splash-less, low dive into the pool.

He does a couple of slow, lazy laps then swims back to the side and lifts himself out of the pool in one smooth motion, biceps bunching, water running down his naked torso, like some citizen of Atlantis rising from the deep.

"Make it stop," Whitney whispers to me out of the corner of her mouth. "I only have so much willpower."

"Just picture him fully clothed," I whisper back.

She sends me an are-you-kidding glance. "Have you seen him dressed?"

Right.

"Then picture him in something completely dorky," I murmur as he walks toward us, water dripping, sunlight gleaming on his tanned skin. "Like socks with sandals."

She nods, her gaze flitting from him to her phone and back to him. The boy *is* magnetic. "Okay, good idea. Um...jorts."

"Jorts that go past his knees."

"Jorts that go past his knees, socks with sandals and one of those T-shirts that's supposed to look like a tuxedo."

We're both silent a moment, imagining it.

She groans. "It's not helping."

"Yeah, that's the problem with the Constable brothers," I say softly, tracing my fingers over the back of Sam's hand. "Too much pretty to be dulled by bad fashion choices."

Max stretches out on his back and puts his shirt over his face.

Whitney and I look at him. His wet board shorts low on his toned stomach. Then at Sam. His wide shoulders tapering to his narrow waist. Then we look at each other and grin.

Sometimes, being stuck between the Constable brothers isn't so bad after all.

41

We stay for dinner, me and Evan—who Sam says has spent so much time at their house this summer they might as well adopt him.

I stay because Dr. Constable-Riester issued the invitation live and in person, coming onto the pool deck after I'd dozed off. The sound of her quiet yet pointed *ahem* woke me with a start and I looked over, expecting to find Whitney, but both her chair and Max's were empty.

Something I knew I'd have to ponder at a much later time when I braced myself and turned to see Sam's mom standing in front of me in a dark blue silky blouse tucked into a pair of crisp white capri pants with a slim, gold belt. Despite the humidity that was wrecking my own hair, hers fell in dark, perfect waves to just above her shoulders. Her makeup was expertly applied and smudge-free. Her gaze sharp. Accusing.

And on Sam's hand.

Which, yep, was still on my stomach.

She probably thinks I put it there and wouldn't let him move it.

Like Devyn, Dr. Constable-Riester preferred it when Sam and Hadley, Hadley and Sam was the Just Friends Show.

I shoved his hand off but he just mumbled in his sleep and put it right back, the tips of his fingers sliding under the waistband of my bikini bottom.

At which point a wave of heat engulfed me as I went into a panicked, full-body blush and stared at his mom in wide-eyed, open-mouthed horror and prayed for a sudden, violent thunderstorm or massive locust infestation, anything to end what was quickly becoming one of the worst moments of my life.

But the sky remained sunny and clear and the yard stayed bug-free and the moment dragged on. And on.

Until finally Dr. Constable-Riester ended it with a stern, "Samuel."

He tensed and then s-l-o-w-l-y slid his hand away, as if by moving at a glacial pace, she wouldn't notice where it'd been.

I wanted to smack him.

More so when he rolled over and sent his mom an innocent grin, which, unlike his brother, he pulled off like a champ. "Hey, Mom," he said all super chill and casual. "What's up?"

Pretty sure Dr. Constable-Riester wanted to smack at him at that point, too.

She refrained. Instead she sent him a pinched-mouth, flinty-eyed look that promised they would be discussing exactly where his hand had been, and why it should never be in that vicinity again, at a later time.

For an ob-gyn, Dr. Constable-Riester has surprisingly rigid views on sex.

Then she'd turned to me as if none of it had ever happened and she didn't hate me with the burning fire of a thousand suns and asked if I would care to join them for dinner.

I blubbered on a bit about how I hated to impose on them and wouldn't want to put her or Mr. Riester out, but she waved aside my polite objections and assured me it was no trouble. It was just a Saturday night cookout and I was more than welcome.

That's when Sam piped in with his own encouragement, saying how I should definitely stay since Whitney's mom was getting her soon, and Devyn was working and Zoe and Taylor had gone to Erie for Zoe's grandmother's birthday, and that way I wouldn't have to eat alone.

Before I could point out that I've eaten by myself many, many times and managed to live through it without choking or stabbing myself with a fork, Dr. Constable-Riester had taken my moment of silence as agreement.

"Wonderful," she'd said, her tone and expression suggesting it was anything but. "We'll finally have a chance to catch up."

Sam rolled his eyes. "I haven't been gone that much this summer."

It was one of the few complaints Dr. Constable-Riester had about her middle son—he didn't spend enough time at home.

"Not you," she said, and swear to God, I heard an unmistakable, *dun dun dun* of doom. "Hadley and me."

Dun dun dun, indeed.

So now, here we are on the huge patio overlooking the Constable-Riester compound—I mean backyard. Just me, Sam, his mom, stepdad and Max. Charlie and Evan inhaled their food—seriously, I don't think they even chewed it—and took off to play video games.

I wish I was with them.

And I hate video games.

Then again, sitting here at this moment in time does have its advantages. Number one being the food. The table is loaded, grilled corn smeared with cheesy butter, huge, tinfoil-wrapped baked potatoes that'd been cooked in the coals of the firepit, toppings for them —butter, sour cream, chives and real bacon bits—sourdough rolls from the Davis bakery (I've had two so far and am eyeing a third) and thick, juicy steaks.

Steaks. Not hot dogs. Not burgers.

But honest-to-God, top-of-the-line, so-tender-each-bite-practically-melts-in-your-mouth-and-makes-you-want-to-cry-it's-so-delicious ribeye steaks.

Because when you're a Constable-Riester, not only do you feed your family freaking steak at your it's-just-a-Saturday-night-cookout, but you can afford to feed the riffraff your children bring home, too.

The last time Sam ate at our place, we had grilled cheese sandwiches and tomato soup.

I mean, he ate two sandwiches, so he must've liked them, but still...

"Sam tells me you're also going to continue working for Glenwood after the summer ends," Dr. Constable-Riester says to me.

All part of her catching-up-with-Hadley plan, which so far has consisted of her asking about how my sisters and Taylor are doing, what classes I'll be taking senior year, and if I've read any good books lately.

I have, but she was probably hoping it was something more like *The Great Gatsby* or *Pride and Prejudice* and not *The Baking Bible*.

Whatever.

What's been left unsaid are all the questions I'm sure she'd really like to ask, such as what did I do that had her sweet baby boy leaving her for the wilds of LA, what are my intentions toward aforementioned precious child, and when will I set him free of my evil clutches?

Or something like that.

"Is that what you'd like to pursue after graduation?" she continues, spearing a piece of lettuce (Dr. Constable-Riester doesn't do carbs unless its wine). "A career in landscaping?"

"God no," I blurt. Loudly. And quite vehemently, if all the weird looks I'm getting are anything to go by. Even Max, who's been nothing but six feet of grunts, shrugs and too much sullen testosterone throughout the meal, raises his eyebrows.

Blushing like mad, I duck my head and set the ear of corn I'd been about to bite into on my plate. Wipe my fingers on my napkin. "I mean, it's a great job. And Mr. G's really nice."

This I direct to Patrick. Lest he think I'm ungrateful that he got Sam and me the jobs in the first place. He gives me a no-foul, no-harm grin.

Even though the only reason we got these particular jobs is because Sam, unlike me, enjoys working outdoors, doesn't mind sweating, sunburns, bugs or dirt and wanted a job where he'd be kept busy.

That boy has an endless supply of energy.

"And I appreciate Mr. G keeping me on," I say, turning to Dr. Constable-Riester. It's not even a lie. Not a full one, anyway. I do appreciate it—mainly because it pays one and a half times minimum wage.

Which was why I accepted his offer.

Well, that and because Sam accepted it first.

It might not even be so bad in the fall, when the work is mostly leaf removal, trimming shrubs and trees and fertilizing lawns. When we'll still be working together.

But in the winter, Glenwood Landscaping turns into Glenwood Snow Removal and Sam's focus will turn to basketball and college applications, leaving me to shovel walks, clear driveways and try not to succumb to frostbite all by my lonesome.

Hooray.

"But it's not something I want to do for a living," I finish lamely. "Not, like, forever or anything."

"No?" Sam's mom asks. "What are your future plans, then?"

To survive this dinner.

And maybe have Sam sneak me a plate of leftovers to take home.

Adults. Always telling us to enjoy our childhoods, not to grow up too fast, and in the next breath wanting us to have our entire futures planned out.

I take a sip of my water. "I'm actually, uh, looking into culinary schools."

It's the first time I've admitted it out loud and hearing it, saying it, makes it more real.

Makes it more realistic, like it could really, truly happen and isn't just some wild, crazy pipedream.

"You're interested in becoming a chef?" Patrick asks. He's the cook in Sam's family and his eyes are lit at the possibility of us bonding over our mutual love of sautéing vegetables and roasting meats.

I smile at him apologetically. "A pastry chef."

Sam slides his hand onto my thigh under the table. "Hadley wants to own her own bakery someday."

Dr. Constable-Riester grimaces. Either she has X-ray vision and knows Sam's hand is, once again, close to the danger zone, or she's dismayed at the thought of sugary, carb-loaded baked goods.

She recovers quickly and even manages a small smile. "So you like baking?"

"I love it."

It's one of the few questions I've been able to answer quickly and honestly.

One point for me.

"And what do you enjoy about it?" she asks.

I blink at her. Several times. No one's ever asked me that before. I've never even thought about it before.

"Well," I begin slowly, "for one thing, I like how...precise baking is. That there are rules to follow and that if something doesn't work out—if a cookie spreads too much or bread doesn't rise or your cake is gummy—you can go back and figure out why and fix it for the next time. And I like that, despite all those rules and precision, how versatile baking can be. How creative you can get using the same basic ingredients—flour, sugar, eggs and butter—and make so many different things. How you can experiment with different flavor combinations or tweak the ingredients to make a cookie chewy or crispy. I like the...the magic of it, I guess." I take a moment to inhale and reach down to link my fingers with Sam's, still on my leg. "But mostly, I love seeing people enjoy what I've made. It just..."

My throat tightens. It's stupid to get emotional over baked goods, but there you have it.

The contestants on *The Great British Baking Show* would understand. There are tears in every episode.

I keep my gaze on my plate. Shrug. "It just makes me happy."

Makes me feel as if I've given them something, some small piece of myself. Like I've showed them, the only way I know how, how much they mean to me. That they're important to me.

Sam leans over and presses a lingering kiss to my cheek. "You make me happy," he murmurs.

"You're not the only one, Sammy-boy," Max says, not bothering to look up from his phone as he speaks. "Hadley and her *cookies* have made many a guy happy."

While I got hot all over, my stomach turning sickeningly, he lifts his head and winks at me. Because he is Satan.

Or at least, he's a mean, overaged brat who loves nothing more than messing with his brother. If only to get a reaction.

Which wouldn't work so well—or be nearly as satisfying to Max —if Sam didn't fall for it. Every. Single. Time.

"What's that supposed to mean?" Sam asks, tensing beside me. He's a bristling mass of protective boyfriend, ready to leap over the table and put his brother in a choke hold.

Being around these two brings my appreciation for my sisters to a whole new, atmospheric level.

"Just that Charlie, Evan and I each ate three of those oatmeal pie things Had brought," he says smoothly. "What else could I mean?"

Yeah. Ha ha. Not going there.

"Three?" Dr. Constable-Riester asks, horrified and thankfully ignorant—or ignoring—her son's unsubtle subtext. "One would've been more than enough."

"You know me, Ma," Max says, typing on his phone. "No self-control."

I slide a glance at his mom, who's giving him the narrow-eyed, pinched-mouth look she gave me and Sam earlier.

Max might not have any self-control but he must have a death wish.

Dr. Constable-Riester is definitely nobody's *ma*.

"No phones at the dinner table," Patrick tells him, his tone quiet but firm.

"I'm done anyway," Max says, pushing his chair back to stand. He tucks his phone into the front pocket of the cargo shorts he'd changed into after his strange and highly suspicious disappearing act with Whitney.

The one where she insisted nothing happened between them.

"You may be done," his mom says, steel in her tone, "but we're not. Sit down."

"Can't," he says simply. Yep. Death wish for sure. "I told some people I'd meet them at seven."

"What people?" she asks.

"You don't know them."

She and Patrick exchange a loaded glance.

"Where are you going to be?" Patrick asks.

"Out."

"What time will you be home?" his mom asks.

He shrugs. "Later."

Her expression turns downright scary. "Maxwell--"

"We're heading out, too," Sam says choosing that moment either because he thinks it's our best chance at escape or he just can't help stepping in and saving the day. Even for his brother. "We're going to the early show at the movies."

We're doing no such thing, but he can hardly tell his mom we're going back to my trailer to where we'll spend the next few hours unsupervised.

He nudges my leg then stands. I give an inner sigh. There goes my chance for a third roll.

"But you were gone all last night," Dr. Constable-Riester reminds him as I get to my feet. "I think you should stay home tonight."

She looks across the table to her husband, who picks up some silent cue and nods. "You can watch a movie here. I'll make sure Charlie and Evan stay out of your hair."

Sam's expression turns mulish. Never a good sign. "I told Jackson we'd double date with him and Fiona tonight."

"I thought Jack was at his mom's this weekend," Max says, all calm and curious, as if he's just bringing up a random fact.

Except his eyes gleam at the prospect of busting his brother for lying.

Dr. Constable-Riester straightens and turns to Sam. "You told me you spent the night at Jackson's house last night."

Last night when he spent the night with me.

And now Max is looking downright cheery.

Crap.

"I did," Sam assures her while I stand there, my stomach in knots, my face flushed, doing my best to become invisible. "Jackson's going to his mom's next weekend."

Sam's mom is not buying this.

Oh, God. We are so dead.

"And if I call Mr. Vecellio," she says, flicking a suspicious, I-know-you're-corrupting-my-sweet-virginal-boy-with-your-wild-and-seductive-ways glance at me before focusing on Sam again, "he'll confirm this?"

So very, very dead.

Because Jack *is* at his mom's place in Columbus for the weekend. He left Thursday and won't be home until tomorrow night.

"Of course," Sam says easily, like it's the truth, the whole truth and nothing but the truth. He even goes so far as to take out his phone, unlock it and pull up Jackson's number. "Here."

And he holds it out to her.

Turns out my boyfriend can be a very convincing liar when he has to be.

Something else to ponder later.

What follows are some of the tensest, most uncomfortable moments of my life, where neither Sam nor his mom moves, gazes locked, each waiting for the other to break.

Seriously. Where are those locusts when you need them?

"You're right," Max says, breaking the silence. "Jack's going to C-bus next weekend. I just texted him."

He, too, holds his phone out to his mother and whatever she reads has her relaxing in her chair, her eyes closing briefly as if in silent prayer.

It's enough to convince her Sam's telling the truth.

Max must've sent Jack a text telling him what to say.

Now it's Sam's and my turn to exchange a quick glance. Max just helped Sam out. Willingly.

That is so not good.

"Fine," Dr. Constable-Riester says, relenting in a way that makes it clear it's anything but fine. "You may go to the movies. But I want you home by eleven tonight."

"Sure," Sam says, quick to agree now that he's got his way. He shoves his chair in. "Eleven. No problem."

"Thank you for dinner," I tell Patrick, as there's no way I can ever, ever look Sam's mom in the eye again. "Everything was delicious."

He smiles at me. *He's* always liked me, anyway. "Anytime."

"Oh, hey," Max says as Sam and I are turning to leave. "Do you have that fifty bucks you borrowed from me last week?"

And there it is.

Max's payback.

That boy does nothing for free.

There's no way Sam borrowed money from Max. For one thing, even though Max makes more than minimum wage working for his stepdad at Patrick's accounting firm, he only works about twenty hours. And he blows his paycheck pretty much as soon as he gets it.

For another, Sam knows better than to owe Max anything.

Yet here we are. Sam getting out his wallet and counting out bills until he gets to fifty. "Here," he says through gritted teeth, holding the cash out.

Grinning, Max takes it. "You ever need anything else, just let me know."

The offer, made to sound all full of brotherly love and generosity, has Dr. Constable-Riester's expression softening.

For someone so smart, she's super gullible.

Eyes narrowed to slits, Sam grunts. Then puts his wallet back, grabs my hand and heads up the walkway toward the garage, his stride long and ticked off. I jog to keep up.

A few minutes later, we're pulling out of the driveway when Sam's phone buzzes from its place in the console between us.

"Can you check that?" he asks.

"It's Max," I say, opening the text. "That'll be another fifty," I read. "Next time, show some gratitude."

Sam's jaw clenches, his hands so tight on the steering wheel they turn white. "Asshole," he mutters.

"If you keep paying him, he'll just keep asking for more."

"He's just yanking my chain. He'll get tired of it eventually. It's not like he needs my money."

Good point. While Max does blow through the cash he earns, he has plenty of his own. Well, not his own really, more like his parents'. And he does get bored easily, hence his endless drive to get drunk or high whenever possible.

"Besides," Sam continues, "he knows if he pushes me too far, I'll push back."

True.

God knows Sam has dirt on Max.

I just can't imagine him ever using it.

Am afraid of Max's reaction if he does.

"Just...be careful," I warn him softly. "Max isn't like how he used to be. The last thing you want is him being the keeper of one of your secrets."

Something I know for a fact.

42

WHEN I HEAR DEVYN'S ALARM GOING OFF IN HER BEDROOM TWO DAYS later, I'm setting the pan of brownies with white chocolate frosting I made after dinner onto the table.

Hopefully they'll lull Dev into a sense of complacency. Or a state of sugar-induced bliss. I'll take either one as long as she hears me out.

By the time she steps into the kitchen, her mouth opened in a huge yawn, hair messy from her nap, I have a cup of coffee poured, doctored up with copious amounts of vanilla-flavored creamer and am holding it out for her. "Hi. You're just in time."

She blinks at the coffee. Frowns. Then finally takes it with way more wariness than the situation calls for. It's not like I spit in it. "Just in time for what?"

Older sisters. So mistrustful.

"Just in time to have a brownie," I say with a sweeping hand gesture at the deliciousness before her.

Eyebrows drawn together, Dev sits at the table. "What do you want?"

Rolling my eyes, I cut into the brownies. "Nothing. God. Suspicious much?"

As she sips her coffee, she eyes me over her coffee cup. "You're not taking another day off work, so don't even ask."

"I don't want a day off." I want all the days off, but now is not the time to bring up how much my job sucks or that I hate it. Plus, she already knows as I may have mentioned it once or twice or a thousand times.

I set a huge piece of brownie on a plate and slide it in front of her. "I just thought you'd like a brownie."

She glances from my face to the brownie and back to my face. But the lure of rich, dark chocolate is too much for her to resist and she breaks off a corner and pops it into her mouth.

I put a smaller brownie on a second plate and sit down. Swipe my finger through the frosting and suck it off as I sneak glances at Dev and try to decide how best to start this conversation.

It's not that she's unapproachable. Or difficult. It's more that she's always busy. And tired. And stressed.

That's her life: working, sleeping and stressing. All because she chose to stick around when no one else would.

I wonder what her life would be like if she'd made a different choice. If she'd had a chance to follow her dreams.

Wonder if I deserve my own chance. If it's selfish to want one.

I wipe my fingers on a paper towel. "Did you see that brochure I left on your bed?"

In the midst of breaking off another piece of brownie, Dev freezes. Then slowly sets the bite down. "Yes. I saw it."

I wait but that's all she gives me. "Did you read it?"

She sits back. "No."

"Oh," I say, determined to be hopeful no matter what. To have a positive attitude, see the glass as half-full and think only the happiest of happy thoughts. "That's okay. I mean, I guess you don't have to read it."

Even if I do say it in a way that makes it clear I want her to read it.

If she notices my bait, dangling there in front of her, all shiny and tasty, she ignores it. Just makes a noncommittal sound and sips her coffee while avoiding my eyes.

"It's just I wanted to get your opinion..." I push my plate forward then drag it back. "I'm thinking of applying there in the fall."

My tone is super casual, as if it's a passing thought I'd had, and not one that's been plaguing me for days. As if I couldn't care less about it, when the opposite is starting to be all too true.

Silence surrounds us. Thick, heavy, oppressive silence, the kind that does not bode well for my happy thoughts.

The kind that smothers those thoughts. Strangles my hopes.

Dev sighs and finally meets my eyes. "Had--"

"They have a lot of really good programs," I blurt out before she has the chance to tell me why that's a bad idea. Before she can list all the reasons I shouldn't want more for my life. "They have degree and certificate programs and both of them are less expensive than a four-year university."

"It's still too much."

"They have scholarships," I point out, feeling like Taylor, trying to defer and deflect. Trying to get my way.

Her mouth twists. "Not everyone can get a scholarship, and even if you do, it probably won't cover the costs of tuition *and* room and board."

"Yeah, but I'll be working at Glenwood all year making good money." Yes, I agreed to stay on after summer to continue working with Sam, but that was only part of it. This, this chance, was the main reason. "I can save most of that money. Use it toward tuition or whatever. And I can get loans."

She stands, her movements jerky, her focus on picking up her plate and cup. "That money needs to go toward living expenses. There won't be any left over to save. And loans have to be repaid. Whether you finish school or not."

"I would finish."

"How do you know that? You've never taken piano or ballet lessons, have never joined a club or sports team. How can you be so certain that you'll finish something, something this huge, when you've never started anything?"

My head goes back like she's slapped me. Well, in a way, she has. Even if what she said is true.

"I just want to apply," I say, my voice thick with tears. Husky with pleading. "I'll apply and we'll look into the scholarships, the loans. Maybe there's a way to figure out how to make it work."

Dev stares out the small window over the sink, her face in profile, and I notice the faint lines around her eyes. The paleness of her complexion. The way her shoulders are rounded as if she's carrying a great weight.

She's just tired, I tell myself, but it's more than that. She looks defeated. Muted, like an old painting, the colors faded, the canvas worn.

It's partly my fault, I know, for adding to her stress. To that invisible weight. My fault for asking for something out of reach when I'm not supposed to ask for anything.

My fault for wanting even the possibility of more—more than the life she's given me. More than the life she's lived.

It's not fair of me to ask for a chance when she didn't get one. When Zoe didn't.

It's not fair.

But I still want it. That chance. That possibility.

"There's no point in applying," she says, turning to face me. "You'll just get your hopes up."

Hope. The most dangerous thing of all to a girl like me.

I nod but I can't look at her. She's not being mean. Or at least, she's not being mean on purpose. She just doesn't want me to be disappointed.

Like she is.

"It was just an idea," I say, soft and small.

A stupid, useless, hopeful idea.

The worst kind.

———

I don't tell Sam.

He'll just try and cheer me up. Will reassure me that there's a way to make it work, that we'll figure out something. In Sam's world, everything he touches turns to gold.

Must be nice, living in that fantasyland.

But I live in the real world. So I don't tell my boyfriend I won't be applying to PTC or any other school. That I won't be moving to Pittsburgh with him after graduation. That all the dreams and plans we'd made the past two weeks will never come true.

I'm not going to be a pastry chef or own a bakery someday. I'm going to stay right here, in this town.

I don't tell him I threw away the brochure Whitney brought me. That I deleted all the sites I'd searched for and saved on my phone—sites for other schools in both Pennsylvania and New York, that offer programs in the arts and restaurant management.

I don't tell him how excited I'd gotten about the possibility of going to PTC, of going anywhere. How hopeful I'd let myself get about having a different future. It'd been stupid, thinking I could change my circumstances. Selfish, wanting more than what I already have.

I don't tell him any of that.

And I try really, really hard not to blame him for getting my hopes up. For pushing me in a direction I can't go.

I keep it all to myself.

No more hoping. No more dreaming.

No more wanting things I'll never have.

I've always known what my future looks like. Living in this trailer with my sisters, helping take care of Taylor. Doing my share. Working two or three jobs and scrimping and saving.

It means never having enough.

Not enough money for anything other than the basics.

Not enough time for a social life.

Not enough energy to even hope for something more.

For people like Sam and his friends, the four to eight years after high school mean college and grad school. Summers off and

Christmas break binge-watching Netflix. Spring breaks in Mexico. It's travel and parties and friends. All leading to some fabulous life working an exciting, well-paying, fulfilling job.

I've always known Sam wouldn't be a part of my future. It's why I fought my feelings for him for so long. This time next year he'll be making plans to leave me. Again. He'll start a whole new life on some college campus I'll never see, filled with people I'll never meet. He'll have a routine I'll never know. New friends who'll replace Jackson and Graham, Kenzie and Tori. New girls who'll replace me. Girls who are smarter. Who have goals and ambitions and bright futures. Girls who aren't afraid of their feelings. Who are open and honest and willingly give their hearts, trusting they won't be broken.

Girls who are so much better than me.

The next time he leaves, he won't come back. Oh, there'll be visits, but those will become less and less frequent, his time spent here shorter and shorter until it simply ends.

It's a truth I've always known. A reality I've always been aware I'd face. I let myself forget it for a few days. Let myself get carried away with stupid, useless dreams.

It won't happen again.

Of course, I could guarantee that by texting Sam right now.

By breaking things off between us.

I should. All we're doing is delaying the unavoidable:

Our ending.

But I can't. And it has nothing to do with my being brave or wanting to keep the promise I'd made Sam to give us a chance. And it's not because I believe Sam and I will somehow find a way to stay together after graduation.

I'm not delusional.

Just selfish.

Sam isn't going to be a part of my life forever. I accept that. But he's a part of it now.

And I'm going to hold on to him, to us, for as long as I possibly can.

The more time I spend with Sam, the deeper I fall for him. And the harder it's going to be when he leaves. But I don't care. I want that time. I want today and tomorrow and every minute between now and then.

And when the end comes, I'll move on with my life.

Just like I did the last time Sam left.

43

S<small>AM'S QUIET AS WE WALK HAND IN HAND DOWN THE LONG DRIVEWAY</small> toward the Vecellios' lake house, his phone in his free hand, the light from it guiding our way in the twilight. There are so many people here we had to park on the main road, but luckily the house is close to the water, surrounded by trees and set far enough away from any neighbors that we shouldn't have to worry about having the cops called on us.

We pass a seemingly endless line of cars, trucks, SUVs and even a lone motorcycle as we head down the steep, winding slope. The sounds of the party—music and laughter and happy shouts—that were muted and dull when we got out of Sam's Explorer grow louder, sharper, with each step we take.

And Sam gets quieter. Or at least, more withdrawn.

"You okay?" I ask him.

He glances at me. "Huh?"

"Are you okay?" I say again, slower this time and with more care, a touch more volume and a surplus of patience.

I've gotten this part of our evening down pat after our hour drive out here, where I became quite the chatterbox, yammering on and on about Taylor finally using the potty, Zoe acting weird and secretive, spending most of her time at home on her phone like she has some secret boyfriend, and the latest chocolate chip cookie recipe I tried, because the long, empty silences made me antsy, like my skin was too tight.

Anxious, like we were heading straight for imminent doom and the only way to delay it was to talk and talk and talk.

Which turned out to be easy enough as I got double use out of my words because whenever I brought up some new topic or mentioned another scintillating tidbit about my life or shared one of my thoughts, Sam frowned slightly at being torn from his internal musings and *huh?-ed* me.

"I'm fine," he tells me.

That, too, has been said many, many times since he picked me up, as I've asked him some variation of that same are-you-okay theme a few times now.

And we keep walking.

Silently.

All the better to let that anxiousness dig a little deeper. Grow a little bigger.

I chew on my bottom lip. I should've stayed home.

I wanted to. When Sam mentioned yesterday that there was going to be an end of summer blowout party, I told him I would skip it since Tori was throwing it along with Jackson. But he insisted that Tori specifically said I was invited and, between his pestering me to go even though I told him to go without me, and Whitney wanting me here as well, I gave in.

That doom-and-gloom cloud has been hanging over my head ever since, a premonition of things to come. Namely several long, awkward and painful hours of me standing by myself while Sam's friends ignore me or, in the case of Abby and Macy, try to incinerate me with their death glares.

So, yeah. Should be a blast.

The music gets louder and the glow from the party reaches us as we near the last curve. Sam turns off his phone's light and sticks it in his pocket as the house comes into view. It's huge, three stories with an A-line shape, wide, wraparound upper and lower decks and floor-to-ceiling windows, all ablaze with light.

There must be at least one hundred people here, gathered on those decks and around the roaring bonfire as well as inside the brightly lit house.

Pretty sure this isn't what Tori's parents and Jack's dad thought she meant when she asked if they could host a small, intimate gathering of a few close friends here before school starts next week.

Then again, Tori's parents and Jackson's dad are both out of town at some distant aunt's funeral. What they don't know won't hurt them.

Or get Tori and Jackson grounded for life.

Our steps slow. I know why I'm dragging my feet—I'm in no hurry to join the festivities. Straightforward and simple, that's me.

But it's unusual for Sam to hesitate. To hang back.

I chew on my lower lip. Rub my thumb along the back of his hand. Okay, something is obviously up with him. Just as he obviously doesn't want to talk about it.

I should let it go. Trust him to come to me when he's ready, to tell me what's bothering him on his own and in his own time. That's what I'd want from him. Time and space to deal with my problems on my own.

Except this isn't about me. And one thing I learned from what happened between us last year is that if you're not careful, if you insist on too much space, too much independence, you wind up alone, surrounded by emptiness.

And I never, never want that sense of isolation, of loneliness for Sam.

"I know something's bugging you," I say, tugging his hand to get him to stop—which he does with a drawn-out sigh.

I tug again so he'll look at me and I search his eyes. "Talk to me," I continue softly. "Tell me what's going on."

Let me help you.

He frees his hand from mine and shoves it through his hair. "It's nothing. Just some family stuff." Someone shouts and laughter breaks out and Sam glances over his shoulder at the party. "I don't want to get into it tonight. Let's just have some fun, okay?"

He holds his hand out and for the first time in a long time—days or weeks or possibly even months now—I hesitate. Like I used to.

But then I take it, linking my fingers with his because even though it's only been a few months, even though I swore I wouldn't let myself fall back into the same old pattern of counting on Sam to always be in my life, even though I promised myself I'll be just fine when Sam leaves for college next year, I can't help but accept every tiny bit, piece and morsel of his time, attention and affection while I still have them.

Can't help but hold on to them. For as long as I can.

44

A FEW HOURS LATER, I WATCH THE PEOPLE GATHERED AROUND THE FIRE from my spot on the upper deck. The party has not calmed down in the least, but from this spot, it's much quieter, the music a dull thrum that vibrates the deck floor, the laughter not nearly as sharp, the voices muted.

I lean both elbows on the railing, holding my Coke can over the edge. So far my night has consisted of me following Sam from the living room to the kitchen to the lower deck to the fire as he made what I've come to think of his "rounds." Seriously, that boy works a crowd like a politician. Smiles are doled out, laughter ensues. There were even three—yes, I counted them—slaps on the back.

Gone was the silent, moody Sam I had the pleasure of spending an hour with in the car. The moment we stepped through the doorway, he transformed into Golden Sam, all good cheer, jokes and charm.

Which wouldn't bother me so much if he hadn't brushed off my attempts at getting him to talk to me.

If his sudden and drastic transformation didn't remind me so much of Max.

I tagged along as Sam chatted and joked. And he was so busy

schmoozing and acting like there was nothing but happiness and joy in his heart, it didn't seem to matter that I stood by his side like a lump of coal.

A silent lump of coal.

Ignoring how only a few people greeted or acknowledged my existence. That most of their gazes skipped over me like I was a huge pimple marring Sam's beauty—something you know is there but pretend not to see.

Something you figure will be gone soon enough.

I couldn't even hide out in some corner with Whitney as her time has been fully occupied by Colby doing some hard-core flirting.

Since she didn't seem to mind in the least, I just said hello then left her to it.

No sense going from being a lump of coal to third wheel.

Especially since Whitney seems pretty into him. Not that I blame her. Colby is a total babe, but way too slick for my taste.

The door opens behind me and I turn, expecting it to be Sam looking for me (I may have slipped away to use the bathroom, oh, twenty or so minutes ago) but it's Tori who looks just as surprised—and disappointed—as I feel.

Guess my boyfriend hasn't missed me yet.

Or noticed I'm gone.

Not that that's the reason I'm up here or anything.

"What are you doing out here?" Tori asks, stepping onto the deck. "Bedrooms are off limits."

There's a loud thump from the room next door followed by a girl's giggle and a guy's deep murmur. I cross my arms, shoulders hunching. "Off-limits for everyone? Or just me?"

She stalks over to the door of the bedroom. Pounds on the glass with the side of her fist. "Jackson! Knock it off!"

Well, that makes sense. Jackson is one of the few people brave enough to go against Tori's wishes.

Plus, it's just as much his family's house as it is hers.

And that is, technically, *his* bedroom when they're here.

There's another thump followed by a muffled curse and more femi-
nine laughter. Then Jack opens the door and sticks his head out, his
brown hair mussed, his shirt on inside out. "I was just making sure no one
broke our nonnegotiable rule about not going upstairs." His gaze slides
to me and he frowns in mock outrage, setting his hands on his hips. "How
dare you break our sacred rule? Have you no morals? No honor?" He
shakes his fist. "Goddamn millennials and their sense of entitlement."

Tori and I exchange a look. Jackson is the drama queen in her
family.

"We're not millennials," his girlfriend Fiona says as she steps up
behind him, putting her glasses on. It's tough to tell if her hair is
mussed—it's huge and curly and always looks pretty wild. But her
shirt is on the right way. Though the buttons are done up wrong.
"We're Generation Z."

He glances at her with a fond smile. She's sort of literal—about
everything—and way smart. "Doesn't have the same ring, babe."

She looks thoughtful. "No. I guess it doesn't."

"Anyway," he says, sliding his arm around her waist and pulling
her up to his side, "I was just telling my favorite cousin--"

"Last week when you wanted Adam to buy you beer, you said he
was your favorite," Tori says of her older brother.

"Ah, but he declined to help me out in my hour of need and therefore fell a spot in the rankings. Congrats. You're now my
number one."

"Hooray," she deadpans.

"As I was saying," he continues to Fiona, "I was just telling my
very favorite cousin how you and I were only up here, in this room
that is clearly off-limits to everyone during party time, on a recon-
naissance mission because we thought we spied an interloper making
her way up here." He nods in my direction. "And there she is." He tsks
at me. "For shame."

Fiona frowns and leans toward him. "I thought we were going to
tell her we were up here looking for my phone," she says in a loud
whisper.

He pats her hip, not the least bit perturbed at her outing them. "Change of plans. Let's just go with it."

I cover a laugh with a cough. This is the most fun I've had since Sam picked me up.

I wonder if, instead of trailing after him the rest of the night, I could tag along after these three?

"If you're going to lie to me," Tori says, not nearly as amused at I am, "at least have the decency to get your stories straight. And next time try to come up with something more original."

Jack grins then gives her a little salute. "Will do, cuz."

And he ducks back into the room, tugging Fiona with him, shutting the door behind them.

At which point there is yet another thump.

And more giggling.

Then a loud thud.

"You wouldn't think Fiona would be that...rambunctious," I say.

Tori stops glaring at the door to face me. "Fi's not very coordinated," she says tightly. "But she's super sweet. And Jack's really into her."

Tori may be the first person to tell you off, but she's also the first person to stand up for someone if she thinks they're being mistreated, misused or picked on.

Especially if she cares about you.

"I wasn't saying anything bad about her," I point out. "Just that things sound pretty--"

There's another sound from the room, this time a bang followed by a crash. We both wince.

"—intense in there," I finish.

"If they keep that up," she mutters, "they're going to destroy his room and break a body part or two." She pauses. "Then again, I wouldn't mind being there when Jack tries to explain how he broke his femur to Uncle Rick."

We smile at each other and say, "Bright side," at the same time.

For a moment, it's like it was between us, when we used to say that exact same thing when one of us was trying to find the happy in a crap situation.

Then her smile fades. Her expression cools.

And the moment passes like it never even was.

Sort of like our friendship.

My throat goes dry and I take a sip of pop. When I lower the can, Tori's studying me through narrowed eyes.

Expecting her to ask me again what I'm doing up here, I work on coming up with a plausible excuse like I had to go to the bathroom and the one downstairs was occupied or I came up here to snoop through her stuff, maybe rifle through her dresser drawers, or that I thought I left my favorite beach towel here the last time I was here well over a year ago and wanted it back.

Anything but the truth.

That I needed a few minutes of peace. That I wanted to hide, if only for a little while.

That even though I'm surrounded by people, I still feel incredibly lonely.

"Where's Sam?" she asks instead.

Well, that's simple enough.

I gesture at the fire and she takes the few steps needed to stand next to me at the railing. We both look down at the small crowd but I don't see Sam.

"Idiot," she says under her breath and when I finally spy Sam, I'm not sure if she's talking about me or him.

Because he's not with the others. He's a good fifty feet away under the lights of the dock at the water's edge. Bending his head to hear whatever it is Abby has to say.

She's touching him. Her hand on his forearm as she speaks, her body angled toward him so that the slightest movement will have them brushing together.

She's touching him. Is standing close to him. Closer than a girl who's not his girlfriend should stand.

And he's not backing away.

A lump forms in my throat and I straighten and turn away. Take another, longer swallow of pop.

No. My boyfriend hasn't missed me at all.

"You just going to ignore that?" Tori asks.

I take another drink. Pretend I don't know what she's talking about. "What?"

She rolls her eyes so far back she probably saw yesterday. "That," she says, jabbing her finger in Sam's direction.

I stiffen. "I trust Sam."

It's why I haven't asked him if he ever really did tell Abby not to text him anymore. Why I haven't asked if she has.

"Well, of course you trust Sam," she says. "He'd never cheat on you. But that doesn't mean he won't do stupid things once in a while. Like talk to his ex-girlfriend alone on a dark dock."

"It's not dark. And they're not alone." More like...separated from everyone else. "And he can talk to whoever he wants."

"Even if it bothers you?"

"I didn't say it bothered me."

Except it does. It bothers me so much.

I bite my lower lip and glance over my shoulder.

Still there, on that dock. Still talking. Still standing close.

Still with her hand on his arm.

"God, you don't fight for anything, do you?"

I bristle. "What's that supposed to mean?"

She shakes her head. "Doesn't matter. Have you seen Kenzie?"

"What?"

"Kenzie. I'm looking for her." Her mouth turns down. "Last time I saw her she was sitting on Jacob's lap."

I give an inner groan. For the past three years, Jacob Rothschild has been Kenzie's on-again, off-again, please-please-please-don't-let-her-get-back-on-again boyfriend.

Yes. Three. Years.

Tori and me? Not members of Team Jacob.

"I haven't seen her," I say, leaving out the fact that I've been up here going on half an hour. "If I do, I'll tell her you're looking for her."

She nods—Tori's grudging version of thanking me. "Make sure this door is locked and my bedroom door closed when you leave."

I frown as she walks toward her bedroom, surprised she's letting me stay up here.

As if she knows I'm hiding and isn't going to force me out into the open. Not yet.

But that wasn't my only surprise tonight. Not even the first.

"Why did you invite me?" I ask, stopping her as she reaches the doorway. "Here. Tonight."

She faces me, is silent a moment then admits, "I was afraid you wouldn't let Sam come if you weren't invited."

"I wouldn't do that."

"Yeah? Well, I didn't know that so..." She shrugs.

"You knew," I say, stepping forward. "You knew because we were friends. You know me."

Leaning against the doorframe, she smirks. "I never knew you."

"That's not true," I whisper, switching my Coke can from my right hand to my left. I wipe my damp right palm down the front of my shorts. "Before, you said you and Kenzie thought you were my friends but that I thought differently, but I didn't. I didn't," I repeat firmly. "You were my friends."

"Yeah. We were," she says with a slow nod. "But you weren't ours. You never trusted us, not really. And you can't be someone's friend if you don't trust them."

I'm stunned. It's like an electrical current has gone through me, zapping my ability to move. To breathe. "I trusted you."

But even as I say it, even as I want to believe it, I know it's not true.

"Please. You never opened up to us. We shared everything with you—what was going on in our lives and with our families. If we liked a boy or had our hearts broken by one. You never talked about your mom or if you were fighting with your sisters. You never told us how you really felt about Sam. You never made any overtures. You never called or texted first or asked one of us to do something," she continues, her words coming faster. Growing louder. "We were your friends for six years. Six. Years. And you never once had either of us over to your house. How do you think that made us feel?"

There's a roaring in my head, a scream of denial that wants to break loose but I hold it back. I hold it in.

"We told you everything," Tori says as she straightens. "We gave you everything. But you always kept a piece of yourself separate. You didn't trust us. Not with your secrets. Not to be your friends. And you never trusted that we really wanted to be yours."

She's breathing hard, her voice unsteady, but her gaze on mine is rock solid. "Kenzie and I were your friends," she continues, softer now. More resigned. "But you?" She shakes her head. "You were never ours."

45

I DON'T KNOW HOW LONG I STAND THERE, HEART RACING, STOMACH churning, as I stare at the door Tori pulls shut behind her.

Kenzie and I were your friends. But you? You were never ours.

I shake my head to clear it of her words. To rid myself of the memory of how hurt she'd sounded. How sad she'd looked.

Like maybe, just maybe, she'd missed me as much as I'd missed her.

But that can't be right.

Because if it is, it means everything she said was true. It means I was wrong, so very, very wrong, about Tori and Kenzie and the others being my friends only because of Sam. About them blaming me for him leaving.

About them being the ones who ended our friendship.

It means all the times I spent by myself last year, spending every weekend at home, being alone, was my own choice.

My own fault.

But it doesn't matter. Doesn't change anything. We can't go back. And it's pointless to go forward when in a year they'll all be leaving anyway.

They'll leave. And I'll stay.

That's the only truth that matters. The one I need to focus on.

The one I need to remember.

I turn and take the few steps needed to go back to the railing but the dock is empty. Sam is gone.

He's gone and I don't see him in the crowd around the fire.

I don't see Abby, either.

I whirl around and cross the deck. Shut and lock the door. As I step into the hallway, Jack and Fiona do the same from his room. Jack's shirt is on the right way and Fiona's buttons have been redone correctly.

We all size each other up for a moment. "Glad to know you both survived whatever that was in there," I tell them.

Fiona flushes.

Jack grins. "It was touch-and-go for a moment," he says, "but we managed to pull through."

I shut Tori's door and the three of us head for the stairs, a trio of rule-breaking soldiers marching back to obey our commander.

"Sorry for throwing you under the bus like that with Tori," Jack says.

"He's afraid of her," Fiona pipes up from Jack's other side. "And he told me we had to divert her attention off us and onto something—or in this case, someone—else. You were convenient."

"Now, now," Jack says good-naturedly as he pats her hand. "I'm not afraid of Tori." There's a beat of silence during which Fiona and I both just look at him before he cheerfully admits, "I'm terrified of her. The last time I pissed her off, her head did a full three-sixty, her eyes turned red and she called upon the demons of the dark to disembowel me. A guy can't mess around with power like that." He glances at me. "I knew you could handle it, though. You're one of the few people brave enough to stand up to her."

I snort as we reach the stairs. "More like dumb enough."

"That, too," he says, taking Fiona's hand and tugging her down the stairs.

I watch them descend and rejoin the party to smiles and laughter and jokes.

Welcomed back into the fold.

I start down the stairs slowly, scanning the huge living room for Sam's dark head while I have the advantage of height. Not seeing him, I pick up my pace. When I reach the bottom, I turn left and head into the kitchen.

Not there, either.

I search for a good five minutes, going from room to room. No one stops me. No one says *hey* or asks me who I'm looking for. No one says anything to me.

Not until I step outside onto the deck facing the dock.

"Well, well, well," a deep, familiar voice drawls from the shadows and I stop in my tracks. Stiffen. "If it isn't Hot Hadley." I turn slowly to find Max giving me a pointed, heavy-lidded up-down look because I'm a female and it's impossible for him not to take me in. Especially since I'm wearing a jean miniskirt and white tank top. "In the flesh."

I roll my eyes. Yes, I'm showing my legs and—gasp!—arms and shoulders. Skin is visible. Get over it.

There are a couple of chuckles from the two guys he's sharing a joint with—Brad Lyons and Alex Dryer. Max Constable is all sorts of hilarious with his unsubtle innuendos and smarmy tone.

Ugh.

I take a step toward the stairs leading to the yard only to stop and face him. "Have you seen Sam?"

"What? Baby brother's not trailing after you like a well-trained puppy? How unlike him."

"Never mind," I mutter and start walking again.

I make it to the edge of the grass when Max catches up to me and slings his arm around my shoulders. "Why the rush?"

I shrug him off. "Go. Away."

He puts his arm back around my shoulders. Leans into me. "And let Sammy's girlfriend wander around a party by herself in the dark? What kind of brother would that make that me?"

"The kind you usually are?" I ask, shoving his arm off once again and taking two steps to the side, putting some distance between us. I pick up my pace.

He catches up to me easily. "Haven't you heard? I'm a changed man. Mending my ways and all that. Being my brother's keeper is just a small part of me becoming a better version of myself. From here on out, I'm just like Sammy boy. Always doing what's right. Walking the straight and narrow. Et cetera, et cetera."

I stop so suddenly he takes three steps before he realizes it and stops, too. "You were just smoking pot," I say. "Like, literally one minute ago."

"Ah," he says, solemn and wise, like he's a six-foot, one-inch, completely ripped, floppy-haired Buddha, "but I didn't inhale."

I press the fingertips of both hands to my temples, if only to try and stop my brain from exploding.

I can't even with him right now. I just can't.

Dropping my hands, I start walking again.

He falls into step beside me. Again.

"It won't work, you know," I tell him as we approach the crowd at the fire.

"Don't give up hope. I'm sure we'll find Sam soon. Just look for the throng of adoring fans."

I do a double take. But I haven't been cloned and am walking beside a replica of myself. It's just Max sounding exactly like me.

At least, the things I say in my head, said in the same exact snide tone.

Not a pretty realization.

"No," I say. "I mean it won't work, the whole you-pretending-to-walk-the-straight-and-narrow thing. Whitney's not going to believe it. She's not going to believe it," I repeat, "but even if she did, it won't matter. She's not into you. And it's not because of how often you get wasted. It's *you*."

I expect him to get angry, or maybe to deny that he's interested in Whitney, but this is Max and Max Constable never does what you expect him to do.

He laughs. "You sure know how to hurt a guy. But this new even greater version of me isn't so I can win the girl. It's not even a choice. It's an order. One that came straight from a higher power."

"Please do not try and tell me you had some kind of religious epiphany."

"Oh, this edict wasn't from God—although the old man likes to believe he's right up there with any and all holy deities."

That has me stopping again. Frowning. "Wait...you talked to your dad?"

From what Sam has told me, ever since Max got back from LA, he's refused to even read any of the texts their father has sent him and won't take any of his calls.

"I didn't have a choice—a recurring theme when it comes to that bastard," he says lightly. "Flew across the country to deliver his ultimatum personally."

"Your dad was here?"

Max nods. "He showed up at the house this afternoon spouting orders and issuing threats." Someone shouts Max's name and he lifts a hand but his attention, sharp and intense, is on me. "Sam didn't tell you?"

"No. I mean...yeah, he did." Sort of.

Family stuff.

That's how he described it to me when I'd asked him to tell me what was wrong.

Right before telling me he didn't want to talk about it.

That he didn't want to share what was bothering him with me.

"Hey, now," Max says, tugging on the ends of my hair playfully. "No worries, Hot Hadley. I'm sure Sammy will think of some way to get out of moving back to LA."

I inhale sharply. "What?"

"Sam left that part out?" he asks with fake surprise. No, he knows exactly how little his brother told me. He knows and he's loving every second of this.

"You're lying," I manage to say, but my voice is thick and unsteady.

"Now, now. No need to disparage my honor. The old man showed up today and threatened to cut me off financially if I didn't get my head out of my ass—that's a direct quote, by the way."

"So? Your mom can still pay your tuition and buy you all the pretty things you've become accustomed to having in life."

"Ah, but dear old Dad convinced her that tough love is the only way to stop me from sliding into a life of excess and depravation. I have one semester to get my life back on track—another quote. After he laid out everything I have to do in order to continue enjoying his financial generosity--"

"Let me guess," I mutter. "Another quote?"

He winks. "You're catching on. Anyway, after I was given my To Dos and a much longer list of To Don'ts, the old man turned his attention to Sam. He doesn't want to take the chance of his golden boy slacking off and thinks the only way he can prevent that from happening is to have him back in LA."

No. *No.* It's not true. Sam isn't leaving me. Not again.

But if it's not true, why was Sam acting so weird earlier? Why wouldn't he tell me what was wrong?

I whirl on my heel and start stomping toward the fire with Max there, right there, by my side, whistling softly, like we're on a freaking stroll to some sunny beach.

I circle the crowd, ignoring Max as he gives out *Heys, How's it goings* and winks like they're confetti and he's the Head Fun Meister of tonight's festivities. I pass Tori, T.J. and Kenzie (guess Tori found her) but don't so much as slow down.

I'm on a mission and will not be deterred.

Not even when Graham is pushed forward by one of his idiot buddies and bumps into me.

Before I can shove him out of my way, Max is there doing it for me.

Knight in shining armor, right there.

One who sticks by my side as we approach a small group talking and laughing it up near the boathouse.

A group that includes my boyfriend.

And Abby O'Brien.

46

I stop. Just slam to a halt. Sam doesn't notice me right away. No, he's too busy charming the crowd, gesturing with his hands as he tells some story meant to enlighten or entertain. He's not standing by Abby, but she's staring at him with pure adoration.

My stomach turns.

That's it. No more parties where there's even the slightest chance Abby is in attendance.

I glance at the Constable boy beside me.

Better make that: no more parties where there's even the slightest chance either Abby *or* Max is in attendance.

I am so making that an official Sam and Hadley rule the second we get out of here.

"Told you we'd find him," Max says, delighted to have been right —and no doubt to see the mess his brother has gotten himself into. He brings his hand up to his mouth like a megaphone. "Yo! Sammy!"

Sam turns and when he sees me, there's a definite flash of *oh, shit* that crosses his face.

Yeah. Oh, shit, indeed.

But then Max snakes his arm around my waist and pulls me to his side, giving Sam a happy, happy wave with his free hand, and any guilt or remorse Sam may have felt is gone.

Replaced with a frown.

I wiggle free of Max's hold as Sam reaches us. "What's this?" he asks.

"Just helping your girl find you," Max says with a grin that's way too smug for my liking. "You're welcome."

Sam's mouth thins and he steps between me and Max. "Hey," he says, taking my hand. "I was wondering where you were."

I pull away and step back, not eager to have either Constable brother touching me at the moment. "Really? Because it seems to me like you didn't even notice I was gone."

His expression darkening, he moves closer to me. Drops his voice. "Of course I noticed. I was just about to come find you."

"I don't know, man," Max says. "It didn't look that way."

"Shut it," Sam growls at his brother.

Max is right. It didn't look like Sam was on the verge of searching me out. It looked like he was perfectly content right where he was. Without me.

But I can't think about that now. Can't worry about what he was doing while I was hiding on the deck outside Tori's bedroom, what he and Abby were discussing out on the dock or why I had to hear from his brother and not him that their father was in town.

There's only one thing I care about.

"Are you moving back to LA?"

"What?" He shakes his head. "No." But I must not look convinced because he repeats it. "No. I'm not going anywhere." He whirls on Max. "What the hell did you tell her?"

"I told her the truth," Max says and there's something in his tone, an underlying resentment and anger that has apprehension climbing my spine. "Just like you always do." He pauses, purses his lips. "Except she didn't seem to know the old man had been in town, let alone that he wants you to live with him again. Why is that?"

"I'd like to know the answer to that myself," I say.

Sam turns to me, hand held out as if to stop me from jumping to conclusions. "I was going to tell you."

"When was that going to be?" Max asks. "Before or after you told her about Abby?"

Sam goes rigid, and when he turns and speaks to his brother, his voice is tight, each word ground out as if through his teeth. "Shut. The fuck. Up."

We're gathering a crowd. Well, the crowd was always there, but now it's edging ever closer, quieting down, leaning in so as not to miss a single word.

"What's he talking about?" I ask, but Sam, glaring at Max, doesn't answer. I grab his forearm. Shake it lightly so he'll look at me. "Sam?"

"It's nothing," he assures me, but he says it too fast and he can't maintain eye contact. He does, however, glance over at the people watching us.

Right at Abby.

I throw his arm away from me and turn to storm off, but he wraps his fingers around my wrist, stopping me. "Look, it's not what you think. I'll explain everything later, okay?"

Before I can tell him no, that him withholding information about his ex-girlfriend is the exact opposite of okay and that he'd better start explaining right freaking now, Max steps over to my side. "Don't keep her in suspense. You're so big on honesty. Just tell her the truth. I'm sure she'll understand."

"Ignore him," Sam implores me. "Let's just go. I'll tell you everything on the way home."

Yes, that's what I want. To leave. I want to get as far away from here, as far from Abby and Max and everyone's curiosity as possible. Want to forget this entire night ever happened. Want to pretend I never saw Sam and Abby on the dock. That I never heard Max's words.

But I don't move. I can't. Because I'm too busy staring at Abby as she makes her way to the front of the crowd, Macy by her side. Our eyes meet. Lock. And she smiles. The same smug, triumphant smile she'd given me at Christmas.

I'll tell you everything...

I look down at Sam's hand, his fingers still wrapped around my wrist, then at his face. His handsome, familiar face. I know him better than anyone. I trust him.

But I don't believe him. Not now. Not about this.

I don't believe him and that's a problem because this is Sam and I'm supposed to believe everything he tells me. Because Sam doesn't lie. He's honest and honorable and good.

But maybe he's not *always* honest and honorable and good.

Maybe there are times when he's just as dishonest and imperfect as everyone else.

Maybe, every once in a while, he's just as messed up and confused and unsure as I am.

"Tell me now," I say softly.

His lips flatten and he gives a slight, quick shake of his head.

Sam hates being told what to do.

It's all part of that entitlement thing. Of getting whatever you want, whenever you want it. He's too used to it, having his own way. Way too comfortable being the one who makes the decisions. Who controls things.

Right now, though, I'm going to be the one who decides. I'm going to get what I want. It's only fair.

Even if that means asking the wrong Constable boy to give it to me.

Reaching down with my free hand, I slowly, purposefully unpeel Sam's fingers from my wrist.

Then I slowly, purposefully turn to face Max.

"Tell me."

Sam takes a step forward, "Had--"

"Abby dropped by the house last night," Max says quickly, relishing his role as villain in our little drama. "Spent a couple of hours there."

At first, it's like I don't even comprehend what he's saying. There's a buzzing sound in my head and my thoughts are fuzzy and I'm just completely confused. Last night? No. Last night Sam was with me.

We babysat Taylor and watched *Toy Story 4* and ate the caramel popcorn I made.

But then the buzzing gets louder and I realize it's not in my head —not only in my head—but it's the murmuring of the crowd, surrounding me. I cover my ears. Shut my eyes.

Yes, he was with me, but he left early, before nine. Had said he was tired and wanted to go to bed so he'd be well rested for basketball in the morning. He kissed me goodbye, like he always does. Told me he loved me.

And before he left, before he started yawning and stretching and saying how beat he was, he got a text message. One he'd said was from his mom. One he hadn't responded to.

But he had excused himself to use the bathroom a few minutes later.

Swallowing the sick taste in my mouth, I lower my hands. Open my eyes. I stare at Max, wanting, needing, him to take it all back. To deny his words. To say they're nothing but lies.

Except I'm looking at the wrong boy.

I'm just too terrified to look at the right one.

Sam edges closer, leaning down to speak near my ear. "Nothing happened," he says fast and low and rough. "I swear, Hadley. We just talked."

The air leaves my body in a long whoosh, like I've been punched in the stomach, and I hunch my shoulders, curling into myself.

Nothing happened.

Except something did happen. Abby was at Sam's house last night. She was at his house and he didn't tell me.

He would never have told me if Max hadn't outed him first.

"Did I forget to mention that Mom and Patrick weren't home?" Max asks me, except he's looking over my head at Sam, his eyes full of spite, his mouth turned up in a sneer. "And that Sam and Abby stayed tucked away in Sammy's bedroom with the door shut for over an hour?"

I recoil and cross my arms, digging my fingers into my biceps. The murmuring of the crowd rises like a wave, washing over me, weakening my defenses. I'm on the verge of breaking, beaten down by Max's words and Sam's secrets.

"Don't listen to him," Sam says, shoving Max aside and stepping between us again. Laying his hands on my shoulders, he ducks his head and meets my eyes, his hands warm on my skin, his gaze direct. Sincere. "He's pissed at me and trying to get back at me."

It's not exactly implausible, the idea that Max is just messing with us for revenge or sport or simply because he's bored.

But that doesn't mean he's not telling the truth.

"Was she at your house last night?" I ask hoarsely. He nods. "Was she... Were you two in your room?"

He hesitates.

Then nods again.

"Nothing happened," he says, his grip tightening when I try to twist free. "Hadley, you have to believe me."

That's just the thing.

I don't have to believe him.

But, oh, God, I want to.

"Why was she there?" I ask through barely moving lips.

Another hesitation. Another quick glance in Abby's direction.

"I can't tell you," he says, remorseful. Anguished.

But it's not enough. Not nearly enough to make up for him keeping another girl's secrets. Not enough to make this right.

And I am done.

"Let go of me," I say, quiet and firm.

He edges closer, his voice dropping to a soft plea. "Hadley..."

Max slams his hand on Sam's shoulder. Hard. "You heard the lady, Sammy boy."

Sam's jaw tightens, but he doesn't shake his brother off. Just searches my gaze. Whatever he sees there has him inhaling deeply and dropping his hands from my shoulders. He takes a step back, head down, throat working as he swallows rapidly.

I stand there, feeling everyone watching me, waiting for my next move, except I have no idea what that is. All I want is to go home, but there's no way I'm getting in a car with Sam. Not tonight. And

Whitney rode with Kenzie so I can't ask her, and it's way too far to even think about walking.

That leaves me only one choice.

I pull out my phone.

"What are you doing?" Sam asks as I start typing.

I don't look at him. "Texting Zoe to come get me."

It'd be easier if I asked Devyn since she's home with Taylor, but it'll be less painful for my psyche to have it be Zoe. Far fewer *I told you sos*. But it will mean waiting—I check the time, give an inner whimper—two hours before she's done with work.

Maybe I will start walking after all.

"You don't have to do that," Sam says quietly. "I'll drive you home."

I sear him with a not-happening look then go back to my message.

"No need to have your sister come all this way," Max says, because unlike the rest of our audience, he's not giving us one inch of space. Nope, he gets even closer and puts his arm around my shoulders. Again. "I'll take you home."

Before I can shove Max's arm off, again, Sam growls—the boy literally growls—and does it for me by putting both his hands on Max's chest and pushing him. Hard.

Max straightens. "What's the problem?"

"She's not going anywhere with you," Sam grinds out, stepping closer.

I frown. God. It's like I'm a bone in a dog fight.

"I'm just helping out," Max says. "Making sure your girl gets home safe and sound."

Sam steps closer. "You've done enough."

"Hey, all I did was tell the truth. You really need to learn to take responsibility for your actions, Sammy."

"It wasn't the truth! And it wasn't yours to tell."

Max shrugs. "Payback's a bitch, isn't it?"

I bristle. Oh, my God. That's what this is about. What it's really about. No wonder Max was so eager to help me find Sam. So insistent on making sure I knew that Abby was at Sam's last night. Sam was right.

Max is pissed at Sam. Like, really, super pissed.

And what better way to get back at Sam than through me?

They're toe to toe now. Nose to nose. Puffed-up chest to puffed-up chest. They're evenly matched, the Constable brothers, as they do that whole stare-down thing guys do when they get in each other's faces.

I take a hesitant step toward the two snarling boys. "Sam..."

He doesn't even glance my way, just keeps glaring at his brother. "I told you, it wasn't me."

"Bullshit," Max snaps, for the first time his composure slipping. "At least have the balls to own up to it."

Sam tosses his hands in the air. "Fine. Believe what you want, but this ends it, okay? We're even now."

"Not quite yet," Max says. And there's something in his soft tone, an underlying threat, that doesn't seem to affect Sam, but has me taking a quick step back. "There's one more truth to be revealed."

Sam turns to me. "There's not. Swear to God, Hadley."

I can't look at him. Can't tell him that on this, I do believe him. That I believe him because I know what truth Max is talking about. What secret he's about to reveal. And it has nothing to do with Sam or Abby.

And everything to do with me.

I give Max a small, desperate shake of my head, a plea for him not to do this.

But he's gone too far to back down. Has the attention of everyone around us, all silent and still, waiting for the tension to finally break.

Eager for what happens next.

"No worries, little brother," Max says, and though there's a flash of remorse in his eyes before he slides his gaze from mine, it's not enough to stop him. Not nearly enough for me to ever forgive him for what he's about to do. "This isn't one of your secrets. It's one of mine. Well, mine *and* Hadley's."

Sam goes rigid, his jaw tight, the muscles in his neck standing out. "What's that supposed to mean?"

"It means that for years, the one thing you wanted most was Hadley. And while it took you a while, you finally got her because when have you not gotten something you want? But here's the thing, Sammy..." He leans in closer, lowers his voice and says the words guaranteed to rip my world apart. "You may have her now. But I had her first."

47

I'M FROZEN. MY THOUGHTS ENCASED IN ICE. MY HEARTBEAT SLUGGISH.

Time seems to stop, and for several long, precious moments, I'm able to stay in this space between Before and After.

Before everything changes.

Before Sam and I end.

After, when I'll be alone again.

I wish I could stay here, right here, right now, forever where everything is still and silent and safe.

But wishing doesn't work. And nothing good lasts forever.

Not for Jones girls.

I exhale and the world around me rushes back to life and I'm bombarded with images and sounds and feelings.

The glow from the fire highlights Max's smug, cocky grin. Paints Sam's furious expression in red and orange.

There's a soft, almost sympathetic, "Oh, Hadley," from behind me that I think comes from Kenzie. A shouted "What did he say?" that could only be Graham. More than a few gasps and growing murmurs and a disgusted, grumbled "Jesus, Max" that sounds like Tori.

I'm suffused with fear and heartbreak and remorse.

Sam lunges forward, knocking Max back a step. "You're a goddamn liar."

Max stumbles then catches his balance. "You go on and believe that. But Hadley and I know the truth about what happened between us last Christmas."

Jerking upright, Sam whips his attention to me. Shakes his head. "No." He swallows. "No."

"You want to know the best part of all this?" Max taunts softly, but neither Sam nor I so much as glance his way. Our gazes stayed locked. Sam is breathing hard, his chest rising and falling rapidly, his expression a mask of pain and fury. "Hadley ended up with me that night because you sent her away. So, really, the only person you have to blame for this is yourself."

Sam roars and I make a grab for his arm. "Sam! No!"

But he shakes me off and practically flies through the air, his punch snapping Max's head back with a sickening crack. The crowd surges forward as Max retaliates with a blow to Sam's chin. Their fight lasts only a minute before they're separated by T.J., Colby and Brad—Max's shirt ripped, his lip cut and bleeding, Sam's eye swelling.

Max steps back and spits blood onto the ground. Wipes his hand across his mouth. "*Now* we're even."

Sam lunges for him again, but T.J. has a hold of one of Sam's arms, Colby the other, and they drag him away. His entire body trembles with rage, thrums with unchecked violence. They stop near a white pickup and Sam yanks free and slams the flat of his hand against the passenger-side door again and again until Jack stops him. Sam drops to a crouch, hands on the top of his head, face hidden by his arms.

T.J. and Colby take a few steps away as Jack squats next to Sam, not saying anything, just keeping his hand on Sam's shoulder.

"You didn't have to try and protect me, Hot Hadley," Max calls from behind me. "I can handle Sammy boy."

Scalp prickling, I turn slowly. Max is leaning against a wide tree at the edge of the grass, ankles crossed, as if he's king of the freaking world and we're all just here to suit his needs. To pleasure him when he demands it. Entertain him when he's bored.

Shield him from his own flaws and weaknesses.

I feel everyone watching me as I storm over to him, but I no longer care what they see. What they hear. Why should I?

I've already lost everything.

I stop a few feet in front of him, my body rigid and aching with the need to lash out at him, to scream at him until his smugness is gone.

But there's one thing I need more than to hurt him. One question I have to have the answer to.

"Why?"

For once, he doesn't put on an act. Doesn't pretend not to understand what I'm asking.

"I wanted him to know," he says, as if there's no better explanation.

And maybe to him, there's not.

After all, what a Constable boy wants, a Constable boy gets.

"You wanted to hurt him."

He inclines his head, all the agreement he's willing to give. "I want him to think about it." He uncrosses his ankles and pushes away from the tree. "Every time Sam is with you, I want him to remember I was there first."

And he walks away.

Because he can. He can drop a bomb on his brother, humiliate me and expose my deepest secret and then just saunter off without a care in the world. No remorse. No worries about what's been said or done.

Boys like Max—selfish, spoiled, entitled boys—don't have to face the consequences of their actions. Don't have to pay for their mistakes.

But girls like me do.

Taking a deep breath, I head toward Sam on unsteady legs. When I'm near the fire, Jack spots me. Says something to Sam that has him dropping his arms and lifting his head. Our eyes meet as he stands.

I want him to think about it. I want him to remember I was there first.

I stop, my heart racing. I get it. What Max meant. Why he really wanted Sam to know what happened between us.

It's about so much more than just hurting Sam. More than just bruising him.

Bruises heal. In time, they fade and disappear. They're forgotten.

This, what happened tonight, isn't a bruise.

It's a scar.

A scar stays with you forever. It's a constant reminder of the pain you suffered. The hurt you endured.

T.J., Colby and Jack pass me without a word, giving Sam and me as much privacy as we can expect at a party this size with the majority of the people still watching us. Still, we're far enough away that they can't hear us, can't see our expressions clearly.

A fact I'm incredibly grateful for when I get close enough to see Sam's face. There's a streak of dried blood on his eyebrow, his eye swollen and red.

And filled with tears.

Like the night of Beemer's party when Sam stood on my porch, when he was lost and hurting, I want to sooth him. To offer some comfort. To take away his pain.

Unlike that night, I don't stop myself from reaching for him.

But before my fingers can so much as graze his cheek, he steps back, out of my reach.

"It's not true," he says, his voice thick. "Max is lying."

I wrap my arms around my aching stomach, fighting the urge to puke. Struggling to stay whole, but it feels as if my body is made up of splintered fragments, pieced back together, fragile and wrong.

I could tell him Max lied. I could deny it all.

And Sam would believe me.

He'd believe me. But he'd always wonder. There'd always be doubt.

I could lie to Sam, as I've done before.

But I won't.

There's no point. The truth is out. It can't be taken back. Can't be hidden from.

Sam and I don't have a year. We don't have anything.

This is how we end.

"Hadley," he says, gruff and pleading. "Tell me it's not true."

"I can't," I whisper.

Sam blanches, his expression stricken.

With two words, I irrevocably break the connection between us.

Tipping his head back, he gulps in air, fighting his tears, and when he has control of himself, he doesn't so much as spare me a glance. He doesn't say anything. He just walks away. Toward the party. Toward his friends. Toward Abby.

He doesn't look back.

I'm left there, in the dark, alone.

I'm left. Again.

———

I don't cry.

I don't cry when Whitney finds me, still standing in the same spot I was when Sam walked away from me for the last time and pulls me into a warm, silent hug.

I don't cry in the backseat of Colby's car while he and Whitney take me home.

I don't cry when I'm in my bed, exhausted and sick to my stomach, staring blankly at the ceiling, eyes so dry they burn.

This is my fault. It was my choice to have sex with Max. To keep it from Sam. My choice to believe that Sam and I could somehow make it work despite everything that's happened.

My choice to believe Sam meant it when he said the past didn't matter. That we were starting new.

I don't cry because I don't deserve the self-indulgence of tears.

I don't cry because I've cried over Sam Constable more than enough.

I don't cry because there's a niggling sense in the back of my brain, sharp and persistent and elusive. Something I can't quite wrap my head around.

Something like anger.

Except I don't have the right to be angry. I was the one who did this. Who ruined things.

But I can't rid myself of this feeling that maybe it wasn't all my fault. That Sam has his share of the blame in this.

Yes, I messed up.

But I wasn't the only one.

It's a crazy thought. Delusional. A way for me to protect myself from the pain.

It's one I can't get rid of.

So I push it to the side. I ignore it.

And I do not cry.

48

OUT OF ALL THE MISTAKES I MADE, THE BIGGEST ONE, THE WORST ONE, was going to Sam's house last Christmas. Not because he was with Abby. Not because he was so horrible to me.

But because of what happened after.

Christmas night, I let Sam go.

Like so many other areas of my life, I didn't have a choice. I'd gone to his house to talk to him. To apologize. To tell him how much he meant to me.

But he wouldn't listen. He'd moved on.

I waited too long. I was too late.

I stood on his front porch that night, wet and cold, snow clinging to my hair, nose running, hand reaching for him—and watched helplessly as he stepped back into the warmth of his house, drawing Abby with him.

And slowly shut the door.

The pain came swift and sudden, stealing my breath.

Four months ago, he told me he was in love with me. That he wanted to be with me.

Guess I wasn't the only liar in our relationship.

I stayed there, right there, on his porch, staring at that closed door, for one minute. Then two. I waited.

But the door stayed shut.

Sam didn't come back.

Tears filled my eyes, blurring my vision, making the huge wreath on the door look distorted, the red bow fading into the deep green. The twinkling lights merged with each other, all soft and unfocused and surreal.

But there was a hard lump in my throat. And my thoughts were crystal clear.

The life I'd lived since Sam left was my new reality. Nothing was going to change it.

There was no going back.

What had started that hot summer day only a few months ago when he kissed me, what had escalated that night when he showed up at my trailer, drunk and insisting he was in love with me, ended for good the moment he shut that door and left me standing in the cold.

For the past few months, when Sam hadn't returned any of my texts or calls, when he disappeared from my life, I'd known we were over. I'd known it, but I hadn't accepted it. Not fully. There'd been a part of me, a small, stupid, hopeful part that had continued to believe that he'd come back. That we could somehow make us—some new, different version of us—work.

But no more. No more believing. No more hoping. No more waiting.

It was time to move on.

I didn't want to. I wanted to drop to my knees and wail and sob at the unfairness of it all. I wanted to pound against the door, pleading for him to give me another chance.

But I'd already lost so much. Sam. My friends. My hopes.

My heart.

The only thing left of any worth was my pride.

I was going to hold on to it as tightly as possible.

So I stayed on my feet, knees locked, hands at my sides. I turned and went down the snow-covered steps. Slowly. Carefully.

I didn't crumble. I didn't beg. I didn't lash out. I didn't run.

I didn't break.

Not completely.

I was halfway down the driveway when a car approached, its headlights blinding me momentarily. Lifting my hand to cover my eyes, I stepped to the side, ducked my head, as if by me not looking up, if I kept right on walking, I could become invisible to whoever was driving. That they—Sam's mom or Patrick—would pass me without stopping to ask what I was doing there or if something was wrong.

That they could hurry up and get inside the house and catch Sam, alone, with a girl.

Catch him and ground him for eternity.

Seemed only fitting.

But the Fates were having none of it because the car slowed and I realized it wasn't Dr. Constable-Riester arriving home to bust her middle son. It wasn't Patrick and Charlie back from making merry at Patrick's parents' house.

It was Max, behind the wheel of the Jeep Wrangler he'd gotten for his high school graduation.

Just in case my night so far hadn't been horrible enough.

He stopped next to me, the passenger-side window rolling down, and though something told me to keep right on walking, I didn't. I jerked to a halt. The interior light flicked on, illuminating Max's handsome profile.

I expected him to say something flirtatious or give me one of his lame come-ons. Maybe some stupid joke about Hot Hadley being out in the cold. But he just looked out the windshield at his house wrapped in twinkling lights, all bright and joyful. Then at the garage, where I noticed something I hadn't when I'd trudged up the driveway ten minutes before. Something Max obviously saw right away.

Abby's car parked in front of the second stall.

Even an idiot could figure out what Sam and Abby were doing in that house, alone, right this very moment. What had happened when I showed up on the doorstep.

Why I was out there, alone, making my way home.

God knows Max is many things. But stupid doesn't make the list.

Turning toward me, he draped one arm over the steering wheel, studying me in that way the Constable boys had, like they were looking for your secrets. Searching for your weaknesses.

Figuring out the best way to get past your defenses.

Then he leaned across the passenger seat and opened the door.

I blinked. Frowned at that open door. At what it signified. Lifting my gaze, I tried my own version of a deep, seeking look, but it was useless.

Max Constable only let you see what he wanted you to see.

And what I saw was a dark-haired boy waiting patiently for me to make a decision.

Continue walking home in the dark.

Or get in his Jeep.

Stay cold and wet—and get colder and wetter.

Or be warm and dry.

I glanced up at the house. Sam was in there, in the light, toasty warm. He wasn't cold or wet or heartbroken.

He wasn't alone.

I was.

Ever since he left, I'd been so alone. So lonely.

But I didn't have to be.

I looked at the house again—part of me hoping Sam was watching, that he saw what happened next.

And I climbed into the Jeep.

As soon as I closed the door, Max turned the heater up, aimed the vents my way then backed out of the driveway. We drove in silence, but he didn't take me home. Instead, we went through the Sheetz drive-thru where he bought me a hot chocolate and himself a black coffee and two hotdogs.

When he went right instead of left on Orchard Drive—the opposite direction of Hilltop Estates—I didn't ask where we were going, just huddled deeper into the seat, both hands wrapped around my cup. Five minutes later we turned onto Langley Lane, driving past the few houses to the baseball fields, bouncing in our seats as we went from pavement to the rutted dirt road. He backed in behind one of the dugouts, turning off the headlights but leaving the motor running.

It was at that point, as we sat there, surrounded by darkness, listening to non-Christmas music, that I knew my night could not possibly get any weirder.

But who knew? Maybe it could get better.

God knew it couldn't get any worse.

Max ate his hot dogs while I sipped my cocoa. Eventually, I warmed up enough to stop shivering and turned the heat down a few degrees. Unbuckled my seat belt and unzipped my jacket. I stole several quick glances at Max, but could only make out his silhouette.

Something was up with him, that was for sure. He wasn't talking. Max was never quiet. He constantly joked and entertained the masses with his charm and stories of his fabulous life.

I'd known him since I was ten and this was the longest I'd ever seen him keep his mouth shut. And that includes when he's completely stoned.

To have him sit there, staring out at the blackness as if I wasn't even in the vehicle with him?

It was unnerving.

And becoming awkward as all get out.

But it was also sort of nice. Sitting with a Constable boy who didn't think I owed him my every thought. Who didn't expect anything of me.

Max hadn't asked me what had happened back at his house. Hadn't made any snide comments about Sam. Hadn't flirted with me. At all. There were no hooded gazes. No touching his upper lip with the tip of his tongue while he scanned my body. No inappropriate comments. No trying to brush his fingertips over my arm or knee or the ends of my hair.

So, yeah, something was definitely wrong.

But I didn't have it in me to ask what.

Couldn't seem to make myself care or ask why he, too, was alone on Christmas.

Finished with his food, Max popped the lid off his coffee and took a sip. Leaned his head back, shut his eyes and sighed.

"So," he said, breaking the silence, his voice a low grumble. "How was your Christmas?"

The sound I made was a cross between a laugh and a sob. "About the same as yours, I'm guessing."

He glanced at me, eyebrows raised. "That bad, huh?"

There it was, the confirmation that his Christmas had sucked, too. Life wasn't always tinsel, cookies and prettily wrapped presents, even for someone like Max Constable.

"Yeah," I said around the tightness in my throat. "That bad."

Head still against the seat, he turned to look at me. "Poor Hadley," he murmured so sincerely, with such kindness and sympathy, tears stung my eyes.

"Poor Max," I whispered and as I did, his gaze dropped. Lingered on my mouth for one long, heart-stopping second.

When our eyes met again, I saw my own longing and grief and sense of loss mirrored back at me. Whether it was real—whether he, too, was suffering as much as I was—or imagined didn't matter.

In that moment, everything changed.

I went from being comfortably warm to almost unbearably hot. The air around us thickened with tension, the space between us seeming to shrink. The back of my neck prickled with a combination of apprehension and anticipation while an inner alarm blared.

It was a warning, loud and clear, that each passing moment spent looking into this boy's eyes brought me closer and closer to danger. Like I was teetering on the edge of a cliff and if I wasn't careful, if I wasn't smart, one small, wrong move would send me tumbling over.

Max set his coffee cup in the console between us. Took my cup from me and did the same. Then, eyes locked with mine, he leaned toward me, the move slow and purposeful and full of intent.

But I refused to let him push me over that edge.

I jumped.

And met him halfway.

Our kiss wasn't magical. Was far from romantic or sweet. It was raw. Angry. Shattered.

Like we were.

But mostly, it was a distraction. A balm. One that made it impossible to think. One that dulled the pain.

So when Max pulled back and searched my eyes and asked if I was sure, I kissed him again. And again. He tugged on me gently and I carefully climbed over the console, my knee bumping his cup and sloshing coffee over the side. Settling on his lap, I concentrated on the feel of his hands as he slid one into my hair, knocking my hat off, the other slipping inside the coat and under my shirt, his fingers hot against my lower spine.

We came together wordlessly, the only sounds our harsh breathing and zippers being pulled down and the soft rustle of clothing being removed. The windows fogged up, cocooning us in a shroud, making it seem more like a dream than reality. It was frenzied and wild and desperate.

And when it was over, I knew it was far from a harmless hookup. That it wasn't just a mistake. It was even more than me trying to get back at Sam. To hurt him.

It was the worst thing I could have done to him. The one thing he'd never be able to forgive me for.

The one thing guaranteed to keep us apart.

The one thing with the power to end us forever.

And I couldn't help but wonder if that wasn't exactly why I did it.

49

The morning after the party at the lake, Zoe finds my purse and sweatshirt on the porch in front of the door.

Handing them to me, she asks why they were there, but I just shrug and close my bedroom door, shutting her out.

It's not like I know for sure how they got there. But I could guess.

Sam probably dropped them off at some point during the night, late enough that there was no chance of anyone seeing him do it.

I spend the day in my bed, the lights off, the window shut and the curtains closed. Whitney texts then calls me, but I don't answer. Devyn knocks on my door and I tell her I'm not feeling well. I hear the muffled sounds of Zoe and Dev arguing about something—money more than likely—and put in my headphones, blasting music to tune them out. Taylor sits outside my locked door and cries for me and I cover my ears with my hands until one of my sisters bribes her with a trip to the park.

For the most part, I'm just...blank. No thoughts. No feelings.

For the most part, I'm numb.

For the most part. But not all the time. Not fully. I wish I was, though.

Because in those moments when feeling returns, it hurts just to breathe, each thought of Sam, of how he'd looked at me when he learned the truth, cutting me like a razor, the pain swift and sharp. I curl into myself, knees to my chest, eyes squeezed shut until the memories fade and the numbness returns.

I'm empty. Hollow. But just for today.

Tomorrow I'll get out of bed. Tomorrow I'll leave my room. I'll braid Zoe's hair and go to work and I'll come home and play with Taylor and make dinner and have a cookie or piece of cake with Devyn before she leaves for her shift at the motel. Tomorrow will be the start of my life going to back how it was before Sam came back.

How it'll be from now on.

Tomorrow I'll figure out a way to live without him.

Tomorrow I'll start getting over him. Again.

This time for good.

————

Monday morning, I stumble into the hallway, ready but not quite willing to take on the day. Taylor's screaming in Zoe's room but I hear Zoe trying to calm her down so I go into the bathroom. Close the door, flick on the light and cross to the toilet.

My head hurts and I'm blurry-eyed, my body aching from lying in bed all yesterday. Even so, I'd love nothing more than to crawl back there, pull the covers over my head and shut out everything and everyone. But there's no way I can bear to hear Taylor crying for me like she did yesterday.

Besides, Devyn would never let me skip work just because Sam and I broke up.

Boy problems do not equate a day off in her mind.

Which means I get to spend eight hours sweating in the heat and humidity, mowing and weed-whacking and hating every moment of my miserable life.

Or at least, quite a few of the moments.

And all of the ones having do with my sucky job.

But the worst part is going to be seeing Sam. We don't work

together anymore, but he'll still be there. At the garage before we head out to our different assignments. After work, when we clock out. When we start school next week, it'll be even worse. We've never had many classes together, what with him doing the whole AP and Scholar courses, but I'll still pass him in the hall. See him in the cafeteria.

And thanks to us agreeing to stay on at Glenwood during the off-season, I won't even get a break on the weekends.

That is, if Sam keeps his job.

If he stays in town.

Max said their dad wants Sam to move back to LA. Maybe he'll go again.

Maybe he did me a favor last year when he disappeared from my life. At the time, I was heartsick and wished only that he'd come back. But now?

Now him leaving again would be a welcome reprieve. One where I wouldn't have to face him day after day. Where I wouldn't have to see him. Wouldn't be reminded of what I lost every time I look at him.

He lost something, too, a nagging, inner voice in my head whispers. *He lost you.*

I shush it. That's not the same. Sam Constable compared to Hadley Jones? There's nothing equal in that equation.

I'm washing my hands when Zoe bursts into the bathroom wearing a loose, white T-shirt that falls to midthigh and nothing else.

I scowl at her. "Knock much?"

Pushing past me, she drops to her knees in front of the toilet, the shirt riding up to show the bottoms of her black underwear.

And pukes.

I gag at the sound. Breathe through my mouth as I dry my hands.

I really need to start locking the freaking door.

Taylor pads in next in her princess nightgown, barefoot and bawling, her face red, her nose running, hair crazy.

Forget locking it. I'm buying a deadbolt after work.

"Haddy!" Taylor sobs. She lifts her arms and jumps in place, all toddler agitation and anxiety. "Up! Up, up, up!"

I pick her up and she wipes her nose on the collar of the T-shirt I slept in.

What. Is. My. Life?

I reach over Zoe, who has now progressed to dry heaves, and grab some toilet paper, but as soon as Taylor sees it coming her way, she stiffens and starts shaking her head like I'm coming at her with a fistful of acid. "No! No, Haddy!"

Seriously. I can't. Not today.

"It's not sandpaper," I tell her but she keeps shaking and screeching and shoving at me and I. Have. Had. It.

I set her down.

She screams louder. Jumps and stomps her little feet. "Up! Up, Haddy!"

"No," I snap, stepping back when she tries to climb me like a tree. "I am not in the mood for any crap, okay? And I'm not holding you until you let me wipe your nose. Deal with it."

Eyes wide and glistening, face streaked with tears, Taylor studies me as she whimpers because, yes, I am a monster, not giving her what she wants, when she wants it.

But I give in too often, way, way too often, and I'm tired of it.

So very sick and tired of always being the one who never gets what she wants.

Crossing my arms, I narrow my eyes and give her my best stone-cold expression.

Bring it, kid.

Lower lip trembling, eyes squeezed shut against the impending horror, she lifts her chin, offering her nose up like a sacrifice.

She's a bit of a drama queen. Gets it from her mother.

I wipe her nose, toss the toilet paper in the garbage then wet a washcloth and wash her face.

"Now up, Haddy?" she asks. "Please?"

I pick her up and she lays her head on my shoulder. She twirls my snarled hair around and around and around her finger, the tension of whatever set her off leaving her little body as she relaxes against me.

Wish I had someone's hair to twirl. I could use some soothing.

Zoe groans and sits back on her heels.

"Are you done?" I mutter.

Hair tangled, face pale, she gives me a look, like she's a queen on a throne and not a tangled-haired, half-naked, nineteen-year-old praying to the porcelain god. "Wow. Thanks for the sympathy."

"Yeah, well, I'm all out at the moment."

"What is your problem?" she asks, getting to her feet.

"My problem?" My voice rises, cracks at the end. I feel on the verge of...something. Hysteria or fury or panic. Or a crazy, fun combination of all three. "My problem is I have to get ready for work and I can't do that with your kid on my hip because you're puking up whatever alcohol you drank last night!"

Taylor lifts her head. "No yell at Mama, Haddy. Be nice."

"I'm with Tay on this one," Zoe says as she flushes the toilet. She crosses to the sink and nudges me aside to wash her hands. "Be nice, Haddy. Just because you and Sam are fighting, don't take it out on us."

"Sam and I aren't fighting," I mutter.

Sam and I are done.

Zoe rinses her mouth then grabs her toothbrush and the toothpaste. Cocks a hip and starts brushing her teeth like she starts every morning hugging the toilet.

Not a care in the world, this girl.

"What is wrong with you?"

Frowning, she speaks around a mouthful of toothpaste. "Nothing's wrong with me."

"Really? Because in case you forgot already, you just threw up. Again. This is like, the fourth time in the past month." And those are just the times I've either seen her get sick or heard her in here, like a few days ago. Who knows how many other times there've been? "You're drinking way too much--"

"I'm not drinking."

"Uh, you were drunk the night you brought home that sleazy, tattooed guy--"

"That was weeks ago," she says, now glaring at me in the mirror. "And I wasn't drunk." Rinsing her toothbrush, I see her throat work as she swallows, then she lifts her eyes and meets my gaze in the mirror. "I'm pregnant."

50

Taylor's singing the "You're Welcome" song from *Moana* quietly near my ear, still twirling my hair, her breath hot against the side of my neck. But I barely hear her. Can't even feel her in my arms. It's as if I've lost all sensation in my body. It all just...*whoosh!* melted into the floor.

I'm pregnant.

But those two little words, said in a soft, calm tone lined with resignation? Those I hear loud and clear and over and over again. They hang in the air between me and Zoe. Hovering there for one breath, then two, before slamming into me. I back up a step, as if pregnancy is contagious.

As if I can somehow escape them.

"Are you..." I have to stop. Work moisture back into my mouth but my voice still comes out barely a whisper. "Are you sure?"

With a sigh, she puts her toothbrush back in the holder. "I took six home pregnancy tests so...yes. I'm sure."

My stomach roils.

Oh, God. Now I'm going to be sick.

"Does Devyn know?"

Zoe nods. "I told her yesterday."

Yesterday. That's what they'd been fighting about. I can't imagine Dev was exactly thrilled by this turn of events, especially when Zoe should know enough to use birth control.

"Who's the father?" My eyes widen. "Not Axel. Please, not Axel."

"No, not Axel," she says, facing me. "It's Ethan's baby."

Ethan the Ass, her prick of a boss.

Ethan the Ass, who broke up with her months ago.

"How far along are you?" I ask. Maybe she's been hooking up with Ethan behind his girlfriend's back. Maybe they got back together and she hasn't told me or Devyn because she thought we'd be upset.

Maybe she hasn't been keeping this from us.

"Fourteen weeks."

I gape at her. *Fourteen weeks?*

"But you just found out," I say, making it more of a statement I'd very much like her to agree with and less like a question she should give a negative answer to.

She shakes her head, her gaze dropping to the floor. "I've known for a little while."

"How long is a *little while*? And please," I add, lifting a hand, "don't say a few days or weeks or whatever. Be specific."

Her eyebrows lift. "Sorry," she says in a very not-sorry tone—my sisters don't like it when I'm bossy, though they both feel free to tell me what to do whenever the mood strikes them. "But I don't remember the exact date. It was sometime at the end of June."

"June?" But that was literally months ago. And suddenly, it all makes sense. All those times she got sick. Her being more tired than usual. Looking so run-down. Being so sad. "Did you tell Ethan?"

Another nod, this one curt. "Let's just say he's not all that excited about the prospect of becoming a daddy."

"Are you two getting back together?" I ask.

Her mouth twists. "No. He's out of the picture."

"You don't need him. You have me and Devyn."

I mean, yeah, as a family we're completely strapped—financially and emotionally—but we'll get through this. Together.

Just like we always do.

"We can move Taylor's bed into my room," I continue. "Put a crib up in yours." Except we don't have a crib. We sold the one we used for Taylor because we don't have space to store it. "Taylor and I can hit up a few garage sales next weekend. See if we can find some baby stuff."

Because we're going to need everything, just like we did when Zoe was pregnant with Taylor.

Which only reminds me of all the ways having a baby in the house changes life. The crying—oh, God, the constant, shrill crying—and endless diapers and every shirt covered in spit-up and sleepless nights.

"You don't have to do that," Zoe says.

"I want to."

"No. I mean, you really don't have to do it. My aunt Claire has a crib the baby can use."

I frown. "Oh. You...you told your aunt?"

Had she told her before me and Devyn?

"I mean, that's nice and all," I add quickly, hiking Taylor up higher. She's falling back asleep and getting heavier by the second. "About the crib. But will it fit in your car? Even unassembled? And do you really want to make another trip up to Erie to get it?"

It's only ninety minutes but it seems easier to just find a used crib in town and use Devyn's car—which is bigger than Zoe's—to get it home.

"Actually," she says slowly then stops. Clears her throat. "I'm moving there." She nods at Taylor, dozing in my arms. "We're moving there. To Erie," she adds when I stare at her blankly.

I laugh, a quick bark of sound that's more disbelief than humor. "What?"

"Taylor and I are moving to Erie," she repeats, tone soft, expression sympathetic. Understanding. But that can't be right. She can't possibly understand what I'm thinking. What I'm feeling. If she did, she'd never say these things. Wouldn't even pretend that this was true.

"Did Devyn say something to you? Did she kick you out? I'll talk to her," I say in a rush. "She's probably just upset about the baby but she'll get over it."

"Dev didn't kick me out. This is my choice."

Her words settle in, the reality of them. I start sweating. My stomach cramps. "You can't move. You're just upset. Once you've thought it through--"

"I have thought this through. I've been thinking about it ever since I found out I was pregnant. Believe me, this wasn't an easy decision and it wasn't one I made lightly."

"Where will you live? What about your jobs?"

What about me?

"We're moving in with Gram," she says of her grandmother. "She's going to watch Taylor and the baby for me while I work at one of the doctor's offices my aunt Carla manages. And Aunt Claire's going to watch Taylor nights so I can get my high school equivalency diploma and Gram offered to help me pay to attend community college or business school."

I tighten my hold on Taylor. "You can go to school here," I say, my voice hoarse with unshed tears. "I'll watch Taylor whenever you want. I'll help you study--"

"I can't keep living like this," she says gently. "Expecting things to be different while repeating the same patterns, the same mistakes. This is my chance at something better and I have to do this. Now. Or I never will. I have to do it," she repeats, "for me. For Taylor and the baby. And for you."

"Me?" I ask incredulously. I try to laugh but it comes out closer to a sob. "You're not doing this for me."

She steps forward, intense and serious and very, very adult. "I'm doing this to prove that none of us—not me or you or Devyn—has to settle for less than what we deserve. That we can break free from the cycle. We're not Mom or Gigi. We're better. We can do better. But we can't do that thinking there are limits on what we can achieve. We can't be afraid to go after what we want. If we want a different life, we have to be brave enough to fight for it. No matter how scary it is."

"Are you scared?" I ask softly.

"Terrified," she admits, her eyes glassy with tears. But I easily recognize the determined, stubborn tilt of her chin—I should. I see it every day on her daughter. She's going to do this.

She's really going to leave me.

I tighten my hold on Taylor and brush past Zoe, needing some air. Some space to just breathe, to catch my breath.

But it's worse in the hallway, I don't know what to do. Where to go. I just feel trapped, like the walls are closing in on me. My eyes sting. My chest is tight. I want to run. To hide. To make all of this—this moment and last night and what happened at Christmas and the whole summer of Sam and Hadley—disappear.

But there's nowhere to hide. Nowhere to go. Not for this Jones girl.

I sense Zoe step up behind me and I take in a shuddering breath. "When?"

Her hesitation has me bracing but it's worse, so much worse than I even realize.

"Saturday."

I jolt hard. "Saturday?" I repeat in a loud squeak. "This Saturday?"

Taylor jerks her head up, eyes closed, then turns her head to the other side and lays it back on my shoulder. I rub her back, attempting to comfort us both.

"Yes."

"So soon?" I cry.

"The longer I wait, the more I put it off, the harder it's going to be to actually do it." She licks her lips. "It won't be that different," she insists, fast and insistent, but her voice is thick with unshed tears. Full of emotion. "We'll come back as often as we can. And you can visit us anytime you want, stay for a weekend or a week or...however long you want..."

It won't be that different...

Maybe not. But it won't be the same. Not nearly the same.

Nothing's ever going to be the same again.

51

After Zoe's bombshell, I put Taylor in my bed and get dressed.

Then I go to work.

Because that's what Jones girls do.

We don't wallow. We don't weep and shake our fists at the unfairness of it all. We accept whatever life throws our way.

And we do whatever it takes to get through it.

Even when everything is falling apart.

Or maybe, most especially then.

All week I follow my usual routine.

Get up. Get dressed. Go to work. Come home. Watch Taylor. Make dinner. Go to bed.

But I let Taylor stay up late, reading her book after book, cuddling with her on the sofa watching Disney movies. I don't put her in her own bed, just let her snuggle with me in mine, scratching her back long after she's asleep.

I don't bake anything. No cookies or brownies or cupcakes. Not even a pan of marshmallow rice cereal treats.

I don't respond to Whitney's texts, telling myself I don't want to be distracted from spending time with my sister or niece. I don't get on social media.

I don't help Zoe pack, but I do sit on the bed while she goes through her clothes and knickknacks and decides whether or not they're worthy enough of going with her when she starts her new life.

I don't cry.

I don't cry because I don't want to upset Taylor, who's too little to understand anything that's going on, and I don't want her to be scared. I don't cry because Zoe cries enough for the both of us, and every time she does, Dev starts crying, too.

I don't cry because I'm afraid if I do, if I let even a single tear fall, I won't be able to stop.

And I don't hear one word from Sam.

He wasn't there when I got to work Monday morning.

It was a huge relief.

It was a crushing disappointment.

But that's me. Always with the confusing emotions.

He sent Mr. G. an early-morning text claiming he was sick, some mysterious ailment that lingered into Tuesday and Wednesday. By Thursday, he stopped pretending and quit over the phone.

I got what I wanted. What I suspected would happen, him quitting. Again.

It should have made it easier, not seeing him. Not hearing his voice. But it didn't. Even with everything going on with Zoe and Taylor leaving—or maybe because of it—I thought of him constantly. Wondering what he was doing. Who he was with. If he was thinking of me.

If he missed me even half as much as I missed him.

He was the first thing on my mind when I woke up. My last thoughts as I drifted off to sleep.

I knew this would happen. I knew the saga of Sam and Hadley didn't have a happy ending, but I tricked myself into believing I could handle the outcome.

Getting involved with him again was stupid.

Believing I had some small piece of control over what happened between us, that I was in charge of when and where and why we ended was delusional.

But by far my biggest mistake—bigger than going to Sam's Christmas night, worse than what happened in Max's Jeep—was forgetting the most important thing of all.

Sam and I weren't meant to be friends.

Now we're nothing.

Like we should have been from the beginning.

———

"I have to admit," Dev murmurs Saturday morning, sounding both surprised and admiring, "I didn't think she had it in her."

We're sitting on the front steps side by side, my head on Dev's shoulder, Eggie lying in the middle of the sidewalk soaking up the sun. Tori's car is parked in Whitney's driveway but even though we've been out here for half an hour—first loading the last of Zoe's stuff into her car, then saying our goodbyes and finally, Dev and I sitting in silence, both of us lost in our own thoughts, doing our best to accept our new reality—I haven't seen Tori or Whitney.

Thank God. I'm way too emotionally fragile to come face-to-face with either of them.

"Do you think she'll stick it out?" I ask.

It'll be a lot for Zoe to handle. Having another kid as a single mother. Working full-time. Getting her high school equivalency diploma. It'll be different and new, living with her grandmother. Navigating a new city. Making new friends.

It'll be a lot for us, too. Not being there to help her.

It'll be different and new, not seeing her and Taylor every day. Not being an integral part of their lives.

Them not being such a huge part of ours.

"I don't know," Dev says. "Maybe." As always, my eldest sister is honest and skeptical. But then she adds a soft, "But I hope she does."

Which shows she can also be optimistic. Hopeful.

Even if only for one of her sisters.

"I thought it'd be you," I tell Devyn.

"You thought what would be me?"

I straighten. "I thought you'd be the one to leave."

She frowns. "What?"

"I thought you'd be the one to leave," I repeat. "I figured once Zoe turned eighteen..."

"That I would...what?" she asked, tone dry. "Take off like Mom and Gigi did?"

Biting my lower lip, I stare down at my hands. "I wouldn't have blamed you."

"Are you serious?" Keeping my gaze down, I lift a shoulder. "Hadley, why would you even think that?"

"You gave up everything for me." The words I've kept buried so long, the guilt I've tried to hide burst out of me. "You were, like, literally weeks away from getting out of here."

Dev bends her knee, tucking her leg underneath her as she turns toward me. "I didn't give up anything. It's not like I had huge plans of setting the world on fire."

"You gave up Bryan."

Her lips roll inward. "No. He gave up me."

"But you were going to go with him. And you could have if you hadn't had to take care of me and Zoe."

"Look, plans change. That's life. And instead of waiting for me—like he promised he would—he found someone else." She shrugs. "That is also life."

I trace my thumbnail along the edge of the floorboard. "Do you still think about him?"

"Hard not to when he texts me at least once a month."

I freeze. "He texts you? I thought he was married."

"Oh, he is. According to him his wife doesn't understand him, not like I did. They barely knew each other when they got married. It was a mistake, but he doesn't know how to fix it. Maybe the next time he's in town we can get together...blah, blah, blah."

I blink at her. "Wow. Was he always such a jerk?"

"Eh. He had his moments."

"Are you going to do it?" She gives me a curious look and I add, "Are you going to meet him? The next time he's in town?"

"No," she says, emphatic. Firm. "He's just looking to hook up. Or maybe I'm some backup plan in case things don't work out with his wife. Either way, I'm not interested in being his second choice."

"Are you still in love with him?"

She startles. "God. No." She shudders as if my question—or the idea of still being hung up on jerky Bryan—gives her the willies. "What is with you today?"

"Well, it's not like it's out of the realm of possibility. I mean, every time he's brought up, you freak out. Every. Single. Time. And you haven't gone out with any guy since he left. Zoe thinks you're still into him, too."

"I don't freak out," she mutters.

"Please. You practically run screaming from the room whenever his name is mentioned."

"Only because I hate being reminded of how gullible I was. How stupid to believe him. And, yes, after he left, I may have, for a while, thought I still loved him. And maybe I really did. Or maybe it was just habit, from us being together for so long. But then one day I realized I wasn't thinking of him every day. That I hadn't thought about him in weeks, and when I did, there was nothing. No twinge. No pain. No longing. No hope that he'd come back."

Stunned, all I can do is stare at her. She could be describing me last year and how I felt about Sam. How those feelings eventually shifted and changed.

Or maybe they hadn't changed at all. Maybe I'd just done a good job of convincing myself they had.

If I'd truly been over him, if there hadn't been at least a tiny spark of hope that we could still be together, I'd have been able to resist him when he came back.

"And I haven't gone out with any other guys," she continues, "because I haven't met any guys *to* go out with. The nursing home isn't exactly swarming with interesting, gainfully employed, good-looking, twenty somethings and the men I meet at the motel are all in town temporarily. Besides, I work two jobs. I'm tired. All the time. When I'm not working, the only thing I want to do is put on sweats, sit on the couch and read a good book."

Good God, she sounds like a grandmother.

Not *our* grandmother, mind you. Gigi took any and all opportunities to go out. That woman had the busiest social life out of any of us.

"You wouldn't have to work two jobs," I say, trying to come off as if it's just a throwaway, means-nothing comment, but my guilt manages to thread its way through, "if you weren't stuck with me."

"I am not stuck with you," Dev says with an exasperated breath that has Eggie lifting his head and looking back at us. "I'm not living in a cage. No one forced me to stick around. When Gigi left, I made the choice to stay."

"Why did you, though?" I can't help but ask. "Stay, that is."

It's one of the questions I've always been afraid to ask. One of the questions I've been afraid to hear the answer to.

The other being, *do you regret it?*

No way I'm strong enough to hear the truth about that one. Not today.

"I stayed because you and Zoe needed me. Because it was the right thing to do." Dev's mouth quirks into a self-deprecating smile. "And because I refused to be like Mom."

That makes sense. Dev has some major issues with Mom, more so than Zoe or me. I think it's because she was the closest with Mom, both because of her being the oldest and Mom treating her more like a kid sister than a daughter.

"But mostly," she continues, "I stayed was because I wanted you and Zoe to have one person, just one single person, who didn't leave. I wanted you to know what it was like to have someone love you enough to stay." She takes my hands in hers, squeezes them as she holds my gaze, looking as serious, as solemn and sincere as I've ever seen her. "You need to know this and you need to believe it. I've never, not once, thought I was stuck with you. *You're* stuck with *me*. And you always will be."

You're stuck with me. And you always will be.

It's one of the best things anyone has ever said to me and I exhale a shaky breath then throw myself into Dev's arms.

She holds tight.

Unlike when Sam told me I'll always be his girl, I don't ask for Devyn's promise that she's telling the truth.

I don't need it.

And it doesn't matter what Mom did or how she lived her life, or how many people have let me down in the past. Doesn't matter that Zoe will be living ninety-miles away or that one day I'll be moving out of this trailer, too.

Doesn't matter whether we see each other every day or only once a year.

Devyn, Zoe and I are Jones girls.

And Jones girls stick together.

Forever.

52

D EV LEAVES HALF AN HOUR LATER—SHE SWITCHED SHIFTS AT THE motel so she could be home last night and this morning—but I stay on the porch after she backs out of the driveway.

I don't want to go inside. It's too quiet. Too empty.

With a completely pitiful, wholly woeful sigh, I set my elbows on my bent knees and rest my chin on the heels of my hands. A few minutes later, Whitney's front door opens and Tori steps out followed by Kenzie and Whitney. They're all smiles and glowing faces and cheery laughs in matching outfits of yoga pants and tank tops, Whitney's hair in a messy bun, Tori's slicked back into a ponytail.

I straighten slowly, stretching my legs out, bringing my arms to my sides. Holding my breath, I wait for them to look over. To see me.

None of them do.

And the sudden onslaught of disappointment almost crushes me.

My breathing gets heavy. My heart starts to race. Cold sweat forms at the back of my neck. It's like I'm having a heart attack or something.

If I did, maybe that would, at least, get their attention.

As it is, they only have eyes for each other and the joyful time they're having basking in each other's company.

Not that I'm jealous or anything.

Or dying inside a little bit at a time for every moment that passes where they don't even notice me.

Kenzie reaches Tori's car first and waits for Tori to unlock the passenger side door. Whitney rounds the back of the car and I lurch to my feet, causing her to stop and look up.

To look at me.

And I see it in the tightening of her expression. The tip of her chin. Her hesitation. Her doubt.

Her hurt and anger.

I've ghosted her for a week. Have ignored her calls and texts. I did to her exactly what Sam did to me last year.

I pushed her away.

Whitney was my friend.

But I wasn't hers.

And now I've lost her, too.

We're staring at each other, gazes locked, when Tori comes up behind Whitney and pauses, then follows Whitney's gaze to me. Tori leans closer to Whitney, saying something that has Whitney nodding, her mouth lifting in a small, sad smile. Tori squeezes Whitney's arm then walks around the back of the car to the driver's-side door.

Without acknowledging me at all.

But Whitney is too polite, too kind to give me an outright snub. She lifts her hand in a half-hearted wave then walks to the rear driver's-side door, turning her back to me.

No, really, I think I'm having a heart attack. As I watch them all climb into the car, my heart pounds and I can't catch my breath. It's wheezing in and out of my open mouth like I've just sprinted the entire hill leading to Hilltop Estates. I bend over slightly, hands on my upper thighs, but it doesn't help.

It's for the best—no, not me having some sort of physical, mental and emotional breakdown, but the Whitney finally giving up on me part.

It would happen eventually, I assure myself. It was only a matter of time before she got tired of trying to get past my defenses time and time again. Before she realized she's better off with people like Tori and Kenzie, girls who know how to trust others and be vulnerable and open.

It was only a matter of time before she left me.

Just like everyone else has.

And that's exactly what they're going to do. Tori starts the car and I'm bombarded by memories: of the last time I saw my mom. Of Gigi standing over my bed, telling me she was leaving. Of Sam walking away from my trailer that night last summer. Of him turning his back on me at Tori and Jackson's party.

Of Zoe's car pulling away, Taylor waving from the backseat.

That's when I finally give up. When I finally stop fighting.

And I break down and cry.

It's like a tidal wave of pain and disappointment and loss hits me, knocking me back. I stumble and fall, landing on the top step hard. Covering my head with my arms, I bend over my knees, press my face to my thighs.

I'm sobbing, my entire body shaking, my breathing so ragged it feels like I might pass out. Eggie whines and pads over to press against my legs and that makes me cry even harder. He nudges my arm with his moist nose. Licks my elbow.

I lift my head. Sniff mightily.

And see Tori's car backing slowly into the road.

My pulse thrums in my ears. Adrenaline suffuses me and I shoot to my feet.

"Wait." But my whisper is too soft. Too broken for them to hear. So I swallow and try again. "Wait!"

It's a shout this time, more plea than demand. But it works.

The car stops.

Only to start rolling forward down the road.

Away from me.

That's when I run.

I take off like a rocket, crossing diagonally through our front yard, Eggie racing after me, barking up a storm. They pick up a bit of speed but I don't give up. I swear I will chase them wherever they go. No matter how far.

I'm done giving up.

I push myself harder than I ever have. Run faster than I've ever gone, legs and arms pumping, bare feet slapping against the sidewalk, vision blurry with more tears.

They're almost at the stop sign and I put on a burst of speed that I dig out from some previously untapped, hidden inner reserve.

Tori starts to slow.

I do a quick glance left, then right, then dart across the street as she rolls to a stop--

Please, please, please...

--and plaster myself against the driver's side door as I slap my palm against the window repeatedly.

Tori jumps and swears. Kenzie screams and flaps her hands. I'm not sure what Whitney says or does as I can't see her in the backseat but I'm sure there are no cusswords or theatrics involved.

Tori rolls her window down. "Are you crazy? I could've run you over!" But then she gets a good look at me and whatever she sees has her frowning. Then again, Tori often frowns around me. Or she has for the past year. "Are you okay?"

But all the running and the crying have made it impossible for me to breathe, let alone speak. And I'm too weak, too utterly emotionally exhausted to even try lying. All I can do is shake my head and gulp in air.

"What's going on?" Whitney asks, leaning forward between the front seats. Her eyes widen. "Hadley?"

"She's crying," Kenzie tells Whitney in a stage whisper. "I think Sam broke her."

Tori snorts softly. "More like Max did. The asshole."

I shake my head again. Sniff. And when I speak, my voice is tear-free. Loud. Strong.

And clear as a bell. "They didn't break me."

The Constable brothers have used me, lied to me, left me and broken their promises. But they didn't break me.

I won't let them.

Tori studies me. Then nods slowly. "What's this all about?" she asks, and though it's not exactly brimming with patience, there's a definite note of compassion.

If you listen carefully enough.

"Could you..." I stop and swallow. Wipe the wetness from my face. "Could you come to my place? I just...I have some things I need to tell you." I let my gaze move from Tori to Kenzie and then, finally, to Whitney. "All of you."

Things I'd rather not say in the middle of the street with my dog sniffing the corner house's rosebush. Besides, I have a point to make and I can't do it here.

It's silent inside the car as the three of them share some wordless message conveyed only through eye contact, the raising of eyebrows and the pursing of lips.

And I want to be a part of it so badly, want to belong to them so much, I start crying again. I blink rapidly, try to wipe the tears away as soon as they fall but it's no use.

So I just let them flow.

More than that, I let them see.

A red pickup approaches from behind us and Tori glances in her rearview mirror at it. Then she faces me, already putting on her turn signal. "We'll meet you there in a few minutes."

53

EGGIE AND I ARE WAITING AT THE END OF THE SIDEWALK WHEN TORI'S car approaches from the opposite way they'd left, then pulls into Whitney's driveway.

The walk back to my trailer gave me enough time to catch my breath and stop my tears, so when Tori, Kenzie and Whitney all get out of the car, I'm at least outwardly calm.

On the inside? I'm still a freaking mess. Still unsure and scared.

But I'm not letting that stop me.

I'm not going to ever let fear stop me again.

Or at least, not today. Let's face it, I'm not that great at the whole *be brave and go after what you want* thing. Not for long periods of time, anyway.

But I'm going to keep trying. Build up my endurance.

And maybe, one wonderful, magical day in the future, it won't be so freaking hard.

Eggie races to the edge of the sidewalk to greet our unexpected guests and the three of them all crouch down to give him enthusiastic pats and rubs and coo about how cute he is, how sweet, what a good dog.

He flops onto his back, wiggling in ecstasy.

But all good things come to an end and they eventually straighten and make their way toward me, Tori in the middle and slightly ahead, Kenzie to her, Whitney the farthest behind.

When Tori stops a few feet from me, they all stop. All the better to stare at me like I've lost my mind and they're not quite sure what to do with this development.

"Well?" Tori asks, hip cocked, tone bored. "You wanted to tell us something?"

"Would you..." I stop. Clear my throat, but I feel tears forming again. "Do you want to come in?"

Whitney takes a step forward, used to coming and going from my place, but Kenzie's words stop her in her tracks.

"Like...in your house?" Kenzie asks. "I thought that was strictly prohibited."

My face heats. Great. I'm sure a beet-red blush is doing wonders for my probably blotchy, tear-streaked cheeks.

I straighten my shoulders and meet each of their eyes in turn. "Would you please come inside with me?"

Tori and Kenzie share another silent look—always with the looks, those two—then Tori flicks her gaze to the trailer, then back to me.

And nods.

We march up the walk, all stiff and silent, like we're heading off to our group execution and not the relative comfort of my somewhat air-conditioned home.

I hold the door open. Eggie's the first one in followed by Whitney and then, after a slight hesitation, Tori and Kenzie. Once inside, I shut the door.

And I dive in.

Starting with Whitney.

"I'm sorry," I say quickly, my voice husky. Honest. "I'm so sorry I didn't return your calls or answer your texts."

"Why didn't you?" she asks, clearly more hurt than angry. Which makes me feel worse. But then, that's nothing less than what I deserve. A hefty dose of guilt and remorse. "I thought we were friends."

"We are. At least...I hope we still are."

Her lips roll inward as if she's stopping her innate kindness and politeness from taking over and agreeing that, yep, we're still the best of buddies no matter how crappy I treated her.

She's being cautious. Smart. Careful not to put herself out there without some guarantee she won't get used or hurt or left again.

She's acting just like me.

I understand that. I understand it and I'm willing to put in the work to get through to her.

Just like she tried to do with me.

"Just, please, hear me out, okay? That's all I'm asking."

She gives a reluctant nod, but instead of continuing our conversation, I turn to Tori and Kenzie because this part is for them, too.

"So...uh...this is my home. Living room" –I gesture to the room in which we're all currently standing then wave to my left— "kitchen. Beyond that is Devyn's room and a bathroom. My room is at the end of the hall," I continue, pointing that way. "There's another bathroom and Zoe and Taylor's room.

"This is my home," I repeat. "And the reason I never invited you over before, the reason I never wanted you to see it was because I was embarrassed." Shame fills me, has the tears falling yet again. I keep talking as I wipe them away. "You both live in such beautiful houses filled with all these perfect, pretty things and I...I didn't want you to see our ancient furniture and stained carpets. I didn't want you to know that it gets so hot in here in the summer because we only have one air conditioner and can't buy a second one, or that in winter we have to wear sweatshirts and two pairs of socks to bed because our walls are paper thin and not properly insulated and we can't turn the heater up because we can't afford a higher gas bill."

"Do you really think we care about any of that?" Kenzie asks, sounding baffled. Insulted.

And yes, hurt. That seems to be the running theme for the day. Me saying things and acting in ways that hurt the people I care about most.

Well, that and bawling my eyes out.

"I cared," I say. "But I shouldn't have. I should have had more faith in you" –I look at Tori— "in both of you. I should have trusted you. And I should have been proud," I continue, softer, my tears still flowing, "of how hard my sisters work to give me a home where I'm safe. Where I'm loved. To give me a place where I'm accepted, fully."

I haven't appreciated that. Not nearly enough.

"But you didn't," Tori says quietly. "You didn't have faith in us. You didn't trust us. Not with anything. And now...?" She shrugs. "Now it doesn't matter." She looks at Kenzie then Whitney. "You both ready to go?"

Kenzie nods and while Whitney hesitates, it only lasts a moment before she steps toward the door. Tori reaches it first and pulls it open.

"Zoe moved out," I blurt, my voice cracking. "She and Taylor moved to Erie."

Whitney's the first to react, facing me with a shocked, "What?"

"Zoe's pregnant—again—and she wanted a fresh start. They're going to live with Zoe's grandma. They took all their stuff."

It's a dumb thing to say—that's what people do when they move, right? Take their belongings with them—but it just seems so final.

Like their existence here has been erased.

Like there's no hope of them ever coming back.

"They took their stuff," I repeat, "and now I can't even look in Zoe's room because it's empty and they've only been gone two hours and I already miss them and it hurts" –I press my fist against my chest — "here. So much."

"Hadley..." Whitney says, her own eyes shiny with tears, "I'm sorry. Truly."

She gets it. Other than Sam, she's the only person I've let in—as much as I let anyone in. She knows better than most what my sisters mean to me, how much I love my niece.

I want to wrap Whitney's sympathy around me like a blanket, let it calm me, comfort me, but this isn't about making me feel better.

This is about me doing better. Being better.

It's about me finally be honest. With my friends. And with myself.

"I don't know my dad," I say, and if any of them are jarred by the abrupt change in topic, they don't show it, just watch me patiently, as if they understand how important this is to me.

As if it's just as important to them.

And what they've been waiting for.

"He left town the minute he found out my mom was pregnant," I continue. "Like, literally, the minute he found out." My palms are clammy and I wipe them down the front of my shorts. Swallow to try and soothe my sore throat. "My mom stuck around, but even as a little kid, I knew it was only a matter of time before she took off, too. Some people aren't cut out for staying and she's one of them. I was ten the last time I saw her, the last time I spoke to her. She didn't say goodbye. Didn't tell us she was leaving, she just...never came back."

"That really sucks," Kenzie says.

"It does," I agree. "But I'm not telling you this so you'll feel sorry for me."

"Oh, I don't. Well, I mean I *do* because I'm not a monster or anything, but mostly I just feel like maybe I understand you a little more. And why you're so messed up."

Whitney inhales sharply.

Tori groans. "Mackenzie."

Kenzie blinks, all wide eyes and good intentions. "What?" She glances at each one of us in turn. "It's not like we all don't know she's got some issues."

And for some crazy reason, I suddenly feel like laughing.

Seriously, this emotional roller coaster of a day is going to do me in.

"I do have issues," I agree. The past twenty minutes—make that the past seventeen years—have proved that, so no point arguing. "I thought that everyone would leave me because, for the most part, everyone had. My dad. My mom. My grandmother."

"And Sam," Tori adds gently.

Our eyes meet and in hers I see that she gets it. She's starting to get me. And because she is, my first inclination is to drop my gaze, shutter my expression. To hide what I'm feeling.

To close myself off.

Sam once accused me of always being scared. He said I was too afraid of opening up or letting someone see the real me. That I was scared to let anyone get close to me.

He was right.

But all that changes. Now.

No more crying.

No more excuses.

No more running scared.

I'm fighting for what I want.

Starting with these three girls.

"And Sam," I agree, letting her see exactly what his walking away from me did to me. How much it still tears me up inside. "Everyone left me," I continue, my voice husky. Unsteady. "But not you." I look from Tori to Kenzie and finally Whitney, keeping my gaze on her when I continue. "You didn't leave. You reached out to me and tried to be my friend and I'm sorry—I'm so, so sorry that I wasn't a friend to you in return. Any of you," I add, glancing at Tori and Kenzie. "I thought the only way to protect myself from getting hurt was to keep people from getting close to me. You were right," I say to Tori. "I did ditch you after Sam left, but not because he left. Not like you think, anyway. I just...I thought with Sam gone, you'd realize what a lost cause I am, and I couldn't handle having you both walk away from me, too."

"Oh, I get it!" Kenzie says, clapping her hands in excitement at her discovery—which has Eggie barking with joy and running over to her. "You ditched us before we could ditch you."

"Yes. That's exactly what I did. That's what I did with you, too," I tell Whitney. "But it's not the only reason. I...." I stop and take a deep, fortifying breath. "I couldn't face you. Didn't want to face anyone, not after what happened at the party."

"Are you talking about the Max thing?" Tori asks. "Because if anyone should be ashamed to show his face, it's that asshole. He had no right telling everyone you two hooked up."

"Max was a giant jackhole that night," Kenzie says with a scowl, which makes her look about as fierce as a kitten but it's the point that counts. "I mean, he's a jackhole all the time but he really stepped up his game at the party."

"Hadley, I don't care that you were with Max," Whitney says.

"None of us cares," Kenzie agrees.

"I mean, I wouldn't recommend hooking up with the brother of the boy I'm in love with," Tori adds dryly, because leave it to her to lay it all on the line. "And honestly, I don't think hooking up with Max Constable is ever the best use of a girl's time—any girl. But it's not like you and Sam were together when it happened."

"Right. You didn't cheat on Sam," Whitney agrees. "And even if you had, and even though I'm Sam's friend, too, I'm your friend first. I wouldn't have judged you for it."

"Uh, considering he was hooking up with Abby," Tori puts in, "he had no right to act like you *had* cheated on him. He was almost as big of an ass that night as Max."

And that's it. The combination of hearing Whitney saying *I'm your friend*—present tense—and having Tori and Kenzie sticking up for me...

So much for that whole no-more-crying thing.

I knew once I started I wouldn't be able to stop. This is obviously my life now.

"I missed you," I say in a rush because it's still easier to let out these personal truths in short, quick bursts where I don't have time to overthink them. "I missed you all so much. You were—are," I amend, looking at Whitney, "such good friends and I'm not. I wasn't. But if you give me another chance, if we can just start over, I promise I will be."

It's hard, it's so very, very hard admitting that, asking for another chance.

Risking their rejection.

But I do it. I do it because they're worth it.

And so am I.

Whitney is the first to relent. And forgive. "You're doing fine," she tells me with a small, kind smile. "Don't be so hard on yourself."

"No," Kenzie says. "She's right." She looks at me. "You weren't horrible or anything, but you've got a long way to go to be on par with us." She gestures back and forth between herself and Tori. "We're pretty awesome friends. But I think with some time and lots and lots of practice, you might just move up to our level. And if you start to slip back into your old ways, we'll just yank you back on track."

"Sounds good," I say, my voice coming out like I've swallowed gravel.

That's two down.

One to go.

Holding my breath, I look at Tori but she's impossible to read.

I'm guessing she's doing it on purpose, the whole stoic, expressionless, making-me-wait thing.

I might even deserve it.

"We were heading to Baldwin's for brunch," she finally says of the local diner, completely monotone. "Before you acted like a crazy person and body-slammed into my car, that is."

I wait some more. She is really milking this payback for all it's worth.

And the gleam in her eyes says she knows it.

But then her lips twitch, and while it's not quite a smile, it's the least hostile she's looked at me in almost a year. "Would you care to join us?"

I almost deflate with relief.

"I'd love to." Hey, maybe this honesty thing isn't so bad after all. "When we're done, we can come back here and hang out. Maybe bake some cookies? Or a cake?"

I haven't baked anything in a week, and while it didn't bother me during that time, it's like I'm suddenly in sugar withdrawal.

"Ooh! Can we do both?" Kenzie asks, clapping her hands in delight.

Right there is a girl after my own heart. I smile for what seems like the first time all week. "Absolutely."

I grab my phone and purse and we head out, two by two—Tori

and Kenzie in the lead, me and Whitney, arms linked, picking up the rear.

I still have no idea how I'm going to get over losing Sam or handle not seeing Zoe and Taylor each day, and God knows my future after high school is one great-big question mark.

I do know that I'll survive it. All of it. And it won't be because I'm hiding from the pain and loss and regret. I'm going to go through it. I'm going to learn from it.

I'm going to survive it.

But I won't have to do it alone.

54

Turns out, trying to change one's entire perspective on life is harder than you'd think.

At least, it has been for me.

Or maybe it's just going to take some time. Longer than the two days I've been working on it.

But I've been doing my best not to revert back to the Hadley of old.

It hasn't been easy.

Especially when I start to miss Zoe and Taylor so much I spend an hour sitting on the couch crying into Eggie's fur. Or when my thoughts drift to Sam and the way we ended.

And I hate it. I hate feeling so lost. So hurt. I just want it to go away.

That's when I start to think that my life would be so much easier if I just went back to who I was: a girl who stayed safe, never took chances and protected her heart above all else. A girl who accepted whatever life sent her way.

But then I remember what I promised myself. How far I've already come.

I remember what Zoe said the day she told me she was leaving.

About how she was moving to Erie to prove that the Jones girls don't have to settle for less than what we deserve. That if we want a different life, we have to fight for it.

I definitely want a different life.

I want more. More out of life. More from myself.

And I want Sam.

So very, very much.

Which is why I'm standing on the pedals of my bike, slowly and steadily pumping my legs, trying to make it to the top of Sam's driveway.

Sam's long, steep driveway.

So far, this isn't one of my better plans.

Then again, it was less actual plan and more spontaneous decision. Even though school starts tomorrow, I still went to work today. There I'd been, riding my bike home from a long, grueling day of weeding and mowing when, instead of taking a left onto State Street, I'd gone straight.

Now, ten minutes later, here I am, sweaty and tired and breathless.

Following my heart and going after the boy who means everything to me.

I finally reach the top and immediately spy Sam in the basketball court, playing one-on-one with Charlie.

Saves me from having to ring the doorbell and the possibility of having the door slammed shut in my face.

Or worse, having his mother answer.

But she's not home. The garage doors are open—allfour of them —but only Sam's SUV is parked inside. Hopefully his mom and Patrick are both at work and will stay there until after I'm long gone.

Max isn't home, either. Pitt started classes last week, which means that after he dropped the bomb about us hooking up, he got to pack up and leave. No sticking around to face the consequences of his actions. No trying to work things out with his brother. No remorse or making amends.

He gets to go on living his life, free and easy. Gets to go right on doing whatever he feels like, saying whatever he wants without any consequences or accountability.

Those are all left to me.

I reach the far corner of the basketball court when Charlie gives Sam the heads-up that I'm here—as in Charlie spies me first and jerks his head in my direction causing Sam to look my way.

I'm too far away to see what, if any, emotions fill his eyes, but the way he goes completely, rigidly stiff and then slowly, deliberately turns away gives me a mighty big clue.

He's not happy to see me.

I'm not welcome here.

It's almost enough to have me doing a U-turn in front of the garage and zooming myself right back down that driveway.

Almost.

But the new, hopefully improving—if not quite all the way improved—Hadley doesn't give up so easily.

Pressing my lips together, I stop my bike next to the entrance to the court and swing off before I change my bold, brave mind.

I'm taking off my backpack, watching Sam ignore my presence, when he says something to Charlie, the words too low for me to hear.

Charlie's eyebrows rise and he looks at me. Frowns thoughtfully. Then turns to Sam. "Make it twenty."

Okay, that was clear enough.

Sam hesitates then nods and Charlie heads toward me in that loping way preteen boys have, all bouncy strides and swinging arms. He stops in front of me—probably because I'm blocking his way.

"Did he offer you twenty bucks to tell me he doesn't want to talk to me?" I ask.

"Nah. He's paying me to get lost." Charlie scratches the side of his nose. "I would've gone anyway," he says in an undertone. Not that he needs to bother being quiet since Sam is now on the other side of the court shooting layups. "No way I want to stick around and watch you two fight."

"Did he tell you we're fighting?"

He rolls his eyes, like I'm just way too lame for him to even deal with. "No. Duh. But it's kinda obvious. You haven't been around and he's been acting like someone died or something."

I glance at Sam. "He has?"

I may have sounded a bit too happy about it because Charlie scrunches up his face. "Uh. Yeah. Anyway," he says with a one-shoulder shrug, "good luck. You're going to need it."

No kidding.

We part ways—Charlie heading toward the house, me entering the court. Sam continues with the layups, shooting them one after the other, switching sides, grabbing his own rebounds and dribbling several times in between before shooting again.

But these aren't just drills he's doing. It's like he's playing some invisible opponent, his movements crisp and aggressive. Giving him a wide berth, I cross to stand behind the basket to the right, where I know he can see me.

He keeps right on acting like he doesn't.

"Sam," I say. But there's nothing. No slight pause. No glance my way. I try again. Louder. "Sam."

This time I know he hears me because his mouth thins and he dribbles harder, sweat dripping down the side of his face, his expression all harsh lines.

I bite my inner lower lip. This was such a mistake. It's been nine days since Sam found out about me hooking up with Max. Nine days. And he hasn't texted or called me once. He didn't stop me from leaving the party last weekend. Hasn't tried to talk to me or see me since.

He quit his job—again—so he wouldn't have to be around me.

He wants us to be through.

Again.

My coming here wasn't bravery.

It's lunacy.

I should let him go.

But I've let so many things go without a fight. Too many things. Including Sam.

Plus, he's really starting to tick me off.

So when his next shot bounces off the rim, I dart out and snatch the ball before he can, twisting away when he reaches for it.

We stare at each other. Well, his is more a burning glare than a stare and it's not actually aimed at me but at a spot over my head. His hair is damp at the temples, his shirt clinging to his chest, his jaw working as if he's doing a fine job of grinding his molars to dust.

And when he speaks, he does so through barely moving lips. "Give me my fucking ball."

Heart racing, mouth dry, I tuck the ball behind my back as I face him, holding it with both hands. Shake my head.

If possible, his expression gets darker. His eyes colder as they flick to mine then away. "What do you want?"

This is so much worse than I thought it'd be—and I'd imagined it was going to be completely awful. But I hadn't counted on how I'd feel, being this close to him and not being able to touch him. Having him look right through me as if I'm not even here.

Barely worth his notice.

"Can we--" I stop. Lick my lips and try again. "Can we talk?"

"We have nothing to talk about."

"Please," I say, swallowing the tiny bit of pride I have left, shoring up my courage. "Please, Sam. Just give me five minutes."

He flicks a quick, cool glance over me, from the top of my ballcap to the tips of my sneakers. "I don't want to talk to you."

And he walks away.

It trips something inside of me, that dismissive look. His flat, frigid tone.

Him turning away. Leaving me yet again.

Heat fills me—not from the sun but from somewhere inside me. It builds and builds, like a volcano ready to erupt, flowing through my veins like lava. My skin feels too tight. Itchy. There's a pressure in my head, beating like a pulse at the base of my skull, insistent. Unrelenting.

How dare he act so indifferent? How dare he stand there and look down on me? How dare he act like I'm nothing to him? Like I was never anything to him? Like he's a king handing down a royal decree —*I don't want to talk to you.*

How dare he walk away from me again.

Except, the whole reason he's on that invisible throne is because I put him there.

I put him there, I realize and let the ball drop behind me. It bounces, hits the backs of my calves then rolls into the fencing. I pushed and pushed Sam to the top of a golden pedestal, high above me, where I could always look up to him.

Where he could stay untouchable and perfect.

"It's all about what you want," I call, voice trembling, but loud enough to stop him in his tracks at mid-court. Strong enough to have his spine going ramrod straight. "You never cared about what I wanted. Not as long as you got your way."

He's breathing heavier, his shoulders rising and falling rapidly, his hands flexing and clenching at his sides. But he doesn't respond.

Doesn't look at me.

Stubborn, stubborn boy.

Except I'm discovering that I can be stubborn, too.

I march over to him, grab his arm and whirl him around. "Damn it, Sam. Look at me!"

"I can't!" His anger and bitterness hit me like a tornado, swirling and whirling around me, stealing my breath, sucking my courage, my own anger into its vortex. I rear back, my hand going to my throat, the erratic, hard thump of my pulse beating against my fingertips.

"Don't you get it?" he says, his voice breaking. "I can't look at you. Every time I do, I imagine you with him and--" He presses his lips together and grabs the back of his neck with both hands. Shakes his head. "I just...I can't."

Max's words from that awful night come back to me.

I want him to think about it. Every time he's with you, I want him to remember I was there first.

Max got what he wanted.

The Constable brothers usually do.

"I'm sorry," I whisper. "Sam, I'm so, so sorry. I'd do anything to take it back."

He lowers his arms. "You can't take it back and you can't fix this. Nothing you do can change what you did. You need to leave. Now. There's nothing, not one goddamn thing, that you have to say that I want to hear."

I reach for him. "Sam…"

Only to slowly draw my hand back when he gives me a look frigid enough to have my fingertips turning blue with frostbite, his lips curling in disgust.

Like he never used to look at me like I was something precious. Something special.

Like he never told me he loved me.

Like I'm nothing.

"It's never enough, is it?" I ask quietly, having to push the words through the constriction in my throat, because even though I've cried at least three times a day since Zoe and Taylor left, I'm obviously not done with the tears yet. "No matter what I do, what I say, how I act… it's never enough."

The look he gives me is so condescending, so freaking arrogant, it takes all I have not to kick him in the shin. "I don't want anything from you."

"Please. You want everything from me. I give you everything I have but you still want more. You want it all. You demand it."

"That is such bullshit," he snarls. "You always held back from me. Always. And you never gave me anything. I had to beg and fight and pull every measly scrap from you!"

"At least I listened to you," I remind him hotly. "When you came back, I listened to you and I gave you a second chance. I forgave you and this is how you're going to treat me now?"

"Forgave me? I didn't do anything that needed forgiving."

"You. Changed. Everything! You decided you were in love with me and that was it. I was just to go along with it. You showed up at my house drunk and issued an ultimatum, and when I didn't give in, you ran off like a spoiled brat throwing a temper tantrum." My voice is shaking but I can't stop the words, hadn't realized they'd been inside of me this whole time. How badly I need to let them loose. "You took the choice from me. Then you left me. And when I came to see you at Christmas, you treated me like shit. Just...brushed me off like so much dirt on your shoe. But you never said you were sorry. Never apologized. Not for any of it."

"Don't," he says, a low warning as he towers over me, arms crossed, shutting himself off from me. From accepting any blame in what's become of us. "Don't even try and turn around what happened Christmas night on me. Don't blame me for what you did."

"I'm not. I made a mistake. I made a million of them. But so did you. See, the thing I'm just now getting is that you're not perfect. But you want me to be."

"What I want is for you to not fuck my brother," he grinds out and I go light-headed, like all the blood has drained from my head. "Guess that's too much to ask for, huh?"

My stomach roils and I take long, slow breaths through my mouth until the sick feeling passes. I study Sam's face, searching for the boy I've known since I was ten. The boy who's had my heart for so many years.

But that's not the Sam Constable standing in front of me. This Sam is mean. Unforgiving.

This Sam doesn't care about me. Doesn't respect me.

After everything we've been through, after everything we've both done, I deserve better than that.

For the first time, I think I just might deserve better than Sam Constable.

"When I came here Christmas," I say softly, "it was to tell you that I changed my mind. That I was ready to be with you. That I *wanted* to be with you." He flinches and makes a low sound, like he's been hit in the stomach, but I keep going. "You wouldn't even hear me out. Tell me, Sam, did you and Abby hook up that night? Huh?" I prod when he remains silent, mouth a thin line. "If I look at your phone right now, how many texts from her am I going to see? How many texts *to* her are on there? How many times did you text her, talk to her in private after you told me you wouldn't?"

He turns a dull red, the blush creeping up his throat. But it's the only admission of guilt he'll give me. The only confession Sam is willing to make. "Is that why you hooked up with my brother? Revenge?"

My first instinct is to deny it, but one of us should be completely honest here.

"I don't know," I say quietly. "Maybe. But I didn't plan it. When I saw you were with Abby, when you chose her over me...it tore me apart. So, when Max pulled in as I was leaving and offered me a ride, I accepted. The rest" –I lift my hands, let them fall— "just happened. I wish it hadn't, but it did. And I'm sorry. I really am. But that doesn't give you any right to treat me this way. To talk to me like that."

"You did it on purpose," he insists. "To get back at me. You could have been with anyone, any other guy, and you picked him because you knew it would kill me."

"It wasn't like that! Why can't you see that? Why can't you see that what you did ripped me apart, too?"

He swipes a hand through the air as if erasing my words. My feelings. "You've been fucking around with me all summer. You knew how I felt about you." His voice cracks and he stops. "You knew and you kept stringing me along. Why? Why couldn't you just let me go?"

My shoulders tighten and I gape at him, fury skimming along my skin, prickling the nape of my neck. "Are you kidding me right now? *I* wouldn't let *you* go?"

Pure rage pushes me forward and I take the two steps needed to bring us toe to toe, but the brim of my hat blocks my view of him so I rip it from my head. Shake it at his stupid, too-handsome face. "I tried to keep my distance but you wouldn't let me. I knew this would happen. I knew we'd both end up getting hurt, but that didn't matter. What I wanted didn't matter. It's about you. It's always been about you. Your wants. Your feelings. From the beginning, you made all the choices and I was just to go along with them. You made me trust you.

You became the most important person in my life and then, when you didn't get your own way, you left me. You. Left. Me."

"I left you," he agrees, gaze flat, tone cold. "But that wasn't my mistake. My mistake was coming back." He steps up to my side, keeps his head down. "We're done. Don't come here again. Don't talk to me in school. Don't look at me. Don't even think about me. Because I am through thinking about you."

This time, it's me who turns away. Who walks away, but I'm blinded by my tears and I only make it two stumbling steps before stopping.

There's one more thing I have to do. One thing I need to give him. The whole truth.

"You were right," I say, forcing myself to face him. "I did hold back from you."

Admitting that is next to the hardest thing I've ever done.

Telling him the rest is going to be the hardest.

But I don't do it for him.

I do it for me.

"June twenty-first."

He scowls. "What?"

"June twenty-first. That's the day you caught me about to go swimming in your pool when we were ten. That was the day I decided to give you a chance. That's the day," I continue, my voice hoarse, unsteady, "I fell in love with you."

He inhales sharply, his body twitching as if it wants to move—either toward or away from me—but his brain won't let it. "It doesn't mat--"

"I love you, Sam." And saying it isn't nearly as hard as I thought it'd be. Not nearly as scary. The truth really does set you free.

Or maybe it's because he won't look at me, his head down, his hands on his hips.

But he hears me. I know he does.

And that's all that matters.

"I should have told you that on Valentine's Day when we were sophomores," I continue, my hands twisting my ballcap so hard the brim bends, "when I was so jealous of Abby I could have screamed. I should have told you the first time you kissed me. I should have told you a hundred times, a thousand times before. I love you. I've loved you for seven years. I thought I'd love you forever but now..." I trail off, uncertain, because this is the part I'm not sure I can get out. The truth that's been bubbling inside of me ever since Sam walked away from me at that party. "Now, I think maybe it's time I stopped. For both our sakes."

I somehow manage to make it out of the court and over to my bike. Feeling him watching me, I shrug on my backpack, climb onto my bike and, my hat crushed between my right hand and my handlebar, I coast down the driveway. At the bottom, I keep going, making it another mile before my vision is too blurry to ride safely.

That's when I stop and call Devyn and ask her to pick me up.

That's when I sit cross-legged on the sidewalk, elbows on my knees, face in my hands.

That's when I cry over Sam Constable.

For the very last time.

55

I TRIED. I WENT AFTER SAM. I GAVE HIM MY TRUTH. AFTER SO MANY years, after all our time together, I finally told him everything.

It wasn't enough.

Or maybe it was, but it was too late.

Either way my fears held me back. Cost me Sam. My best friend. The only boy I've ever loved.

But it wasn't just my mistakes that ended us. Sam has his share of the blame, too.

Even if he refuses to admit it.

I guess that's all part of it. Part of life. Mistakes made and lessons learned. Fears, if not conquered, then at least overcome, bit by bit. Fighting the battles most important to you. Winning some.

Losing others.

Trying for something important. Celebrating when you get it.

And surviving when you don't.

───────

During the first month of school, I learn to live without Sam again. You'd think it would be easier this time. He was only back in my life for the summer, barely enough time for me to get used to him being there once again.

But it's not easier. It's harder.

I thought it was bad when he was in LA. When I couldn't see him every day. But passing him in the halls? Seeing him daily in the cafeteria?

Much worse.

I get through it, though. I mean, what other choice do I have? It's not like I'm going to drop out of school just so I can avoid seeing the boy.

Although I may have considered going the whole homeschooling route, but Dev wouldn't go for it.

So, yeah, it's hard. But each day gets just the teeniest, tiniest bit easier. At the rate I'm going, I should be able to walk past him without wanting to break down in tears by spring break. And I'm sure I'll no longer think about him every single minute of every single day by the time graduation rolls around.

Until then, I just keep moving forward.

Unlike last year, I'm not going through my emotional pain and upheaval alone. I hang out with Whitney, Tori and Kenzie as often as our schedules allow, which is usually two to three times a week. Tori and Kenzie are both on the varsity volleyball team so they're busy with practices, matches and weekend tournaments, and Whitney just started working part-time at the hospital gift shop, while I put in eight hours during the week at Glenwood and another eight on Saturday.

But the three of us sit together at lunch every day, making sure to keep plenty of people—usually T.J., Colby, Jackson and Fiona—between me and Sam.

Yep. Sam and I sit at the same lunch table. In the beginning, it was super weird, and the first day of school, when I took the empty seat next to Whitney, I thought for sure Sam would get up and leave, but he didn't.

He also didn't look at me. Something I know for certain because I may have snuck a quick glance or two—or twelve—his way.

I stopped doing that by the end of the first week.

Hey, two can play the You Don't Exist To Me game.

He's just way better at it than I am.

But I think we're both getting used to it. This New Normal where I'm here and he's here but we're not together. Where we don't talk. Don't look at each other. Where we pretend the past seven years never happened.

That *we* never happened.

You'd be surprised what you can accept when you don't have any other choice.

I have a New Normal at home, too, but Dev and I are slowly adjusting to Zoe and Taylor being gone. I still miss them like crazy—talking to them almost every day on FaceTime is not the same as them being here, especially when Taylor starts crying for me and there's nothing I can do to comfort her—but it helps to know them being in Erie really is for the best.

We've also had to tweak our finances now that it's just us. Without Zoe's income, things are tighter than usual, so I've had to push aside my wild, secret dream of quitting Glenwood Landscaping and using all my free time to focus on my baking.

I've pushed it aside, but I'm keeping it alive by mulling over some different ways I could possibly make money doing what I love, like maybe starting a dessert blog or, as Whitney suggested, trying to sell some of my desserts, either to local stores or out of our trailer.

If those ideas don't pan out, I'll think of something else.

That's who I am now. A girl who doesn't give up. Who takes charge of her life.

For the most part, anyway.

What can I say? I'm a work in progress.

And I'm no longer content to wait around for life to happen *to* me. I want to be the one in charge. Going after my dreams. Making things happen. Starting with my future.

I've been looking online at different culinary arts programs. There are a couple close to home like PTC and Erie County Community College in Buffalo, but not even those are going to be doable.

Not right after graduation, anyway.

Devyn was right. Even if I were to get a scholarship to help with tuition, it wouldn't be enough.

But in a few years (three if I'm lucky, five more realistically) after I've worked a full-time job and one or two on the side, after I've saved as much money as possible, I'll go.

It's not a foolproof plan. Life is still going to happen, the bad and the good. And when it does, I'll have to, once more, adjust accordingly. There may even be a few times when I'll have to do whatever it takes to get through.

But that's okay. Because for all the other times, I'll be the one in control.

The one making things happen.

56

"I'M GOING TO HAVE TO HAVE A LOBOTOMY," KENZIE SAYS, ALL heartfelt melodrama and weary acceptance. She looks like a forlorn fairy, her hair parted on the side, her bangs held in place with a sparkly barrette. The top of her short, light blue dress is shiny and formfitting, the bottom flaring out from her waist, like cotton candy. "That's the only way I'll ever be able to go on."

We're in the girls' bathroom—yes, we are the types of girls who not only attend homecoming as a group, we also stick together like glue all night and only pee when we're all together—down the hall from the gym where approximately four hundred of our classmates are gyrating as one sweaty mass to "Bottoms Up."

Washing her hands, Kenzie sends Tori a pleading look in the mirror. "Your dad works for that neurosurgeon, right? Can he get me on the schedule?"

"First of all," Tori says, reapplying her hot pink lipstick, "my dad is renovating Dr. Montgomery's offices. He's not the receptionist there. Secondly, I'm pretty sure lobotomies are illegal now, what with the whole turning-people-into-lifeless-zombies thing. And if they weren't, I'm guessing they wouldn't be, like, elective surgery."

Kenzie rips a sheet of paper towel from the dispenser with

enough force to tear the whole thing from the wall. "I'd rather be a lifeless zombie! At least then I wouldn't have this awful, horrible, disgusting memory in my head."

"I think it's sweet your parents are still so into each other," Whitney says, adjusting the bodice of her silver strapless dress. "You're lucky."

"Lucky?" Kenzie repeats, all gaping mouth and crazed, heavily made-up eyes. "*Lucky*? They're my parents. And they're...old."

"They're not even fifty," Tori points out, tossing her lipstick back into her black clutch. Her dress is long, black, slinky and so tight it took two of us to tug it down after she went to the bathroom.

But the best part is the glittering, plastic homecoming queen tiara on her head.

Royalty in our midst.

"They were doing it in the living room," Kenzie mutters with a full-body shudder. "Like, right there. Out in the open like wild animals."

We'd just arrived at the football game when Kenzie realized she forgot her high heels—we all wore jeans to the game and changed into our dresses at Fiona's since she lives closest to the school. When Kenzie ran home right after Tori was crowned homecoming queen, she walked in on her parents having sex.

She is now extremely traumatized.

"You're lucky you haven't caught them before this," Tori says as we make our way to the door.

"That's true," I say because I've never seen any man—none over the age of twenty, anyway—as into a woman as Mr. Porter is Mrs. Porter. Then again, she's really hot. "The way your dad looks at your mom? I'm surprised they're not hooking up every minute of every day."

Kenzie covers her ears. "Ahh! Stop! Bad enough I have to have my brain bleached to rid myself of the image of them...of *him*...of *her*... doing...*that*." She shoves the door open. "I am never, ever walking into my house again without ringing the doorbell first."

"I'm never, ever sitting on your couch again," Tori says and we all crack up, just die, right there, as we walk single file out of the bathroom.

We're still laughing when Kenzie—the engine of our sparkly, high-heeled, heavily mascaraed train—stops without warning. Tori runs into her. I run into Tori. And Whitney runs into me.

"Shit," Tori mutters and I immediately know something is up, something big. Whitney peers around my shoulder and reaches down to link her hand with mine in support. In comfort.

Kenzie and Tori step aside—Tori to the left, Kenzie to the right—and that's when I see him next to the gym's doors, slouched against the wall, head down, hands in the pockets of his black dress pants.

Sam Constable, big as life and darkly handsome in a suit and tie, his hair slicked back from his face.

Sam Constable standing between me and the gym.

My heart stutters and swells at the sight of him, conveniently forgetting how he smashed it into a thousand pieces.

But I haven't forgotten.

My friends haven't either. They flank me, all silently congregating to my right, putting their bodies between me and Sam.

My sisters aren't the only ones who have my back now.

As if sensing me staring at him, he looks up. Across the distance, our eyes meet and hold, and my heart simply leaps.

I sigh. Stupid, forgiving heart.

But then, I broke his heart, too. Something I need to remember so I don't get sucked into the who-hurt-who-more game.

Knowing my friends are waiting for me to make the decision of whether we go back to the dance or duck into the bathroom and hide out there until Sam's gone, I take a step toward the gym.

I don't run from Sam Constable. Not anymore.

He straightens as we approach.

And heads our way.

Crap.

Just because I don't run from the boy doesn't mean I want to torture myself by getting close to him.

"Hey," he says.

As I'm not supposed to talk to him—or look at him or think about him—as per the stipulations he gave me that day at his house six weeks ago, I keep my mouth shut while my friends return his greeting.

I don't talk to him, but I *do* look at him.

If only to prove he's not the boss of me.

Also, because he keeps looking at me. Well, he keeps sending furtive, nervous glances my way then, as soon as he sees me looking back, jerks his gaze to the floor, the ceiling or my friends.

"Uh...congratulations," he tells Tori, gesturing to the tiara on her head.

Tori grins. "Thanks. It was a surprise. I thought for sure you and Brynn were going to win."

Sam was on the homecoming court, too, because of course he was. He'd been paired up with Brynn Ellsworth, a well-liked member of the marching band and track team.

One side of Sam's mouth kicks up into that stupid, adorable grin that gets me every time. "Nah. You and Timmy always had it in the bag."

And then we all stand there for what has to be the longest, most awkward minute of my life, glancing at each other as the music pours out of the gym, the bass so loud it vibrates the floor.

"Okay, well, this is, like, super uncomfortable," Kenzie says, giving Sam a friendly pat on his arm. "We're going to go now because I want this to be over."

Tori laughs, Whitney presses her lips together to stop a smile and I just start tugging Whitney forward.

Sam touches my wrist. "Hadley..."

It was barely even a touch, that brush of his fingers against my skin, but I jerk to a stop.

It was hardly more than a whisper, the sound of my name, but it reverberates through my head.

I look up at him.

His throat works as he swallows. "Could...could I talk to you?"

"I thought we weren't supposed to talk," I can't stop myself from saying.

Okay, I probably could have, but I don't want to.

He blushes but doesn't back down. "It'll only take a minute," he says holding my gaze, his eyes lit with stubbornness, jaw set with determination. "Please, Hadley."

I tell myself I could resist him if he hadn't said please, but it's not his politeness that gets to me. It's the thread of nerves in his tone. The slight tremor in the word *please*.

The way he says my name again, soft and almost tender.

Like he used to.

I am such a sap.

"I'll catch up with you in a few minutes," I tell my friends, earning me a pursed-lip perusal from Tori, an eyebrow wiggle from Kenzie and a worried frown from Whitney, who asks, "Are you sure?"

Tori and Kenzie are my friends, but they're Sam's friends, too. Were Sam's friends first.

But Whitney is *my* friend first.

I give her a quick, grateful hug. "I'm sure."

I watch them leave, Tori and Kenzie in the lead, Whitney bringing up the rear, her feelings about leaving me alone with the boy who broke my heart clear in her reluctant, feet-dragging walk. In the way she keeps glancing over her shoulder to give Sam the ol' stink eye.

They disappear through the gym's doorway and I force myself to turn and face Sam.

Only to find him staring at me, the look in his eyes so raw, so full of longing and need and something else, something deeper and so much more dangerous to my hard-earned peace of mind, to my healing heart, I take an automatic step back.

He notices—Sam notices everything. But he doesn't try and hide what he's feeling. Doesn't shutter his gaze or smooth his expression. Doesn't clear away the husky timbre of his tone when he murmurs, "You're so beautiful. That dress..." He rubs his palms together. Shakes his head as if in wonder as he slides his gaze over me. "That dress is amazing."

My skin prickles with heat. It's not a dress. Not really. It's two pieces: a cropped halter top done up in sequins and a snug, floral skirt that ends well above my knees. Zoe found it at a thrift store in Erie and sent it to me as a surprise, knowing I'd love it.

Did I mention it's green?

Sam's favorite color.

I try to swallow past the lump in my throat but it's no use. That sucker's staying there. "Thank you." I look at the gym door. "I should probably--"

"Are you having fun?" he blurts, taking a quick step toward me. "At the dance, I mean?"

Squeezing his eyes shut, he groans softly, his face scrunched up in a wince.

Well, that was an extremely lame question.

"I *was*," I say, and by the way he nods, solemn and accepting, it's clear he gets my meaning that I'd been having an enjoyable evening up until now. "You?"

"I wasn't."

My breath catches.

His meaning is just as clear as mine.

Gets even clearer when he continues.

"Talking to you," he says, taking another step closer to me, "being this close to you, is the best part of my night so far. The best part of the last six weeks."

"Sam--"

"I miss you. I miss you so much, Hadley, and I'm sorry," he says in a rush, voice trembling. But his gaze is steady. Earnest. "I'm sorry for everything—for being selfish last summer and giving you that ultimatum. For being a spoiled brat and shutting you out the way I did and moving to LA without a word. For the things I said when you came to my house the day before school started. But what I'm the sorriest about is being such an asshole at Christmas. I never should have said those things to you. I never should have sent you away."

"Because of what happened after," I say slowly. "With me and Max."

He shakes his head. "Because I hurt you." He drops his gaze to the floor for a moment. Inhales deeply then meets my eyes. "Because I did it on purpose."

I flinch and he hurries on, his words quiet but quick, as if they're bubbling out of him, as if he's been holding them back all this time.

"I'd convinced myself I did the right thing, moving to LA. That I was over you and then I came back here and you're all I thought about. I picked up my phone at least a hundred times to call you. Christ, Hadley, I drove by your trailer three times, like some crazy stalker, and I just...I wanted one night, one night where I could pretend that it hasn't always been you." He inhales a shaky breath, his voice dropping. "I wanted to pretend, for one night, that it wouldn't always be you."

I lick my lips. "So you called Abby."

"I was an asshole to her, too," he says, shame filling his voice. He stabs a hand through his hair, causing it to wave wildly above his right ear. "I had no right calling her. No right spending time with her or" –his cheeks turn red— "or being with her, when the only girl I wanted to be with, the only girl I ever want to be with, is you."

"No."

The word bursts out of me, loud and adamant, before I even realize it. Like there's some separate force inside of me, an internal defense mechanism that's still chugging along, doing its best to protect me from having my heart broken yet again by this boy. Determined to save me from his words. From why he wanted to talk to me now, after all these weeks.

From what he's going to say next.

Saving me from myself.

"No," I repeat, softer now.

But it's as if Sam expected nothing less than full-out resistance and has prepared a counterattack, one using his honesty and feelings and hope to chip away at my resistance.

"When you showed up Christmas night," he says, "when I saw you there on my doorstep with snow clinging to your lashes and your cheeks pink from the cold...it was like my heart" –he rubs a hand absently over his chest— "started beating again. Like it'd been silent and still for four months, but one look at you and I came to life again."

There's an ache in my own chest because that's how it'd been for me, too. Like I'd been underwater ever since he left, holding my breath, but as soon as I saw him, I could breathe again.

"I saw you," he continues, his voice hoarse, his eyes shiny with tears, "and it was like God or the universe was laughing at me, showing me exactly what was really going on, how little control I had over my own thoughts and emotions. I was so pissed. So hurt. And instead of realizing it was all my own fault, I blamed you. For showing up at my house, for being everything I wanted. For not wanting me back."

"I did want you," I say, and despite my vow not to cry over this boy again, tears are filling my eyes. "You pushed me away. You were with Abby."

"I was wrong. I was so wrong and I'm sorry. I'm so sorry, Hadley." He takes a step toward me but I shift back and he stops. "I know I changed things between us without giving you a choice, I know I had to have everything my way, but I don't want to do that now. So if you tell me to go, I will. I promise I will. And I won't bother you, won't ever bring this up again. I love you. I love you, Hadley. Will you please give me another chance to show you how much? To treat you the way you deserve to be treated?"

I want to. It terrifies me—the new bolder, braver me—how much I want to. How badly I want to jump into his arms and pretend the past six weeks never happened. That I was never with Max. That Sam hadn't been with Abby.

But in the end, I can't. I can't put myself through that pain again. Not when I've finally started healing.

"It won't work," I say. "Too much has happened between us. Too many mistakes have been made."

"We can get past them."

He sounds so certain. So sure of us both that I almost believe him. Almost.

"You said that before," I point out. "You said that we were starting fresh, that the past didn't matter, but it does. What we do matters. And you'll never be able to forgive me for being with Max. Not completely."

"Do you forgive me? For being with Abby?"

"I don't know," I answer honestly.

He nods. "Maybe...maybe that's something we could work on. Together. Getting past what we both did."

"How?"

"I don't know." And it's the best thing he could say to me because it's the truth. And it's not a promise, but his next words are. "But I'm willing to try, to do whatever I have to in order to make us work this time. Forever."

"I'm scared," I admit, hugging my arms around myself. "More so than when you first asked me to give you a chance. Having you leave me hurt, but losing you? Sam, it tore me apart. I don't know if I can put myself through that again. Not even for you."

"I know," he says, and this time when he steps forward, I stay where I'm at and he leans his forehead against mine, his voice thick with tears. And I remember the first time I admitted I was scared, how he told me he was, too. But isn't that what being brave is all about? Doing something despite your fear?

"You said you loved me," he says, lifting his head so he can meet my eyes. "At my house, you...you said you've always loved me. You still do, right? You didn't stop?"

"I didn't stop. I wanted to, but I couldn't."

He shuts his eyes on a long exhale. "Thank God," he murmurs.

"But love isn't always enough."

We loved each other before and we still made so many mistakes. Hurt each other so badly.

"No," he says, surprising me with his agreement. "It's not. It might not be enough for us. In the end, we may end up right back here, broken up. Broken-hearted. But what if we don't? What if somehow, despite everything we've done and everything that's against us, we make it? Together? That's a risk I'm willing to take. Are you?"

"I don't know."

Doing so is crazy. Risky, like he said. It's the complete opposite of careful and safe.

But then love, like life, often is. Full of joy and heartache. Wins and losses. It's about forgiveness and acceptance. Fear and courage.

"Why don't we..." I stop. Clear my throat and blink back the last of my tears. "Why don't we start with a dance and go from there? No promises. No expectations."

His grin starts slow then builds and builds until I can't help but smile back, then he nods and holds out his hand, palm up.

Sometimes, to get the most out of life, you need to steer it in the direction you want it to go.

And sometimes, I think as I take Sam's hand, you need to hold on and just go along for the ride.

EPILOGUE

CHRISTMAS NIGHT I'M HIT WITH DÉJÀ VU.

Same holiday. Same boy. Same girl.

Except this year, I'm not standing on Sam's porch, waiting hopefully, anxiously to be let in.

He's standing on mine.

Also, it's not snowing.

We've had an incredible lack of snow this winter, which has been a curse for certain local businesses, such as the ski resort forty miles outside of town and Mr. G, who relies heavily on people needing his snow removal services to help get through the winter.

For me? Total blessing.

I got fired.

Well, not fired, exactly. Laid-off was what Mr. G called it the day after Thanksgiving when I went into work only to find I shouldn't have bothered. Since there wasn't any snow to be cleared, and since he already had two full-time employees who could handle what little work they did have, I got the boot.

I could have kissed him. On the mouth. And he's old enough to be my grandfather. And has a seriously gnarly beard.

Without even thinking it through, I went to the Davis Bakery and begged the owner to give me a job.

Like, literally begged. It was a bit pathetic.

But it worked.

Marjorie, the owner and my boss, appreciates my passion for baked goods and has been teaching me a lot about both baking and owning a small food-based business.

The hours suck, though. I go in at four thirty a.m. three times a week before school and on Saturdays and Sundays.

But it's totally worth it.

"Hey," I say to Sam softly, as a tail-wagging Eggie greets him with some good old-fashioned Christmas joy. The air is cold and smells like burning wood from Mr. Keane's woodstove. "I thought you were in lockdown all day."

During Thanksgiving dinner, Sam's mom told his family the only way one of her sons was leaving their house on Christmas was in the back of an ambulance.

Or a hearse.

At least, that's what Sam said she said.

I highly doubt she used those exact words, but I bet that was pretty much her true meaning.

Petting Eggie, he grins up at me. "I got paroled. And I wanted to see you."

And just like that, my entire body seems to light up from within.

Forget Christmas cheer. Hearing those words from this particular boy, seeing him, being near enough to touch him, is all I need.

"I'm glad you did," I tell him, because that's something I'm working really hard on lately. Telling my truths. Sharing my feelings.

It's not easy—opening up, letting myself be vulnerable. But with all the practice I've been getting these past few months with Sam and my friends, I'm slowly getting better at it.

I shiver and wrap my long, thick cardigan around me tighter.

It might not be snowing, but it's just as cold as it was last year. So cold, Sam's cheeks and the tip of his nose are pink.

Almost as if he's been standing there for longer than the thirty seconds it took me to walk from my bedroom to the door when I heard him knock.

He's also fidgeting, like he's nervous and when I lean out the door, he quickly steps forward, blocking my way.

And my view.

This whole scene is becoming quite suspicious.

I step aside and open the door wider. "Come on in," I whisper.

Even though it's barely nine, Zoe and Taylor—home for the holidays—are already in bed. And can I just say it's a Christmas miracle they lasted as long as they did. Taylor had us up three times during the night and we finally gave in and let her unwrap her presents at five-thirty. But even with two naps, she was a monster all day.

Whoever said this was the most peaceful time of the year never sat on the couch at five-thirty-five a.m. while an over-stimulated toddler tore the wrapping off a dozen presents, then screamed her head off when there no more left to open.

Sam shifts his weight from side to side. Clears his throat. "Actually, could you...would you mind meeting me out back? I have a surprise for you," he adds quickly, probably trying to tempt me because I am looking at him like he's lost his holly jolly mind.

Like I said, it may not be snowing, but it's really cold out.

And I'm already in my pajamas—thick, fleece pants, a thermal, long sleeve Henley topped with my cardigan and two pairs of socks.

But for the past few months, Sam hasn't asked anything of me. Not more of my time than I'm able to give. Not more of my thoughts and feelings than I'm ready to share of my own free will.

And I can't refuse him. Not tonight of all nights. As always, I have a very hard time saying *no* to Sam Constable.

Even when it means I'm going to freeze my butt off.

"Let me get my boots," I say with a resigned—and yes, grudging —sigh.

I may not be able to say no to the boy, but that doesn't mean I'm happy about it.

Sam, on the other hand, is thrilled. He smiles, wide and bright. "I'll meet you out there."

"Okay," I say, drawing the word out.

He's still grinning when I shut the door on his handsome face.

Yep. Very suspicious.

I button up my cardigan then get dressed like I'm about to embark on an epic journey across the tundra—boots, puffy coat, winter hat tugged down low, mittens and scarf—before heading into the living room where our Christmas tree twinkles brightly.

Not from the lights. But from shiny, silver tinsel.

So. Much. Tinsel.

For some reason, Dev's always loved it and since Zoe wasn't here to complain about it, Dev went to town, tossing the flossy strands with all the abandon of a fairy high on drugs and drunk with the power of her pixie dust.

Seriously. The tree is literally dripping with the stuff. You can barely see any green.

Which is fine. It was Gigi's tree, she just left it here when she took off. It's older than Devyn and gets scragglier each year, so the abundance of tinsel helps hide the bare spots.

My present for Sam is the only one still under the tree, wrapped in bright, red paper and topped with a festive gold bow. It's a photo album I filled with pictures of us, spanning the years from when were kids to now. It's a physical reminder of everything we've been through. Of what we've always meant to each other.

It's our story.

Tucking it under my arm, I make my way through the kitchen, stopping long enough to grab the plate of cookies from the table then open the door and step outside.

And into a magical, winter wonderland.

Sort of.

I mean, it's still my backyard with our broken grill in the corner and Taylor's plastic wading pool leaning against the side of the trailer. But now, it's all lit up. What seems like hundreds of tiny, white lights have been strung from the corner of the roof to the top of the neighbor's wooden fence, crisscrossing in the air, creating a twinkling canopy of faux stars. A crackling fire burns in one of those portable, metal firepit things in the center of the yard, surrounded by two camping chairs and a portable, rectangular table covered in a blue and gold tablecloth and topped with a thermos, two Christmas mugs and what looks like a small buffet. Music is playing. Not Christmas carols but "Hard Place."

The song we danced to at Homecoming.

But the best part by far is standing off to the side, his hands tucked into his coat pockets, a goofy, expectant smile on his face. "Merry Christmas, Hadley."

I slowly make my way down the few steps. "How did you even do all this?"

He shrugs, all nonchalant and cool, but he's studying me in a completely anxious way. "Jack helped. And I asked Zoe to keep you occupied and out of sight of the backyard while we got everything set up."

I laugh, my breath coming out in a soft puff. "I wondered why she kept wanting to watch baking videos with me."

We'd curled up on my bed, a sleeping Taylor between us and Zoe's new laptop on my knees. Stayed that way for almost an hour before Zoe's phone had buzzed with a message. She checked it, muttered *thank God* and promptly shuffled off to her old room to sleep.

A minute later, Sam knocked on the front door.

"I brought hot chocolate," Sam says, gesturing at the table. "And some snacks. And there are blankets and plenty of wood for the fire."

I'm stunned. Speechless.

And so full of love for him I can barely breathe.

But he takes my silence for something else entirely and his expression falls. "But if you're cold, or you don't want to sit out here, we can just go inside."

"I'm not cold. And I don't want to go inside."

"You don't?"

"No," I say, closing the distance between us. I set his present on one of the chairs, the cookies on the table. "This is the best present ever. Thank you."

"You're welcome. But it's not your present."

"It's not?"

He shakes his head. Tugs on his left earlobe. "I just...I wanted to do something to replace the memory of last year with something better. Something new."

"It's perfect," I murmur huskily, tears stinging my eyes.

Rising onto my toes, I brush my lips against his cheek and his breath hitches. His skin is cool and I linger there, warming it with my kiss for one heartbeat. Two.

Over the summer I kissed Sam at least a hundred times.

But I haven't kissed him, haven't so much as held his hand since that party at the lake.

Ever since Homecoming, Sam and I have been making our way back to each other. Steadily. Slowly.

Like, glacially slow.

That's how it had to be in order for us to truly get past our fears. For us to learn to forgive each other—and ourselves—for the mistakes we made. The hurt we both caused.

To finally, fully move past it.

But I think we both always knew we were headed to this spot.

That it was only a matter of time before we ended up here.

So instead of lowering to my heels, I slide my mouth over and press it against his because I can.

Because I so badly want to.

Settling his hands lightly on my waist, Sam kisses me back. It's soft and sweet and hesitant.

It's the perfect first kiss.

Because that's what it is. The old Sam and Hadley, Hadley and Sam are gone. What we are now has changed. Just like we've changed.

We're something better. Something new.

That doesn't mean things are going to be easy going forward. Sam and Max still aren't speaking to each other and I don't know when, or if, that'll ever change. The Constable brothers are both extremely stubborn and who knows what goes through the minds of boys?

They are a strange and fascinating breed of humans, that's for sure.

There were so many things we had to work through—our insecurities and jealousies and trust issues. So many

He also doesn't talk to Abby. Not like he used to. There are no more texts or phone calls. No more secret meetings. He even tried to tell me why Abby was so upset at that party, why she called him and went to his house that night, but I stopped him.

It's not his story to share.

I know better than anyone how it feels to have someone else tell your secret. And I wouldn't wish that on anyone. Not even Abby.

We also have no idea where Sam will be this time next year. He's applied to Pitt and OSU as well as UPenn and Cornell because his dad pressured him to try a couple of Ivy League schools.

But none of that matters. What matters is here. Now.

What matters is being in the arms of this boy. Loving him. Being loved by him in return.

Sam and I were never meant to be friends.

We were always, always meant to be so much more.

———

Thank you so much for reading The Art of Holding On! If you loved Hadley and Sam's story, you'll also love **Counting Flowers**, book one of my Flowers on the Wall Duet.

When Natalie's perfect life starts to spin out of control, she finds herself turning more and more to her little "quirks" - like repeatedly counting the flowers painted on her wall - to help her focus and stay calm. But nothing is the way it used to be, and as her carefully arranged life unravels, she's forced to face what's real. And learn to accept it might not be what she thinks it should be.

Available at your favorite online retailer!

COUNTING FLOWERS SNEAK PEEK

I WAKE UP FIVE MINUTES BEFORE MY ALARM, LIKE I DO EVERY DAY.
Rolling onto my side, I turn on the bedside lamp then grab my phone, unplug it and shut off the alarm before putting in my earbuds and selecting a Beyoncé song.

Like I do every day.

I prefer my mornings to proceed in a specific, organized way. And that specific, organized way starts with my listening to Beyoncé.

And no, Destiny's Child doesn't count. Neither do movie soundtracks or anything where she's the featured artist.

It has to be one of her songs from one of her albums. Period.

It's good luck, starting my day with Queen Bey.

Today's song is "Drunk in Love" and I turn up the volume before sitting up. Leaning back against the headboard, I stretch my arms overhead, yawn, then focus on the wall opposite me.

And I count the flowers there.

Like I do every morning.

I start at the light blue tulip in the top left corner—like I always do—then scan the wall, left to right, like reading a book. But when I get to the orange coneflower at the bottom right corner, I frown.

Eighty-two.

I've missed one.

Now I have to start again.

Crap.

There are eighty-three flowers in the mural on my wall, that is a given. I know this, I've counted them hundreds...thousands...of times. But I can't *not* count them again. Not because I want to.

I have to.

There's a knot in my chest, and a fluttering, unsettled feeling in my stomach. And neither will go away until I count the flowers and get eighty-three.

The song switches to "Goner" by Twenty-One Pilots and I kick off the covers and crawl to the bottom of my bed, then settle on my knees on the mattress.

And I count the flowers again, slower, more carefully, this time saying each number under my breath.

Eighty-three.

The knot loosens. The fluttering eases. But I'm not done. I repeat the process, this time in reverse order, starting at the orange cone-flower and ending with the light blue tulip, right to left, bottom to top. Up and up, side to side until finally, eighty-three.

Then I start again, this time counting color by color. Blue first (19), then purple (17), red and pink (14 and 14), yellow (11) and orange (8).

Eighty-three.

Once again, I reverse the order. Orange, yellow, pink and red, purple then blue. The blues aren't just blue, of course, they're aqua-marine and cobalt, navy and sapphire. The purples are violet, plum and mauve. Reds as bright as fresh blood and as dark and deep as a rose. Pinks both soft and neon. Sunflower yellows and golden oranges or a combination of the two, like the burst of colors in a sunrise. Melding like the warm glow of a sunset.

I keep it as simple as possible, though God knows I could make this even more complicated. But I fight the urge to break the colors down even further, consider it a personal victory that I'm able to do so.

Besides, it's not so much the counting or grouping that's important. It's the familiarity. The repetitiveness. The order to it.

Each time I reach eighty-three I'm able to breathe a bit easier.

But honestly, I hate that number. Eighty-three. Not only does counting and recounting that many flowers take up a good chunk of my time, the number itself makes me uneasy. You can't divide anything into eighty-three evenly. It drives me crazy.

Something I'm trying like to mad to avoid at all costs.

I could always ask Mom to paint another flower, but then I'd have to explain why I want the flower added. And while my mom gets me better than anyone else, and I hate keeping things from her, I can't tell her. It's embarrassing how often I perform this particular habit. How I can't start my day without it. That I can't fall asleep at night until it's done.

If Mom knew that, she might get the wrong idea. She might think it's a problem. Or worse, that there's something wrong with me.

So, nope. Not going to ask for another flower. Yes, eighty-four is a much stronger number and can be divided by so many other numbers evenly (2, 3, 4, 6 and 7) but if there were eighty-four flowers, I'd probably think of even more ways to drag out my flower counting. It might go from being a quirky, slightly OCD-ish habit into a full-blown obsession.

It's a shame, though. A new flower wouldn't take long to add, and it would make the entire mural better. I even have the perfect spot for it; on the left, about halfway up the wall between a pink rose and purple aster. Of course, the new flower would have to be blue because the number of colors increase by three—except between purple and blue.

And the fact that I'm thinking of this, that I've contemplated it, oh...once or twice or one hundred times before...makes me think I'm not doing all that well with the whole *avoid going crazy at all costs* thing.

Luckily, right now, my flower counting is still just a quirky, slightly unusual habit. One I can manage just fine, thanks all the same.

For the most part, at least.

To prove it, I get to my feet, determined not to start the entire process all over again. Afraid if I do, I'll be here all day, counting and recounting flowers, until my secret is revealed to the world.

Counting and recounting until I lose my ever-loving mind.

I'm not sure which would be worse.

Either one of them would put a damper on my senior year and I have too many plans, have set too many goals to let anything get in my way now.

I head toward my adjoining bathroom, a woman with places to go, things to do, and worlds to conquer. A woman in control of her thoughts. Her mind.

But not, it seems, in control of her body. Because as I walk past the mural, I can't help but trail my fingertips along the wall, tracing the edge of a butterfly. And imagine that perfect blue, eighty-fourth flower filling that tiny, empty space.

ABOUT THE AUTHOR

Beth Ann Burgoon lives in northwestern Pennsylvania where she pens young adult novels that are emotional, sharply written and relatable. She loves coffee, the Pittsburgh Penguins hockey team and '80s teen movies.

———

Let's keep in touch!

Want all the updates, sneak peeks of upcoming releases, cover reveals, exclusive excerpts, giveaways and more? Sign up for my newsletter at: www.bethannburgoon.com

email: beth@bethannburgoon.com
www.bethannburgoon.com
www.facebook.com/bethannburgoonauthor
www.instagram.com/bethannburgoonauthor

Made in the USA
Middletown, DE
14 January 2021